THE WORKS OF

Karlheinz Stockhausen

THE WORKS OF
Karlheinz Stockhausen

ROBIN MACONIE

Second Edition

With a Foreword by
KARLHEINZ STOCKHAUSEN

CLARENDON PRESS · OXFORD

1990

Oxford University Press, Walton Street, Oxford OX2 6DP

Oxford New York Toronto
Delhi Bombay Calcutta Madras Karachi
Petaling Jaya Singapore Hong Kong Tokyo
Nairobi Dar es Salaam Cape Town
Melbourne Auckland
and associated companies in
Berlin Ibadan

Oxford is a trade mark of Oxford University Press

Published in the United States
by Oxford University Press, New York

First published 1976
Second edition 1990

British Library Cataloguing in Publication Data
Maconie, Robin
The works of Karlheinz Stockhausen. – 2nd edn.
1. German music. Stockhausen, Karlheinz, 1928–
I. Title
780.92
ISBN 0–19–315477–3

Library of Congress Cataloging in Publication Data
Maconie, Robin.
The work of Karlheinz Stockhausen/Robin Maconie;
with a foreword by Karlheinz Stockhausen. – 2nd edn.
Includes bibliographical references
1. Stockhausen, Karlheinz, 1928–   —Criticism and interpretation.
I. Title.
ML410.S858M3   1990   780'.92—dc20   89–20989
ISBN 0–19–315477–3

Typeset by Cotswold Typesetting Ltd., Gloucester

Printed in Great Britain by
The Alden Press Ltd., Oxford

Foreword

by Karlheinz Stockhausen

ROBIN MACONIE leads the reader through my work like a travel guide. He offers an overall and coherent view. The music is experienced through his eyes and ears, as one who has inhabited this musical world for many years.

Let no one suppose that the composer may be better able to interpret the musical vibrations transmitted through him, than a commentator who immerses himself, body and soul, in this music. All the commentaries that have ever been, and those yet to be written, all the thoughts and dreams and impressions and visions and actions which my music arouses in its hearers, all these, no less, add up to the meaning of this music—something which must always remain largely a mystery, never totally to be comprehended by a single individual. The resonance is different in every person, for each stands on a different rung of the ladder of spiritual self-enhancement.

Knowledge of this music must therefore come via a mind which has thought long and deeply about it. It must be obvious to everyone that each individual must work out his own view of the music he loves, and that a Maconie by his side can only give him a certain amount of help. But there are very few who can manage it with no help at all . . .

Maconie has left many questions open, and these the lover of my music must find out for himself:

Am I a newcomer in musical history, or am I a reincarnation of an earlier composer? Are the superficial parallels between my music and the music of other cultures perhaps grounded in experiences of my earlier lives on this planet?

What are the distinctively *new* vibrations and rhythms in my music, and what laws of the Universe are transmitted in them? To what spiritual planes do the different works, or isolated events from individual works, aspire? To what level of awareness do they bring us?

What are the underlying moods of particular works? Which is the appropriate state of feeling for listening to a given work? Which works are expressly spiritual in tone, that is to say music of praise, prayer, and thanksgiving to God? In which is the spirituality more hidden?

Which works appeal more directly to the physical being, the feelings and sufferings of sensory existence, and which more to the transcendent life of the spirit?

Or is a balance of sorts discernible overall between the vibrations and rhythms of the beast and the angel in man?

Which pieces *sing* more than others, which transport us to worlds far removed from our planet? Which works allow us to experience the way of life of much smaller creatures, down to the smallest micro-ogranism? Which enable us to traverse great distances with the stride and breath of giants, to fly with giant wings?

In which work has the Prince of Satania, Master Lucifer, insinuated himself with his brilliant wit and glittering alchemy? Which works, which parts of works allow us, like a child seeking protection, to cling to God's foot, snug and content in the certain knowledge of complete security?

Where sounds the voice of Prophecy?

Where the voice of Divine Humour?

Kürten, 30 January 1976

Preface

AMONG living composers Karlheinz Stockhausen remains pre-eminent. A prodigiously hard-working and inventive composer, he is also agent, publisher, author, lecturer, and conductor, and recording artist and technical and production supervisor of his own works. His music and ideas have influenced a new generation of composers in every decade since the fifties. Most serious composers of today's middle and younger generations will admit to having fallen under the Stockhausen spell at some stage in their development. On a broader front, through the startling imagery of his electronic and intuitive music, he has caught the imagination of the larger culture of creative artists in sound whose anonymous work reaches the public via film, television, radio, and studio-produced pop music. His process compositions of the sixties, which many of us found a hard act to follow, are ready for reappraisal as composition by computer grows apace in the eighties and nineties.

Despite the range and strength of loyalty his music inspires, it is still true, I fear, that the impact of Stockhausen's music is something difficult for most listeners, including composers, to comprehend. In part this is a problem created by a consumer culture. People are disturbed by the music and they want to know why they can be profoundly touched by a musical experience that is not entertaining in any conventional way. This is the stereotype reaction to modern art, and any book aiming to introduce a wider public to an important figure in modern art such as Stockhausen is bound inevitably to address the philosophical issue of what music is for, what kind of ideas it is equipped to convey, and how a listener may come to terms with them.

It is certainly true that conditions for understanding Stockhausen's music have greatly improved over the decade since publication of the first edition of this study. The list of Stockhausen's music on record is greatly enlarged (indeed, virtually up to date), ranging from the earliest pieces for unaccompanied choir to some of the most recent pieces from the opera epic LICHT. Stockhausen's sleeve notes to his recordings have also become clearer and fuller, assuming less on the part of the reader, and giving much more. As a result, today's reader has ready access to better information about individual works, and to the works themselves in recorded form.

The welcome availability of background information has allowed the new edition to abandon its earlier, somewhat fragmented format, for one better adapted to broader analysis and overview. One obvious change has been the removal of information on past and present recordings to a separate discography.

A further windfall of information from other sources has been provoked, much as anticipated, by the first edition's speculative and factual errors. I am grateful to all those experts who have seized the opportunity of publishing valid criticisms which otherwise might not have seen the light of day. Their advice has been noted and is acknowledged.

The purpose of an overview is twofold. Firstly, to give information and encouragement to potential listeners and students of Stockhausen's music; secondly, to consider the philosophical and procedural questions which arise from the music as a whole or in particular instances. The second area of concern is aimed particularly at the practising musician and composer, though it ought also to interest the student of aesthetics. It has to do less with the historical and external facts of the music or of the composer's life, and much more with analysis of the impressions the music may arouse, and how they may be related to matters of musical design, to notation, to technology, to performance practices, and so on.

Certain works are clearly going to interest some listeners because they make use of compositional procedures, or address technical or psychoacoustical questions, which are interesting in themselves. The question is not only how a piece sounds, and what visions those sounds may arouse, but equally why it sounds as it does, in terms of its production. What can be learned about the practical aspects of musical design from the particular impression? Is the sound impression we get consistent with the means employed? These are valid questions because new notations, new concepts of performance, and new combinations of live and electronic sound are features of music since 1950; performers need guidance on their interpretation, and Stockhausen's involvement in these practical matters is better informed, more consistent, and more credible than most. By and large, Stockhausen's scores are models of rational notation of aleatoric and indeterminate practices that are widely accepted in today's music but plagued by notational inconsistency. This aspect of his music deserves to be emphasized.

Not only has more information become available about Stockhausen's music, and more music been written, since the publication of the first edition a decade ago, but the music-technological climate has also changed dramatically. Digital audio has brought studio-quality music reproduction within the reach of the ordinary listener. A record-buying public which is rapidly acquiring a taste for high-quality sound is likely to become increasingly responsive to the refined aesthetic of the recording studio which Stockhausen's music embodies. *Invisible Choirs* is an especially appropriate first release for Stockhausen on compact disc, being music for sixteen channels of choral polyphony, a perception of polyphony enlarged by multichannel recording technology, and geared to the improved definition and directionality of digital sound reproduction. Needless to say, it will sound even better when surround-sound digital audio becomes the norm for home listening.

The domestic microprocessor is another significant new arrival. Home computing and associated music synthesis is an expanding activity. If we leave questions of musical quality aside, as we surely must at this stage, it is nevertheless clear that the conceptual basis of music for computer is radically different from anything one might obtain from a conventional musical education. For example, the programmer needs descriptive tools for sounds and sound processes which go beyond reproducing a particular pitch at a particular time to address the wider questions of how sound identity is maintained over a range of pitch and intensity, and what decides the position of a given note in a musical context. It is now the right time to look afresh at the procedures in use among the avant-garde composers of the fififties and sixties. To give only one example, Stockhausen's problematic process compositions of the sixties acquire new relevance as a result of these developments.

The present decade has also seen fractal mathematics come into intellectual prominence as a speculative and recreational mathematical tool for modelling dynamic processes in the natural world. Fractals offer a rationale for structures and processes until recently considered as random or indeterminate and thus beyond the reach of rational description. It has also stimulated interest among scientists in the aesthetics of naturally indeterminate structures. The distinguishing feature of fractal phenomena is structural self-similarity (as, for example, the small tributary resembles the river, the bare twig, the tree, or a small patch of stars seen through a telescope, the greater night sky). There are now precise mathematical descriptions for phenomena which express this property of self-similarity.

Fractal mathematics is of especial importance to composers and students of new music. It disposes of the imaginary gulf which has been thought to separate chance and determinism in music since the fifties. We can now reconcile the serialism of pointillist music with the I-Ching-derived music of Cage as examples of music occupying different positions on a scale of structural indeterminacy. This will bring great relief to many critics, as well as inspiration to computer-based composers. And it brings yet further endorsement to Stockhausen's pioneering investigations, in this case into self-similar musical structures. From the time of *Mantra* through *Inori* and *Sirius* to *LICHT*, he has dedicated himself with increasing daring and subtlety to the invention of complex self-similar musical structures whose every dimension, from the whole to the smallest particle, is configured to the same formula.

In his foreword to the first edition Stockhausen challenged the reader (and through the reader, the author) to identify the spirit of the music. As the music and the composer become more familiar, it is possible to discern his moods and intentions with more ease. There are powerful opposing forces at work in the music: the one and overwhelming tendency to organize everything according to some master plan, the other an equally powerful readiness to change everything on a moment of impulse. The doctrinaire rigidity of serialism gives rise to explosive intuitions. Each stimulates and subverts the other in an unpredictable alchemy which confounds intellectual analysis as much as it astonishes the unprepared ear. Which element is the divine, and which the mischievous, is not as obvious as it may seem. The series or formula may be a divining rod on one occasion, and on another the classic emblem of divine perfection. A musical intuition may be an extravagant indulgence, or it may be the moment of illumination for which everything else is merely self-preparation. To ask which is to ask the wrong question: the mix, the humour, is all.

Swansea
5 October 1987

Acknowledgements

I AM profoundly grateful to Karlheinz Stockhausen for his continuing generous and unconditional support over many years, and to Suzee Stephens for her patience and prompt assistance in transmitting and answering numerous requests and inquiries. My thanks are due to the Leverhulme Trust for valuable assistance in the form of a research award, and to Bruce Phillips and Pippa Thynne of Oxford University Press for sustained help and encouragement. I am grateful to Universal Edition (London) Ltd., the copyright holders, for allowing reproduction of the excerpt from *Mikrophonie II*, and the complete score of *Dr. K-Sextett*. The reproduction of excerpts of all other works written prior to 1969 is by kind permission of the copyright holders Universal Edition AG, Wien; reproduction of excerpts of compositions dating from 1970 is by kind permission of Stockhausen-Verlag, 5067 Kürten, West Germany. I am grateful to Jonathan Cape Limited, London, the Estate of Hermann Hesse, and translators Richard and Clara Winston for permission to reproduce passages from the published English translation of Hermann Hesse's *The Glass Bead Game*. Particular thanks are owed to Richard Toop for his friendly and expert advice and encouragement over the years, and for permission to reproduce arguments and insights from his many writings on Stockhausen. I am also deeply obliged to Robert Slotover for allowing me ready access to Allied Artists' films of the composer's 1971 British lecturers, and to transcripts of these and other conversations.

Notes on the text

UNLESS otherwise stated all quoted remarks are by Stockhausen and all citations from sources not in English are translated by the present author; the Foreword was translated by Sally Wright.

In the listening of instrumental forces, the following convention has been adopted: Woodwinds 0.0.0.0.0 (flute (piccolo, alto flute), oboe (cor anglais), clarinet (E flat, A, bass), bassoon (contrabassoon), horn); 0.0.0 (trumpet (piccolo trumpet, bass), trombone (alto, bass), tuba (euphonium, Wagner tuba)); percussion are listed; strings 0.0.0.0.0 (violins I, violins II, violas, cellos, double basses). Non-standard instruments are named and located appropriately (e.g. saxophones with the woodwinds, electric organs with orchestral keyboards).

Pitches are indicated in American standard notation: C1 (lowest C on the piano, 32Hz)–C2–C3–C4 (middle C)–C5–C6–C7–C8.

Contents

I *An Introduction*

KARLHEINZ STOCKHAUSEN was born on 22 August 1928 in Mödrath near Cologne. His father was Simon Stockhausen, his mother Gertrud, née Stupp. He was the first of three children. The family was poor. His father was a village schoolteacher, descended (so he believed) from noble forebears, the Stockhausens of Asbach in the Westerwald; he was proud to be the first of his family in many generations to gain an education and rise on the social ladder. The Stupps, for their part, were an old and wellrespected Neurath farming family, and quite well off. Gertrud, a handsome woman, was evidently musical; the household piano had been bought for her as a child, and her family allowed her to work at home instead of in the fields, both of which were considerable sacrifices at a time of economic hardship. Stockhausen père had some natural musical ability himself: he played the violin passably well, and could pick out a tune on the black keys of the piano.

Early life was unsettling. The pay of a teacher was poor and life was grim. As a newly-qualified schoolteacher the father was obliged to move from one temporary post to another, on average twice a year, so for some years the young family lived a peripatetic existence, moving from village to village. Poverty, instability, and the strain of having three children in rapid succession proved too much for Stockhausen's mother, and she entered a sanatorium when he was four years old, suffering from acute depression. Shortly afterward Simon Stockhausen obtained the position of head teacher at the village school at Altenberg, on the outskirts of Cologne. It was a permanent and respected post, but obliged him to accept the less pleasant title and responsibilities of being local organizer for the Nazi party.

Simon Stockhausen was a registered party member and he fervently believed, as a poor man and devout nationalist, in the rebuilding of a strong Germany. What he feared was having his personal loyalties and fervent Catholic faith compromised by his political duties. Matters were not made any easier by Gertrud's illness and incapacity, and the death in infancy of the second son, 'little Hermann'. There was also the case of Simon Hansen, a forester and self-appointed revolutionary, who attempted unsuccessfully to blow up the beautiful twelfth-century Altenberg Cathedral as a gesture of protest, and whose capture would certainly have cost the elder Stockhausen his job, and possibly his liberty. At great personal risk, and having no real alternative, Simon Stockhausen concealed the culprit from the authorities. On another occasion the young Stockhausen composed and recited a poem in honour of a bishop visiting the Altenberg cathedral. The poem declared, with youthful idealism, the endurance of faith in times of trouble. That evening the Gestapo arrived at the Stockhausen home and took the father away for questioning, accusing him of being responsible for the poem's anti-Party sentiments. Simon returned home badly shaken, and made the boy swear never to do anything that might implicate him again.

Stockhausen remembers as a youngster having to deliver leaflets and collect dues on his father's behalf for the various funds administered by the Party, his father being obliged to work after hours as a farm labourer in order to make ends meet. The postman image is one he likes to use to explain his role as a bearer of musical messages to the rest of mankind: 'I am the postman who is bringing the mail without knowing what is in the letters.'[1] He entered primary school in Easter 1935, and began taking piano lessons with the local organist, Franz-Josef Kloth, from the age of six. He made rapid progress, and practised diligently. At ten, following extensive research into his family history, he was admitted to the Pastor-Löhr-Gymnasium, a 'humanistic' grammar school at Burscheid, where he studied Latin, mathematics, and English. That year he took communion for the first time. 'It made an enormously deep impression on me. Confession is like practising music. You have to practise confession, again and again.'[2]

Meanwhile at home the politicization of village life became more oppressive, school prayers were forbidden, and his father was forced publicly to renounce devotions he continued to practise privately at home. His family life shattered and his public position increasingly compromised, the elder Stockhausen sought to free himself from domestic and community pressures by marrying a young local woman who had been keeping house for him. Restless and anxious about the future, he saw the approaching war as a chance of redeeming himself by heroic action, and marriage as the key to personal liberation. Luzia Stockhausen bore him two daughters, Waltraud and Gerd. At the first opportunity, Simon volunteered for active military service.

In 1942 Karlheinz became a boarder at the LBA (teacher training college) at Xanten on the lower Rhine, established in a converted monastery and run on strictly military lines. He was the youngest student of his year. It was a totally regimented existence, he later recalled: everything was organized down to the last fingernail, one had no privacy, and one was never alone. There was nevertheless a considerable emphasis on music: in addition to regular Sunday processions, in which he played oboe, and for whose regular beat-patterns he retains an abiding loathing, the college provided a symphony orchestra, a salon orchestra, and a jazz band, in all of which he took part, playing piano and also violin. Occasionally he and a few friends would listen in secret to late-night BBC broadcasts of American jazz. During his first year at Xanten he returned to Altenberg to see his father on special leave, and learned that

[1] Hans Oesch, 'Interview mit Karlheinz Stockhausen', *Melos/Neue Zeitschrift für Musik*, 1 (1975), 460.
[2] Michael Kurtz, *Stockhausen: eine Biographie* (Kassel, 1988), p. 5.

his mother had died, put to death as an act of Government policy to relieve pressure on hospital accommodation and to save food.

Stockhausen remained at college until 1944 when, too young for combat duty, he was transferred to the teacher training college at Bedburg on the Erft, soon afterward converted into a military hospital. He became a stretcher-bearer; as a fluent English-speaker, he was called upon to attend wounded and dying English and American soldiers, and translate for them. There was a piano on which he would play requests. 'When everything else was gone, music seemed to them still to have value.'[3] Some would ask for Beethoven, others for ballads or music-hall songs. Shortly before the end of the war Stockhausen saw his father for the last time. Fearful of the consequences of a return to civilian life, and determined to seek a hero's death, he returned to the battlefront somewhere in Hungary, and was lost in action.

For a few months after the war Stockhausen worked in Blecher as a farm labourer to support his stepmother and two half-sisters. He practised piano and studied Latin at night for the entrance examination to the Bergisch-Gladbach Gymnasium. When his former piano teacher Kloth took charge of an operetta production for the Blecher Theatre Society, he asked Stockhausen to take over the choir rehearsals. Stockhausen remained as repetiteur, later music director, for the society for three years. He also played piano for dancing sessions round the villages. In February 1946 he entered the Bergisch-Gladbach Gymnasium as a mature student. Completing his *Abitur* in Easter the following year, he moved to Cologne with a sense of relief, joining the piano class of Hans-Otto Schmidt-Neuhaus at the Musikhochschule. In 1948 he enrolled as a full-time student in the music education (school music) course, with piano as his main subject. Among his fellow students in the piano class was Doris Andreae, daughter of a prosperous Hamburg industrialist, who later became his wife. At this time he was also enrolled in classes in musicology, philosophy, and German studies at Cologne University, and supported himself by taking a variety of student jobs, among them car-park attendant, night-club pianist, and night watchman.

From 1948 he began studies of harmony and counterpoint with Hermann Schroeder, a conservative teacher of the old school. An altogether livelier mind at the Musikhochschule was Hans Mersmann, whose appointment as director in 1947 introduced a welcome spirit of adventure to the music education course. As co-publisher of *Melos*, the leading new-music periodical, Mersmann had experienced the unwelcome attentions of the authorities during the Third Reich. He introduced his music education analysis students to Hindemith, Stravinsky, Bartók, and other composers whose music and ideas had long been suppressed.

Perhaps surprisingly, Stockhausen felt no special inclination to compose at this stage, still less to make composing his life. His passions were writing poetry, reading plays, and debating the philosophy of modern art with other like-minded students. It

[3] Karlheinz Stockhausen and Robin Maconie, *Stockhausen on Music* (London, 1989), p. 22.

was not the work of art which fired his deepest convictions, as much as the evident power of new art to inspire awe, and (significantly) to alienate evil. Hermann Hesse's novel *The Glass Bead Game* impressed him enormously, and Stockhausen too wrote a novel, *Humayun*, using the life story of the sixteenth-century Mogul emperor as a pretext for a philosophical inquiry into the meaning of birth and death, which he interpreted as points of transition from the spiritual into the material world and from the material world back to the world of the spirit. These processes of change, 'the whole mystery whereby beings come into existence in time and space, and then return once more into the realm beyond space and time', were a major preoccupation—far more interesting to contemplate, so he thought, than the life between, the achievements of which at best are of merely anecdotal significance.

Not until 1950, towards the end of his third year, was he introduced to free composition exercises in various classical styles. He clearly enjoyed the challenge, writing additional pieces in imitation of more advanced composers than those set in the syllabus. In February 1950 the composer Hermann Heiss, a former pupil of Josef Matthias Hauer, gave a concert of his own works at the Musikhochschule, followed by a lecture on the principles of twelve-tone composition. It was Stockhausen's first real encounter with serial technique in practice, and he eagerly approached his composition tutor for further guidance. Schroeder was against the idea, but his colleague Fritz Schieri proved more amenable: he had developed a personal system of composing tonally using all twelve chromatic pitches in a regulated fashion, and this hybrid idiom, it seems, may have provided Stockhausen with a basis for his own early excursions into serial composition. The *Choral* and *Chöre nach Verlaine* (later renamed *Chöre für Doris*) for unaccompanied choir are among a number of works he composed at this time for the student choir, of which he was a member. Among a number of compositions which have not survived are a Scherzo for piano in the style of Hindemith, a set of six piano studies, and a successful student pantomine, *Burleska*, for which he wrote the libretto and some of the music. Both the concept and its instrumentation (for speaker, four solo singers, chamber choir, string quartet, piano, and percussion) seem to prefigure *Momente*.

Nevertheless, his attitude to composing remained ambivalent. Poetry was still his preferred medium of expression. His verses of the period are rough-hewn in texture and express an intense, often mordant and prophetic vision. Composing, by contrast, seems to have awakened calmer and deeper contemplative powers, as well as offering him the possibility to explore and enlarge his range of expression well beyond the bounds of language. His music is purer in tone; there is a certain surgical objectivity, both to the sound and movement of the music itself and, as we shall see, also revealed in his freedom of manipulation of the musical material on the way to the finished work. He tells of showing an unnamed supervisor a sketch of two bars of music seething with notes, possibly an early attempt at transcribing the 'swarm of bees' sound image to which he often alludes, certainly a promise of textural and statistical complexities to come. His tutor was appalled. 'Who can hear all these notes?' 'I don't want you to count them' was the reply. 'You don't control what you are writing,' came the answer. 'Just put one note, be precise.'[4]

During the summer of 1950, in an effort to prove to himself that he could write at least one extended work, he composed the *Drei Lieder* for alto voice and chamber orchestra, to poems by himself. It was his first piece for solo voice, also his first for instrumental ensemble. 'The *Drei Leider* are dedicated to my wife Doris, to whom I brought the score from my refuge in 1950, flushed with success, who certainly could not make much out of the manuscript and until summer 1975 could not yet hear how the piece actually sounded. "Was lange währt . . . [wird endlich gut]." '[5]

He sent the score to be considered for performance at the Darmstadt International Vacation Courses for New Music. It attracted the attention of the Cologne music critic Herbert Eimert, who was on the jury, and the two subsequently met. Eimert was responsible for the evening music programme on Cologne (North-West German, later West German) Radio: his influence and encouragement was destined to play a decisive role in launching Stockhausen's career.

Late in 1950 the Swiss composer Frank Martin came to Cologne as visiting professor in composition at the music high school. Stockhausen showed him the *Drei Lieder* to gain admission into his composition class. He was duly accepted, and had 'four or five' lessons. Stockhausen's final year at the music high school was devoted mainly to analysis and composition. He completed a *Sonatine* for violin and piano (he original manuscript reads 'for piano and violin') in March 1951, and immersed himself in an analytical thesis on Bartók's *Sonata for Two Pianos and Percussion*. Eimert arranged for the Sonatine to be performed on his evening programme by Wolfgang Marschner, concert-master of the Cologne Radio Orchestra, with the composer as accompanist; he also invited Stockhausen to condense his Bartók thesis into a form suitable for broadcast as a radio talk.

Stravinsky remarked:

The ordinary musician's trouble in judging composers like Boulez and the young German, Stockhausen, is that he doesn't see their roots. These composers have sprung full-grown. With Webern, for example, we trace his origins back to the musical traditions of the nineteenth and earlier centuries. But the ordinary musician is not aware of Webern. He asks questions like: "What sort of music would Boulez and Stockhausen write if they were asked to write tonal music?"[6]

For some twenty years Stockhausen's compositions of his student days remained out of bounds, and may indeed have survived only because of their special association with his wife Doris, their dedicatee. Until 1971 Stravinsky's 'ordinary musician' in search of Stockhausen's tonal origins had no way of knowing what transpired before *Kreuzspiel*; not only was the question of antecedent influences unanswerable, therefore, it was also unthinkable. Asked that year by a concert

[4] Ibid. 44.
[5] Karlheinz Stockhausen, *Texte zur Musik*, iv (Cologne, 1978), p. 42.
[6] Igor Stravinsky and Robert Craft, *Conversations with Igor Stravinsky* (London, 1959), p. 127.

organization in Paris for a work to première, and curious to hear how these 'early works' would sound after so long, Stockhausen agreed to revive the *Chöre nach Verlaine*, renamed *Chöre für Doris*, the *Choral*, and the *Drei Lieder*.

Chöre für Doris

1950: *Choir Pieces for Doris.*

Three movements after Verlaine for unaccompanied mixed choir.

1. 'Die Nachtigall' (The Nightingale)
2. 'Armer junger Hirt' (The Poor Shepherd Boy)
3. 'Agnus Dei'

Duration 15′.

Stockhausen's themes are faith, hope, and love: faith in an uncertain future, hope after suffering, and the anxieties of undeclared love. The liquescent clarity of Verlaine's original verses flows rather less smoothly in translation, the German text tending to wrestle with emotions which the French language is content simply to resonate. Stockhausen's settings come to grips, if not entirely to terms, with the resulting discrepancy between word-setting and interpretation. First he treats the texts with the kind of neutral respect that assumes the poet's tone of voice will take care of itself; then an additional layer of performance indications, typically dynamic and tempo changes, is imposed on the basic setting to draw out the meaning more clearly. In all three songs we can observe this separation of the text and the drama, as it were. In 'Die Nachtigall', for instance, the four-part choir provides a restless harmonic background over which a solo soprano dips and soars at twice the speed. The oppositions of solo and group, of register, tempo, and characterization, are clearly drawn.

'Armer Junger Hirt', in lighter vein, is rhythmically more impulsive and varied, though harmonically still lacking in direction. Stockhausen turns the lyric about a shepherd boy with a 'terror of kissing' into a mini-cantata. The choir is divided in two, in a dialogue of male and female, high and low voices, which is more a commentary on the theme of love than an interpretation of the text. A dramatic interplay of opposites is already emerging as characteristic of the young Stockhausen; his choral idiom in this work is interestingly recalled in the 1974 version of '*Atmen gibt das Leben . . .* '. Tonal cadences play an important, but unconventional role. Normally one would expect successive points of harmonic repose to link up in a greater progression; in this case, their function appears to be disruptive, both rhythmically and tonally. Rhythmically, because they are so emphatic in arresting the musical flow; harmonically, because they veer off in such unexpected directions. Now here, now there, the music opens a tonal window into a blazing root-position chord with jazz or Stravinskian overtones, only to start off again from another tack. Of course the image matches the irresolution of the subject; it is even possible to see Stockhausen's free association of elements of traditional harmonic progression as an early anticipation of moment-form.

The 'Agnus Dei' alternates some real two-part counterpoint between widely-separated female and male voices, with four-part chorale-like harmonizations of a melodic setting of the verse. There is a greater sense of progression in both melody and harmony, a longer line to the soprano melody, and quite a serial complexion to the underlying chromatic harmonies. There is also more rhythmic independence to the part-writing. Stockhausen ignores the austere, symbolic triplets of the poetic form in favour of an episodic structure responsive to every perceived change of mood and imagery, though it in turn incorporates elements of traditional church ritual. Once again, tonal cadences appear out of the chromatic web unexpectedly.

Drei Lieder

1950: *Three Songs* for alto voice and chamber orchestra.
1. 0. 2. 1. 0; 1. 1; percussion, xylophone, piano, harpsichord; strings 8. 0. 6. 4. 4.
   1. 'Der Rebell' (The Rebel)
   2. 'Frei' (Free)
   3. 'Der Saitenmann' (The String Man)
Duration 19'.

After the pastel tones and polite atmosphere of the choir pieces, Stockhausen's remarkable first essay in orchestral composition reveals a totally different side to his character. This is an ironic, mordant world, a Georg Grosz image of peacetime Germany in moral decline. The art-song form is turned upside down: instead of celebrating the finer things of life, Stockhausen turns his attention to the rebel spirit, the jester, and the poor street musician. Eimert told Stockhausen that the Darmstadt jury rejected the piece as 'too brutal and old-fashioned'. Finer sensibilities among the jury may well have been offended by the composer's subject-matter; 'old-fashioned' however, seems a surprising description for a piece so kaleidoscopic in mood, and so refined, even exquisite, in its use of orchestral colour. The sheer technical fluency of Stockhausen's instrumentation, its vital and volatile character, cannot easily be appreciated from a mere reading of the written score, but it certainly transforms the literal predictabilities of a student exercise into a musical experience of considerable passion and wit.

It also marks Stockhausen's introduction to composing with a series. The row (Ex. 1) has marked tonal implications, and is employed with evident success as a basis for melody and harmony (and also counterpoint), in comparison with the earlier choir pieces. The intervals formed by 1–6 are virtually symmetrical with those formed by 6–11. Serial repetition is allied to rhythmic variation and

Ex. 1

Drei Lieder: the series.

permutations of note and rhythmic orders are frequent. The opening bars of 'Der Rebell' (Ex. 2) are an obvious example. Seven 5-note segments of the series enter in sequence, gradually compressing an initial interval shape in rhythm and time to form a 7-note chord, a foretaste of similar time-compression procedures in *Sirius* and *Jubiläum*.

Compared to the *Chöre Für Doris*, the texture of the *Drei Lieder* is remarkably light, the small orchestra laid out unconventionally, in family groups of four woodwinds, two brass, strings in four parts, percussion, piano, and amplified harpsichord. Each timbre group is treated as a separate layer of colour, which, in a manner comparable with colour separation in a printing process, allows for great richness of polyphony and polyrhythmic combination without sacrifice of transparency.

'Der Rebell' takes the form of a dialogue between the solo voice and the trumpet, whose toy-soldier image, with side-drum flourishes, sets an ironic tone at the beginning of each song. The same toy soldier, an allusion no doubt to the composer's exerience of military life at Xanten, turns up again in *Trans* and *Herbstmusik*. One can also point to some remarkable writing for xylophone and startlingly beautiful cluster resonances in the middle and upper reaches of piano and harpsichord.

'Frei' is more confident, at times even jaunty. There are many interesting features. Stockhausen's rhythms assume a freedom and fluidity of expression, both individually and in combination, which point the way ahead to *Kontra-Punkte* and *Gruppen*. The vocal writing is also more spacious and eloquent, for instance the extended melisma of the setting 'am süssen Ort' at 13. No less impressive are the orchestral glissandi at 13 and again at the climax before 24, where Harlequin's

Ex. 2

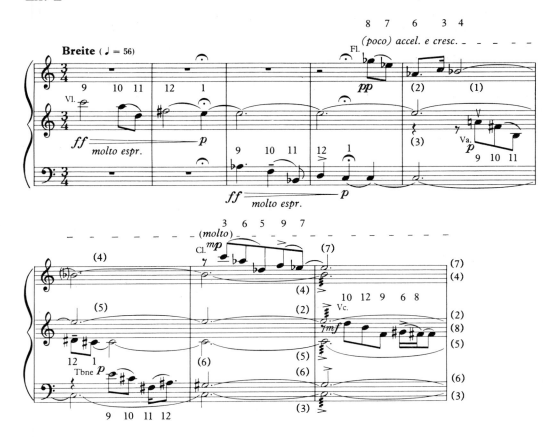

Drei Lieder: opening bars of 'Der Rebell'.

© Universal Edition AG Wien.

mocking references to *la dolce vita* immediately summon up sinful, luxuriant big-band jazz harmonies, in an expression of musical rectitude much later recalled in *Der Jahreslauf*. There are also indications of a desire to combine 'free' and 'measured' tempi in advance of *Zeitmasze and Zyklus*.

'Der Saitenmann' is certainly the most expressionistic setting of the three songs. The vocal style is unexpectedly impassioned in places, and where the text wells up with emotion, Stockhausen turns to the violins, though even here the tone remains ironic (and the sonorities ravishing).

It is an extremely accessible work, one which deserves to take its place in the repertoire along with, say, Stravinsky's *Renard*. It even allows for the possibility of balletic or mime interpretation. Stockhausen draws on his experience of salon orchestra and jazz music in a filmic treatment of poems which for all their outward formal indications (especially the interlacing intricacies of 'Frei') are used principally as narratives on which to hang interpretative flashes of musical imagination. As Schoenberg borrowed the newsreel idiom to give dramatic concentration and immediacy to *A Survivor from Warsaw*, so Stockhausen seems to have adapted the rapid-fire techniques of animated film music to create a modern stream-of-consciousness concert idiom.

The work's considerable charms do not disguise Stockhausen's underlying seriousness of purpose, or the strength of his defence of the social outcast. Harlequin, the fool, has the wit to cut the king's line of Gordian knots and escape the gallows; the string man cradles his fiddle in his torn hands and hears music that passers-by, busily 'buying a new world', cannot imagine. In all Stockhausen's music one finds the two aspects of prankster and prophet, mischief-maker and visionary; understanding the two sides of the composer's personality is essential to understanding his musical thought-processes.

Stockhausen's idiom implies a degree of conspiracy between voice and orchestra here as in *Momente* and now in the opera cycle *LICHT*.

Choral

1950: *Chorale* for four-part unaccompanied mixed choir.
Duration 4'.

Stockhausen's word-settings normally follow a natural speaking rhythm, the pace being determined by the meaning of a text rather than its poetic structure. There is thus little of the tension usually found between the artificial form of a verse and the sense of a text imposed on its pattern and timing of stresses. Rather, as we have seen, the composer will stretch or condense the outer form the better to accommodate the sense he wishes a text to convey, speeding up or slowing down the pace as intuition dictates, and thereby introducing a restless and impulsive energy into otherwise inert material.

Choral follows the composer's usual practice, but refines it too. His two-stanza poem, with five lines per stanza, the fifth line echoing the first, is authentically Lutheran in character. Stockhausen has also followed convention in setting the text as a melody and then harmonizing it in four parts: the evidence being the series, again diatonic in interval structure, which appears in original, inverted, and retrograde forms in the soprano voice only, the other three parts filling out a chromatic harmonic progression in traditional stepwise movement. (Although the row (Ex. 3) starts and ends in D, the lasting impression is of a D waiting to resolve into a G which never arrives.)

The rhythmic construction of the soprano melody is interesting. While the pace varies from line to line in a natural speaking rhythm, there are nevertheless precise formal symmetries among the lines of a clearly intentional kind, and on a separate plane from the normal verse structure. So while the melody rhythm follows an ABABA pattern, and while the written time-scale is a traditional four beats to the bar, the pulse rate is constantly changing: the first line being in crotchets, the second in quavers, the third compressing the line 1 rhythm into quaver values, the fourth permutating line 2, and the fifth expanding the line 1 rhythm into minim values. The effect, as one might expect, is of a controlled variation of expression in the rhythmic domain, within a consistent time structure. Rhythm and tempo are in fact the principal means of expression: the four-part chromatic harmony providing moment-to-moment continuity to the musical flow, but little in the way of overall tonal direction. It is significant that the same music is used twice, virtually without change, for the two verses. This is new for Stockhausen and unusual in the context of his entire output. And to this observer, in the way the fifth-line refrain builds to the final cadence, an impression is created that not only the series, but also time itself is reversed, like a tape played backwards. The idea of a real correspondence between time-reversed structures and classical cadences is quite intriguing, given the composer's frequent use of time-reversal in electronic and instrumental works of the mid-fifties.

Sonatine

1951: *Sonatina* for violin and piano.
1. 'Lento espressivo'–'vivacetto irato'–'tempo 1'
2. 'Molto moderato e cantabile'
3. 'Allegro scherzando'

Duration 11'.

These are three disparate 'studies in style' related by a common series (Ex. 4) in which thirds and fifths predominate. Though later in date than the *Drei Lieder*, the score looks like an earlier composition, which suggests that the orchestral songs were considerably worked over at a later time (its elaborate tempo-changes are possible evidence of this). The first movement, 'Lento espressivo', is the most Schoenbergian in line, though the violin is curiously limited in range, only once soaring as high as a three-line E♭. In fact, there is only one place, at 28 in the second

Ex. 3

Choral: initial statement of the series as the soprano melody.
© Universal Edition AG Wien.

Ex. 4

Sonatine: the series.

movement, where the violin writing appears truly idiomatic, and even that looks like an afterthought.[7] So the choice of solo instrument appears to have come later; there is enough of the 'song without words' in the piece to suggest Stockhausen initially had texts in mind, or at least a vocalize. Certainly the Schoenberg style detectable here is more that of the piano pieces, Opp. 11 and 23, than of the *Phantasy*, Op. 47.

Be that as it may, this is Stockhausen's first composition for instruments alone, and one looks with interest at his approach to form in the absence of a text. Each piece tries a different approach. The first movement alternates precise three-part counterpoint and more irascible outbursts; its interest is primarily abstract and architectonic. Irony emerges in the second movement, based on a grotesquely slowed-down boogie-woogie, in which the two partners gradually separate and go their own ways. While the piano accompaniment gets ever more ponderous, the

---

[7] Kurtz (op. cit. 330) lists a *Präludium* for piano solo from 1951 as 'identical with the piano part of the first movement of the *Sonatine*'.

lightweight sound of the muted violin becomes increasingly buoyant, and ends by floating off in its own time of six against the piano's four beats to the bar.

The third movement, longest and liveliest of the three, is a highly dramatic 'altercation without words'. The two instruments are highly contrasted, and the writing very physical in gesture, the violin leaning towards a 'feminine', emotional, more reflective character, while the piano takes a more articulate, dynamic, even brutal 'male' character (in accordance with Stockhausen's own interpretation of the sexes). Wild fluctuations of mood, which towards the end even incorporate a burst of Beethovenian triplets, defy ordinary logic. During 1951 Stockhausen worked as accompanist to a touring magician ('I improvised on the piano and distracted the audience at crucial moments').[8] Perhaps this movement is music to accompany magic, with its high level of spontaneity, impulsive gestures, and distracting turns. The *Sonatine* as a whole asks for balletic interpretation as three studies of couple relationship.

[8] Interview, in 'Notes and Commentaries', *New Yorker*, 18 Jan. 1964.

2 *Orientations*

THE argument that hindsight brings insight is well entrenched: if new ideas are to be explained, they have first to be put into historical context. Normally, a historical context can be found for any new discovery. It neither foresees, nor explains it. But for a majority the knowledge that something new is nevertheless part of the cultural mainstream suppresses any anxieties it might otherwise arouse. Cook's sailors amazed welcoming tribes of South Pacific islanders by rowing towards the shore while facing back the way they came, instead of in the direction they were actually moving. Even now the idea persists that looking back is a requirement of navigating into the unknown.

Whatever the merits—which Stockhausen frankly disputes—of sifting through a composer's life history for clues to his creative development, the debate over the origins of post-war new music is infinitely more complicated than what sort of tonal music a given avant-garde composer might have written. Of course Stravinsky's remark quoted in the previous chapter is as much intended to provoke as to explain. The avant-garde had indeed sprung fully armed, but then so in his time did Stravinsky himself, and so would any composer making his critical début. A composer's reputation is made by a first masterpiece, not by deduction from works of immaturity (unless of course he happens to be British). The point is not that individual composers of the post-1945 avant-garde had no obvious stylistic affiliations with the past. It is rather more momentous and unprecedented than that: the fact that an entire generation was united in wishing to sever all connection with the history of music, and with conventional ideas of musical taste and function.

Even a seasoned practitioner like Stravinsky found it impossible to discern any real continuity between the modernism of the inter-war years, which could still be construed in terms of existing musical orthodoxies, and the new music of the fifties, which burst on the scene with annihilating energy, and evaded every attempt at defensive rationalization. Young composers on both sides of the Atlantic spontaneously aligned themselves with a philosophy of radical disaffection with Western history and tradition, and they expressed themselves in a collective musical regime of particulate notes and gestures. They defended their music with intelligence and designed it with architectural precision. In practice, much of it did not sound in the least intellectual, unleashing visceral energies and emotions from performers and audiences alike. For an anonymous musical idiom to have so immediate and powerful an impact on the culture of the time had to indicate a degree of historical necessity and aesthetic integrity, even if the latter could only be characterized in broadly negative terms. New music in the early fifties was certainly a mystery to most 'ordinary musicians', as it tantilized many a composer of Stravinsky's generation. It has remained a mystery, by and large, to subsequent generations.

For a number of leading young composers there was a private dimension to their public alignment with a policy of rejection of history. Family sufferings and wartime tragedy toughened the resolve of particular personalities, among them Stockhausen, Boulez, and Xenakis, to sever their music from all risk of contamination with the past. All three in their several ways came to maturity armed with a formidable conviction of having been chosen to survive, and to lead music to a new level of consciousness.

Intellectual considerations sufficed, however, for the greater majority of young composers and artists of Stockhausen's generation. Quite simply, cultural roots and artistic tradition had lost their relevance and their authority to determine where music ought to progress. Nazism had all but severed the cultural roots of Germany and Austria: leading composers had been persecuted and forced into exile; their works had been suppressed. For as long as the younger generation could remember, music itself—classical, popular, and folk—had been used as a medium of political propaganda, for fomenting nationalism, underscoring the war effort, and gilding the neo-classic ramparts of dictatorship. As far as the young were concerned, a postwar civilization could not be reconstructed on the same principles that had ripped civilization apart. Indeed, any contemporary composer who had avoided persecution or had flourished under a regime which sought to limit artistic expression, or any contemporary music which had been encouraged or merely tolerated by such regimes, were by definition tainted, either by impotence or by collaboration. There was thus no tradition for young idealistic composers to acknowledge. Even Stravinsky and Hindemith did not escape suspicion of compromise. As for those few composers whose reputation and persecution gave the post-war generation something with which to identify, composers such as Schoenberg, Webern, or Varèse, as long as they remained unpublished and unheard and the possibility of a real continuity of ideas remained unfulfilled, there could be no question of a sense of tradition being restored.

It was a moral as well as a practical repudiation of the role which music had come to fulfil. On the one hand, after a war which had brought the holocaust and the atomic bomb, there was the moral argument that new music could no longer justify serving partisan interests, whether of class or of national allegiance. Instead, it was bound to aspire to the same dispassionate and humane collectivism which characterized the best scientific endeavour: transcending national boundaries, dedicated to the common good of all mankind, and expressing itself in a common international dialect. On the practical side, however, the post-war generation had no option but to start totally afresh and to tackle the immense problems of creating a new musical dialectic on an international basis. Ignorant of the music they wished to know, and suspicious of what they had been taught in its place, they were faced with a real cultural vacuum which had in some way to be filled.

The past lay in fragments, the fragments belonged in a museum. Music needed new precepts and new principles. In common with many other fields of intellectual and artistic endeavour, the watchword was 'back to fundamentals': fundamental propositions, in the manner of Wittgenstein, fundamental principles, in the manner of Einstein, fundamental canons of beauty, in the manner of Le Corbusier. There was little in all of this ferment of ideas for the composer directly to seize upon: no theory for new music directly comparable, for example, with Paul Klee's theory of art. Schoenberg's system of twelve tones related only one to another was intellectually attractive, but his music did not appear to match it in novelty of idiom. Webern's music, on the other hand, did: but his account of the creative process proved to be woefully subjective. Messiaen's system of modes and theories of rhythm were certainly very promising, but did not protect his music from lapses of taste, while discussion of his theories was impeded by the composer's preoccupations with bird-song, the colours of harmonies, and other expressions of religious and romantic sentiment.

Hermann Hesse's novel *Magister Ludi*, published in 1943 (and available in English as *The Glass Bead Game*) depicts a future civilization in which music has become the most refined and universal expression of human thought. The Game itself is an elusive amalgam of counterpoint, medieval disputation, chess, astronomy, abacus, rosary, staff notation, and a vague premonition of computer machine code. Hesse not only conceived an intellectual climate with which young post-war composers could identify, he also intuited (which is probably more to the point) the culture of information technology now upon us. Hesse's intellectual world is abstract and esoteric, medieval and modern, and can be construed as a defence of intellectual values lately condemned by bourgeois authority as degenerate or subversive.

The novel outlines a new art of music, allied to mathematics, which has renounced the decadent '*feuilleton* culture' of a previous age to embrace 'a new, monastically austere intellectual discipline':

These rules, the sign language and grammar of the Game, constitute a kind of highly developed secret language drawing upon several sciences and arts, but especially mathematics and music, and capable of expressing and establishing interrelationships between the content and conclusions of nearly all scholarly disciplines. The Glass Bead Game is thus a mode of playing with the total contents and values of our culture . . . . [It] was played both in England and Germany before it was 'invented' here in the Musical Academy of Cologne, and was given the name it bears to this day. . . . Mathematicians brought the Game to a high degree of flexibility and capacity for sublimation so that it began to acquire something approaching a consciousness of itself and its possibilities. This process paralleled the general evolution of cultural consciousness, which had survived the great crisis. . . .

What it lacked in those days [of the early twentieth century] was the capacity for universality. . . . There was a passionate craving among all the intellectuals . . . for means to express their new concepts. They longed for philosophy, for synthesis. It required half a century before the first step was taken toward spanning these gulfs. . . . A Swiss musicologist with a passion for mathematics gave a new twist to the Game. . . . He invented the principles of a new language, a language of symbols and formulas, in which mathematics and music played an equal part, so that it became possible to combine astronomical and musical formulas, to reduce mathematics and music to a common denominator, as it were. . . . The Game rapidly evolved into what it is today: the quintessence of intellectuality and art, the sublime cult, the *unio mystica* of all separate members of the *Universitas Litterarum*. Indeed, in the days of Plinius Ziegenhalss, it was often called by a different name. . . . That name, which for many a prophetic spirit in those days embodied a visionary ideal, was: Magic Theatre.[1]

The hero, or 'Magister ludi' of the novel's original title, is the character Joseph Knecht:

No knowledge has come down to us of Joseph Knecht's origins. Like many other pupils of the elite schools, he either lost his parents early in childhood, or the Board of Educators removed him from unfavourable home conditions and took charge of him. . . . But we do not really read [the qualities of great composers] from their biographies and from such facts about their private lives that have come down to us; we read them solely from their works, from their music. . . . We regard his life, in so far as it is known, as built up in a clear succession of stages. . . . As Magister Ludi he became the leader and prototype of all those who strive toward and cultivate the things of the mind. . . . It seems to us perfectly appropriate, and in keeping with his life, that his biography should also have passed the usual dimensions and at the end passed on into legend . . .[2]

Stockhausen has named Joseph Knecht as one of two favourite literary heroes (the other being Novalis' Heinrich von Ofterdingen).[3] While the coincidences between the real and the fictional life are astonishing, what is perhaps more significant is the extent to which Stockhausen seems to have determined, early in his career, to model himself on the character, as well as embracing the underlying philosophy and musical symbolism, of Hesse's creation. With *Kreuzspiel* the fictional persona has been taken on board; today, in *LICHT* both the subtle counterpoint of the Glass Bead Game and the dual character of Knecht/Stockhausen are effectively mythologized.

During the summer of 1951 Stockhausen attended the Darmstadt Vacation Courses in New Music. The previous year Professor Werner Meyer-Eppler and Robert Beyer had lectured on 'The Sound World of Electronic Music': in 1951 they led a seminar entitled 'Music and Technic', in which Eimert also had a say. Stockhausen made the acquaintance of Luigi Nono, the Italian composer and son-in-law of Schoenberg, and of Gottfried Michael Koenig; with the young Belgian Karel Goeyvaerts he formed

[1] Hermann Hesse, *The Glass Bead Game* (London, 1972), pp. 15–39, 47–8.
[2] Ibid. 47–8.
[3] Interview, *Frankfurter Allgemeine Zeitung*, 18 July 1980.

a particular friendship. Goeyvaerts was a long-time student of Messiaen at the Paris Conservatoire. He introduced Stockhausen to the radical new ideas of the Messiaen circle of young composers, and to the music of Webern, whose scores had been circulating in manuscript and studied in secret in Paris since the occupation, but had long been unavailable in Germany.

Goeyvaerts introduced an eager Stockhausen to the attractive implications of comprehensive serialism in Webern's handling of pitch, intensity, register, and touch as independent variables, particularly the concentration of information in the isolated notes and perfect symmetry of the second movement of his Piano Variations, Op. 27. Approving of Webern's treatment of register and time as vertical and horizonal co-ordinates of a uniform musical space, Goeyvaerts nevertheless seized on the apparent inconsistency between the composer's sophisticated treatment of pitch and pitch-associated parameters, and his comparatively rudimentary treatment of the time dimension. (This was a largely symbolic criticism of the Viennese triumvirate on the part of a rising post-war generation of Paris-based composers, and probably originated with Messiaen himself, who had pioneered a new and promising approach to musical time. Boulez' valediction to Schoenberg, 'Schoenberg is Dead', was to make a similar issue of the discrepancy between Schoenberg's advanced serial language and his use of out-of-date classical forms.)[4]

Goeyvaerts also showed Stockhausen one of his own compositions, the Op. 1 *Sonata* for two pianos, an example of the use of 'register-form', his own invention, to resolve the discrepancy. The problem with time as a dimension is that it is one-directional: we can reverse structures in time intellectually, but have to experience them always 'from left to right'. (Stockhausen returns to this conundrum in *Dr. K-Sextett*.) Register form introduces the notion of octave displacement to serial calculation. In the case of the second movement of Goeyvaerts' *Sonata*, every time the same note of the series reappears it is shifted to a higher octave, folding back to the lowest extreme when it 'goes over the top', Register form therefore conceives of the pitch realm in a new way. The traditional keyboard image of pitch is of a continuous space within which one can move freely; in terms of register form, however, it becomes an aggregation of distinct layers or bands, each an octave in width. The conceptual basis for composing in terms of octave-width bands leads naturally to the conception of pitch-space itself as a variable. In the second movement of the sonata, Goeyvaerts gradually compresses the available pitch space from the extremes to the middle octaves; a reverse unfolding of register space is heard in the third movement. Both techniques, of octave displacement and modulation of the pitch space, contrive to introduce a sense of direction to a serial idiom that was proving stubbornly and intractably static.

Stockhausen was deeply impressed by this first encounter with Webern's music. He was also fascinated by Goeyvaerts' ideas on register form, if less so with the actual

---

[4] *The Score*, 6 (1952).

music. This was a sound and a conception of music he had never encountered before; he identified with Goeyvaerts' quasi-mystical account of serial music as an image of pure knowledge, and even with the static imagery of Goeyvaerts' own music as an aesthetic of the stars. The two of them decided to make a stand and perform the second movement of the *Sonata* (the outer movements were altogether too complex and unfamiliar for Stockhausen to master in a few days) at the open seminar on composition. The seminar was to have been conducted by Schoenberg, but he was forced to withdraw because of illness—his last illness, in fact—and his place was taken by Theodor Adorno, the philosopher of music, who had studied composition with Berg and was author of a number of influential texts, the most recent being *The Philosophy of the New Music*. Goeyvaerts and Stockhausen duly performed the movement, only to have it was savaged by Adorno, who did not understand the new idiom at all. His response provoked an equally spirited defence by Stockhausen on behalf of the composer, who could not speak German. Adorno, he said, was 'trying to see a chicken in an abstract painting'.[5]

Stockhausen also heard Messiaen's *Mode de valeurs et d'intensités* for piano, in a recording made by the composer which had been brought to Darmstadt by the French music critic Antoine Goléa:

I will not readily forget that extraordinary moment, one summer day at Darmstadt, . . . when I played the disc of *Mode de valeurs et d'intensités* for the first time, in the presence of a number of young pupils, among whom was Stockhausen. I had no score, for the work was not yet published, but listening to the disc was enough for Stockhausen and for the Belgian Karel Goeyvaerts to realise its unique and prophetic qualities; they played it again and again, a score of times, totally engrossed, their eyes shining, and kept repeating 'This is the first integrated and systematic exploration of pitch space! This is what we have been dreaming about!'[6]

Stockhausen returned to Cologne to prepare for his final examinations. He kept closely in touch with Goeyvaerts by letter, beginning a correspondence which was to continue through to 1954. The Belgian was a true kindred spirit, the only other composer of his own generation in whom Stockhausen felt truly able to confide. His examinations successfully completed, he set to work planning compositions to embody the new-found principles of serialism and form. *Kreuzspiel*, completed on 4 November 1951 and again dedicated to Doris Andreae, marked his professional debut as a composer, and for many years remained his acknowledged Opus 1.

Events moved quickly. Through Eimert the new score came to the notice of Henrich Strobel, director of the Donaueschingen Music Festival and always on the look-out for promising new composers. Strobel proposed a commission for an orchestral work, for a fee which Stockhausen realized would enable him to study in Paris for a year. A piece for orchestra was already germinating, with the provisional

---

[5] Karlheinz Stockhausen and Robin Maconie, *Stockhausen on Music* p. 36.
[6] Antoine Goléa, *Rencontres avec Olivier Messiaen* (Paris, 1960), pp. 246–7.

title *Spiel*; in the time available to him between engagements as accompanist to the magician Adrion, he finished the first movement, which now has a separate existence as *Formel*, and a reduction of the score for two pianos was passed to the conductor Hans Rosbaud. Strobel duly confirmed the commission for an orchestral work to be premièred at the 1952 Donaueschingen Festival. Stockhausen married Doris on 29 December, and set off for Paris a fortnight later.

Kreuzspiel

1951: *Cross-play*
For oboe, bass clarinet, piano (and woodblock), and 3 percussionists (6 tomtoms, 2 tumbas or congas, 4 suspended cymbals).
Duration 10′.

Stockhausen describes this first pointillist composition as an example of dramatic form. The description 'dramatic' is meant in a classical sense, of a developmental process governed by the arrow of time. His earlier compositions are 'dramatic', but in the popular sense of conveying action and emotion; what emotional content there is in the new piece is expressed in a very much more refined manner, depending on the listener's prior awareness of its terms of proportion and equilibrium, and of subtle disturbances and distortions which are introduced into the flow from time to time.

The drama consists in the 'cross-play' of pitches from high to low and vice versa. In the DG recording, the piano bass register is panned to the left speaker, and the treble to the right, enabling the displacement of individual pitches (for listeners with perfect pitch) to be heard as audible movement to left and right. As pitches enter the middle octaves, they are picked out and sustained by the two woodwinds, and as more and more notes come to occupy the mid-range, they begin to acquire the contour and character of somewhat hesitant melodies. The drift continues however, through the mid-range and out to the extremes, so the woodwinds' potential melodies evaporate again, and the first movement, or first version of the 'game' ends with the pitches once more confined to the piano extremes of range, albeit transposed.

Two further movements follow: the second being what Messiaen would call an 'interversion' of the first, the development this time starting in the mid-range and gradually spreading outward to the pitch extremes, and a third which combines the two previous processes. (The idea of creating new material by aggregating earlier movements is employed by Berg in the *Chamber Concerto*, also by Bartók and Milhaud, but in a pointillist context as here, an audible counterpoint of structures is likely to be perceived simply as an increase in the density of events.)

Stockhausen's procedural starting-point is Goeyvaerts' *Sonata* for two pianos, and there is also an interesting parallel with Messiaen's pitch orders in 'les yeux dans les roues' (*Livre d'Orgue*), composed the same year, 1951, and similarly influenced, it is suggested, by Goeyvaerts' concept of register form.[7] There is a degree of cumulative impact in the three movements, and dramatic inevitability in the crosswise displacement of pitches in individual movements, but true drama involves human uncertainty as well, and it is Stockhausen's introduction of dramatic tension which distinguishes *Kreuzspiel* from both Goeyvaerts and Messiaen.

For example, the process by which the piano pitches converge and condense into sustained melodies is a palpably dramatic invention: it is not serially preordained, but a perceptually significant transition from notes as abstract data to melodies capable of expressing emotion and time in human terms. A similar dramatic conception underlies *Gesang der Jünglinge*, in the manner in which the child's voice condenses out of the plasma of electronic sounds. Stockhausen's original conception, as communicated to Goeyvaerts, was in fact for high (e.g. boy treble) and low male voices, piano, and tambourines and snare drums for their noisier attack. On reflection, however, he decided the percussion lacked resonance, and replaced them with tom-toms and tumbas arranged around the open piano, hopefully to gain extra resonance from the latter. Goeyvaerts for his part was opposed to the use of voices on account of their 'imprecision' of timbre, and also because a text would introduce extrinsic sounds.[8]

The percussion contribute an additional dimension to the drama. They represent first of all a relatively unpitched complementary sound-world to that of the piano and woodwinds, a shadowy region offsetting the precision and brilliance of the serial pitches. In the first movement the tumbas also provide a tempo reference for the piano attacks, which would otherwise be impossible to quantify. Thirdly, percussions convey physical action, and thereby heighten dramatic tension. The accentual structures of the percussion parts also describe processes of convergence and divergence, but between states of maximum order and disorder. These processes occupy and articulate larger segments of the opposing pitch-structures; they also interfere with and disturb the pitches in their appointed courses: 'Each time notes and noises occur at the same point of time—which happens fairly frequently—the note in some way or another drops out of the series, alters its intensity, transposes into the wrong register or takes a different duration from the one preordained.'[9]

In movement I, (Ex. 5) tumbas first beat out an identificatory series 2 8 7 4 11 1 12 3 9 6 5 10, then the additive duration series 1 2 3 . . . 12. Each statement of the duration series occupies 13 crotchet beats or $6\frac{1}{2}$ bars, against which the

---

[7] Jonathan Harvey, *The Music of Stockhausen* (London, 1975), pp. 16–19. According to Richard Toop, 'Goeyvaerts showed his piece to Messiaen around September '51, and apparently M. was extremely interested in the X-forms etc.' (Private communication).

[8] Hermann Sabbe, *Karlheinz Stockhausen: ' . . . wie die Zeit verging . . .* (Munich, 1981), pp. 18–19.

[9] Karlheinz Stockhausen, *Texte Zur Musik*, ii (Cologne, 1964), p. 11.

Ex. 5

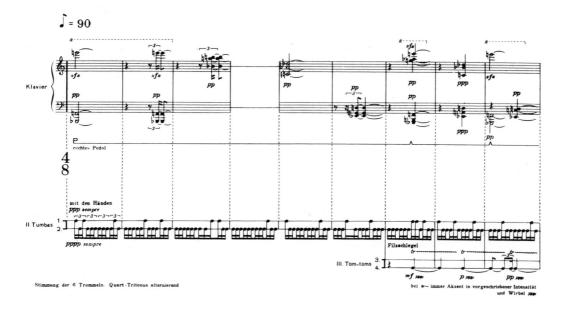

Kreuzspiel: the opening bars.
© Universal Edition AG Wien.

lower-pitched tom-toms play overlapping contrary rhythms. At bar 14 a tempo-change to quaver = MM 136 signals the end of the introduction; after two more statements of the duration series the woodwinds appear at bar 28, and following three further rotations a woodblock signal from the pianist begins a serial accelerando leading the music to its half-way point at the end of bar 52. From there on the form is retrograded and inverted, so that at bar 91 ((2 + 6 + 6) × 6½ bars) the starting piano pitches have reached their destinations.

In movement II, cymbals replace tumbas and tom-toms. Originally the tempo returned to the opening quaver = MM 90, but in the published 1959 version this has been doubled to crotchet = MM 90. (He also abandons an original serialization of attacks, and the piano chords in II are also a 1959 addition. The score looks intriguingly like a precursor, incidentally, of Boulez' *Mallarmé Improvisations* I and II.) Here the woodwinds are naturally more to the fore; the movement lasts through (6 × 6½) bars to bar 138, ending with a two-bar codetta which balances the opening woodwind exchange. Movement III brings a change to compound time and a return to the quaver = MM 136 pulse. An opening statement of the series (bars 146–50) defines the unit of duration as 13 dotted-crotchet beats. Six further rotations lead to the mid-point in bar 176, marked by an encircled accented tumba beat; thereafter through five further rotations the music gradually loses complexity, returning to the pitch distributions of the first section proper (after the introduction, at bar 14). Over a last piano chord the tom-toms play a measured rallentando-decrescendo statement of the duration series which, with a final beat added for good measure, makes six units for the mirror and thirteen for the movement as a whole.

Formel

1951: *Formula* movement for orchestra

3. 3. 3. 3. 3; glockenspiel, vibraphone, harp, celesta, piano; strings 6. 0. 0. 3. 3. Duration 11′.

Kreuzspiel is about musical elements in transition; the drama of the conception resides in the inevitability of the process. But the work also contains a particular revelation: in using sustaining wind instruments to highlight pitches as they pass through the mid-range, Stockhausen has brought about a situation in which melodic formulations are spontaneously generated. These melodies are not serially ordered, though they are produced as a consequence of serial operations. Nevertheless, they are an intimation of how the vertical (harmonic) and horizontal (melodic) dimensions of serial music might begin to be reconciled. A natural corollary of that discovery would be to compose a work which seeks to express the transition of groups of pitches, rather than invididual pitches, from the vertical to the horizontal in a serially more systematic fashion. This indeed was one of Stockhausen's intentions for the orchestral commission which came after *Kreuzspiel*; the new piece was also going to explore a fuller and richer palette of orchestral timbres, and refine and develop the implications of register transposition.

Formel is the first of a projected three movements, and remains the most hermetic in character. All three depict processes out of which melodies appear and grow; in II and III, which were completed after Stockhausen's move to Paris, the processes are overtly dynamic and continuous, in contrast to the crystalline structures and permutations of I, which Stockhausen eventually decided to withhold as a separate 'Study for orchestra'. Though he has since explained in his forweord to the 1974 published score that he felt he movement to be 'much too thematic', it would perhaps also be true to say that *Formel* is complete in itself.

The music describes a chevron-shaped expansion process from the mid-range to the extremes of pitch, first building outward to fill the pitch space, then

Ex. 6

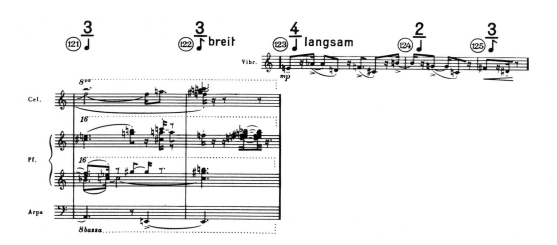

Formel: bars 117–25. Each layer of the instrumental texture is rigidly confined to an octave register. The two extreme octave registers are occupied; piano and celesta in the upper extreme articulating 9 × 4 then 10 × 3 semiquaver values, while harp and pizzicato basses in the lower extreme play the complementary 4 × 9 followed by 3 × 10 semiquaver values. The solo vibraphone in the middle register also plays 10 × 3 semiquaver values. Note that the harp melody is a transposed, segmental rotation of the vibraphone melody (Ex. 7).

© Universal Edition AG Wien.

systematically withdrawing from the middle to the outer limits. Where *Kreuzspiel* orders pitches, *Formel* orders 'blocks'. Each block has two aspects, the horizontal and the vertical. The number of pitches per block (ignoring repeated notes) in the horizontal dimension increases serially from one to twelve, as the duration of each constituent pitch division reduces from 12 semiquaver units to one; simultaneously the distribution of pitches in the vertical dimension rotates from a starting succession of 12 one-note groups, each of one semiquaver duration, through 11 two-note chords each of two semiquavers' duration, 10 × 3 × three semiquavers' duration, and so on to a final state of 1 twelve-note chord, twelve semiquaver units in length. Every horizontal component is always found in association with the same corresponding vertical component. For example, a sequence of 10 × three-note chords is always heard simultaneously with a section of melody based on a three-note structure, and one of 3 × ten-note chords with a ten-note segment of melody. The 'cross-play' of duration structures is therefore similar to Messiaen's duration crab-canons in the piano piece *Cantéyodjayâ*, and in much the same way one senses a certain imbalance in favour of the middle values at the expense of the extremes.

The requirements of register form account for the piece's unusual stratification of harmonies and melodies: if the serial transposition of blocks to different octave spaces is to work, the pitch space occupied by each component is bound to be restricted. A consequence is that the music conveys in performance a tangible, at times almost overwhelming, sense of suppressed violence, a perception if anything intensified by Stockhausen's strict allocation of orchestral timbres to particular pitch layers (Ex. 6). The orchestra forms a symmetrical structure of forces pivoting to either side of the vibraphone at the middle, representing the intersection of instantaneous (vertical) and continuous (horizontal) dimensions. Six violins are balanced by

Ex. 7

Formel: bars 1–10, vibraphone melody. The note content follows the series 1 × 12 semiquaver values, 2 × 11 (bars 2–3), 3 × 10 (bars 4–6), 4 × 9 (bars 7–9), 5 × 8 (bars 10 ff.).

© Universal Edition AG Wien.

3 cellos and 3 basses; 3 oboes and 3 clarinets in A are balanced by 3 bassoons and 3 horns; glockenspiel, celesta, and piano are less obviously counterpoised by pizzicato cellos, basses, and harp. The musical data progresses outwards by stages, but passes through regions of tone colour which are fixed; and since they are fixed in treble and bass registers according to the range of the appropriate instruments, once more the impression aroused over a period of time is one of instruments pacing about like caged animals. It is a disturbing, but, one is bound to admit, powerful impression, whatever its theoretical basis.

Within a strict framework Stockhausen repeats, ornaments, and elaborates his melodic line as if to demonstrate the liveliness of effect which can be derived from serial processes (Ex. 7). Twenty years later, with the composition of *Mantra* in 1970, he was to rediscover a similar suppleness of melody in a context of counterpointed transformations of register. *Formel* is thus the archetype of a long line of melody forms which continues today with *LICHT*. Indeed, its strongest echoes may be found in the *Tierkreis* melodies, 'Aries' and 'Capricorn' in particular, of 1975.

3 *Paris, 1952*

PARIS was the cradle of the new music, and Paris in 1952, celebrating the year of *L'Oeuvre du XXe siècle*, was at a peak of creative excitement, with Messiaen, Boulez, and Pierre Schaeffer all producing some of their most innovative and exciting work. The stir created by Cage, whose visit in 1949 introduced the prepared piano and its spiculated timbres to fashionable society, was still to be felt. Public interest was high in the music of the Three Viennese in the year following Schoenberg's death; his pupils René Leibowitz and Max Deutsch were actively teaching, writing, performing, recording, and above all defending the sacred principles of twelve-tone composition which had so long been proscribed.

Some idea of the excitement of the period may be gained from the high level of dissension, from the personal and polemical battles, and from the rivalries that existed among the principal factions of new music. Schaeffer, *agent provocateur* for *musique concrète*, proclaiming the dawn of a new era of tape music; Lasry and Baschet, sculptors in sound, constructing new shapes in metal, glass, and inflatable plastic for the aware composer; Leibowitz, resisting any challenge to his newly won authority as keeper of the serial keys; Messiaen, welcoming every new development and thereby innocently wreaking havoc among the established as well as the new conventions of musical order; and Boulez, wearing the colours of total predetermination, in the midst of the fracas lashing out at all and sundry. It was a euphoric, pentecostal tumult; as Boulez himself remarked, 'Rarely has there been a time of such sheer exaltation in the history of music.' It was happening against a background of a noisy popular battle being conducted in the press and on the concert platform between the defenders of tonal neo-classicism under the banner of Stravinsky, and the apostles of 'progressive atonality' (whose standard had no recognizable image but which bore the name of Schoenberg).[1] The arguments that raged then are still evident today, and Stockhausen's music continues to address the conceptual challenges encountered during his time of study in Paris.

In April 1952 *La Revue musicale* published a special edition, *L'Oeuvre du XXe siècle*, to coincide with the International Festival of Twentieth-Century Arts.[2] Among its contents two essays stand out: Pierre Schaeffer's 'L'Objet Musical' and Boulez's more

---

[1] See 'Open Forum: Variations on the Theme—Tonal or Atonal?' in Rollo Myers (ed.), *Music Today: Journal of the International Society for Contemporary Music*, (1949), 132.
[2] 'L'Oeuvre du XXe Siècle', *La Revue Musicale*, Numéro Spécial No. 212 (1952).

celebrated piece 'Eventuellement . . .'. The importance of Schaeffer's contribution to new musical thought has been largely overlooked (though it has not been helped by the dogmatic and often querulous tone of his writings). For the new musician, 1952 was the year of the tape recorder. Its impact can be summed up in the terms of an advertisement which appeared in the selfsame edition, inviting readers to consider its advantages to the teacher of music, composer, or music critic: 'to enable your pupils to judge for themselves the quality of their interpretation; to note at speed an idea, or a musical theme; to preserve a very precise recollection of a recording or of a live performance'. Pinpointed are three decisive areas of innovation in compositional thinking which Schaeffer had identified and, abetted by his students, was actively investigating.

First, tape added a new dimension to musical objectivity. Radio had assisted the rise of an earlier style of objectivity: neo-classicism, an aesthetic impartially receptive to and critically aware of classical idioms. Now tape introduced the possibility of a similarly objective appraisal, description, and creative manipulation of natural sounds and noises. Moreover, continuous sounds recorded on tape could be dissected into smaller and smaller segments of time, the parts rearranged, and even reversed in direction. The technological revelation of the inner life of sounds, directly comparable to Muybridge's photographic revelations of the dynamics of movement and their impact on the graphic arts,[3] meant that composers could no longer shelter behind the convention that natural sounds and noises were 'non-quantifiable': henceforth, all were equally open to analysis and, ultimately, to precise notation. New music was therefore bound to include sounds and noises of every kind, natural or contrived: a new science of sound was destined to evolve to meet this new challenge. The atomization of organic sound was part of the same atomization of knowledge already exemplified in pointillist music, but with the significant difference that for composers working in the tape medium the process was audible, demonstrably real, and 'concrete'.

Secondly, a tape recorder can 'objectify'—render intelligible—normally ephemeral sound (as well as musical thought) processes. Disordered or transitional processes become interesting, and even beautiful. The relationship between the tape medium and improvisation, or between tape and chance processes, further introduced to the young composer the possibility of a musical aesthetic based on chance procedures, both for the production of sound textures on tape, and equally as a medium for developing performance skills of improvisation and indeterminacy to a point where they could be freely employed in concert performance. Such skills have developed and flourished today in the oral culture of studio-based popular music, where music is composed directly to tape without necessarily starting from or going through a written stage. They are skills which have flourished less among classically trained composers, partly through lack of access to and training in sound recording, but

[3] Aaron Scharf, *Art and Photography* (London, 1968).

largely from the persistence of visual modes of thought. Stockhausen's continuing study and refinement of performance and notation conventions to determine specific degrees of musical indeterminacy, is the outstanding exception. Many respected figures of avant-garde music from both sides of the Atlantic took up the challenge of indeterminacy during the fifties, only to abandon it when it proved too difficult to resolve in a rational way (as the history of graph notation makes only too clear).[4]

Instant recall, the third advantage, is a corollary of the second, and carries the message that repetition, in so far as it is there for the simple purpose of aiding recall, is no longer a requirement of musical form. (The argument does not apply in quite the same way to dance music, although dance's structured repetition of step patterns is arguably just as much an aid and expression of a memorization process: all the same, we observe a tendency at this time for avant-garde music to retreat from dance simultaneously as it embraces the other implications of non-repetitive form.) With the loss of formal repetition there comes a corresponding loss of conventional awareness of the passage of musical time on the part of the listener. In its place a dynamic of action, or of music theatre, may arise, or a composer may give his music a sense of continuous development in other ways. Stockhausen is in no doubt about his own objectives: 'What I am looking for, and what I am working toward, is always the same: the *dynamic of change*, revealed as the passage of time, expressed as music.'[5]

As a result of acclimatization to recorded music, the listener also absorbs new memory and processing skills for music which function independently of its inherent oral conventions of repetition, shape, and sequence. These evaluative skills are typically exposed in broadcast quiz programmes where players are expected to identify a composition, artist, and even a particular recording, from a momentary burst of recorded music.

Schaeffer's essay on 'The Musical Object' is full of enthusiasm, but his ideas are not always clearly consecutive. To be sure, it is not easy to define a musical object in general terms which can apply as well to a musical note or phrase as to a sound or noise. Having determined a tape-recorded 'sound-object' as a starting point, he examines a number of mechanical options for varying and developing it. These include cutting and rearranging the sound material on tape to create a range of different but related sounds, altering the speed of play-back to transpose a sound in pitch and change its duration, and varying its dynamic envelope.

Among the concepts especially pertinent in relation to Stockhausen's music are what Schaeffer describes as 'the correspondence of duration as a function of pitch'. This is an interesting remark, because it is not strictly accurate. If a taped fragment of music is altered in speed, its perceived pitch is changed, and its overall duration is also changed. So far so good. But we have to distinguish duration, the outer dimension, from tempo, the inner measure of time, because it is tempo, and not

---

[4] See Erhard Karkoschka, *Notation in New Music* (London, 1969).
[5] Karlheinz Stockhausen, '1952/53: Orientation', in *Texte zur Musik*, i (Cologne, 1963), p. 37.

duration, which relates to frequency. The same criticism arises in Stockhausen's seminal essay ' . . . how time passes . . . ', dating from 1956[6] where duration and tempo are also treated as equivalent. Again, when we come to Stockhausen's process compositions of the sixties, in particular the plus-minus scores from *Prozession* to *Pole* and *Expo*, the theoretical basis for this music of transformation, as it is argued in the composer's notes to the performer, is once more consistent with Schaeffer's prescriptions for the musical object and its transformation, published fifteen years previously.[7]

Boulez' essay 'Eventuellement . . .' is also extremely fertile ground. Whereas Schaeffer is always attentive to the sounds that one hears with the new equipment, Boulez shows himself by contrast to be much more concerned with 'l'écriture'. The electronic medium is seen as an ideal instrument for the realization of abstract formal concepts, not as an instrument with its own sound qualities and limitations. (If only that were true.) His discussions of serial instrumentation (apropos *Polyphonie X*), serialization of tempi, and the generation of harmonic density by interval 'multiplication', on the other hand, are especially pertinent.

While in Paris, Stockhausen shared a room with a temperamental Turkish student in the Cité Universitaire Maison des Provinces de France, and divided his time between Messiaen's classes at the Conservatoire, and the studios of Schaeffer's Club d'Essai. Messiaen's course in analysis and aesthetics for 1952 centred on 'rhythm', a fortunate choice in view of his innovative theories of rhythmic identity and transformation. The French composer's dual nature, part medieval visionary, part machine-age designer, must have appealed to Stockhausen, whose own exceptional musical intelligence is complemented by equally decisive spiritual convictions. Among the subjects examined in Messiaen's course Stockhausen recalls 'rhythmic analysis of all Mozart's piano concerti, the rhythm of Gregorian chant, Indian rhythm; analyses of Debussy's, Webern's and Stravinsky's music, and of Messiaen's own works, from the original sketches to the final score'.[8] Stockhausen was later to publish his own analyses of cadence rhythms in Mozart, statistical processes in Debussy, and serial permutations in Webern.

Spiel

1952, revised 1973: *Play*, two movements for orchestra.

0. 3. 3. 3. double bassoon, 3; glockenspiel, vibraphone, celesta, electric organ, piano, strings 6. 6. 0. 6. 6.

[6] *Die Reihe* (English Edition), 3 (1959), 10–40; essay revised and edited by Georg Heike in Stockhausen, op. cit. 99.
[7] See below, p. 159–60.   [8] Stockhausen, op. cit. ii (Cologne, 1964), p. 144.

Seven percussion players, instrumentation for each movement as follows:
- I. 1: small Indian bell, small triangle; 2: 2 suspended cymbals, 2 tom toms; 3: woodblock, temple block; 4: hihat; 5: African garland rattle; 6: ratchet (e.g. washboard), 2 antique cymbals; 7: 2 tam-tams, pedal timpano.
- II. 1: 5 tuned cymbals (cinelli); 2: 2 suspended cymbals; 3: 2 suspended cymbals; 4: hihat; 5: large sizzle-cymbal; 6: 3; tom toms; 7: pedal timpano. Player 1 employs two, players 2–7 four grades of beater.

Duration 16′.

The surviving two movements of *Spiel* compare with the first two movements of *Kreuzspiel*, both in treating the theme of musical 'points' converging and condensing into melodic lines (this time forming a complete series), and in their instrumentation, which expands the limited palette of timbres of the earlier piece into the orchestral domain, while preserving the earlier distinctions of accompanying percussion. The choice of pitched instruments is the same as in *Formel*, but with a strengthening of the bass register by addition of double bassoon, a doubling of strings (though violas are still omitted), and a substitution of the substaining electric organ for the less powerful harp.

Stockhausen has imparted a more palpable dynamic of change to both pieces, compared to *Formel*. Characteristically spare in instrumentation and lean-sounding, the first movement depicts a process of continuous accretion of pitches and timbres, highlighted by the cell-like growth of a vibraphone melody in the mid-range, against a ringing background of glockenspiel and piano chords at extremes of register (Ex. 8). The contrast between foreground action and static background sonorities is stark: the score suggests a meditative piece, but the audible consequences of Stockhausen's choice of instruments and range of serial dynamics are considerably more assertive (in *Trans* one finds a similar amalgam of 'aggressive' and 'meditative' sounds).

In the second movement point-formations condense out of a resonant background of sustained metallic percussion. The change of percussion instrumentation to sounds of a more diffuse character results in less masking of quieter background elements by foreground accents, and allows the gradual mutation of amorphous resonances into sustained distinct pitches to be clearly appreciated. A resounding note struck on a glass goblet originally marked the point of contact of the two sound-worlds (Ex. 9), after which the process reverses and the pitched sounds are gradually absorbed once again into the background of percussion resonances. For the first performance under Rosbaud at Donaueschingen, Stockhausen agreed to end the piece with the struck glass sound. 'Rosbaud gave a uniquely massive downbeat for such a fragile instrument, and the percussionist eagerly responded with a blow so intense that the goblet burst into a thousand pieces.'[9]

[9] Ibid. iv (Cologne, 1978), p. 53.

31

Ex. 8

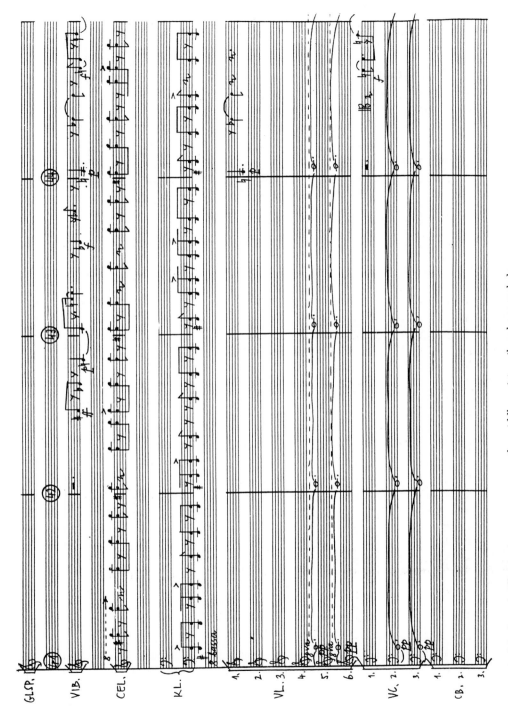

Spiel 1: the pointillist texture converges on the middle-register vibraphone melody.

© Universal Edition AG Wien.

Ex. 9

Spiel II, bar 56: the climax where in the original version a crystal goblet was struck.

In the 1973 revised score high triangle and small cymbal create a bright halo of metallic resonance as a substitute for the original glass.

Although the musical action is still determined according to the principles of register form, the relationship of percussion and pitched instruments suggests a more systematic approach, based on an awareness of attack and decay as separate components able to be transposed, by analogy with tape-recorded examples, to create new sounds. Stockhausen's serialization of durations is also more sophisticated than that of *Formel*. In *Spiel* the full orchestra is divided into four instrumental subgroups defining individual registers, and each is assigned a different but related scale of durations (Ex. 10). The result is an evident improvement in the distribution and flow of events. The graduated association of longer durations with softer dynamics, shorter with louder, is devised to maintain a balance of energy relative to time.

Ex. 10

$(\flat=1)$												
I	$11\frac{2}{3}$	$10\frac{1}{2}$	$9\frac{1}{3}$	9	$7\frac{2}{3}$	$6\frac{1}{2}$	$5\frac{1}{3}$	5	$3\frac{2}{3}$	$2\frac{1}{2}$	$1\frac{1}{3}$	1
II	$11\frac{1}{2}$	$10\frac{1}{3}$	10	$8\frac{2}{3}$	$7\frac{1}{2}$	$6\frac{1}{3}$	6	$4\frac{2}{3}$	$3\frac{1}{2}$	$2\frac{2}{3}$	2	$\frac{2}{3}$
III	$11\frac{1}{3}$	11	$9\frac{2}{3}$	$8\frac{1}{2}$	$7\frac{1}{3}$	7	$5\frac{2}{3}$	$4\frac{1}{2}$	$3\frac{1}{2}$	3	$2\frac{2}{3}$	$\frac{1}{2}$
IV	12	$10\frac{2}{3}$	$9\frac{1}{2}$	$8\frac{1}{3}$	8	$6\frac{2}{3}$	$5\frac{1}{2}$	$4\frac{1}{3}$	4	$2\frac{2}{3}$	$2\frac{1}{2}$	$\frac{1}{3}$

Spiel: duration scales of the four orchestral layers.

Schlagtrio

1952, revised 1973: *Percussion Trio.*

For piano and 2×3 timpani.

Duration 16′.

Music arises from Measure and is rooted in the great Oneness. The great Oneness begets the two poles; the two poles beget the power of Darkness and of Light. . . . Perfect music has its cause. It arises from equilibrium. Equilibrium arises from righteousness, and righteousness arises from the meaning of the cosmos. . . Music is founded on the harmony between heaven and earth, on the concord of obscurity and brightness. . . For a long time one school of players favoured the technique of stating side by side, developing in counterpoint, and finally harmoniously combining two hostile themes or ideas, such as law and freedom, individual and community. In such a Game the goal was to develop both themes with complete equality and impartiality, to evolve out of thesis and antithesis the purest possible synthesis.[10]

[10] Hermann Hesse, *The Glass Bead Game* (London, 1972), pp. 31, 41.

Stockhausen's new composition returns to austerity of conception and tone material. Overtly transcendental in theme, it expresses the idea of perfection in music, and the manner of its execution, as envisioned by the narrator of *The Glass Bead Game*. Like *Kreuzspiel*, the piano articulates a converging of pitch material from extremes to the centre. The pitch material is melodic, however, and the temporal counterpoint more closely interlaced, suggesting a fleeting comparison with Boulez' *Structures Ia* for two pianos. Stockhausen's serial orders describe clear trajectories, not only in register, but in duration, dynamic, and (in the original at least) attack character, from extreme differentiation to relative homogeneity (Ex. 11). The play of elements in the six-octave pure-pitch domain of the piano is mirrored by an equivalent process in the confined one-octave 'contrary sound space' represented by the six timpani. Each timpano corresponds to an octave register of the piano; the timpani are tuned to a whole-tone scale, a quarter-tone lower in pitch than the piano, occupying as it were the interstices between alternate pitches of the chromatic scale. Originally, both piano and timpani parts incorporated analogous series of 8 modes of attack; in the 1973 revision these were considerably simplified.

The meeting of opposites, which occurs when the reciprocal pitch spaces are filled and contrasts most nearly neutralized, distils a new serial melody, combining features of both as after an exchange of chromosomes in a newly fertilized cell. This third voice remains when the parent melodies symmetrically withdraw to their original positions, finally passing, in the composer's words, 'beyond the realm of the physically representable or perceivable'.[11]

Schlagtrio represents a considerable challenge to the performer and to the listener. Much of the interpretative difficulty arises from the use of timpani as an alternative timbre to the piano. First, their sheer physical assertiveness in performance threatens to overwhelm the piano, even though the dramatic complementarity is exact and the third section of the piece, where the timpani play alone, is extremely effective, a distant recollection perhaps of the sounds of wartime. Second, the timpani are perhaps too precise in pitch to be truly 'alternative', added to which the louder the instrument is struck the more the quarter-tone offset in pitch is distorted by stretching of the membrane. Third, the instruments are not sufficiently resonant at a distance to be heard to sustain pitches to the same specified degree as the piano (we may recall the composer's analogous problem with the smaller drums of *Kreuzspiel*). Fourth, the 'pitch octave' of the six timpani is arguably too low and too condensed in register to be readily identified as complementary to the six-octave range of the piano. In *Kontakte*, by comparison, the further a timbre descends the scale from brightness to obscurity, the wider the interval between adjacent pitches: a prescription which, if applied to the timpani in *Schlagtrio*, might conceivably have resulted in an extension of the contrary pitch space by a further octave or two, and increased the number of instruments to a full twelve (the chromatic scale of bongos

---

[11] Stockhausen, op. cit. ii, p. 14.

Ex. 11

Schlagtrio: opening bars. Once again the music describes a movement from opposite extremes to median values (compare *Kreuzspiel*, Ex. 5 above).

© Universal Edition AG Wien.

in the first version of *Punkte*). As the present instrumentation stands, the requirements of balance suggest that all instruments be amplified; some clarification of the essential dramatic relationship between piano and timpani might also be effected were the piano to be situated in the centre of the auditorium, and the two groups of timpani at either side of the proscenium. A not dissimilar staging is specified for *Kontakte*, if loudspeakers are substituted for timpani (which they resemble physically as vibrating surfaces).

Punkte

1952: *Points* for orchestra (original version: withdrawn)
1. 2. 3. 3 saxophones, 2. 1; 1 cornet, 1; 12 bongos tuned in semitones B3♭–A4 (3 players); 2 pianos ('hard' and 'soft'), 2 harps (II 'muted'); strings 2. 0. 2. 1. 1. Duration 8′ 30″.

Punkte in its original version marks an important time of decision for Stockhausen. His withdrawal of the score is part of its significance, of which the 1962 recomposition (effectively a new work, and considered elsewhere) gives little overt clue. From the circumstances of its composition, and judging by its relationships with *Schlagtrio* and *Kontra-Punkte*, as well as from its instrumentation, it is possible to draw conclusions which make its non-appearance in original 'pointillist' guise a matter of regret.

Stockhausen withdrew many compositions after their first performance at this time, partly as a result of adverse public reaction, parly also in a spirit of intense self-criticism. Scores were burned. That difficult and awkward works like *Formel*, *Spiel*, and *Schlagtrio* have been reinstated, as it were, whereas the *Punkte* of 1952 remains in limbo, indicates the growing doubts he was beginning to feel about the musical principles and procedures in which he had invested so much faith and effort. We deduce as much from the fact that *Kontra-Punkte* begins again with point formations from *Punkte*, but this time they are gradually transformed into group formations. Stockhausen was also in doubt about the viability of the orchestra as a suitable medium for composing in serially related timbres: 'Any attempt to subordinate the different structures of the different instrumental tones to a general rational principle of proportions is bound to fail', he wrote.[12] The 'rational principle' he valued could only be implemented satisfactorily, it seemed, in the electronic medium.

The score nevertheless survives (Ex. 12). It differs from *Spiel*: the music does not

[12] Seppo Heikenheimo, *The Electronic Music of Karlheinz Stockhausen* (Helsinki, 1972), p. 15.

Punkte 1952: page 1. The texture is more aerated than *Spiel*, and has inner serial 'echoes' (compare Boulez' *Polyphonie X*). Note the cancelled bongo parts: 'Bongos weglassen—"Stuck"' ('Omit bongos throughout').

germinate continuous melodies from a pointillist flux; nor of course does it evolve in timbre from diversity to unity, as *Kontra-Punkte*. Unprecedented pitch repetitions and interval symmetries in the opening few bars suggest an unprecedented approach, as though a veil of silence were drawn over the music and one could only hear through a pattern of perforations in the veil.

Punkte's instrumentation is highly interesting: richer in sonorities, less doctrinaire, and more aware of the practicalities of ensemble balance and blending of timbres. It is also unusual for Stockhausen in specifying exclusively instruments of precise pitch. The role of percussion as a complementary pitch space is taken by a scale of tuned bongos in the middle register, a clear indication of the work's conceptual affinity with its transcendental predecessor *Schlagtrio*. After finishing the score, however, Stockhausen decided to omit them. Their presence may not however have been entirely necessary, as the subgroup of two harps and two pianos express a complementary relationship with the sustaining goups of woodwinds, brass (including saxophones), and strings (including violas).

Kontra-Punkte

1952–3: *Counter-Points* for ten instruments.

Flute, clarinet in A, bass clarinet, bassoon, trumpet, trombone, piano, harp, violin, cello.

Duration 12′.

Kontra-Punkte is an exuberant, colourful, outgoing, and impatient piece, its dynamism in marked contrast to the serially constrained energies of its immediate instrumental predecessors. Its theme is 'integration', drawing pointillist diversity of instrumental colour and contrasts of dynamic and attack into individuality, continuity, and similarity. The focus of all this gravitational attraction is the piano, whose leading and integrative role Stravinsky much admired (his own *Movements* for piano and orchestra of 1959–60 employs the instrument in a similar way). The essentially happy mood of the piece, its playfulness and richness of invention, are experienced like a release: it is as though, having decided that conventional instrumental timbres did not submit to serial prescription, Stockhausen was suddenly able to enjoy them for their own sakes.

The new work uses a much-reduced ensemble, compared to *Punkte 1952*, but again exclusively of instruments of tempered pitch, in pair formations (flute—bassoon, clarinet—bass clarinet, trumpet—trombone, piano—harp, violin—cello). The musical texture, at times unusually dense, appears to derive from preordained blocks of pitches distributed and combined in a manner not dissimilar to the electronic studies. These groups of pitches are shared among groups of instruments, to be revealed in the interplay of time-point structures which 'disturb' them into life, creating repetitions, *Klangfarben* conjunctions, and echoes of pitch. In this respect it plays the scherzo to Boulez' *Polyphonie X* for seventeen instruments, whose pitches form similar constellations. Combinations of attack and sustaining instruments abound, articulating lines and phrases of enormous length; here more clearly than ever the listener is made aware of a polyphony of time structures, the very large simultaneously with the very small.

As the work proceeds, one by one the instruments stop playing; while the gradual reduction of timbres is scarcely noticed except in retrospect, the gradual rise of the piano to supremacy, asserted in cadenzas of ever-increasing length (offset by ever-decreasing dynamic levels) is impossible to miss. The writing for all instruments is brilliantly virtuosic: here too Stockhausen's idiom is perhaps closer to Webern than ever before (though with a far greater sense of humour). Emotionally, it is the opposite pole of the *Schlagtrio*, whose 'levelling out' of contrasts it shares; in rhythm and tempo it shows an elegance and flexibility equally in opposition to *Formel*, with which it has obvious affinities in timing and tendency to expand from the centre to extremes of register.

Kontra-Punkte passed through many revisions during and after publication. The underlying structure suggests two sections of twelve units of 22 dotted-crotchet bars. The basic 22-bar division is articulated in the structure of superordinate tempo-changes, alternating a reference quaver = MM 120 tempo (corresponding to middle C, Stockhausen's central pitch, final resting-place of the flute at 508, and also central pitch of *Formel*) with six faster tempi, quaver = MM 126, 136, 152, 168, 184, and 200, corresponding approximately to the first group of six pitches with which the work begins.[13] The number 22 is interesting as the sum of the series $(1, 2, \ldots 6) + 1$, and also (in terms of 66 quaver pulses) as the sum of the series $1, 2, \ldots 11$. Stockhausen's choice of a dotted-crotchet bar unit inevitably suggests division into twelve demisemiquavers. The possibilities of serially determined super and subordinate tempo variation are considerable.

Rather optimistically, Stockhausen originally demanded an incandescent MM 60 *per bar* (equivalent to twelve demisemiquavers per second), and was prevailed on by Scherchen, who conducted the première at the 1953 ISCM Festival in Cologne, to reduce this tempo to a more manageable level. Even so, the pianist was unable to negotiate the ending, and the first performance had to be curtailed. Only after this were the published changes of metronomic tempo introduced.[14] The structural integrity of Stockhausen's original plan, relying on notated tempo relationships reviewed at a *constant* speed, is to that extent compromised. The smallest time

[13] Dieter Schnebel, 'Karlheinz Stockhausen', *Die Reihe* (German Edition), 4 (1958). Much of the author's analysis of *Kontra-Punkte* is omitted from the English edition (1960).
[14] Heikenheimo, op. cit. 22–3.

Ex. 13

Kontra-Punkte: bars 87–91. First published version.

Ex. 14

Kontra-Punkte: bars 87–91. Revised published version.
© Universal Edition AG Wien.

divisions within the bar, however, are nearly always strictly the same for every player, so a listener can still follow Stockhausen's tempo changes visually, by looking at the note values, if not so easily by ear, listening to the music.

At 88 a major revision has taken place between publication of the first and second printed scores. In the earlier version (UE 12207) the minor ninth interval defined by piano and trombone is filled out by a dynamic cluster (Ex. 13), an example of the composer's favourite 'swarm of bees' image which also appears in *Gesang der Jünglinge* and is itself a subsequent addition to the original score. This cluster starts as a tutti and tapers away in density, and belongs conceptually to his 'statistical' phase of development, being an instrumental equivalent of filtered noise.

For the revised published score (UE 12218), Stockhausen rewrote this 'insert' entirely: in its place he substitutes a 'firecracker' of points (Ex. 14), equally 'statistical' in effect, but using serial principles this time to achieve maximum differentiation. Instead of being restricted in dynamic to minimum values, and in register to a narrow octave band in the mid-range, the pitches are scattered across a much wider bandwidth, from mid-range to upper extreme, and across the whole dynamic range. Here too (Fig. 1) the serial orders can be esaily identified.

Fig. 1

Pitches: 2 4 5 3 6 1   5 6 1 4 2 3   5 1 2 6 3 4   3 5 6 4 1 2

Attacks: 3 4 5 2 6 1   4 5 1 6 2 3   5 1 2 6 3 4   3 5 6 4 1 2

Intensities: (*pp* = 1, *p* = 2, . . . *sfz* = 6)

```
5 4 2 4 5 6    5 6 6 4 5 4    2 6 5 4 4 6    6 6 5 5 6 6
6 6 6 6 6      4 1   5 6 6    5   6 1 5 5    4 4 1 4     5
  3 5 5 4      3 2   3   5 4      5 6 4  5 2 6 6
  5 4   3      6 5   6       3      2   3   5 2 3
    3   2      2 3           6      6         3 4
        1      4                   3
```

Incidence of intensities (per unit of six demisemiquavers):

pp × 1	*mf* × 4
p × 2	*f* × 5
mp × 3	*sfz* × 6

With *Kontra-Punkte* the pointillist phase of Stockhausen's career comes to an end, subsumed into a wider matrix of organizational categories increasingly sensitive to aural perceptions. The question dominating his next instrumental works, piano pieces, *Zeitmasze* for woodwind quintet, and culminating in *Gruppen* for three orchestras, is a new one: the perception of time.

4 *The Path to Electronic Music*

STOCKHAUSEN became acquainted with electronic music synthesis through Herbert Eimert. Between 1948 and 1952 the focus of experimentation in composition using prerecorded material was the Paris Club d'Essai, run by Pierre Schaeffer, an initiative whose origins lay in radiophonic drama. Electronic tone synthesis was nothing new. From the turn of the century inventors and instrument manufacturers had been active in developing instruments powered by electricity and utilizing the most up-to-date audio technology, to supersede the player piano and harmonium in the domestic keyboard market. The theory and technology of tone synthesis was therefore well established in 1950, but it had largely evolved in relation to traditional keyboard applications, and to market forces conditioned by an uniformed public taste. From time to time exceptions, such as the ondes Martenot, theremin, and trautonium, appeared alongside conventional orchestral forces on the serious concert platform to perform new works by Messiaen, Varèse, Hindemith, and others. But the traditional master and servant relationship between composer and electric instrument remained: composers accepted or rejected the new sonorities as they came, and were neither able, nor saw it as a creative necessity, to become involved in the theory or practice of timbre synthesis. Messiaen perhaps came closer than most, with his experiments with exotic organ registers in the *Messe de la Pentecôte* and the *Livre d'Orgue*, but that too was intuitively based, and limited to pre-existing components of organ timbre.

A composer and music critic of long standing, Eimert had been an advocate of new music from the 1920s, publishing a monograph on the teaching of atonal music in 1923, and acquainted with German developments in electric musical-instrument technology from the thirties and forties. He was thus in a position to recognize the compositional implications of new researches in phonetics instituted by Werner Meyer-Eppler at the University of Bonn after the war.

Since the late nineteenth century the study of speech sounds had developed in close partnership with that of sound recording. (Indeed, George Bernard Shaw, an amateur of British research in this field at the turn of the century, indirectly based his play *Pygmalion* on the subject.) After the end of the war, with the arrival of tape recording and the sonagram (a voice-print device), phonetics research was able to focus on analysis of continuous speech, with a view to isolating the basic components of spoken language. Similar research in the United States and elsewhere had already acknowledged the close relationship between music and the organization of speech sounds, both as timbres and in their temporal succession. Statistical and probabilistic analysis of the distribution and degrees of change of units of spoken language in time were also relevant, as an aspect of information theory, to early computer-based research in artificial intelligence, voice recognition, and automatic translation. (Ironically, experimentation in music was frequently encouraged among researchers as a stepping-stone to the higher complexities of language analysis and synthesis.)

As part of his investigations Meyer-Eppler dissected individual speech sounds from tape recordings, and reassembled them to form synthetic words and phrases. It was hearing the fruits of such experiments that persuaded Eimert that a sound theoretical basis existed for setting up an electronic music studio where a new art of music, grounded in pure research in tone synthesis and on fundamental principles of musical organization and perception, might be created. It was out of this conviction that the Cologne Radio electronic music studio eventually came into being.

Robert Beyer, Reader in New Music at Cologne Radio, and Meyer-Eppler presented papers on 'The Sound-World of Electronic Music' at the Darmstadt Summer School for New Music in 1950 and they were joined by Pierre Schaeffer in 1951, when the latest ideas in electronic and concete music were again reviewed. That was the year Stockhausen first attended; he struck up a friendship with Meyer-Eppler, which continued afterward by letter and was eventually to lead to his studying with Meyer-Eppler from 1954. It is thus reasonable to assume that by the time he arrived in Paris, Stockhausen was sufficiently *au fait* with the theoretical principles of both *musique concrète* and electronic music for his first practical experiments in the medium to be seen as a considered response to the alternatives represented by Paris and Cologne. Effectively, the choice facing the composer of tape music was either to follow Schaeffer in intuitive manipulation of preformed materials, following only instinct, totally lacking in scientific rigour, and offering no real hope of arriving at any systematic method—or to aim toward a compositional system grounded in science, but for which neither a comprehensive and intelligible theory nor suitable technical means yet existed. There was no doubt where Stockhausen's inclinations tended: as he wrote to Goeyvaerts, 'From day one I sensed that musique concrète is nothing more than wilful capitulation in the face of indeterminacy, a perversely amateurish game of chance and unbridled improvisation.'[1] For the time being, the suprematist principles shared by Stockhausen and Goeyvaerts provided a theoretical defence against aesthetic anarchy; Stockhausen also found an ally in Boulez, who had come to the same conclusion and was developing his own radical serial methodology for handling the new medium.

Toward the end of March 1952, Stockhausen visited the Club d'Essai studios for the first time at the invitation of Boulez, then engaged in the preparation of a tape

---

[1] Hermann Sabbe, *Karlheinz Stockhausen*: ' . . . *wie die Zeit verging* . . . ' (Munich, 1981), p. 42.

étude. A few months later, he was writing to Goeyvaerts about Messiaen's concrete study *Timbres–Durées*, about which he and the composer had exchanged words. Stockhausen was not convinced that the tape medium was 'necessary' for the purpose expressed in the composition. Not only rhythmically, but in every other way: dynamics, range of timbres, variations within a timbre, combinations of timbres—Messiaen would have been better served, said Stockhausen, by conventional instrumental forces.

Stockhausen continued to attend the Club d'Essai as an observer, while at the same time keeping up a correspondence with Goeyvaerts on the theoretical goals of electronic music synthesis, and referring practical questions to Meyer-Eppler from time to time. In November an opportunity arose for some hands-on experience in a small studio in the basement of the PTT building on the rue Barrault. There, at Schaeffer's behest, he spent some weeks recording and codifying instrumental sounds, both European and non-European, on to disc. He also made tape recordings of ethnic instruments in the Musée de l'Homme. The studio was poorly equipped, but did have a sine-wave generator. Goeyvaerts encouraged him to begin experiments in synthesis by superimposition of sine tones:

The work was infinitely arduous; as there was no tape-recorder in the studio I had to copy each sine tone on to disc and then re-copy it from one disc to another! This first 'composition of sounds' by electronic means was witnessed by the Fench scientist Abraham Moles, who thought me totally starry-eyed . . . [Goeyvaerts and I] wanted absolutely pure, controllable sounds without the subjective emotional influence of interpreters.[2]

In fact, Stockhausen's aim and approach to electronic tone synthesis were entirely orthodox; what was unusual was their application to the production of non-standard timbres, and in their being 'handmade' rather than mechanically produced.

The first attempt at a 'Study on one sound' proved abortive. It seems that Stockhausen wanted to reproduce a range of typical attacks; he would know from his observations of *musique concrète* that the initial attack or onset of a musical tone is the portion richest in partials, the decay portion being generally simpler; also that the attack is the feature by which the ear normally distinguishes one timbre from another: it 'defines' the tone. However, it proved impossible to define the attacks of these sine-wave complexes in a satisfactory manner. As he later confided in a letter to Eimert—whose plans for an electronic studio in Cologne were aimed precisely at satisfying these objectives—the technical means available to him in Paris were simply not up to the task: 'the possibility of realising a "sound-atom" is completely beyond me.'[3]

A compromise solution was eventually discovered: six different timbres were prepared by introducing damping materials between the strings of a piano at specific

---

[2] Karlheinz Stockhausen, *Texte zur Musik*, iii (Cologne, 1971), p. 342.
[3] Herbert Eimert, 'How Electronic Music Began', *Musical Times*, Apr. 1973, pp. 347–9.

47

nodes to suppress unwanted harmonics. These prepared timbres were recorded on tape, and identical sections cut 3 cm. into the attack, where the sound was richest in harmonics, relatively stable in amplitude, and free of initial action noise; these sections could then be spliced together to give usable lengths of relatively static timbres.

Konkrete Etüde

1952: *Concrete Study.*

Tape original, of which an acetate copy survives in the GRM archives, Paris. Duration 2′ 45″.

His plan for a concrete *étude* then involved combining these basic timbres in serial orders, so that a correspondence would exist between the instantaneous harmonic proportions of the sounds (their attack characteristics) and the time proportions of the piece as a whole. The normal tape speed in 1952 being 76 cm./sec., it was possible to create different attack characteristics by splicing short segments of different timbres in séquence, in various serial permutations, which would pass so rapidly as to appear instantaneous. Stockhausen went further, permutating not only the six constituent timbres, but also their durations, to reproduce in microcosm at the instant of each attack a version of the essential structure of the entire work.

Each of the basic compound timbres was then transposed to six pitch levels (Ex. 15). Toop[4] gives these as I = C″, II = F″♯, III = B″, IV = F′, V = B′♭, VI = E, (i.e. C0, F0♯, B0, F1, B1, E2), which appears improbable as it would put I and II below piano range and the whole piece in the bass register. Given that similar interval-complexes based on middle C occur in later electronic works, one may assume an intention to have the entire piece finally transposed to the mid-range, even if for the purposes of achieving the best possible sound, as well as for precise editing of attacks, the initial work had to be done at these much lower pitches. Transposition would normally be effected with the aid of the *Phonogène*, a device to alter pitch without stretching or squeezing time values; in the event Stockhausen speeded up and edited each transposition afresh to preserve the time proportions of the attack sequences. The final assembly on to disc could then take place.

The 6 × 6 'magic square' of serial orders and permutations from which Stockhausen determines the distribution of musical events in pitch and time, both in microcosm and in macrocosm, is an important development in his serial thinking.

[4] Richard Toop, 'Stockhausen's *Konkrete Etüde*', *Music Review*, 37 (1976), 297.

Ex. 15

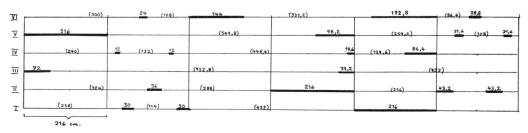

Konkrete Etüde: score, page 1 (after Richard Toop). The six-line stave indicates the six levels of transposition, thick lines representing sound, thin silence. Each block is 216 cm. in length; tape speed is 76 cm./sec. Both the linear order of transpositions (5 3 4 1 6 2 . . . etc.), and the number of layers in successive blocks (2 6 1 4 3 5 . . . etc.) are serially determined.

© Universal Edition AG Wien.

Also significant is his use of 'modes' to decide how the sounds within a macro-time unit (a tape length of 216 cm., or approximately 3 seconds' duration) are to be combined:

1. Start together, end separately;
2. End together, start separately;
3. As (1), durations related to pitch (the higher the shorter);
4. As (2), durations related to pitch;
5. Sounds in linear succession, followed by pauses;
6. Sounds in linear succession, preceded by pauses.

Modes and magic squares were to form the basis of Stockhausen's compositional procedures in electronic and instrumental fields for many years thereafter.

The sound of the completed *Etüde* did not live up to expectations—Toop describes a characteristically 'shuffling, vaguely ethnic sound, . . . at times like a refugee from the Unesco folk-music project'.[5] Recopying on to disc, and from disc to disc also gave the final recording a prominent underlying rumble (though Stockhausen quite liked

[5] Ibid.

49

that aspect, and seems to refer to it in the thundering passages of *Kontakte* at X and elsewhere). Although Stockhausen described it in a letter to Pousseur as 'a negative result', the procedural and conceptual gains achieved in the *Etüde* are of the utmost significance.

Toward the end of his life Eimert complained[6] that Stockhausen misrepresented history in claiming to have been the first to compose synthetic sound spectra, on the grounds that Stockhausen had himself written to him from Paris to confess that his first attempts at realizing a 'sound atom' had failed, and that by the time of his first successful efforts in Cologne the following year, Eimert and others had already produced several pieces. But on the evidence of Stockhausen's original plan to create synthetic timbres by superimposing sine tones, and of the procedures perfected in the *Etüde*, it is obvious that the major conceptual breakthrough of a consistent methodology for electronic music had in fact been achieved before his return to Cologne. On the well-known falsification principle, then, Stockhausen's claim to priority must be accepted, for had a hypothesis not existed, his attempts at realization could not have been deemed to fail.

Elektronische Studie I

1953: *Electronic Study I.*
Duration 9′ 30″.

Following his return to Cologne in March 1953 Stockhausen was appointed permanent collaborator in electronic music in the newly founded studio for electronic music at Cologne Radio. He joined Eimert, appointed studio director, and sound engineer Heinz Schütz, who had previously assisted Meyer-Eppler as well as Eimert and Beyer in their electro-acoustic researches. The studio was equipped with a melochord (an electronic keyboard), a trautonium, two ring modulators, an octave-filter, two in-house W49 filters developed for radio drama applications, two full-track studio tape recorders, and a *four-track* tape recorder:

After a number of experiments I decided not to use electronic sound sources (melochord, trautonium) producing predefined spectra, but to limit myself to sine tones ('pure' tones, without overtones) produced by a frequency generator. Sine tones differ from one another only in frequency and amplitude. It follows that a combination of frequency and amplitude relationships will yield a sound result specific to that combination.[7]

---

[6] Op. cit.
[7] Stockhausen, op. cit. ii, p. 23.

Studie I returns to the original goal of a musical structure of 'pure, controllable sounds' determined in every aspect by a consistent series of proportions. The static character of the finished work is no error of judgement, therefore, but quite intentional. Although the studio equipment in Cologne was manifestly superior to that available to him in Paris, Stockhausen nevertheless found the task of combining sine tones one at a time into vertical complexes far from easy. Because of their extreme purity of form, sine tones are extraordinarily revealing of defects in transmission or recording, and distortions are compounded by recopying from tape to tape. Stockhausen found that tape recorders were not neutral at all: each had its distinctive sound character, each was an 'instrument', and their inconsistencies relative to one another could appear even greater than between two conventional musical instruments such as violins. He was nevertheless able to report to Goeyvaerts in July 1953: 'I am putting together sine tones to make sounds for a new piece . . . and have just composed some examples of superimposed sine tones, which are totally still, but out of which individual partials emerge into the foreground one after another at predetermined times.'[8] The absolute stillness for which he strived is the outward expression of an ideal condition of equilibrium, a *Gleichberechtigkeit*, or absence of hierarchical inequalities of emphasis, among the sound elements in their various aspects. Through his studies of acoustic literature it became clear that he would also have to take account of the limitations of human hearing for that ideal to be perceived. This meant, for example, organizing his seial prescriptions to take account of Fletcher and Munson's curves of equal loudness level this a number of years before the recording industry introduced sound metering adjusted to correspond more nearly to the human ear's speed of response and perception of loudness in relation to frequency.

The tone complexes of *Studie I* (Ex. 16) are bell-like combinations of sine-tone partials ultimately derived from a germinal symmetrical series of intervals from the overtone scale: descending minor tenth, rising major third, descending minor sixth, rising minor tenth, falling major third, expressed in the harmonic ratios $\frac{12}{5} : \frac{4}{5} : \frac{8}{5} : \frac{5}{12} : \frac{5}{4}$. From a starting frequency of 1920 Hz, a series of six frequencies is derived in accordance with the interval succession. This series forms the basis of a magic square, and from the remaining frequencies in order a further five serial transpositions and magic squares are derived. The organization and dsitribution of frequencies is similar in principle to the *Etüde*, though more elaborate and far-reaching in practice. Each tone group has one dominant frequency, louder than the others, which determines the duration of the group. Six dynamic envelopes are rotated, based on straight-across or painstaking diagonal tape-cutting, without or with reverberation. 'This music sounds indescribably pure and beautiful! . . . You cannot imagine how happy I am at the moment', Stockhausen wrote to Goeyvaerts in August 1953.[9] 'It is unbelievably beautiful to hear such sounds, which are

[8] Sabbe, op. cit. 44.
[9] Ibid. 45.

Ex. 16

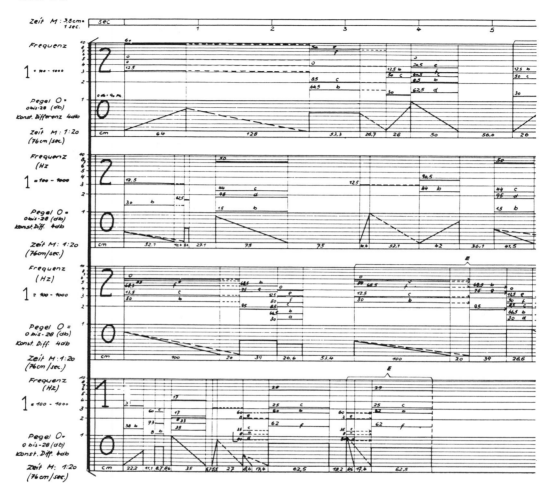

Elektronische Studie I: sample pages of score representing the first 12.8 seconds. There are four layers, each system comprising an upper logarithmic stave for pitch, and a lower stave for amplitude. Solid lines refer to unreverberated, dashed lines to reverberated pitches and amplitudes. Sections with E-brackets above are 'Echo-sections' of previous pitch material. Numerical signatures refer to pitch (I = range 100–1,000 Hz., 2 = 200–2,000 Hz., ½ = 50 Hz., etc.) and maximum amplitude (in Germany studio potentiometers are negatively calibrated from an optimum 0 dB to infinity: −8 therefore means a scale of amplitudes rising to a maximum of −8 dB).

© Universal Edition AG Wien.

completely "calm", static, and "illuminated" only by structural proportions. Raindrops in the sun . . .'.[10]

Like the later instrumental piece *Refrain*, *Studie I* appears to inhabit the treble register, an effect of the subjective preference the ear has for higher frequencies. A gentle, transparent piece, its meditative, slightly tremulous air is enhanced by frequent small echoes; the range of synthesized timbres, extending from low drum-like reverberations at close range (at times almost decompression effects) to small chimes in the middle distance, creates an overall impression of a dynamic plane that slopes up and away from the listener like a di Chirico perspective. On the night of 24

[10] Richard Toop, 'Karlheinz Stockhausen, Music and Machines', Introduction and programme notes, BBC concert series, Barbican Centre, London, 8–16 Jan. 1985, p. 23.

September Stockhausen's wife Doris was admitted to a maternity clinic, and gave birth to their first daughter early the following morning. The happy event is commemorated in *Studie I* by a serially unauthorized 108-Hz 'one-gun salute' which momentarily breaks the stillness.

Elektronische Studie II

1954: *Electronic Study II.*
Duration 3′.

Studie II is complementary to *Studie I*. It is dynamic (Stockhausen's provisional title was in fact *Bewegungen* (Movements)) where the earlier study is stationary sounds, and noisy where the earlier was harmonious. Once again, the composer builds anew on his Paris experiences; whereas *Studie I* took the production of sine-tone spectra as its starting-point, *Studie II* looks again at the production of differentiated attacks. A letter to Goeyvaerts of October 1952 shows that he was already considering the possibility of manipulating complex electronic sounds with the aid of filters:

In general, the density of electronic sounds can be specified by the use of sine and filtered sounds. But remember, with electronic sound material you're not dealing most of the time with tones any more, but with more complex sounds, and the production of different sounds already implies the creation of inherent density differences, over which we are still a long way from having any influence. I'm going to talk it over thoroughly with Dr Meyer-Eppler again next week.[11]

Superimposition of sine tones was only one of two classic tone synthesis techniques employed by the electronic-organ designer: the alternative, 'subtractive' synthesis, operates on the basis that since electronic 'white noise' is compounded of all frequencies, any desired individual frequency or frequency combination could theoretically be extracted from a white-noise source by filtering.

Theoretically, a noise source offered certain advantages. In principle, it should be easier to work with filters on dense sound material than to assemble sine tones painstakingly one by one, a procedure not only extremely time-consuming in itself, but virtually restricted to the production of complexes of unnaturally few partials. Furthermore, all natural and musical sounds incorporate some noise: on the one hand, action noise (breathing, bowing) from the performer, or mechanical noise from the instrument; on the other hand, a natural smearing or indeterminacy of

---

[11] Sabbe, op. cit. 40.

pitch and tone quality arising from human inexactness and the contribution of an acoustic environment to the perceived quality of tone. The use of filtered noise could lead to the production of sounds with an apparent 'inner life'. By far the greatest attraction, however, was the theoretical advantage of a synthesis procedure able to range freely along a continuum between the extremes of pure tone and noise. Such a procedure would enable every type of sound event to be precisely determined in relation to every other, each one occupying a specific region of a serially specifiable sound universe.

The sound-world of *Studie II* occupies an intermediate region between the tone complexes of the earlier study, and filtered ('coloured') noise. A frequency scale ascending from 100 Hz and based on a constant interval ratio of 1 : 25th root of 5 (standard equal temperament is based on the constant interval ratio : 12th root of 2) provides an inharmonically tempered range of pitches. Groups of five pitches are combined to form tone mixtures: there are five 'densities' of tone mixture, of constant interval 1, 2, 3, 4, or 5 degrees of the scale. These mixtures are all synthesized in the same fashion, reminiscent of the method employed in *Etüde* for generating attacks: individual sine tones of the required frequencies were recorded on to tape, and edited together in ascending order of pitch in a sequence of 4 cm. segments; the resulting arpeggiated attack was then rerecorded via an echo chamber, allowing the synthetic partials to combine and interact to produce a complex sound. The original tone sequence was then edited out of the copy, leaving a shadowy, indeterminate, and occasionally tremulous sound with certain character- istics of cavity resonances.

The distribution, dynamic shaping, and superimposition of tone mixtures follows serial procedures of a generally similar kind to *Studie I*, but based on orders of five rather than six components. *Studie II* explores an ambiguous area of aural response between inflection and tone: between awareness of the dynamic shape of sounds and groups, that is, and the inner composition of individual tone mixtures. In this composition time asserts itself: the longer the interval between changes, the more a listener is aware of the harmonic content of tone mixtures; when changes are more rapid, the more one tends to be aware of the group rhythm. Thus the succession of 'blocks' linking pages 1 and 2 of the printed score resemble a Debussyan chord progression (for example, the woodwinds which introduce *Le Martyre de Saint Sébastien*), whereas the complex group in the middle of page 12 has a more syllabic character.

A rising intensity seems to assist, and a falling intensity retard momentum, though this effect varies with the duration and complexity of a group. Interestingly, one perceives the frequency content of complexes more readily when they are rising than when they are falling in intensity (compare for example the rising group on page 11 with the falling group on page 9). Where blocks overlap vertically the result, surprisingly, is often 'choric'; contrariwise, those vertical aggregations that do not overlap (e.g. the final complex of page 16) sound noisier *and* more like real timbres. On pages 13–15 short, crisply articulated sounds in rapid succession create a jazz-like mood, and the surprise 'drum-roll' ending is also amusing and impressive.

Stockhausen's score for *Studie II* (Ex. 17), a remarkable achievement in itself, quickly assumed the status of a new-music icon. In this score all layers are superimposed on a master stave-system which follows the same convention as *Studie I* in indicating pitch on an upper, and amplitude on a lower stave. In the segment illustrated the sounds are of short duration (horizontally) and relatively broad band width (vertically). Each block is a reverberated composite of five

Ex. 17

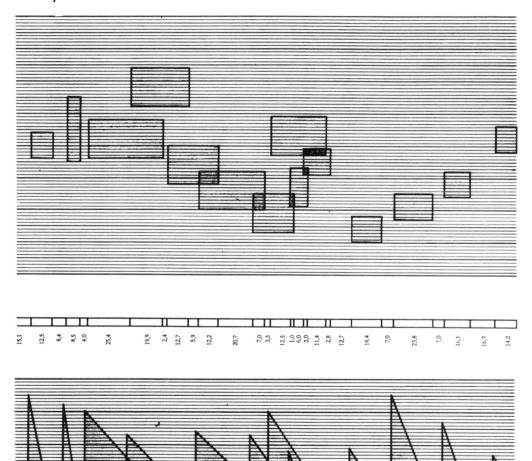

Elektronische Studie II: from page 13 of the published score (UE 12466).
© Universal Edition AG Wien.

inharmonic pitches, height indicating relative range and thus size of the interval constant separating adjacent pitches. The lower stave aligns envelope amplitudes with each block. Instantaneous attacks and rapid decays (acute angles) create a percussive texture. Triangle peaks indicate amplitudes up to a threshold somewhat below the maximum attainable. Taken together, the two electronic studies offer coherent images of the passive and active modes of musical response, the first expressing the contemplative mode, the second the gestural mode. Some years later *Refrain* and *Zyklus* expressed the same complementary relationship in live-performance terms.

Gesang der Jünglinge

1955–6: *Song of the youths.*

Electronic music.

Duration 13′.

Gesang der Jünglinge is the eloquent consummation of this first long love affair with the electronic medium. After three *études*, Stockhausen longed to realize a major composition. From the time of its first conception in late 1954, he intended a work incorporating the human voice alongside electronic sounds. 'The plan for a Mass (intended for liturgical use in church, or at least via the radio) was short-lived—approaches to the relevant authorities left the composer in no doubt that such a project would be condemned by the church hierarchy (a real blow to someone whose daily routine during the realisation of *Studie II* had been: "rise early, go to church, work hard all day and go to sleep in prayer").'[12] In its place Stockhausen chose the benedicite from the Apocrypha, sung by the three young men Shadrach, Meshach, and Abednego after they refused the command of Nebuchadnezzar to bow down before brazen images and were cast into the fiery furnace.

   Incorporating the human voice was no simple task of adding sung elements to the kinds of electronic sounds Stockhausen had already produced for the earlier electronic studies. A coherent rationale for integrating vocal and electronic sounds had to be devised. In one sense, this was a radical step from an idealized world of proportional relationships to a synthesis rationale deriving from 'pre-formed' speech; in another sense, however, it was a progression the logic of which becomes apparent in the context of his progress in acoustics and resumption of university study.

[12] Toop, op. cit. (above, n. 10), p. 26.

In 1954 Stockhausen began attending lectures and seminars in communication theory under Meyer-Eppler at Bonn University. For two years he travelled up to Bonn two or three times a week to take part in a range of studies in acoustics and phonetics; he later described Meyer-Eppler as 'the best teacher I ever had'. These research studies centred on language perception: for example, whether the rules governing written language could transfer to spoken language (in the sense that a computer might be programmed to understand continuous speech given the normal rules of grammar and syntax); if not, whether alternative rules more appropriate to auditory perception could be found. It was clear from analyses of tape-recorded speech that spoken language did not conveniently resolve into intelligible units of sound corresponding to words on the printed page. Considered objectively as differentiated sound, speech typically consisted of a more or less continuously modulated skein of sound, which had to be sorted out into words in the mind of the listener, though their interpretation thereafter was undoubtedly conditioned by acoustic factors such as pitch and dynamic inflection. The determining factors in interpreting speech sounds were not absolute and precise, therefore, but relative and approximate. It is Stockhausen's mastery of this new relativistic sound universe that distinguishes the new work:

[Meyer-Eppler] was a teacher who had come from phonetics, had given up analysing the different sounds of language in order to devote himself to studying statistics, because he wanted to know more precisely what all the different noises were, and analysing the wave structure of noises and consonants in language led him to use statistical methods of description and analysis. He would give us exercises demonstrating the principles of Markoff series; in one we were given cut-outs of individual letters from newspaper articles, and we had to put them in sequence by a chance operation, and see what sort of a text came out.[13]

Such explorations of the frontiers of perception between chaos and form were immensely significant. They are the basis of organization of *Gesang der Jünglinge*; they symbolize, to a religious disposition, the divine act of creation itself and the work of human imagination. In addition, they suggested the possibility of an intellectual reconciliation between the 'opposite poles' of European serialism and the indeterminancies of Cage and his colleagues in the United States.

It is often remarked that Stockhausen makes a concession to popular opinion in incorporating vocal elements. Certainly there were allegations of impenetrability brought against his earlier works to which he was not insensitive.[14] Most of his compositions to 1954 had in fact been wihdrawn from circulation after their first performance. Certainly there was a period of self-examination about whether the original ideals which had sustained him (and Goeyvaerts) through a period of unprecedented upheaval in Western music, and enabled his music after *Kreuzspiel* to steer clear of all temptations, from neo-classicism to anarchy, needed all the same to

[13] Karlheinz Stockhausen and Robin Maconie, *Stockhausen on Music* (London, 1989), p. 50.
[14] See Seppo Heikenheimo, *The Electronic Music of Karlheinz Stockhausen* (Helsinki, 1972), pp. 34–42.

present so intractable an image to the general public. But in reality his rationale for music was always developing, always open to change, and always recognizing that the ultimate, logical, and appealing alternative to an arbitrary system would be one founded on scientific principles. Such a system, just as rigorous, drawing its strength from the world of everyday human experience, would be more likely as a matter of course to connect with the perceptions of the 'ordinary listener'.

No sudden crisis of conscience at all, therefore, rather a gradual and inevitable progression from a suprematist position toward a scientific aesthetic, bearing out the view that Stockhausen was as ready to modify his intellectual position as he was apt to revise his manuscripts. The considerable flutter which greeted *Gesang der Jünglinge*, therefore, can be regarded as doubly unjustified: neither was it a philosophical U-turn away from 'pure' electronic music back to *musique concrète*, nor was it a Pauline conversion to representational music. It was simply an inevitability that the composer's increasingly sophisticated knowledge of acoustics and phonetics should find expression in a music with words. For Stockhausen, to compose with words signifies a particular moment of self-assurance.

The task of mediating between sine tones and the voice is approached with typical thoroughness. Twelve categories of sound element are distinguished: they refer equally to synthesized and preformed phonemic elements, and are rated on a scale of aural comprehensibility. Vowel-like sounds, for example, correspond to stationary sine-tone complexes; diphthongs to non-stationary sine-tone complexes; consonants to filtered noise. For each sound component of spoken language there exists a synthesized equivalent. In addition the 'macrostructural' features of the composition, such as the clouds of impulses which burst forth from time to time, derive from statistical features of the microstructures of speech sounds. Thus a continuum between electronic sound and vocal sound is established at every point between the extremes of tone and noise (Ex. 18).

The scale of sound elements describes a continuum between the horizontal and the vertical, that is, between elements perceived as successive or melodic, and those which are perceived as instantaneous or harmonic:

    SK = pulsed sine-tone complexes
    IK = pulsed complexes of filtered noise
    LS = tones and syllables
     R = noises filtered to c. 2% frequency bandwidth (e.g. [f] [s] [sh])
     I = single impluses (e.g. [t] [b] [k] [g])
    SV = synthesized vowel sounds
    RO = broad-bandwidth filtered noise (1–6 octaves) (e.g. unvoiced vowels)
    IO = pulsed complexes of fixed density (e.g. voiced [r] [x] [z])
    IA = single impulses (chords of predetermined scales)
    RA = chords of 2% bandwidths of filtered noise
   S(A) = sine-tone chords (inharmonic or transitional scales)
    GA = sung chords (aggregations of sung tones)

Ex. 18

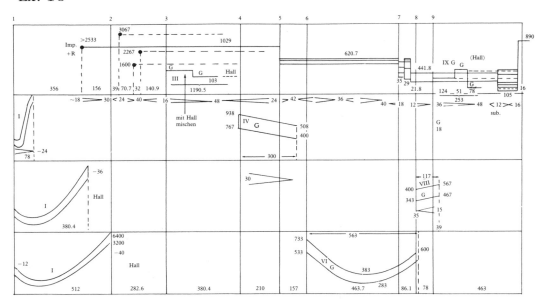

Gesang der Jünglinge: sample pages 1 and 2 of score (after Richard Toop). Statistical 'impulse-showers' are indicated by curved outlines in this four-layer score; straight lines and dots signify precise pitches. 'Hall' means 'Nachhall', i.e. reverberation; 'verhallt', 'reverberated'. Five-line staves may indicate spoken or sung material. The graphic conventions anticipate *Kontakte*.

© Universal Edition AG Wien.

The sequence could be folded over, static chords merging with pulsed chords, to make an endless cycle (such a progression is the basis for *Zyklus* for solo percussion). Stockhausen has chosen a series of orders, however, expressing a generally straight-line trajectory from particulate sound and noise to intelligible song. The recurring phrase 'Praise the Lord' ('Preiset den Herrn', 'Jubelt dem Herrn') acts as a textual refrain, also as a point of attraction, cadence-like, for the electronic sounds: 'wherever speech momentarily breaks through the air-waves of the music, it praises God'.[15]

Like his two previous electronic studies, *Gesang der Jünglinge* is a multi-layered musical structure. For the first time, however, the polyphony is associated with multichannel sound reproduction. His first thoughts were for a six-channel system: five speakers encircling the auditorium, and one speaker carrying the boy's voice suspended over the heads of the audience.[16] This was later reduced to the five in a horizontal array, sounding in essentially antiphonal relationship (not until *Kontakte* are static and continuously moving sounds combined).

[15] Stockhausen, op. cit. ii, p. 49.
[16] Karlheinz Stockhausen, 'Actualia', *Die Reihe* (English Edition), (1958), i 45; Mya Tannenbaum, *Conversations with Stockhausen* (Oxford, 1987), pp. 23–4.

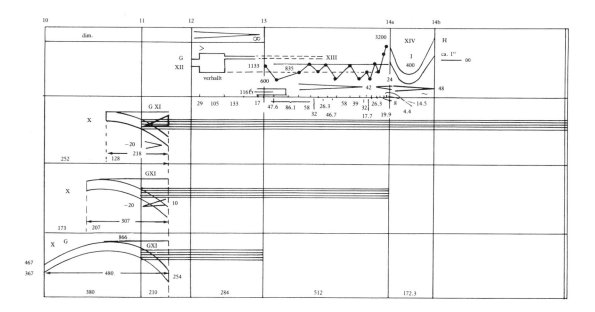

Considering the enormous technical and intellectual demands it made on the composer, it is not surprising to learn that Stockhausen had to bring the work prematurely to an end, in order to meet the deadline for the first performance. Even though the original schema is incomplete by the loss of the seventh and final section, however (it was to have lasted a full twenty minutes), the work is a masterpiece.

5 *The Piano Pieces*

To composers of the Renaissance and Baroque, keyboard instruments were a means of speculating in the abstract about pitch, time, structure, and improvisation. Temperament aimed to render, and the keyboard to represent pitch as a uniform continuum; standard five-line stave notation reproduced that uniformity in graphic form, and extended it also to the time dimension of music. With the aid of these newly precise co-ordinates, a composer could chart the course of a melody unaffected by human limitations of range or intonation. Any point on the keyboard was equally accessible by hand and its equivalent note as easy to plot on the musical map. It provided a new stimulus to experimenting with melodies and groups of notes as objects able to be freely moved from place to place in pitch and time; they could also be inverted, played backwards, stretched and compressed in relation to the beat, and the result played back immediately.

Keyboard instruments were therefore a natural choice for music expressing intricate structural concepts involving precisely interlocking pitch and time relationships. Later generations of keyboard composers began to reconsider the implications of 'human' factors in performance, such as improvisatory uncertainties of timing and ornamentation. Reacting against the mechanical uniformity of standard pitch and notation, they set out to devise alternative notations to allow for natural indeterminacies of virtuoso performance; examples include the paradoxically named 'unmeasured preludes' of d'Anglebert and Rameau, and Couperin's extraordinary range of ornamentation signs. Among keyboard composers one observes a constant give-and-take relationship between pure speculation (the visual, the intellectual), leading to the invention of new ways of organizing music, and performance practice (the aural, the physical), which hinders, but is also extended and enhanced by, the demands of speculative form. Precisely this give-and-take is observable in Stockhausen's pieces for piano 1952–61.

Stockhausen trained as a pianist, was an accomplished improviser, and had composed the *Sonatine* for violin and piano as a student. For many newcomers, the piano pieces are a point of first direct contact with Stockhausen's conceptual and practical world. The encounter can be disconcerting, because there is no sign in the earliest set of four piano pieces of any idiomatic connection either with the composer's pianistic education, or with the piano music of the contemporaries he admired. So no jazz, and no irony either; and despite procedural links with Messiaen and Boulez, neither the sonorous clangour of the former nor the physical ostentation of the latter. This laconic and purposeful music, totally engaged in itself, makes even Cage's *Music of Changes* seem self-consciously artful. 'They are my drawings', says Stockhausen, and they relate to concepts and aural impressions arising from his experiences in concete and electronic music.

Klavierstücke I–IV

1952–3: *Piano Pieces I–IV*
Duration I 3′, II 1′ 45″, III 0′ 30″, IV 2′.

Pieces I–IV date from his arrival in Paris. III and II were written first, and he later added IV and I: the set was intended as a birthday present for his wife Doris, in the optimistic expectation she would be able to play them (remembering they had met as students in the same piano class in Cologne). According to the composer, they mark a transition from pointillism to group composition, that is, from a procedure of maximum contrast characteristic of his instrumental music up to *Punkte 1952*, to one of clustered relationships and values, reflecting his observations and experiences of concrete music, and also a growing consensus among his contemporaries that continuous contrast is ultimately self-negating.

The tempo of each piece is 'as fast as possible', simply meaning that time is an external co-ordinate; it is also means, to paraphrase a favourite Stockhausen quotation from the German biologist and philosopher Viktor von Weizsäcker, 'the notes are not of the time, but time is in the notes'.[1] The time values indicate are to be exactly realized, but in the absence of phrasing any resulting impression of tempo will depend on how the relationships of the notes are executed and perceived (whether they are related by conjunction or by dynamic, for example). Temporal ambiguity is a feature of other composers' piano music at this time.

The 'group' composition of III (Ex. 19), outwardly simple, actually works on four different levels: pitch, group duration, rhythmic organization within a group, and dynamics. The piece is modular in construction. Pitches are organized in units of four adjacent semitones: initially D–D♯–E–F, F–F♯–G–G♯, and G♯–A–A♯–B, an arrangement leaving C and C♯ as 'free radicals' (they define the pitch space of the second half of the piece)[2]. The order and octave transposition of pitches within a

---

[1] Karlheinz Stockhausen and Robin Maconie, *Stockhausen on Music* (London, 1989), p. 37.

[2] According to Harvey (*The Music of Stockhausen* (London, 1975), pp. 257, who likens the pitch organization to the Webern *Geistliche Lied*, Op. 15 No. 1, the pitches are grouped in fives: four adjacent semitones plus a terminal minor third. But that analysis also becomes less plausible as the piece progresses, and, for the pianist, no more useful a guide to detecting the tonal drift of the piece from white notes to black, and back to white again.

Ex. 19

Piano Piece III (complete).

© Universal Edition AG Wien.

group is subject to variation: occasionally at first, more frequently as the piece progresses. Notes from adjacent groups are interchanged (the D in group 1 anticipates group 3, for instance, and the B♭ and F in groups 5 and 6 have been exchanged). At 8, the half-way point, the 'wild' D♮ introduces a shift to mainly black notes (one hears this as a change of key); the final sequence of seven pitches, measuring in semitones from the C♯ of 13, forms the interval series 3 5 6 1 4 2.

The pitch content is projected on to independently organized sequences of durations, corresponding to the 'modes' of the *Konkrete Etüde* and related in spirit to the 'personnages rythmiques' of Messiaen and rhythmic procedures described by Boulez in the article 'Eventuellement . . .'. Taking the first bar as a starting-point,

64

Ex. 20

Ex. 21

the first six durations form a sequence (Ex. 20). We divide this into two groups of three durations, and define them in relative terms as a note followed by a rest, then two notes of equal value, then an unbroken group of three unequal values: short, long, medium (Ex. 21). Applying the same numbering, we see that in 2 the sequence is permutated to 4 5 6 3 2 1; then follows a succession of 'block' combinations of three unequal durations, which develop the linear relationship of the subgroups of the original sequence in various orders and superimpositions. The modal options differ from the *Etüde*, and are as follows:

1. Six-note linear succession
2. Three unequal durations, start together (4 5 6)
3. Three unequal durations, end together (4 5 6)
4. Two durations start together, a third ends (2 + 3 1)
5. One starts, two follow and end together (1 2 + 3)
6. One starts, two follow and begin together (1 2 + 3)

Linear sequences return with the F at 8, and continue to the end, sometimes combined with 'block' modes. The orders (Fig. 2) appear playful rather than systematic.

Fig. 2

```
6 5 4 1 2 3
1 2 3 6 5 4
6 5 2 3 4 1
```

The dynamics of III form another layer, though the group relationships are defined by the durational modes. A range of four adjacent dynamics is employed. In 1 we find two only, *p* and *mf*, each appearing three times, while in 2 a group of three *f* indications is followed by a group of three different dynamics: *f*, *mf*, and *p*. In 3–4 the three dynamics are inversely related to duration, while in 5 the reverse applies, the longest note of the group also being the loudest. The final B, the highest pitch of the piece, attracts an exceptional *ff*.

Piece II is ampler in sound, and introduces 'non-retrogradable' rhythms, that is, symmetrical patterns of division within a structural unit; the sustaining pedal is also employed to define individual groups. Five dynamic levels are used (a sixth, *ppp*, appearing at the last chord). Four groups of three pitches are rotated, two of them diatonic: D E♭ F, and its retrograde inversion B A G♯, and two chromatic: C C♯ D and its inversion G♯ G F♯. The notes D and G♯ link diatonic and chromatic pairs at a tritone distance. At 8 and 9 the diatonic triplets become whole-tone; other interval and order permutations appear as the piece proceeds. The piece unfolds mainly in the treble and mid-range; bass notes have the effect of large-scale punctuation, whether or not this is Stockhausen's intention. About the final B♭, however, there can be no doubt: it has been saved up, like the highest pitch of III, to end the piece on a note of surprise.

Forward and reverse combinations of durations, of which non-retrogradable structures are a special case, give II an idiosyncratic charm. If we reverse the group in 3, for instance, a structure resembling that in 22 appears, and vice versa (Exx. 22–3).

Piece IV is based on the two linear modes where each note in succession is followed by a rest, or alternatively is preceded by a rest. This may appear to be an academic distinction; in Webern's Op. 27 piano Variations, however, one finds ample precedent for structural syncopation (for instance III at bars 45 ff.), and here again it allows a composer to make the end of a note the structural reference point, as an alternative to the point where it begins sounding. The note itself is merely the sounding portion of a duration which may be larger in extent; the ratio of sound to silence then becomes a matter of serial proportioning within the duration. It follows that an otherwise regular off-the-beat succession can be made to appear irregular by varying the antecedent rest from note to note: they will still terminate at regular intervals, but on an instrument like a piano that is less easy to hear than in the case of tape-recorded sounds. In Piece IV two wide-ranging lines interact in a lively counterpoint which is generally emphasized by well-contrasted dynamic labelling which, apart from occasional excursions, remains *ff* or *pp*. The surprise ending is a two-part diminuendo.

Piece I (Ex. 24), written at great speed in only two days, has excited controversy over its difficulties of execution, some of which are real, but many of which arise from the fact that the notation is a little harder to read than normal. This complexity comes from the fact that one set of measurements is used to determine the larger 'phrase' structure, and other sets to determine the scale of subdivision of each structural duration. The latter provide the frame of reference for the modal organization of pitches, which in this piece are grouped in adjacent hexachords, C–F, F♯–B.

Barring and time signatures are guides to the phrase structure, which is based on a

Ex. 22

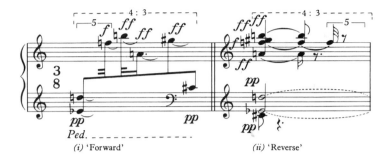

(i) 'Forward'   (ii) 'Reverse'

Piano Piece II: bar 3 'forward' and 'reverse'.
© Universal Edition AG Wien.

Ex. 23

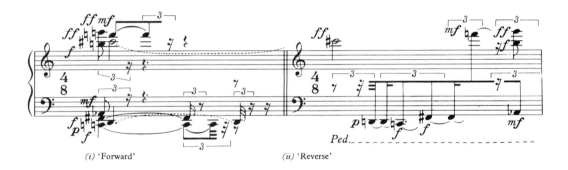

(i) 'Forward'   (ii) 'Reverse'

Piano Piece II: bar 22 'forward' and reverse'.
© Universal Edition AG Wien.

six-value 'magic square' rotated like a combination lock (Fig. 3).[3] Pitch and large-scale time orders are reasonably clearly visible on the page: in the first row, 1 is actually $1\frac{1}{2}$ (a 3/8 bar); elsewhere in the fourth row 2 is actually slightly less (a total of 7/16 instead of a full 4/8). The different modes are also quite visible: in bar 1 notes entering separately and ending together, in bar 2, left hand, a linear mode with successive beats initiated by rests in varying proportions (5:0 (no note), 1:4, 0:5 (no rest), 3:2, 2:3). Though it is not overtly indicated, in bars 2, 5, 7, and 8 a third pedal can be seen as necessary to sustain the starting notes without affecting the

[3] Richard Toop, 'On Writing about Stockhausen', *Contact*, 20 (1979), 25.

Ex. 24

*) Das Tempo jedes Stückes wird vom kleinsten zu spielenden Zeitwert bestimmt: So schnell, wie möglich. Wenn dieses Tempo ermittelt und metronomisch fixiert ist, können alle komplizierteren Zeitproportionen in Klammern (⌐----⌐ ┌───┐) durch Tempo-wechsel ersetzt werden.

The tempo of each piece, determined by the smallest note-value, is "As fast as possible." When the player has found this tempo and determined it metronomically, all the more complicated time-proportions under the brackets (⌐----⌐ ┌───┐) can be replaced by changes of tempo.

Piano Piece I: first page. The pedalling of bar 1 indicates a division of pitches into two hexachords.

Fig. 3

```
5   2   3   1   4   6
3   4   2   5   6   1
2   6   4   3   1   5
4   1   6   2   5   3
6   5   1   4   3   2
1   3   5   6   2   4
```

separation of following note groups. Dynamic clustering is particularly pronounced, and made easier to hear and articulate because a wider range of dynamics is employed, though one can't help feeling that loud accents among the quieter groups—for instance, the *fff* in bar 1 and *ff* in bar 4—might have been introduced principally to confound analysis and disconcert the performer.

What distinguishes Stockhausen's groups from his pointillist style is that emphasis is laid on various degrees of statistical uniformity within each group: an average dynamic, for example, or a fundamental regularity of tempo, or a generalized up or down movement. Density of notes is a prerequisite, of course, for perceiving group similarities, and the unaccustomed density of Piece I is a principal feature marking it out from post-Webernian pointillism. The music has none of the underlying metrical regularity of Boulez or Messiaen, being altogether more impulsive and unpredictable in mood; on the other hand, one is always aware of the composer being in control, simply because every detail has been consciously decided.

Klavierstücke V–VIII

1954–5: *Piano Pieces V–VIII*
Durations V 6', VI 26', VII 7', VIII 2'.

Toward the end of 1953, having completed the electronic *Studie I*, Stockhausen began a second cycle of piano pieces. His studies with Meyer-Eppler were opening his mind to possibilities of systematic control of group phenomena at different levels of internal organization. These possibilities were to be explored in the electronic *Studie II*, and with even greater consequence in *Gesang der Jünglinge*; but for day-to-day purposes the piano was obviously ideal. Having rung the serial changes on a first set of four piano pieces, he hit upon the grand idea of an extended cycle projecting the same series in macrocosm, adding to the initial set five more sets to make a total of twenty-one pieces forming a super-series 4 6 1 5 3 2. The second set was therefore intended to be of six pieces, Pieces V–X, and the third would consist of the single Piece XI. Pieces V–VIII of the second set were realized in 1954–5, XI in 1956; IX and X had to wait until 1961 to be composed, by which time Stockhausen's thinking had considerably advanced.

Unlike the slow and often frustrating labour of electronic music, writing for piano was simplicity itself: ideas could be set down very rapidly, evaluated, and as quickly revised. The underlying complexities and theoretical inconsistences of Pieces V–VIII reflect the experimental freedom with which Stockhausen approached them, and the rapidity with which his ideas changed and developed. For this reason, work on V–VIII was initially rapid: the basic outlines of each piece were decided more or less by logical extrapolation, after which the detailed interpretation of each schema became a matter of aesthetic judgement. As one might expect of pieces related in outline and proportion to the earlier set I–IV, the new pieces were all fairly short, and if anything, given the sharper focus of his ideas, rather more single-minded and hermetic in expression. Piece V was a study in far-flung 'constellations' of grace-notes, set in opposition to a foreground of long, measured pitches. In VI, originally the shortest of the set at little more than a minute in length, grace-note figurations were interwoven into a Webernian structure of fixed intervals packed into a two-octave space, while the original version of VII was an equally Webernian exercise in metrical invariance. VIII, the only piece to survive unscathed, is also the most complex:

. . . at least a dozen simultaneously operative serial levels: two for pitches (grace notes and 'main notes'), and the others for such things as number of superordinate groups (groups of groups) per section, number of groups per superordinate group, number of attacks per grace-note group, number of notes in each grace-note attack, dynamic level of the grace-note groups, and an even larger number of specifications for the main notes.[4]

These four were in various stages of completion—indeed, V and VI had already come back from the engraver—when Stockhausen encountered the American pianist David Tudor, on his first European tour, performing solo piano works by Boulez and Cage, particularly the latter's *Music of Changes*. Stockhausen was impressed by Tudor and gave him copies of Pieces I–IV and V–VIII as they became available; he was eventually to dedicate them to him.[5] He was also, one suspects, impressed by hearing the Cage pieces, and by the visual appearance of the scores, which convey so precise an impression of objective detachment from the sound-events they contain. These pieces are projections of random selection procedures applied to as many parameters as may be separately identified; the resulting music is thus an aggregation of separate layers, each of which expresses a certain limited unpredictability. Today we might describe such pieces as fractal compositions, applying the mathematics of indeterminacy formulated by Benoît Mandelbrot. In

[4] Ibid. 27.
[5] David Tudor, 'From Piano to Electronics', *Music and Musicians*, 20. 12 (1972), 24–6.

1954 Cage's use of the *I Ching* might have appeared to put him at an opposite extreme from Stockhausen's serial determinism. But that is to gloss over profound similarities of intention and technique, which Stockhausen's aesthetic sense would recognize even if his intellect disapproved of the lengths to which Cage was willing to go:

In [*Music of Changes*], for example, charts are made up of sounds—noises, as available on a piano, or pitches, and these are taken singly or in conglomerates (chords, tremelos, flourishes); of durations; of dynamics; of tempi; and of superpositions (the number of possible series of events going on simultaneously within a given structural length: from zero to eight). Tossing coins . . . determines the combinations of the various elements on the various charts: how many superpositions; at what tempo; what particular durations; whether a duration be expressed by a silence or a sound; what sound; at what dynamic. . . . The outlines of the piece's structure, however, are planned at the start (like the elements on the charts) and not left to chance (as the configurations of the elements are); though these outlines are space lengths—a number of measures—whose time lengths are in turn dependent on the chance-determined tempi.[6]

Tudor was able to bring his performer's experience to bear on the issues of time perception which Stockhausen's new pieces were examining from a more theoretical viewpoint, and to demonstrate that there were degrees of accuracy in performance related to complexities of notation and to the physical and mental limitations of the human performer. These subjective factors are of course related to other well-known performance uncertainties which give music its expressive humanity: agogic accents, subtleties of intonation, and so on. They are however not the same as Meyer-Eppler's degrees of probability, since the latter can be objectively determined (as the electronic pieces prove) while the former cannot. This is why Pieces V–VIII in their revised form look so different from pieces I–IV, which their earlier versions, with barlines and time signatures, more closely resembled; they now begin to identify with the imagery of Cage's barless space-time notation.

Stockhausen's change of orientation is reflected in his 1955 remarks concerning the revised Pieces V–VIII:

If after a year and a half spent working exclusively on electronic compositions, I now work on piano pieces at the same time, it is because in the most strongly structured compositions I am brought up against essential musical phenomena which are non-quantifiable. They are no less real, recognizable, conceivable, or palpable for that. These I am better able to clarify—at the moment anyway—with the help of an instrument and interpreter, than through the medium of electronic composition. Above all it has to do with conveying a new sense of musical timing, more truly expressed by the infinitely subtle 'irrational' nuances, stresses and agogics of a good interpreter, than by any measurement in centimetres. Such 'statistical' criteria of forming will open up a completely new, hitherto unknown perspective on the relationship between instrumental and performance factors.[7]

[6] Christian Wolff, 'New and Electronic Music', *Audience*, 5 (1958), 125–6.
[7] Karlheinz Stockhausen, *Texte zur Musik*, ii (Cologne, 1964), p. 43.

Stockhausen's doubts can now be seen in context. The earlier versions were too limited in scope to do what he now wanted them to do; they were also visually inappropriate for the perceptions he wished to express; and they were not rich enough in incident to match the level of drama Tudor had shown to be possible.

Piece V was recast, and fleshed out with new material unrelated to its original scheme of relationships; VI and VII were discarded. Only VIII was allowed to stand. VI was completely rewritten, at considerably greater length, as a comprehensive review of the techniques of group composition in place of a miniature exposition of a single aspect. Following its New York première in December 1954, he again rewrote it completely, redistributing the pitches in alternative registers. The Vega recording by David Tudor is of this version; the piece was less drastically revised again in 1960, in which form it is recorded by Kontarsky on CBS. VII was replaced by a new piece based on orders of five rather than six, unlike all the other piano pieces in the set but in line with *Studie II* and *Zeitmasze*, and giving new prominence to assisted resonances.[8]

Piece V is in six sections, identified by tempo: quaver = MM 80–90–71–113.5–101–63.5; the tempi representing whole-tone divisions of a chromatic 'tempo octave' MM 60–120: we are to see more of this tempo scale in future. Since the music lacks a regular pulse, these metronomic tempi are more psychological than real (added to which, the tempo often fluctuates between successive attacks). One is reminded of Boulez' remark 'tempo is simply a quality of speed in the passing of time'.[9] Tempo aside, the measured note structure of 'main notes' is both distended in time-scale and short on material: the amount of main-note data on which a performer or listener could base a sense of regular tempo is calculatedly insufficient (though pitch repetition undoubtedly helps maintain awareness of the measured note structure as a separate component). When the grace-note material is taken into account, however, each section is seen to be characterized by a density of events in inverse relation to its chronometric duration (*not* its tempo). The question is whether average density is perceived for relatively long durations, as it is perceived for the relatively short structural durations of, say, Piece I. Stockhausen's use of half- and full-pedal sustain is certainly designed to help the listener hear particular constellations of grace-notes and main notes as structural entities (Ex. 25).

Piece VII is in five tempo-defined sections (quaver = MM 40–63.5–57–71–50.5). Its distinctive feature is an attention to piano resonance notated as silently depressed notes and chords, forming a continuously varying background of assisted resonance, which the sounded notes jar into sympathetic (sometimes reluctant) vibration. These resonances are a pianistic equivalent of vocal 'formants', which express the shape of the vocal cavity and are excited by the sound impulses emerging from the larynx to create a combination of tone and tonal halo perceived as a

---

[8] The surviving original Pieces VI and VII, now redesignated V$\frac{1}{2}$ and VI$\frac{1}{2}$ by Richard Toop, are described in some detail by him in op. cit. 26 and in 'Stockhausen's Other Piano Pieces', *Musical Times*, Apr. 1983, pp. 348–52.

[9] Pierre Boulez, 'Music and Invention', *Listener*, 22 Jan. 1970, p. 102.

Ex. 25

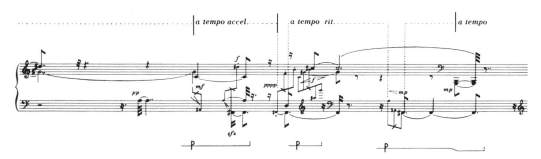

Piano Piece V. Long notes initially obscured by small grace-note flourishes; a new sense of pitch space and an exposed awareness of psychological time are noticeable features.

© Universal Edition AG Wien.

particular vowel. In addition to the interplay of grace-note time and measured time, therefore, there is a further dialogue between musical action and response. Unlike V, where the pedals are used primarily for phrasing, and only exploit artificial resonance as an afterthought (see page 4 of the score, for example), VII treats the notated resonances as a primary element, with the pedal helping out. Third pedal and left pedal ('una corda') make their appearance, the latter however as additional tone colour (e.g. *sforzato una corda*) and not just to dampen the sound level.

Fluctuations of tempo are less in evidence here; in their place we find the beginnings of a flexible system of pauses, distinguished by the length of the note or rest above which they appear. (Pause variants reach a peak of proliferation in Piece XI.) The pitches of VII derive from the same series on which *Gruppen* for three orchestras would shortly be based; once again, chiming repetitions of main-note pitches emphasize fixity of time and place in opposition to a newly aggressive uncertainty of grace-note figurations. The illustrated passage (Ex. 26) from section 4, quaver = MM 71, depicts a slowing down of main notes and resonances to a virtual standstill in the bass register, suddenly shattered by loud and high grace-

Ex. 26

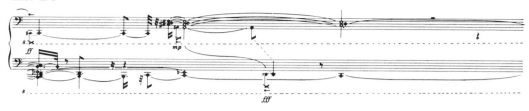

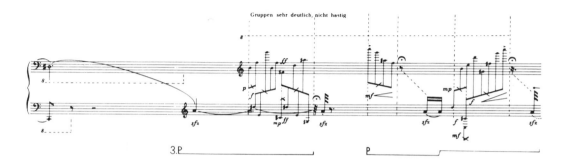

Piano Piece VII. The lozenge-shaped notes represent sustained low-pitched resonances made audible by grace-note attacks (*ff, mp, fff*). Suddenly bursts of notes reappear at the upper extreme above a reference tone A4: their tempo is tangential to that of the larger note-values.

© Universal Edition AG Wien.

notes descending as it were from an ultrasonic region into audibility. It is an image to which Stockhausen repeatedly returns: in *Kontakte* at 19′ 31.5″, *Telemusik* at 16, and *Hymnen*, Region 4 after the words 'Mesdames, Messieurs, rien ne va plus'.

The organizational complexity of VIII has already been noted. In this brief piece of two sections (quaver = MM 90–80) the measured-note density is high and the texture almost toccata-like in mood and metrical regularity; by contrast the grace-note figurations are now so encrusted with notes and performance specifications as to require more time to prepare than the main notes (Ex. 27). The situation is thus reversed; now the grace-notes threaten to slow down the musical flow rather than galvanize it into motion. Dynamics play a particularly high-profile role in the delineation of form. Each major formal unit selects six adjacent values from a scale of ten dynamics, *pppp* to *ffff*. Different dynamic levels within a subset define the internal structure; the average dynamic value distinguishes one group from another. Major structural divisions, as shown here, are indicated by long notes: internal subdivisions, as in Piece V, by grace-note collections, here chord aggregations of one to six notes. In section 2 (quaver = MM 80) these are slightly coloured by half-

74

Ex. 27

Piano Piece VIII.
© Universal Edition AG Wien.

pedalling, but apart from this nothing remains of the harmonic and resonance effects noted in other pieces.

Piece VI is based on the same initial set of proportions as the original miniature, extended into a bravura concert exercise of major length, something that Tudor could impress New York audiences with, and which would hold its own in scale and virtuosity with anything else in the contemporary piano literature. This is no sketch for an electronic composition, but a compendium of brilliant pianistic devices: subtle, rich, and classically remote. It is also perfectly characterized for Tudor himself, in complete contrast to the subsequent overt ebullience of Piece X, which Tudor could not bring himself to accept. Stockhausen returns to the variable tempi of V, which are given new prominence and precision by being expressed in a manner analogous to the dynamic envelopes of his electronic studies. A thirteen-line stave above the keyboard notations offers twelve distinct levels of tempo, and the possibility of indicating a precisely timed transition between any two levels by a sloping line of appropriate length and angle, an upward angle corresponding to an accelerando and a downward angle to a ritardando (Ex. 28). The line vanishes wherever a pause appears. It may not be entirely coincidental that a similar notation is found in

Hymnen to signify the sound of breathing in and out: an upward angle for an intake of breath, and a downward angle for breathing out, and in the pauses between, no line. Some element of respiration is suggested by the way in which the tempo line phrases the underlying notes.

Grace-note groups appear to have a new function in VI, partly as a consequence of the newly precise tempo co-ordinates: rather than heighten or anticipate main-note events, they seem calculated in this instance to blur them, in effects of often iridescent beauty and variety. As in VII, we find 'passive' assisted resonances shaping audible boundaries around specific note groups in a manner complementary to the 'active' visual phrasing conditioned by the tempo stave.

Klavierstück XI

1956: *Piano Piece XI*
Duration 14'.

Piece XI is the most celebrated example of a type of formal indeterminacy which had enormous impact during the mid-to-late fifties. It has been variously described as variable form (because the order of events is freely variable), multivalent form (because the formal chemistry of each event varies according to the chosen sequence), and the formal equivalent of a synthesized non-periodic sound (the sound quality being determined by the aggregate composition of elements, and not by their sequence). To the layman, however, the term 'mobile form' is perhaps the most immediate and meaningful. Piece XI consists of a single sheet on which nineteen sections of music are distributed with careful disconnectedness across the white space: the performer plays sections one after another, choosing at random (Ex. 29). Segment lengths are serially measured, though subject to variation in tempo. At the end of each segment the music pauses momentarily while the player chooses its successor at random, to be played to the tempo, dynamic, and touch values indicated at the junction between them, a device akin to a change of registration in organ music. The analogy with Calder's suspended sculptures is exact. The work does not have a definitive form, it is simply capable of assuming any one of a totality of configurations available to a structure of a limited number of components linked in a limited number of ways.

Piece XI continues the serial investigation of musical time as it is written and as it is perceived and articulated. In Stockhausen's overall plan it is the third of six sets of piano pieces, and the set consisting of one piece only. The idea of one piece containing many is therefore a logical device for redressing the balance as well as

Ex. 28

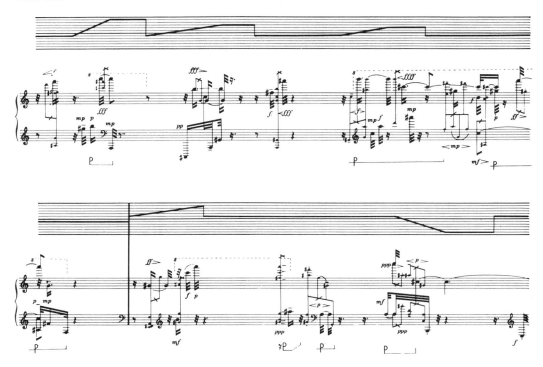

Piano Piece VI. Tempo is treated in a manner analogous to amplitude (the higher, the faster). Time appears fluid and improvisatory; the interaction of mensural and grace-notes is now very subtle.

© Universal Edition AG Wien.

witty and provocative in itself. The imaginative leap required to make the transition from fixed to mobile form is not as great as it may first appear. We have already seen Stockhausen drawing up his basic distinctions of timing in Pieces V–VIII: they include metronomic tempo, chronometric duration, psychological time (accelerando, ritardando), grace-note action time ('as fast as possible'), statistical time (based on a transitional or average density of notes), and acoustically-determined time (governed by pauses or the decay of pedalled notes). We are also by now familiar with Stockhausen's compositional method and his formal priorities. He composes serially in a modular fashion, block by block; each block is likewise divisible into smaller units, and the contrasting grace-note structures are inserted into the serial time structure.

At every level of organization there are serial consistencies which unify the structure; at the same time, there are considerable freedoms to distribute material within preordained limits (not to mention considerable licence on occasion to vary

Ex. 29

Piano Piece XI: a section of the score.
© Universal Edition AG Wien.

the terms of reference when the composer so wishes). While it may seem strange to a musician of orthodox sensibility that, for example, Piece XI allows for a segment to be performed at six different tempi, because we have been brought up to believe (and Stravinsky has told us so) that tempo is inseparable from the meaning and identity of a composition, we have only to look at *Kontra-Punkte* or Piece VI to see that Stockhausen regards external tempo as simply an indication of the speed at which a listener experiences a piece of music. It is therefore not illogical to make a formal argument of the distinction between the musical event and the speed at which it is performed. If the speed is slower, we listen more carefully to the inner detail of the event; if faster, we perceive it more globally: providing the music is calculated to remain interesting at extremes of speed (it is) then varying the tempo of a segment from one performance to another is no different from (say) photographing a building or a flower from a distance or close up: both are legitimate. The notion that music must always be observed, as it were, from the same distance, as though it were a book which one had to hold always at a constant arm's length in order to read, is a visual, literary prejudice.

   In his first book on the Modulor, the architect Le Corbusier describes a game called the 'Panel Exercise'. The 'panels' are flat rectangular shapes based on the Red and Blue series of proportions (they in turn are derived from the 'Golden Mean' $(a:b=a+b:a)$ of which the Fibonacci series 1, 2, 3, 5, 8, 13, 21, 34, 55, 89, 144 . . . is a convenient expression). The game consists of assembling selections of these panels into higher-order rectangles whose outer dimensions are harmoniously proportioned, and whose inner divisions, thanks to the logic of the Modulor, will also form spontaneously harmonious relationships. The 'Panel Exercise', Le Corbusier observes, 'has the satisfying effect of showing that in the very heart of this impeccable geometry—which some might think *implacable*—the personality has complete freedom of action'.[10] What the pianist sees on the page are an equivalent of Le Corbusier's panels. They are visually proportioned to a Fibonacci series; the player is instructed to play them in any order, preferably unpremeditated, the eye roaming freely over the page to alight on whichever is to be played next. At the end of each segment a group of symbols is printed which determine the relative tempo, touch, and dynamic level of the segment which is to follow. There is a certain procedural similarity with changes of registration between sections of organ music.

The piece is an object-lesson in notational precision, clearly distinguishing the permutatable constants of tempo, duration, dynamic level, and timbre (attack) from the relatively fixed local deviations of accelerando and ritardando, pauses and accents. A significant consequence of the piece's mobile form and attendant variability of sectional tempi is that the grace-note figurations, being performed always 'as fast as possible' whatever the surrounding tempo, collectively acquire the status of a tempo constant against which the ever-changing metronomic tempi can be evaluated. Once again, we see a reversal of the normal situation where measured time is the constant and grace-note time the subjective variable.

Mobile form has been a headache to a generation of fascinated composers and musicians. It challenges a basic assumption that music is only meaningful as a logical progression of musical ideas in a certain fixed order, such that to change the order is to vary the meaning and invalidate the logic. We see sonata form as a model of rational discourse, and song, ballet, and opera as musical expressions of sequence-dependent narrative structures. The way music is printed and read on the page reinforces the conventional view that music makes sense only if it is enjoyed in a certain order. This has nothing to do with the internal logic or absence of logic of the music itself: there are familiar musical forms whose sequence is arbitrary, such as the cadenza, variation form, and the fantasia. Messiaen's bird-song compositions set out to imitate the random conjunctions and associations of bird-calls in nature. They are, if you like, implicitly indeterminate in order. And yet, because the music is seen as a continuous sequence on the page, we allow ourselves the comfortable assumption that it must therefore express a logical progression, in the same way as film is perceived as continuous in the face of edits, jump-cuts, and flashbacks.

[10] Le Corbusier, *The Modulor* (London, 1954), p. 96.

Composers have criticized Stockhausen's endorsement of mobile form on aesthetic and theoretical grounds. Stravinsky[11] objects to the performer being permitted to determine the piece's 'final shape', as if the final shape were a priority (this is another form of the literary fallacy). Cage, on the other hand, repeatedly objects to what he sees as a philosophical inconsistency on Stockhausen's part.[12] Since it is determinate in all respects but the order of performance, he argues, Piece XI is not indeterminate enough (he might just as well argue that his own *Music of Changes*, being indeterminate in all respects except the order in which events are performed, is no less a betrayal of principle). Boulez, while clearly impressed (a well-known photograph portrays him gazing at the score of Piece XI, deep in thought), concludes that Piece XI is inherently unstable, because segments do not remain identifiably the same (in duration, tempo, dynamic, and touch) from version to version[13] (though his own essay in pianistic peregrination, *Sonata III*, which reduces the mobile principle to a choice of pathways, is perhaps a more appropriate candidate for Cage's criticism).

Thirty years later, the battle of words appears distinctly irrelevant. Now that we live in a culture where even the classics are subject to programmed random selection on one's home CD player, nobody objects that this invalidates the logical argument of the music (even if it does, the fact remains that we have adapted to listening intermittently in preference to continuously). We acknowledge the existence of information processes such as computer programs, and even literary forms such as computer games, which are by definition multivalent, i.e. designed to allow the user to follow a variety of routes to achieve a particular goal, and in which the behaviour of each segment of the process can vary by inference from the previous stage, or as a result of actions or decisions of the user. In short, the idea of a program as a structure distinct from the information processed, but allowing that information to be processed in a variety of orders, is now perfectly normal. The form of Piece XI should therefore no longer be an issue: what is surprising is that it should have remained an issue for so long.

---

[11] Igor Stravinsky and Robert Craft, *Conversations with Igor Stravinsky* (London, 1959), p. 112.
[12] John Cage, 'Indeterminacy', in *Silence* (Cambridge, Mass. 1966), pp. 35–6.
[13] Antoine Goléa, *Rencontres avec Pierre Boulez* (Paris, 1958), p. 229.

6 ' . . . how time passes . . . '

MUSIC occupies and, in so doing, represents time. The ways in which music is organized on the page are calculated to affect the experience of order a performance may express, and thereby its sense of time. Though not the only art experienced continuously in time, by its comparative abstraction music has certain advantages over other time-dependent art forms such as drama or dance, which are more limited in range. Drama's range of time is the range of human experience that can be conveyed in voice and gesture. Dance is similarly limited to what co-ordinated human action is able to express: its range of time is measured in physical movement. By tradition drama and dance are directed toward a co-ordinated response: a conspiracy of emotion, or integrated action. What they say to us about time has an implicit social dimension: co-operation is good for you. Traditionally music is directed toward a similar goal of integration, the orchestra being a model community, the symphony a sounding together, the concert a social occasion. Superficially, musical order is all about conformity, of which musical time is the crowning expression.

Underneath the surface, however, musical time can be infinitely more subtle and wide-ranging. Compared to the narrative forms of drama or dance, music's field of representation is coextensive with hearing itself, from the virtually instantaneous to the farthest reaches of memory. Thanks to sound recording, music today has also extended its sphere of influence to the farthest outreaches of order, now encompassing unpremeditated invention moment to moment, expressing an infinitely fine time-scale, or imitating the unpredictable patterns of sounds in nature, where the time-scale is infinitely large. Today's art and music are no longer concerned exclusively with conformity of response, but are equally concerned with plurality, the coexistence of alternative perceptions, reflecting the contemporary view that collective agreement may not always be musically appropriate or indeed socially desirable. Creating and interpreting art and music in such a way that many alternative interpretations are equally available brings its own difficulties, though it has transformed and enriched our understanding of the plurality of meanings to be discovered in a great deal of classical art.

For as long as stave notation has existed composers have invented musical structures formed to the same set of proportions from the largest time dimensions down to the smallest figures of melody and rhythm. This is curious because such relationships are not normally audible *en passant*, though they represent a perception of the real world measured in superimposed cycles of the sun and moon, the stars and the seasons. Perhaps the corollary of that interpretation is more to the point: that a music of multiple time-scales in harmonious proportion is an expression of divine order. Philosophical considerations of this sort are not at all alien to music, only neglected at present. They certainly belong to Stockhausen's conceptual world: his preoccupation with music of different time-scales would seem quite normal to a Machaut or a J. S. Bach, and its association with divine perfection entirely logical.

Zeitmasze

1955–6: *Time Measures* for five woodwinds (oboe, flute, cor anglais, clarinet, bassoon).
Duration 14'.

In *Piano Pieces V–VIII* Stockhausen examined the relationship between musical events perceived as grouped and those perceived as discrete. Time relationships loom especially large, not least because so many perceptions of group values are time-dependent. Through meeting the pianist David Tudor, his field of reference opened out to include performance factors, psychological as well as physical, influencing the articulation and thus the realization of notated distinctions. With *Zeitmasze* and *Gruppen* performance factors assume even greater significance. The piano had an a priori advantage of objectivity which Stockhausen was initially eager to exploit; moving to non-keyboard instruments and ensembles brought other advantages and also new challenges. Most obviously, proliferation of performers: since an ensemble can play as a unit, or as individuals, it is possible to compose transitions from an extreme of total co-ordination to the opposite extreme of complete independence of line. When composing for non-keyboard instruments, a composer is obliged to take a variety of physical limitations into consideration which can be ignored in writing for the piano, in particular limits of range, breath, speed, and dynamic. But there are significant expressive compensations. The very existence of physical limits means that a listener can hear them: as the technical demands of a part approach a maximum in any one parameter, both instrument and performer are subjected to strains normally audible as distortions of tone quality or character. The distinctive timbre of each woodwind in *Zeitmasze* acts as an Ariadne's thread leading the ear through the polyphonic maze, while at the same time variations in the quality and consistency of timbre enable the ear to follow the movement of a part within its own particular territory.

All of which makes *Zeitmasze* a strongly characterized, indeed voluble piece. The title means 'tempi' and also measures of time; the choice of title signals, as the music itself confirms, a treatment of tempo relationships which goes beyond the theoretical and addresses real perceptions of performer and listener. The choice of wind instruments is a key. In *Kreuzspiel* it is the woodwind duo which symbolizes integration of points into melodic lines embodying continuity, control, and a human scale of gesture and expression. In *Gesang der Jünglinge* the same integrative role is taken by the boy's voice. That being the case, a composition starting with five instruments all of which emody similarly restricted scales of action and time control is in Stockhausen's terms already highly integrated. Like *Formel*, it can only develop toward greater dissociation. The interest of both *Zeitmasze* and *Gruppen* is observing how the process of dissociation is achieved, and at the same time controlled. The technical problems of notation, for one, are formidable.

Stockhausen has said that his first inspiration for *Zeitmasze* came in the form of a dream of a voice singing to the accompaniment of woodwinds.[1] This initial version of the first four munutes, bars 1–28, composed at speed as a present for the sixtieth birthday of Heinrich Strobel, is indeed a setting for alto voice accompanied by flute, clarinet in A, and bassoon, of an epigrammatic text by Strobel himself:

on cherche	trying
pour trouver	to find
quelque chose	something
mais au fond	but really
on ne sait pas	not knowing
ce qu'on cherche	what to look for
au juste	exactly
et cela est vrai.	and that's the truth.[2]

There is one thing to be said about structures with an inbuilt propensity to disorder, and that is that they are funny. *Zeitmasze* is an enormously funny piece, once players get over their inhibitions and master the inherent difficulties of the writing. From the coyly jazz-like opening to the individual signing-off flourishes at the end, the composer's high spirits are always close to the surface. Joseph Schillinger, the Russian-American composer whose visionary theories were an inspiration to Cage and his circle, aptly conveys the sense of exaltation aroused by a music of different and varying speeds:

The rhythm of variable velocities presents a fascinating field for study and exploration. The very thought that various rhythmic groups may speed up and slow down at various rates, appearing and disappearing, is overwhelming. . . . The idea stimulates one's imagination towards the complex harmony of the universe, where different celestial bodies (comets, stars, planets, satellites) coexist in a harmony of variable velocities.[3]

[1] Hans Oesch, 'Interview mit Karlheinz Stockhausen', *Melos/Neue Zeitschrift für Musik*, 1 (1975), 460.
[2] Heinrich Strobel, '*Verehrter Meister, Lieber Freund . .* '. *Begegnungen mit Komponisten unserer Zeit* (Stuttgart, 1977), pp. 88–9.
[3] Joseph Schillinger, *The Schillinger System of Musical Composition* (New York, 1946), i, p. 95.

Naturally there are two directions in which a five-layer polyphony is able to disintegrate. Within a common time-structure individual parts can be variously differentiated in rhythmic accentuation and ornamental figuration. This strategy characterizes Stockhausen's initial stages of composition, in effect reversing the process of integration represented in *Kontra-Punkte*. Indeed, a major proportion of *Zeitmasze* (bars 1–28, 41–73, 104–53, and 207–92) is virtually monorhythmic, both the rhythm of the bars and their pattern of subdivision being the same for every part, if we allow for minor variations of ornamentation. The ensemble performs as a single organism, of which individual instruments are 'limbs', allowed a limited independence of movement. This is again a similar strategy to *Kontra-Punkte*, though in the earlier work the process of change from points to groups is inevitable and irreversible. *Kontra-Punkte* is 'dramatic' in Stockhausen's terms, meaning it is governed by the arrow of time; *Zeitmasze* by comparison has the freedom to move either way, sometimes tending toward greater integration, at other times toward greater dissociation. Timing is always the principal co-ordinate, and of course Stockhausen's repertoire of time-scales is now enviably large, but differentiations of attacks, dynamics, and phrasing also play their part in assisting or contradicting a trend (Ex. 30). Grace-notes are less, groups much more in evidence, and transitions from staccato showers of points to legato lines and groups particularly so. In the illustrated passage of overlapping tempi, a reference tempo is set initially by the oboe (top stave), then passed to the clarinet (fourth stave) at 164, both 'as fast as possible', up to the bar rest at 164b. Within this time-span, the flute slows down and hands over to the cor anglais at 163 which accelerates to 'as fast as possible'; simultaneously the clarinet accelerates from 161 and hands over to the bassoon at 162, who slows down again. While the starting-point at 161 and end-point at 164 are 'fixed' the intermediate cross-over points between pairs of instruments may vary from performance to performance.

Alternatively, the five parts can move away from a common time structure toward complete independence of tempo. This is the later, and in many respects contradictory development, and a recurrent feature of his electronic music, notably *Kontakte* and *Telemusik*. An obvious parallel can be drawn with the experience of loss of synchronization of tape recorders, of which Stockhausen complained as early as 1953, when working on *Studie I*. Coincidentally *Gesang der Jünglinge*, on which Stockhausen was engaged at this time, is a five-channel tape composition.

In order for a gradual change of tempo to be audible, the part involved has to be evenly pulsed and reasonably uninterrupted; if irregular and broken in texture, what is perceived is simply an alteration of density within a uniform time field. For instance, the unsynchronized cadenza at bars 100–2 has the idea of beginning as a pointillist texture and converting gradually to a legato group texture, but the pointillism is very short-lived, and the transition piecemeal. Elsewhere, at 159–72 and 192–200 the pointillist element is even more strictly contained. The lesson seems to be that multiple time layers and pointillism do not mix well.

84

Ex. 30

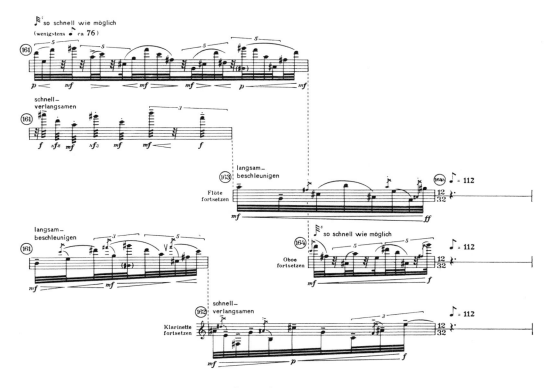

Zeitmasze. Note Stockhausen's 'space-time' notation.

© Universal Edition AG Wien.

Phrasing, or melodic integration over unusually long time units, based on a strict application of breath control, is in fact the distinctive feature of *Zeitmasze's* range of 'time measures'. The first is Stockhausen's familiar chromatic scale of metronomic tempi, crotchet = MM 60–120; the others are all subjective: 'as fast as possible', a ritardando from 'as fast as possible' to 'four times slower', an accelerando from 'four times slower' to 'as fast as possible', and finally 'as slow as possible' (depending on the length of an individual breath). It should be obvious that the first option of metronomic tempi is suitable only for synchronized part-writing, and not at all for unsynchronized; equally, that the four subjective time measures—two extreme, two transitional—cancel out the metronomic options as well as each other. This is not therefore a series in the ordinary sense of the term.

After 293 Stockhausen's structuring of time relationships significantly changes. The music reverts to common time signatures and metronomic tempi, and to that extent to the earlier idea of a unitary ensemble, but now each part articulates at a different 'harmonic' frequency: for example at 323 ratios of 9 : 7 : 6 : 4 : 5, at 327 9 : 7 : 6 : 5 : 4 among oboe, flute, cor anglais, clarinet, and bassoon respectively. We thus enter the world of *Gruppen*, where the microworld of frequency and the macroworld of musical form coincide. The change brings entirely new criteria into operation, which are examined in depth in Stockhausen's essay '. . . how time passes . . . ',

Gruppen

1955–7: *Groups* for three orchestras.

  I. 2. 2. 1. 1. 2; 2. 2. 1; marimbaphone, glockenspiel, percussion (see below); keyboard glockenspiel (or celesta), harp; 10. 0. 2. 4. 2.
 II. 2. 1. 1. alto, baritone saxophones, 1. 3.; 2. 2. 0; vibraphone, tubular bells, percussion (see below), ratchet, 2 triangles; piano, electric guitar; 8. 0. 4. 2. 2.
III. 1. 2. 2. 1. 3; 2. 2 (+contrabass). (or 1); xylorimba, percussion (see below), celesta, harp; 8. 0. 4. 2. 2.

Percussion for each orchestra: 4 cowbells, tam-tam, 3 cymbals, 3 wood drums, 4 tom-toms, snare drum, tambourine (4 players). Cowbells, tam-tams, cymbals, wood drums, and tom-toms are tuned to specific pitches.

Duration 25′.

Stockhausen's essay is predicated on a leap of faith: that organiztion in the frequency domain can be related, indeed interchanged, with musical structure in the domain of rhythm, metre, and form. We are back to the quest for a totally unified musical order-principle pursued so intensely with Goeyvaerts between 1951 and 1954. This time, however, the unifying principle is no arbitrary *donnée*, being inferred on the one hand from textbook accounts of the vibratory structure of complex sounds, and from practical experience of working with impulse generators in the preparation of *Gesang der Jünglinge*. From a knowledge of the harmonic structure of a sound or noise it only requires a motive to construct analogous frequency structures in the formal domain. Practical experience with an impulse generator provides the audible proof that a continuous train of impulses accelerated beyond a frequency of 14–20 Hz changes in perceived terms from a time event belonging to the domain of rhythm to a frequency event belonging to the pitch domain. So tempo and frequency are theoretically and perceptually interchangeable: all that it requires is that they be experienced at the appropriate speeds. That the activities associated with pitch perception and rhythm perception are located in different parts of the brain has no bearing on the relatedness of the two phenomena, but rather on the way the human sensorium is designed to 'receive' vibratory information at differing wavelengths. 'The ranges of perception are ranges of time, and the time is subdivided by us, by the construction of our bodies and by our organs of perception.'[4]

Gruppen was originally conceived as a work for orchestra and three-channel tape. For various reasons that possibility was ruled out. Then in 1956 he made a version for orchestra alone, applying principles of varying co-ordination of different tempi in the manner of *Zeitmasze*. On reflection he decided that the practical difficulties of execution were too great for an ensemble of this size, and in 1957 he rewrote the work entirely for three orchestral groups and three conductors.

Gruppen brings to a peak that preoccupation with groups which had started in 1952 with the *Piano Pieces I–IV*. 'The notion of groups is transcended in *Gruppen*, just as in *Kontra-Punkte* the notion of points was transcended by introducing groups. This is always happening, and it is always interesting. If one concentrates on a certain aspect, then one transcends it, because one cannot be content to remain always within a closed system.'[5] Before *Gruppen* Stockhausen defined a group in either procedural or perceptual terms. In the procedural sense, the group is a serial strategy to replace the pointillist aesthetic of total contrast by a richer hierarchy of degrees of contrast among the various parameters. In the perceptual sense, group composition acknowledges the fact that musical formations exceeding certain boundaries of subtlety, polyphonic complexity, density, noisiness, or speed are perceived globally rather than in individual detail. Neither definition has anything specific to say about the internal structure of a group: indeed, the external criteria of similarity and speed admit a considerable freedom of choice in the internal distribution of group material, manifestly demonstrated in the formal indeterminacy of Piano Piece XI, the impulse showers of *Gesang der Jünglinge*, and the superimposed tempi of *Zeitmasze*.

The groups of *Gruppen* are something new: they are precisely determined in their time structures, and for that reason subject to refined control. Essentially they are microstructures of points, pointillistic microcompositions speeded up into the time domain where group perceptions supersede individual distinctions. The title 'Groups' cannot really be properly understood in isolation: it asks to be read in the context of *Punkte* 'Points' and *Kontra-Punkte* 'Counter-Points'. If *Zeitmasze* is complementary to *Kontra-Punkte*, in that the transformation of points into groups is achieved through performer action, then *Gruppen* is the complement to *Punkte*, both because the groups are pointillistic in conception, and because they are integrated primarily by design.

Essentially a group event is determined by a fundamental frequency or prevailing time value or unit beat (global tempi once again corresponding to a chromatic scale of pitches). Like the vibrating string of a monochord, the fundamental time length can be shortened to correspond to a change of chromatic pitch; as a complex sound

[4] Karlheinz Stockhausen and Robin Maconie, *Stockhausen on Music* (London, 1989), p. 95.
[5] Ibid.

source, however, the monochord is also capable of vibrating simultaneously in progressively smaller divisions of its fundamental length, corresponding to an ascending harmonic series: two halves, three thirds, four fourths, and so on. The choice and combination of harmonic divisions, and thus the metrical complexity of the group, can be calculated to give greater rhythmic complexity or greater simplicity. A group consisting of harmonics in the ratio 1:2:4:8 corresponds for example to a classical 2/4 bar incorporating minim, crotchet, quaver, and semiquaver pulse divisions, and a group consisting of 1:2:6:12 harmonic divisions to a classical compound 6/8 bar of dotted minim, dotted crotchets, quavers, and semiquavers. To define 'noisier' group rhythms one simply uses the so-called irrational values 5:7:11:13 and so forth. However, the inherent complexity of such noisier groups is always kept within bounds: with every new beat the structure repeats—it is periodic—and within each beat the structure is symmetrical: that is, at the half-way point the pattern of pulses reverses, oscillating between extremes of maximum unity (the downbeat) and maximum disunity (the half-way point).

The larger formal determinations relating group to group derive initially in retrospect from Stockhausen's first electronic compositions, and only after that, at the stage of realization, from concerns of the moment: with stereophonic effects of layers of music of different tempi coming from different directions in space, and of musical events 'panning' from one position to another. Like the rectangular tone mixtures of *Studie II*, each group occupies a defined intervallic range and is characterized by a particular distribution of pitch intervals. The basic architecture of groups in relationship one to another, their size, scale, and distribution in register and time, follows a similar rationale to *Studie I*, the pitch content of which also derives from an initial series of intervals expressed as harmonic ratios.

These measurements have their own serial justification, but are essentially fixed; Stockhausen introduces a further range of parameters in order to bring the composition of group proportions dynamically to life. The first is tempo, each group being assigned a characteristic tempo corresponding to its frequency in the series. The logistics of controlling the resulting successions and superimpositions of tempi are enormously complicated, and in fact caused Stockhausen to divide his original single large orchestra into three smaller orchestras with a corresponding reduplication of percussion forces, albeit with contrasting keyboards;

I originally wanted to write a normal orchestra piece, but when I started composing several time layers I had to superimpose several metronomic tempi, and it was impossible to find a solution by which one conductor would be able to lead the three sections of a large orchestra in different tempi. So I finally concluded that the only way was to split the diverse time layers and put each group in a separate place . . . Once I had the idea of separating the three groups . . . I began to think in terms . . . of sound movements.[6]

Instrumentation and dynamics also have a role to play in generating movement.

[6] Jonathan Cott, *Stockhausen: Conversations with the Composer* (London, 1974), pp. 200–1.

The composition of the three orchestras reflects a now familiar distinction between instruments of precise and approximate pitch, also between types of intonation which occupy a middle ground (e.g. pizzicato, *col legno*). While his orchestration is technically very sophisticated, its conceptual basis is much the same as in previous orchestral works. More innovatory is a rhythmic and dynamic delineation of individual group formations, made possible because the underlying structure is so precisely controlled. Having established the 'harmonic' identity of a group, Stockhausen can create a shape within the schema with considerable freedom to serve particular expressive ends or to control its degree of internal coherence or virtual indeterminacy. At times his treatment of groups is represented as playful (Ex. 31):

Whole envelopes of rhythmic blocks are exact lines of mountains that I saw in Paspels in Switzerland right in front of my little window. Many of the time spectra, which are represented by superimpositions of different rhythmic layers—of different speeds in each layer—their envelope which describes the increase and decrease of the number of layers, their shape, so to speak, the shape of the time field, are the curves of the mountain's contour which I saw when I looked out of the window.[7]

Mountain ranges *are* mathematically interesting,[8] but unlike those contemporaries whose drawings are designed to be heard two-dimensionally,—height equal to pitch—these mountain-inspired shapes are simply a composer's aide-mémoire to patterning in the rhythm domain, and are neither directly 'readable' in the finished score nor audible in the music, other than possibly in terms of a mountain-related quality of irregularity. In any event, what the listener hears is interior pitch complexes rather than exterior shape: dynamic processes resembling natural disturbances such as leaves blown by the wind, or waves on the water, rather than contours.

Elsewhere there are indications in the score that Stockhausen has modelled larger sections on the harmonic evolution of particular types of musical sound. Just as the envelope curve of attack and decay describes a characteristic rise and fall in amplitude and harmonic richness, so the rhythmic structure (or 'time spectrum', to use Stockhausen's term) of a group can be made to follow an analogous rise and fall in density and complexity. Stockhausen has used some artistic licence in relating the time-scales of timbre and envelope evolution of a musical sound, in effect reducing the time of evolution of a rhythmic wave-form to a very small number of cycles; the alternative would be complex sounds gradually evolving on a timescale closer to Ligeti than Stockhausen, in fact hundreds of times slower than the present score.

A typical piano or wind sound, of abrupt attack and gradual decay, builds rapidly to a maximum complement of harmonics, which gives the note its distinctive timbre; after which its complexity diminishes to oscillate around a fundamental periodicity

---

[7] Ibid. 141. See also Karlheinz Stockhausen, ' . . . how time passes . . . ', *Die Reihe* (English Edition), 27–8 and Jonathan Harvey, *The Music of Stockhausen* (London, 1975), pp. 70–1.

[8] See Benoît Mandelbrot, *Fractals: Form, Chance and Dimension* (San Francisco, 1977), pp. 210–11.

Ex. 31

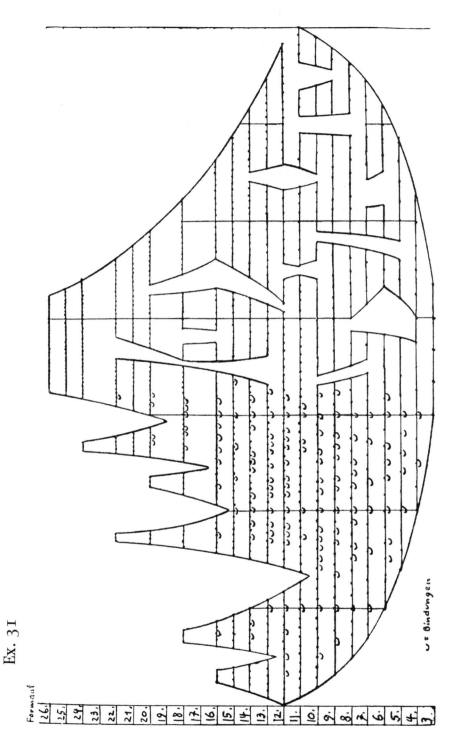

Gruppen. Stockhausen's Klee-like diagram of the rhythmic envelope of the section 7 tutti, showing a 'mountain range' in the first three measures and 'negative spaces' (shaped voids) in the remaining four measures. 'Formant' refers to a given subdivision of an underlying three-beat duration; 'Bindungen' refers to tied values which superimpose a further accentual rhythm on the rhythmic texture. See Jonathan Harvey, *The Music of Stockhausen*, London, 1975, pp. 69–72.

© Universal Edition AG Wien.

which we perceive as the pitch of the note. A short sound the decay of which is suppressed, such as a pizzicato or staccato, translates in the time domain as a short group of relatively consistent rhythmic complexity, more 'statistical' in structure, as indeed its sound-equivalents are more 'noisy'.

The first bars of *Gruppen* feature an accented tritonal cluster allowed to reverberate, followed in bar 2, Orchestra I (Ex. 32) by a similar structure magnified in the rhythmic domain: an initially dense complex of harmonic divisions

Ex. 32

Gruppen: Orchestra I. Rhythmic disintegration of a tritonal cluster. The pattern of divisions is clear. A drum accent provides a time cue for Orchestra II.

© Universal Edition AG Wien.

degenerating into a less complex reverberation, the whole shaped by a periodic fluctuation of amplitude. Fricative (bowed) or iterative (tremolo, rolled) sounds retain a measure of rhythmic complexity and do not decay into simpler patterns; there are many groups in the work which conform to this type. Rarer perhaps is the Orchestra III ritardando at 113–15, a group initially complex and statistical in structure, which gradually resolves into a slow pulsation of simpler metres (Ex. 33). A particularly dramatic form of evolution imitates a tremolo gradually building to a crash on the tam-tam: its rhythmic equivalent is a periodic structure incorporating physical noise and increasing in complexity to a break-off point where the excited timbre is allowed to swing freely, casting its resonance this way and that. Such a pattern of evolution is suggested by the periodicity and crescendo leading to the brass and percussion climax of the entire work, building to the extraordinary moment at 119 where brass harmonies are acoustically 'cross-faded' from orchestra to orchestra.

Ex. 33

Gruppen: Orchestra III. The formant-rhythm at 114 gradually settles into a more or less coherent beat (compare the wave-rhythm of *Dr. K-Sextett*).

© Universal Edition AG Wien.

Gruppen is a monumental achievement, an ingenious hybrid of theory and fantasy. It is Stockhausen's grandest conception to date; though belonging to the same period as *Zeitmasze* and *Gesang der Jünglinge*, and sharing a number of theoretical preoccupations with these two works, its origins penetrate a good deal deeper, as his essay makes clear; its conclusions, in terms of musical form, are also arguably more rigorous and internally consistent than either of the other two works. The musical imagery of *Gruppen* is turbulent and dynamic, its texture of unprecedented sharpness of detail; as one might expect, the role of the conductors as movers and shapers is correspondingly vital. When the three orchestras come together in the same tempo, the music has tremendous *élan*; at other times, when structures in different tempi are superimposed, the effect can be robustly impressionistic, and comparisons with Debussy's statistical forms, of which Stockhausen had written approvingly, are not far away.

Stockhausen's equation of pitch and time relationships may appear fanciful, but it has an honourable lineage. Helmholtz's observations on the Greek tetrachord[9] are a reminder of the importance early theorists from the time of Pythagoras attached to harmonious proportions in both time and pitch:

The musical scale is as it were the divided rod, by which we measure progression in pitch, as rhythm measures progression in time. Hence the analogy between the scale of tones and rhythm naturally occurred to the theoreticians of ancient as well as modern times . . . Alterations of pitch in melodies take place by intervals, and not by continuous transitions. The psychological reason of this fact would seem to be the same as that which led to rhythmic subdivision periodically repeated. All melodies are motions within extremes of pitch . . . Every motion is an expression of the power which produces it, and we instinctively measure the motive force by the amount of motion which it produces . . . How long and how often can we sit and look at the waves rolling in to shore! Their rhythmic motion, perpetually varied in detail, produces a peculiar feeling of pleasant repose or weariness, and the impression of a mighty orderly life, finely linked together . . . But the motion of tone surpasses all motion of corporeal masses in the delicacy and ease with which it can receive and imitate the most varied descriptions of expression. Hence it arrogates to itself by right the representation of states of mind, which the other arts can only indirectly touch.[10]

Carré

1959–60: *Square* for four orchestras and four choirs.

   I. 1. 1. 1. tenor saxophone. 0. 1; 2. 1; choir 2. 2. 2. 2; piano, percussion; 4. 0. 2. 2. 0.

   II. 1. 1. 1. 1. 2; 1. 1; choir 2. 2. 2. 2; vibraphone, percussion; 4. 0. 2. 2. 0.

[9] Hermann Helmholtz, *On the Sensations of Tone* (New York, 1954), pp. 264–5.   [10] Ibid. 250–3.

93

III. 0. 1. 1. baritone saxophone. 1. 1; 1. 1. 1; choir 2. 2. 2. 2; amplified cymbalom, percussion; 4. 0. 2. 2. 0.

IV. 1. 0. 1. alto saxophone. 1. 2; 1. 1; choir 2. 2. 2. 2; harp, percussion; 4. 0. 2. 2. 0.

Percussion for each orchestra: 2 tom-toms, bongo, 3 cowbells, snare drum, bass drum, Indian bells, suspended cymbal, hi-hat, gong, tam-tam (2 players).

Duration 30–34′.

If I speak of a musical development as dramatic, when it is strongly directional, and epic, when it is sequential, then I could use the term lyric to describe a music in which the forming process is instantaneous. In my composition CARRÉ for four choirs and orchestras, I tried for the first time to concentrate on instantaneous forming, or the forming of moments. . . . I worked on the basis of starting with the here and now, and then we will see if there is any past and future.[11]

Carré was conceived during long periods of flying between stopovers on a tour of American university campuses which Stockhausen made in the summer of 1958. Despite superficial resemblances of scale and instrumental forces it is the antithesis of *Gruppen*: if the earlier composition demonstrates the integrative power of positive action, the new composition advocates the contrary power of revelation, aspiring to a state—perhaps even 'united states'—of grace. Having attained a mastery of organizing sounds in the physical domain, now able to navigate with equal confidence between order and disorder, it is perhaps not unexpected that Stockhausen should be on the alert for contrary worlds to conquer. The American composers he still admired represented an alternative view of organization, declaring that the purpose of their purposeless music would be realized if mankind only learned to listen in a fresh, perhaps more innocent way. Something of this attitude to listener sensibility emerges from Stockhausen's account of how the new composition was first conceived:

I was flying every day for two or three hours over America from one city to the next over a period of six weeks, and my whole time feeling was reversed after about two weeks. I had the feeling that I was visiting the earth and living in the plane. There were just very tiny changes of bluish colour and always this harmonic spectrum of the engine noise.

At that time, in 1958, most of the planes were propellor planes, and I was always leaning my ear—I *love* to fly, I must say—against the window, like listening with earphones directly to the inner vibrations. And though a physicist would have said that the engine sound doesn't change, it changed all the time because I was listening to all the partials within the spectrum. It was a fantastically beautiful experience.[12]

The sounds of *Carré* simply are: this is not music of doing, but of being. Whereas *Gruppen* represents a world of natural phenomena disturbed by external forces, the

---

[11] Stockhausen and Maconie, op. cit. 45.
[12] Cott, op. cit. 31.

new work focuses on the rhythms and changes within continuous sounds in such a way as to draw the listener in and obliterate any sense of time. Four orchestras surrounding the listener suggest that the movement of sounds in space as signalled in *Gesang der Jünglinge* and *Gruppen* is going to play a major role; in the event, however, dynamically moving sounds play a specially limited and disruptive role in the compositional drama, and even distance and directional effects are relatively incidental: the principal consequence of distributing sources of sound around the auditorium is to induce a change of mind among listeners conditioned to having their responses led from the front.

The four orchestras are lightweight in composition and evenly matched, identifiable mainly through their respective keyboards (piano, vibraphone, cymbalom, harp). There are sound acoustic reasons for the absence of lower strings, and for the small numbers of strings overall; string sound is typically diffuse and thus difficult to locate precisely, and the problem increases with lower frequencies to a point where distance and directional effects may be masked if not actually overwhelmed. The addition of choir groups is a happy invention, not only strengthening the important mid-range of frequencies, but also adding a richness and variety of articulation to each orchestra which the ear can readily seize upon. The vocal parts, notated in international phonetic script, are abstracted compositions of vowel and consonantal fragments (including occasional recognizable names and ejaculatory remarks) which recreate the vocal fluxes of *Gesang der Jünglinge* and mediate between percussive noise and instrumental tone.

Stravinsky was much impressed by *Carré*, 'although it will no doubt be discovered that my admiration extends only to superficialities'.[13] In his 1963 monograph on the composer, Karl Wörner recalls first impressions which totally confounded conventional expectations. There was nothing recognizable: no texts, no themes or motives, instead 'solo instruments often at the extremes of their range, . . . ecstatic outbursts from dense instrumental groups, and . . . resounding long-held chordal complexes. It is a never-flagging hypertrophy of ideas and impressions which mill round the listener from all sides. . . . One's aesthetic involvement with the work is unceasing.'[14] Wörner's first impressions are interesting not only because they reflect a period sensibility but because *Carré* is a music of first impressions of the most intensely memorable kind. Not going off to sleep with one's head against the window, lulled by the slow drone of a turbo-prop, but a series of cataclysmic jolts into consciousness. The scale of events is monumental and often terrifying. Monumental in the time-scale of events ('I thought I was being very brave', the composer remarks, 'in going far beyond the time of memory, which is the crucial time between eight- and sixteen-second-long events. When you go beyond them you lose orientation'),[15] monumental too in sheer physical impact: enormous tidal waves of sound suddenly

[13] Igor Stravinsky and Robert Craft, *Themes and Episodes* (New York, 1966), p. 12.
[14] *Stockhausen: Life and Work*, rev. edn. trans. and ed. Bill Hopkins (London, 1973), pp. 164–5.
[15] Cott, op. cit. 31.

95

towering above the audience, avalanches sweeping with enormous violence through the auditorium space. This is quite simply music on a superhuman scale:

A work of art [said Sergei Eisenstein] must reproduce that process whereby, in itself, new images are built up in the human consciousness and feelings; . . . The strength of montage resides in this, that it includes in the creative process the emotions and mind of the spectator . . . [who] not only sees the represented elements of the finished work, but also experiences the dynamic process of the emergence and assembly of the image just as it was experienced by the author.[16]

Stockhausen defines a moment as a period of awareness of relative absence of change. Take away the time dimension and a moment is a point; add the time dimension and a moment is a point magnified to such an extent that a listener can be drawn into its inner life. Consider the proposition of instantaneous forming: the idea of a music in which the impression is always of the here and now, and not of what has gone before or what might yet come. The definition of a method to obliterate memory and anticipation is total change from moment to moment. Take away the time dimension and you are back once more to pointillism; add the time dimension and moment form is a pointillism so magnified that the contrasts only cancel the memory of one another out. Long durations of no change or very gradual change, violent contrasts, and silence: Stockhausen frequently 'hard-edits' the musical fabric into silence, and in fact whole sections of the work can be edited out, as the DG recording allows. These silences are not the straightforward breaks or preparatory pauses to be found in Piano Piece XI, but palpable voids.

Music which has a beat can be mentally paced, but music which is airborne has to be timed in relation to events which encroach upon it. There are reference complexes which stay with the listener like the hum of a motor, signifying both our motionlessness and our being transported; against the constant background images pass by: in a flash, suddenly appearing in fortissimo and fading rapidly, or gradually overtaking in slow motion. A door opens, voices are heard (Ex. 34).

The writing-out of *Carré* from the composer's sketch plans was undertaken by Cornelius Cardew in 1959.[17] During this time Stockhausen was chiefly engaged in

---

[16] Sergei Eisenstein, *The Film Sense*, trans, and ed. Jay Leyda (London, 1948), pp. 24, 34.

[17] Cornelius Cardew, 'Report on Stockhausen's *Carré*', *Musical Times*, 1961, pp. 619–22, 698–700.

Carré: Orchestra II. The overall duration is shown in seconds, and is subdivided into irregular subsections A, B, and C. The timing of each beat is relatively to-scale. Choir pitches are notated in a modified form of international phonetic notation, as are the syllabic textures. *Kopfstimme* (head-tone): a falsetto speaking voice. Contrast the sustained tam-tam and bass-voice 'travelling tones' with the B1 voice textures, which seem to be passing at speed from the opposite direction (similar contrasts occur in the electronic soundscape of *Kontakte*, for instance at 18′ 56.5″).

© Universal Edition AG Wien.

Ex. 34

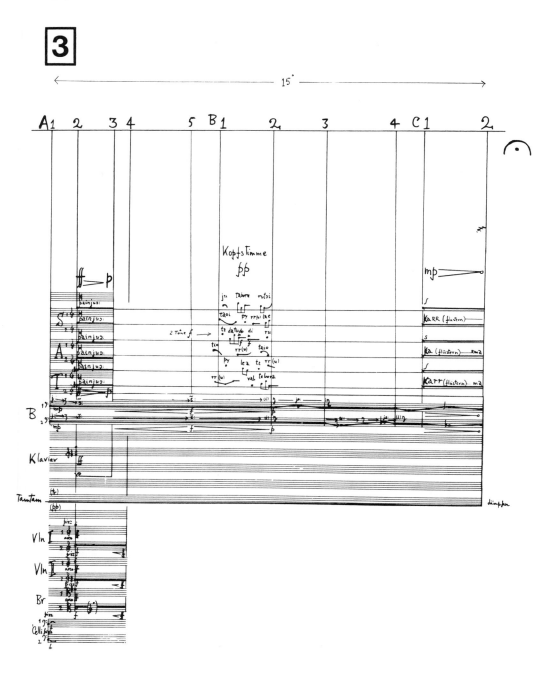

Ex. 35

Carré: the insert at 69X. The chess-board graphics indicate an anticlockwise rotation of the pointillist texture showing in detail for Orchestra II; at the same time a sustained soprano D is pan-rotated in the opposite direction.

the studio with *Kontakte*, and the feedback from the new electronic work to the orchestral domain is noticeable in a number of ways. The imagery of mechanical motion, for example, is more immediately graspable in the electronic medium. *Carré's* slow-changing sounds *imply* an early intention to 'pan' them across the auditorium like the famous brass chords in *Gruppen*. A preliminary version of *Kontakte* involving four instrumentalists with individual potentiometers volleying electronic sounds like tennis players among four loudspeakers was attempted experimentally but abandoned, and it may have been Stockhausen's intention to have the four conductors vary the amplitude of their respective orchestras in a similar way, in the hope of producing a similar effect. There are panning movements of static sounds in the final score, but they rotate around rather than traverse the auditorium space. The most effective dynamic movements occur with the extremely turbulent textures of the X-moments (Ex. 35), inserted into the score at a late stage of realization. Here the four conductors begin to beat synchronously instead of timing events by intuition, and great vortices of sound descend out of nowhere to sweep round the auditorium at enormous speed. These insertions correspond with Stockhausen's development of a 'rotation table' to enable *Kontakte's* layers of electronic sound to be smoothly circulated among the four speakers at different speeds and in different directions. It is perceptually and acoustically interesting that in the orchestral domain turbulent sound masses should succeed in conveying an illusion of movement so much better than static sounds.

Ligeti and Penderecki were both converted to the composition of sound masses by *Carré* and proceeded to exploit the superficial qualities and associations of orchestral texture with enthusiasm. Boulez too appears to have been impressed by the X-moments, employing an imagery of staccato events against a continuous background similar to 32X and 63X in parts of *Pli selon Pli*, especially 'Don' and 'Tombeau'. But whereas Stockhausen's 'sound horizon' is always clearly-pitched and his transitional staccato events percussively clangorous, in Boulez' sound-world it is the staccato foreground which remains clearly pitched, while the background remains an indistinct haze of metallic resonances.

7 Cycles

STOCKHAUSEN's religious devotion to parities of organization at every level of music from timbre to superstructure continues through 1958–60 with the composition and realization of *Kontakte*, electronic music for four-channel tape with optional piano and percussion, and *Zyklus* for solo percussionist. The realization score of *Kontakte*, setting out the way in which the work was actually put together, is a fascinating chronicle of Stockhausen's thought processes. From the outset it is clear that he had in mind a composition using a range of timbres totally defined in their microstructures and accelerated into the pitch domain. *Carré*'s was not the only sound-world to be inspired by listening to the propeller sound on those long air flights over America. Slow aeroplane sounds with infinitely subtle changes of timbre and pitch are among the first and most meditative elements of the new composition. Its conceptual basis changes dramatically, however, during the preliminary stages of synthesis. An early plan, as has been said, involved four performers each controlling the sound level of one channel of a four-track tape in addition to playing their own instruments. The sections of the work realized for preliminary trials consist of long sounds each with a distinctive inner life. The finished tape is dramatic, aggressive, and ecstatic: an enormously rich and volatile cocktail of sounds which bubble and fizz from the depths to the heights of auditory perception.

Stockhausen began work by returning to procedures first employed in the composition of the *Konkrete Etüde* and the two electronic studies in 1952–4. The first entry in the realization score, dated 20 February 1958 (Ex. 36) describes a cyclic microstructure composed of a sequence of ten impulses serially varied in amplitude and distance in time, though not in pitch. It resembles the all-interval series in favour during the fifties (used for instance, by Nono for *Incontri* and by Stokhausen himself for *Schlagtrio*). The figure has interesting internal symmetries that the score diagram does not reveal: principally an underlying 'Victory' motif; alternate time points in the overall duration of 55 units recur at 0, 5, 10, 15, 30, 45 units, a rhythm resembling the scherzo horn entry of the famous motto of Beethoven's Fifth. Cyclic repetition is clearly intended, though similar patterns of tom-tom-like impulses appear in the final composition in real time, for example at VIIF in the score.

Five days later, he is experimenting with a cycle of impulses of varying distances but this time of constant amplitude. On 29 February (Ex. 37) he constructs a sort of contracting tremolo in edited sine-tones of constant 5-cm. tape-length and

Ex. 36

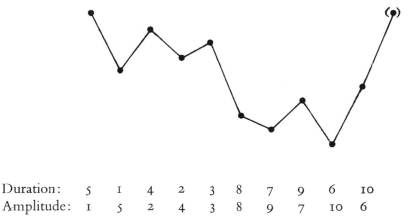

| Duration: | 5 | 1 | 4 | 2 | 3 | 8 | 7 | 9 | 6 | 10 |
| Amplitude: | 1 | 5 | 2 | 4 | 3 | 8 | 9 | 7 | 10 | 6 |

Kontakte, realization score. The ten duration values may be grouped in multiples of 5 (5, 1 + 4, 2 + 3, 8 + 7, 9 + 6, 10 . . .) suggesting a superordinate 'Victory' motif (· · · –), which amplitude fluctuations however are likely to obscure.

alternating pitches related to serial tempi (40–48–60–75 Hz). Doubled in speed and reversed, it sounds approximately as notated in Ex. 38. Doubled again, to sound an octave higher and twice as fast, it can be heard punctuating section XIIB.

Curiously, these experiments in composing the microstructure of a wave go over the same ground as the *Konkrete Etüde* and the two electronic studies, only to reach the same conclusions. First Stockhausen tries and apparently discards the idea of amplitude and duration as microstructural variables, then, changing tack, he reverts to the same method of rotating sequences of sine tones of constant length and amplitude that he used in *Studie II*. 'I have come to realize', he had written to Goeyvaerts in December 1952, 'that one can only work with sounds which have the *same timbre* and the same loudness . . . But even that's not enough. They all had to have *the same rhythmic time-values*'.[1] After a lapse of three months, on 2 June he resumes work to try a number of variations of the two previous methods, observing certain constraints of formal symmetry and sonority. A significant breakthrough is signalled with the production of a particularly elaborate impulse complex on 4 June, which collates independent trains of impulses at five distinct pitches into a single stream (Ex. 39). The five layers accelerate and slow down in periodicity over the same length of cycle, but peak at different points (i.e. are 'out of phase' with one another). Each dot represents a 5-cm. section of tape consisting of an impulse and

---

[1] Richard Toop, 'Stockhausen's *Konkrete Etüde*', *Music Review* 37 (1976), 296.

Cycles

Ex. 37

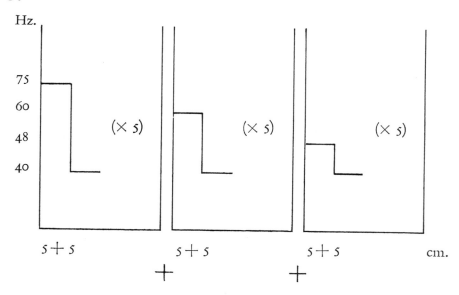

Hz.

75
60
48
40

(× 5)   (× 5)   (× 5)

5 + 5   5 + 5   5 + 5   cm.

+   +

Kontakte. A contrasting loop formation using pitched sine-wave material in a manner reminiscent of *Studie II*.

Ex. 38

♩ = ca. 60

[pitches approximate]

Kontakte.

silence; the aggregate (47 × 5 = 235)-cm. length being copied twice, the two copies joined 'forward' to 'reverse' to form a symmetrical density curve, and the whole copied again and formed into a loop to be accelerated some 1,000 times. The resulting structure is a prototype for *Zyklus* for solo percussionist, which can be understood literally as a 'spin-off' from Stockhausen's electronic researches.

Up to this point Stockhausen has followed the classic 'cut-and-stick' method of assembling tone complexes, which is time-consuming and limiting, in that there is little scope for varying the end-result other than by repeating the process. Now,

Ex. 39

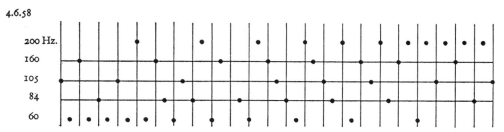

Kontakte.

however, a new discovery comes into play: by changing the order of the three heads in a studio tape recorder from 'erase–playback–record' to 'playback–erase–record' it became possible to overcopy a tape loop automatically, adding new layers of material, and at the same time to modify the sound on tape in real time. This new means of continuous synthesis eliminated the need, and at a stroke the basic rationale, for hand-edited complexes based on serially ordained values. It was no longer necessary to justify accepting a speculative result on the say-so of structural consistency; Stockhausen could now experiment much more freely, and have to choose only the most acceptable results.

After 4 July 1958 the precise notation of microstructures gives way to diagrams of transformation procedures, like flow charts, from sine or impulse sources via filters and other modulators to the final destination on tape. Both the input and output become less precisely defined in advance; instead we observe the emergence of naturalistic criteria for the selection of favoured procedures, for example sounds having distinctive 'wood', 'metal', or 'skin' characteristics. (This range of timbres is already prefigured in the earlier electronic studies, needless to say; what the new work does is to describe continuous aural transitions from one kind of sound to another, the real-world percussion serving to identify points of arrival and departure. It follows that the choice of instruments is dictated by the variety of electronic sounds, not the other way round.) Stockhausen's assistant, the composer Gottfried Michael Koenig, was set the task of analysing the harmonic evolution of sampled percussion sounds during this time, but this complicated work appears to have had little direct impact on synthesis procedures now in use. As if coming to terms with a new instrument, the composer's chief concern seems to be with setting a certain kind of wind in motion, and hoping to disover a 'right sound' as a result. After accelerating the initial sound to up to 1,000 times its original speed, it no longer mattered whether one started from impulses of varying distances, a sustained tone of varying amplitude, or any other particular prescription: 'I'd obtain the same result . . . It's just a matter of obtaining something the quickest way.'[2]

Despite the radical change of method, the original form-scheme was largely preserved. As the published sketches show, it is closed, permutated and ordered in six-by-six magic squares (in contrast to the serial fives of the earliest experiments in synthesis). The sketches indicate a form-plan of eighteen major structures on a scale of six durations of constant ratio 2:3, namely 29″, 43.5″, 1′ 05″, 1′ 37.5″, 2′ 26″. Only fourteen of these were completed, work having to be curtailed through lack of time, but two introductory sections were added at the beginning. The planned time proportions also suffered considerably revision during realization.[3]

Kontakte

1959–60: *Contacts*, electronic music for four-channel tape, or electronic music for four-channel tape with piano and percussion.

Percussion: marimbaphone, 2 wood drums, 3 plywood tom-toms, 2 woodblocks, guero, bamboo rattle; small tam-tam, 4 pitched cowbells, hi-hat, suspended cymbal, Indian bells, scale of 13 antique cymbals; 4 tom-toms, bongo, snare drum, inverted bongo containing dried beans.

Centre stage: large tam-tam, domed gong.

For the pianist: 2 woodblocks, bamboo rattle; hi-hat, suspended cymbal, 4 pitched cowbells, Indian bells, 3 antique cymbals; bongo.

Duration 34′ 30″.

The piece begins and ends with cyclic gestures, on gong and snare drum respectively, which suggest the starting and stopping of a 78-r.p.m. gramophone record. After a short hiatus, the music opens with a vigorous résumé of principal types of sound material, ranging from the dense flux of IB to the comically nasal exclamation of ID and the solitary complex 'aeroplane tone' of IF. This initial burst of energy gradually peters out in both instrumental and electronic activity, leading via a short passage of droning electronic sounds with added Doppler effects to section III, the planned beginning of the work. This section is closely related to the meditative sound-world of *Carré*, but the electronic sounds have that inner life which makes them appear to move in straight trajectories across the listening space. Here the instruments, which are always in direct imitation of the electronic sounds, are sparing and sustained.

---

[2] Jonathan Cott, *Stockhausen: Conversations with the Composer* (London, 1974), p. 88.
[3] Seppo Heikenheimo, *The Electronic Music of Karlheinz Stockhausen* (Helsinki, 1972), p. 152.

After some four minutes, IV cuts in abruptly with a second dynamic interlude, shorter and more concentrated than IB–IF. V reverts to the slow Doppler-effect drones of II, beginning with a sound rather like an electric motor coming up to speed; this time, however, the lengthy continuous transitions of II are dissected into shorter moments and their order is reshuffled. Gradually the lines of sound converge into a single tone which then splits up again in a symbolic gesture of 'contact' which recurs later in more elaborate forms. IN VB the solitary tones of III are overlaid on the continuous transitions of II; again the music moves by increasingly rapid changes to a point where the two elements seem about to merge into a single tone colour. The music cuts again to another anticipatory passage, which this time descends to the same point of confluence to which the previous passage seemed to be rising, namely the deep, loud 'close-up' complex at VI behind or within which staccato saxophone-like melodic fragments can faintly be heard. Unexpectedly, this magnified sound is succeeded by one even more exaggerated in close-up at VIIA, but it recedes fairly rapidly to merge into a gently animated series of exchanges between the instruments and their electronic mirror images. Four such sparring episodes lead to a fugato at VIIF distantly reminiscent of the Stravinsky *Septet*, short-lived and brusquely interrupted by buzzing signals. A series of musical gear-changes leads to more agitated and less sharply focused counterpoint at VIIID, which fades quickly to leave only the high, tinselly rattle of a greatly accelerated pulse complex.

A second fugato-like imitation between marimbaphone and tape occurs at IXA, following grace-note ornamental sequences reminiscent of Piano Piece V. A series of short episodes depicting different aspects of accelerated frequency complexes, including high crotala-like pitches (IXD), a sensation of great speed (IXE), and of great inner energy (IXF), builds to the passage at X which represents a psychological climax of the work, and which is analysed by Stockhausen in great detail in his essay 'The Concept of Unity in Electronic Music'.[4] Here (Ex. 40) a continuous stream of pulsed sound is transformed from a continuous pitched whine into a rapid up-and-down glissando that decelerates all the while into separately perceivable impulses. The original pitch was a percept of the frequency of succession of impulses, *c.* 170 Hz, but that sense of pitch vanishes as the impulse frequency slows down; a second impulse succession fades in imperceptibly, descending in pitch: this time, however, each pulse is heard to have a separate pitch *content*. A brief melody, based perhaps on the mirror series, is heard, the last note bouncing like a ping-pong ball in slow motion, to be joined by the piano, then the marimphone, and finally descending into a timeless resonant limbo. Stockhausen confesses that having reached this point he was reluctant to let the sound go (the section lasts for 4′ 30″ instead of the projected 43″).

This deep, continuous background rumble is crossed at intervals by brilliant ornamental gestures. Gradually a melancholy mood settles, reflected in the

[4] *Perspectives of New Music*, I. I (1962).

Ex. 40

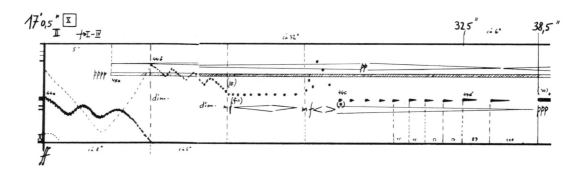

Kontakte, performing score. Graphic representation of the aural illusion beginning at 17' 0.5" where a harsh pitch decelerates into unpitched pulses which then 'open up' to reveal themselves as individual tones.

© Universal Edition AG Wien.

complicated, sometimes angry transformations which follow in XI (Ex. 41). Here the music returns to the notion of meeting and parting lines first encountered in VA. The sound 'splits': a succession of layers peel away from a continuous impulse-tone, each to be transformed into a basic sound category. The first layer moves away upward to turn into bell-like sounds; simultaneously another layer bears downward to become an indistinct drumming. A third spins off to take on a wooden quality in XIC. Further layers peel away as the music gathers pace, its texture thickening then attenuating to allow deep, metallic resonances to emerge into the foreground. These build to the dramatic climax at XIIA, where both instrumentalists ritually cross the stage to strike the great tam-tam and gong, which form the ceremonial centre-piece of the ensemble. (Stockhausen has referred to the impression made on him as a youth by the conjunction of the J. Arthur Rank gong stroke and the MGM lion: since that time the tam-tam has always been associated in his mind with the roar of a lion.)[5]

An explosive disintegration at XIIIC is followed by another low-pitched ornamental exchange structurally similar to VIIIF and IXB but more varied in texture. Once again the music accelerates in pitch and speed, reaching a peak of elevation and tension at XIV, where Stockhausen simulates a progressive 'switching off' of layers of sound from low to high (a similar process is heard in *Gruppen*). From this point the listener senses the end of the piece approaching, but the mood remains strangely exalted. The electronic sounds appear to lose their grip, breaking off and floating separately away, while the instrumental parts remain high pitched, sustained, and generally tranquil. Sudden rushes of noise descend from the

[5] Karlheinz Stockhausen and Robin Maconie, *Stockhausen on Music* (London, 1989), p. 76.

106

Ex. 41

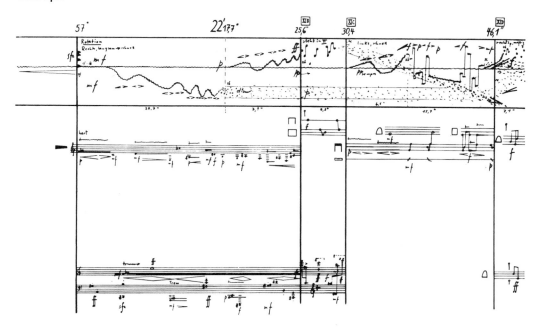

Kontakte: the 'splitting of the sound'. The constant wavy line in the electronic mid-range is the F4 texture which begins to split up after the hammer-blow chord at 57″ into layers which wander away and change in timbre. Four layers can be seen to peel away: at 57″, at 22′ 17.7″, at 30.4″, and just visible at 46.1″.

© Universal Edition AG Wien.

stratosphere to alight on the snare-drum surface and take off again, and the music ends on a note of heavenward withdrawal.

In his essay 'Four Criteria of Electronic Music'[6] Stockhausen identifies the four distinctive areas in which electronic music is able to extend and inform human perceptions of the sound-world. They are: (1) the unified time-structuring or integrated proportioning of micro and macrostructures; (2) the splitting of the sound to reveal its constituent elements; (3) multi-layered space, which is the creation and revelation of depth perspectives in sound; and (4) the equality of tone and noise. *Kontakte* demonstrates more directly what *Gesang der Jünglinge* intimates only obliquely, that our perception of sounds in the real world, whether a boy's voice or conventional musical instruments, is conditioned by a temporal frame of reference which is scaled to human behaviour (one could add, also to a human propensity, from the time of Adam, to make distinctions). Electronic sounds, by contrast, can be

[6] Ibid. 88.

scaled up or down in time, making the transition between form, rhythm, timbre, and pitch with relativistic ease, and demonstrating by example that sound types we identify in completely different ways are indeed the same. So we can learn to follow sounds as they travel from one frequency domain to another, and hear relationships and connections where before we only heard differences.

Of the four criteria perhaps the equality of sound and noise is the one making the greatest immediate impact on the listener. It means that we can also learn to discriminate among noises in the same way as among conventionally 'pure' musical timbres. Noises are also distinguished by their inner structures, which tend to be more complex or indeterminate than pure tones. The sound types of *Kontakte* allow the listener to identify types of noise with particular micro structures, and to discover beauty and order where previously disorder appeared to reign. A noise can be interpreted as a tone magnified to reveal its interior indeterminacies, and one of the impressive features of *Kontakte* is Stockhausen's adjustment of pitch scales to correspond to the degree of determinacy of particular sound types: there are indeed 84 scale divisions, ranging from microtonal intervals for sine tones to a Pythagorean scale of perfect fifths for the noisiest complexes.

A work so rich in implication is bound to conjure up different associations for the individual listener. I can never hear the 'splitting of the sound' section (XI) without thinking of the solo violin tremolo of Bartók's Violin Concerto No. 2, first movement, at 167, which is the same mood, the same shape, and the same pitch; equally, the distant chimes of XIV evoke the same atmosphere as the piano's high-pitched call-signs of Messiaen's *Oiseaux exotiques*. There is a noticeable sense of farewell about the work as a whole, despite its high spirits. One has the feeling that this is the end of an era.

Zyklus

1959: *Cycle* for solo percussionist.
Small drum, 4 tom-toms, 2 wood drums, guero, triangle, Indian bells, 4 cowbells, 2 suspended cymbals, hi-hat, domed gong, vibraphone, marimbaphone.
Duration 10–16′.

Zyklus reproduces the dynamic microstructure of a synthesized tone in the formal domain. It is a nine-layer form modelled on a five-layer impulse structure dated 4 June 1958 in the realization score for *Kontakte*. The instrumental conception is also impulsive, the graphic notation specifying attack characteristics only. The music describes a closed cycle and may therefore start and end at any chosen point.

The score may also be inverted and played in reverse, like its electronic prototype; to this end the score is designed to be read in either direction. Each layer of the skeleton structure is identified with a different percussion instrument and consists of a measured sequence of attacks describing a cycle of acceleration and deceleration. Each of the nine cycles peaks at a different point in the overall form, maintaining an equivalence of distributed energy throughout the piece. The various instruments are grouped around the player in a circle, so that the progress of the piece is expressed as a continuous rotation by the player either clockwise or anticlockwise, following the successive peaks of activity from instrument to instrument (Ex. 42).

Attaching to the skeletal structure is a subsidiary cycle of points and groups which oscillates between complete determinism and various degrees of indeterminacy at twice the frequency of the main cyclic structure, reaching maxima of indeterminacy at the fifth and thirteenth periods, with nodal points at the ninth and conjunction of seventeenth and first periods. There are seventeen equal time periods in all. The variable and fixed structures are distinguished by sound types: for example, the two keyboards are represented by glissandi in the fixed cycle, and by individual notes and note groups in the variable structures; the small drum is similarly identified by rolls in the fixed cycle, and single shots and groups in the variable structures. The following example from the sixteenth period (Ex. 43) gives the performer a choice of inserting the material in one of two bracketed boxes into the main structure which

Ex. 42

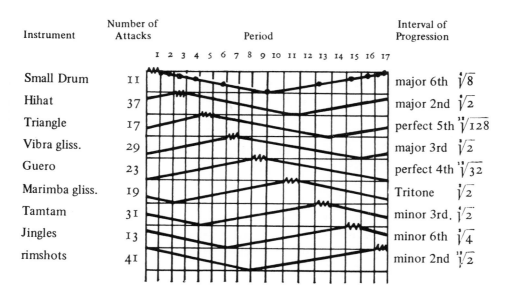

Zyklus. A diagram of the relative densities of attacks of the structural layers.

Cycles

Ex. 43

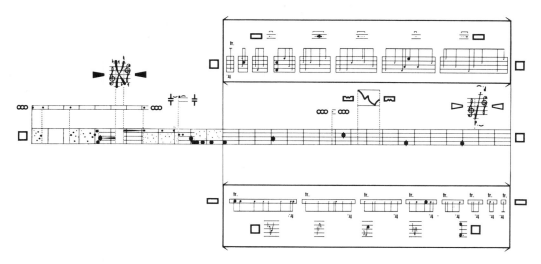

Zyklus: 16th period. The middle stave represents the leading voice (here dominated by the tom-toms). The score is designed to be read either way up (but always left to right), so a performance may tend either toward increasing determinacy of timing, or the other direction, toward ever-increasing temporal ambiguity and freedom of choice.

© Universal Edition AG Wien.

runs through the middle and is characterized by heavy rimshots on tom-toms (indicated by a square symbol). In either case the inserted material consists of ancillary tom-tom and small-drum (rectangle) figurations, but in the top system the drum 'groups' are played as fast as possible, and the tom-tom figures are measured, while in the bottom system this relationship is reversed, the tom-tom groups being as fast as possible, and the drum figures precisely timed. Other degrees of formal indeterminacy involve the random ordering of events at fixed time points, within designated time areas, and among contrasting tone colours. Chromatic pitches play a minor role in this music of timbre, and the accent glissandi of both vibraphone and marimbaphone are frustratingly elusive to listeners eager for tonal markers.

In addition to structural ambiguities, Stockhausen's notation reveals a continuous progression from determinate to statistically quantified events. This ingenious device gives the performance a sense of continuous evolution, towards entropy or towards order according to the chosen direction. At the juncture of periods 17 and 1 (Ex. 44) extreme indeterminacy is succeeded by extreme precision (compare the notations for tom-toms above and below the double line):

Thus one gains the impression of moving in a circle, always tending towards greater freedom

Ex. 44

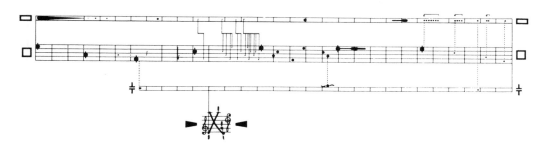

Zyklus: the 'crossover' between aleatoric freedom and fixity. The Caskel recording (on Mainstream 5003) begins from the lower stave (maximum fixity).

© Universal Edition AG Wien.

(clockwise) or greater fixity (anticlockwise), in which nevertheless at the critical meeting-point the two extremes embrace inseparably. . . . To close open form by bending it in a circle, embody the static in the dynamic, endlessness in the pursuit of a goal—not by a process of excluding or destroying one or the other, nor wishing to create a third reality by synthesis of the two: instead an attempt to abolish the dualism and reconcile tendencies apparently so divergent and contrary.[7]

Zyklus is Stockhausen's first piece for solo percussion. It remains an isolated masterpiece in the classical percussionist's repertoire, which is scandalously limited in any case. It is pleasant to think of the work as a gesture of tribute to Varèse, who did so much to legitimize percussion as a medium of serious musical expression.

[7] Karlheinz Stockhausen, *Texte zur Musik*, ii (Cologne, 1964), p. 73.

Refrain

1959: for three keyboards and percussion.

Piano (also woodblocks), vibraphone (also cowbells), and amplified celesta (also antique cymbals).

Duration 11–12′.

Refrain is complementary to *Zyklus*, as *Carré* is complementary to *Kontakte*. Whereas *Zyklus* puts a single sound under the microscope, as it were, drawing the listener into the rhythmic microstructure of a complex wave-form, *Refrain* implies the opposite extreme, a time-scale of perception so magnified that vast formal structures are compressed into ringing tone-mixtures. Following Stockhausen's now well-established convention, high-pitched ringing instruments belong to the class of sonorities corresponding to greatly accelerated frequency structures: this music is the aural equivalent of a satellite view, scanning a continent at a single glance but implicitly capable of revealing extraordinary detail at ground level.

The refrain of the title is a notation of disturbances which discreetly ruffle the surface of the music at intervals. It is engraved on a transparent strip (Ex. 45): the strip pivots like a compass needle over part of the score which is curved to accommodate it; for a performance a fixed position of the strip is agreed among the players, determining the relative times at which the refrain is heard.

For much of the time the three instruments play as a single instrument, producing unison aggregations of crystalline intensity and clarity, varied by careful shifts of balance, pitch sharing, and inflection, and aided by auxiliary percussion and voiced attacks after the manner of Japanese ritual music. The chord aggregations vary from one to six notes, and appear to be based on vertical symmetries; the onset of the refrain comes like a wind of change, causing the still intervals to shimmer, crescendo briefly, crack, and cascade in flurries of small glissandi and single tones.

Chord changes, and the timing of events within the duration of a chord, are measured aurally in relation to the decay in amplitude of a specified tone, or visually in relation to the distance separating attacks (space-time is *not* curved in this instance, but straight and horizontal). For the intervening silences a repertoire of five pause signs gives a range of durations approximating to a Fibonacci series (0.5–1.0–1.5–2.5–4.0 seconds). Silences and rapid arpeggiations of ancillary notes, the latter organized in groups of one to six pitches, gradually invade and break up the reflective surface of the music, but in a different way from the refrains: the image does not dissolve, but appears to revolve like a faceted jewel, as sharp and brilliant as ever, but reflecting many images instead of one or two. These phases of rapid change are animated by syllabic cries and tongue-clicks, adding a vocal-tactile dimension which itself corresponds to highly accelerated percussion attacks.

The music strongly recalls the stationary sound-world of *Studie I*, though with

Ex. 45

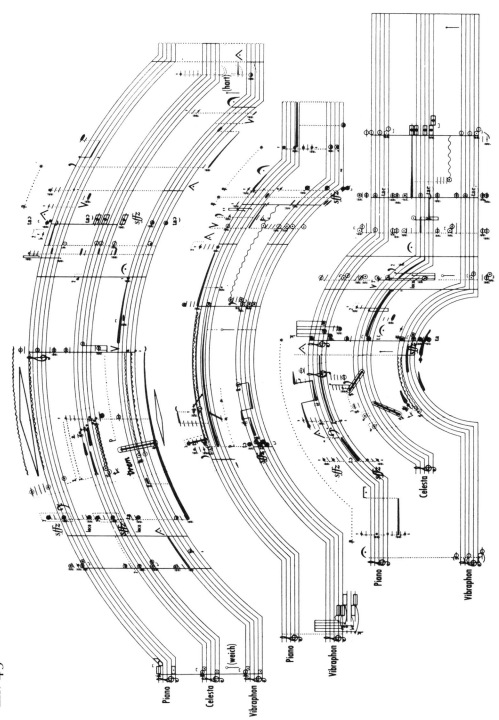

Refrain: upper portion of page 1, showing the 'refrain' plastic strip in the '11 o'clock' position. Durations are measured according to the decay of specified tones from a starting to a finishing loudness degree (indicated by the thickness of the taper).

© Universal Edition AG Wien.

subtle differences. The instrumental tone mixtures belong to a unified time-scale (determined by a fixed rate of sound decay); furthermore there are bound to be interior fluctuations of composite tone as a result of differences of tuning among the three keyboards, the celesta and vibraphone's fixed pitches interfering with the normally slightly divergent tunings of the piano's triple and quadruple strings in the mid to high register. Human performers, no matter how precise their timing, will inevitably introduce subtle uncertainties of co-ordination and phrasing. Like the marvellously poised music-theatre of Japan, therefore, there is a constant uncompromising tension between the timeless inevitability of the drama and the actual indeterminacies of living performance.

There is a wonderful scene in Chris Marker's *La Jetée*, a film about survival after a nuclear holocaust that is depicted unusually as a narrative sequence of still photographs in black and white. These images are all the more powerful and involving for the very reason that, contrary to expectation, they are frozen in time. The scene is a moment where a girl is discovered asleep. The sun is shining through the window on to her face. Suddenly her eyelids seem to flicker, but before the observer can be certain of what has happened the moment passes and the image reverts to stillness. If *Refrain* has a message, it would seem to be that same individual flicker of life, or momentary tremor of human action, measured against a scale of eternity.

Originale

1961: *Originals*, musical theatre with *Kontakte*.
Duration 1 hr. 34 min.

Stockhausen's essay in 'instantaneous actions' translates moment-form from the concert-hall to the stage.

Independent moments in proportional relationships of intensity, duration, density, degree of renewal, richness of activity, simultaneity, sequence.

   Scenic harmony—scenic melody
   Scenic metrics—scenic rhythm
   Scenic dynamics—scenic agogics
   Scenic topics—scenic colours

Selection criteria:

   naturalistic—artificial
   unambiguous—ambiguous
   commonplace—absurd.[8]

        [8] Ibid. 109.

'I = musical theatre', Stockhausen concludes, echoing Schwitters:

The goal he had in mind was not so much the total work of art in the sense that [Hugo] Ball or even Kandinsky meant it—a synchronous combination of all the arts—but rather an unceasing obliteration of all borders between the arts and their integration into one, including the machine as 'an abstraction of the human mind', including kitsch, chair legs, singing, and shuddering. In reality, HE, Kurt Schwitters, was the total work of art.[9]

As might be expected, Stockhausen's prescription for theatrical invention draws on a finely tuned discrimination of degrees of organization in the sphere of musical actions and relationships. The piece is composed in eighteen scenes, collated in seven structures. It unfolds as a polyphony of actions, involving music, drama, film, photography, painting, recording, street theatre (Frau Hoffmann, a local news-vendor with a famous sales pitch) and street music (Lilienweiss, a local street singer) (Ex. 46). Commissioned by the Cologne Theatre am Dom, it was sketched out relatively quickly during a visit to Finland in August 1961, and performed twelve times from 26 October to 6 November. Many of the principal players came from the composer's circle of artist friends: David Tudor and Christoph Caskel (who performed excerpts of *Kontakte*), the Korean performance artist Nam June Paik (who had previous experience of New York 'happenings'), the experimental poet Hans G. Helms, and the painter Mary Bauermeister.

It was a project fraught with danger. Recalling Piscator's triptych-like stage productions in Berlin during the twenties and thirties, Stockhausen intended the piece to be performed on separate stages with the audience in the middle, to allow the theatrical polyphony due space. However, the management objected at the lack of space for an audience, insisting that the action all take place on a single cramped stage. Then, after two controversial performances, the theatre manager was instructed to suspend performances or the theatre's subsidy would be withdrawn. Stockhausen and the players responded by taking on financial responsibility for the remaining ten performances. Altogether strong emotions where aroused on both sides.

For all its congestion of activity, and despite the occasionally provocative behaviour of one or two participants, *Originale* is curiously laid-back. The performers are mostly role-playing: the painter paints, the musicians make music, the recording engineer gets on with his job. What drama arises does so out of the conjunction of activity types, which, being 'real', are expected to project a particular intensity of intention and timing, or are to varying degrees 'subverted' by irrational or impulsive behaviour. A significant feature of the piece is the use of recording media (tape, camera, and film). Wörner[10] describes an uncomfortable moment where the players stand transfixed and observe the audience as though the audience itself were a media

[9] Hans Richter, *Dada: Arts and Anti-Art* (New York, 1965), cited in Udo Kultermann, *Art-Events and Happenings* (London, 1971), p. 37.

[10] Karl H. Wörner, *Stockhausen: Life and Work*, rev. edn. trans. and ed. Bill Hopkins (London, 1973), pp. 190–2.

Ex. 46

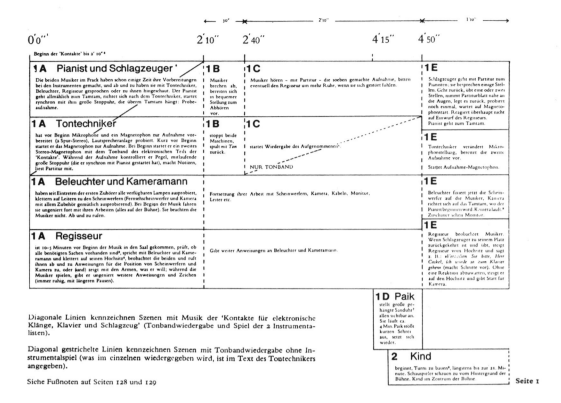

Diagonale Linien kennzeichnen Szenen mit Musik der 'Kontakte für elektronische Klänge, Klavier und Schlagzeug' (Tonbandwiedergabe und Spiel der 2 Instrumentalisten).

Diagonal gestrichelte Linien kennzeichnen Szenen mit Tonbandwiedergabe ohne Instrumentalspiel (was im einzelnen wiedergegeben wird, ist im Text des Tontechnikers angegeben).

Siehe Fußnoten auf Seiten 128 und 129

Originale: page 1 of the score. 'Paik' refers to the Korean performance artist Nam June Paik.
© Universal Edition AG Wien.

event, and a later moment where every player takes photographs. At the very beginning a sound engineer records part of *Kontakte* while a stage manager goes through the motions of preparing the stage for a theatrical performance. The recording is immediately played back with the sound of the stage manager's voice overlaid on the music. Constant reference to studio and recording processes sustain a multi-layered awareness of temporal states: 'past' recording and 'present' action, 'instantaneous' photography and 'future imperfect' film. A further complementarity can be discerned between the 'real time' of studio production and the 'synthetic time' of the recorded artefact (*Kontakte* in its electronic version).

Originale is Stockhausen's first major exercise in music-theatre, though ritual actions and staging have begun to make an appearance in *Kontakte* and *Refrain*. It is the start of a line of compositions invoking the inventive co-operation of performers, which was to lead eventually to the intuitive text compositions *Aus den sieben Tagen* and *Für kommende Zeiten*, and thereafter to the refined choreography of *Inori*, *Musik im Bauch*, and *LICHT*.

8 Moments

DURING 1960 Stockhausen began sketching an orchestral composition entitled *Monophonie*. Wind and percussion instruments, including two pianos and guitar, were to be distributed in groups across a multilevel lozenge-shaped stage, with the string orchestra at the back concealed behind side and rear curtains. The idea was for the strings to produce a 'wall of sound' as a backdrop against which the front-of-stage instrumental polyphony would be heard in relief. The music was going to create diverging patterns from one note (E), entries of instruments to be cued by light at individual desks (like a radio play). A notation system resembling *ars antiqua* mensural notation, and later incoporated in *Plus-Minus*, replaced chronometric with more approximate durations. Owing to contractual disagreements the project was suspended after only one page of the score was sketched. Some ten years later the composition of *Trans* led to a revival of a similar but reversed orchestral scenario, strings creating a visual and acoustic screen at the front of stage, with wind ensembles concealed at the back.

There followed a lengthy period of retrospection in which a number of old scores were literally settled. Preparation of the realization score of *Kontakte*, detailing the entire process of synthesis and assembly of the electronic music, represented an enormous investment of time. The sequence of Piano Pieces I–XI was completed in 1961 with the composition of IX and X, and in 1962 Stockhausen closed another gap by retrieving *Punkte* from the archive and composing it afresh.

Klavierstück IX

1961: *Piano Piece IX*.
Duration 10′.

Though in certain exterior respects they conform to original 1954 specifications, the two piano pieces are essentially compositions of 1961, IX mediating with clipped precision between periodicity and aperiodicity, and X ranging with enormous energy and sense of danger between disorder and order. IX looks like a throw-back to an earlier time. We are back to strict, even simple notation, barlines, and time signatures. Not surprisingly it is among Stockhausen's most accessible and sought-after pieces of his first twenty-five years. The form falls into 33 sections grouped by tempo into two episodes of 24 and 9 sections respectively, expressing a ratio of 8 : 3 which also coincides with the tempi quaver = MM 160 : 60 of the first episode of 24 sections. One obvious feature identifying it as a later composition is the Fibonacci series, which since Piano Piece XI has assumed increasing importance as a serial determinant, typically of section durations and grace-note collections.

Mediation is perhaps not the best description of the relationship between periodicity and aperiodicity, which is more of a contest. The music articulates a progressive intermingling and intercutting of starkly defined structure types, leading from a starting-point of total periodicity (persistent chord repetition) to an end-point of total aperiodicity (bars 117–53). The composer's sketch-notes identify six structural types:[1]

A = a regularly repeated four-part chord;
B = an ascending chromatic melody line;
C = polyphony;
D = staccato chords with damped reverberation (half-pedalled);
E = soft, ringing chords and isolated tones;
F = soft, quick figurations in the treble, some accents.
Isolated bass-notes as fundamentals.

Something very interesting has happened to Stockhausen's concept of periodicity in the intervening years, if we compare it with the Webernian even quaver values of the first version of VII and the latter part of *Zeitmasze*. First, it is a periodicity of chords, and chords imply a further dimension of order, namely simultaneity. 'Everything organized in the vertical, such as chords, is clearly determinate because you would never find notes falling by accident together in a chord.'[2] Second, it is a periodicity of pulsed chords, in imitation of electronic music. A piece which begins with the same chord repeated 139 times, all the while declining in loudness, may just as readily be construed as a single tenuto chord repeatedly interrupted as it were by being passed via an impulse generator. The distinction acquires relevance in relation to later sequences consisting of constantly changing chords with ever-varying attack, duration, and dynamic characteristics, i.e. a maximum of new information. Such passages are relatively discontinuous, the passage in Example 47, for example, resembling segments of prerecorded tape edited together. These overt references to electronic music procedures (another being to define larger time units by use of various types of pedalling in apparent simulation of electronic reverberation), together with an absence of conventional expressive phrasing, add up to a sense of

[1] Reproduced in Herbert Henck, *Karlheinz Stockhausen's* Klavierstück IX: *Eine analytische Betrachtung* (Bad Godesberg, 1978), p. 5.
[2] Karlheinz Stockhausen and Robin Maconie, *Stockhausen on Music* (London, 1989), pp. 48–9.

Ex. 47

Piano Piece IX, bars 94–104. Over a third-pedal sustained bass cluster chord 'impulses' are played, exciting subharmonically coloured resonances.

© Universal Edition AG Wien.

much longer timespans than implied by metronomic values. The repeated chord becomes not many, but a single harmonic constant repeating in perpetuity, 'zerhackt' like the anthems in *Hymnen*, varied in amplitude, fading out and returning like a short-wave call-sign from another planet. At the other extreme, the later isolated short chords can be understood as instantaneous cross-sections of much longer events, blips encountered during random tuning across frequencies. If so, we are once again in the remote time-world of *Refrain*, crossed, however, with the dynamic, impulsive action time of *Zyklus*. In short, moment-form.

With the change of tempo to quaver = MM 120, the character of the music is suddenly transformed to single-line figures and ornamentation. Stockhausen toyed with the idea of using a *Refrain*-like graphic space-time notation, but finally opted in favour of conventional grace-notes and notational consistency. Here again the associations of aperiodicity are updated. It is more than the absence of a regular beat: what it implies is an escape from a musical environment in which every event has a history, into an ideal pointillist world of perpetual renewal.

Klavierstück X

1961: *Piano Piece X.*
Duration 23′.

Piano Piece X is as close to an embodiment of ecstasy as anything Stockhausen has written. Great blocks of polyphony in ceaseless inner turmoil alternate with trance-like blanks in which nothing happens or is heard but resonant after-images. Its sound-vocabulary is impulsive and calculatedly physical in expression, relating to *Zyklus* and *Kontakte*; its affective world identifies with the transcendental character of *Carré*.

The music mediates, in Stockhausen's words, between 'order' and 'disorder'. These terms have a precise meaning in physics, and it is in this sense that they are understood here. In earlier pieces, such as *Kontra-Punkte*, the composer speaks of a situation of maximum differentiation (pointillism) resolving to a situation of relative equilibrium ('Gleichberechtigkeit'), and it might be assumed that the latter represented a higher order, greater control, predictability, and so on. It may come as a surprise, therefore, to learn that undifferentiation in a physical system corresponds to disorder. In that sense, the process of reduction of contrasts articulated in *Kontra-Punkte* is equivalent, not to a gradual imposition of order, but to a gradual decline of a physical system into entropy.

We may also distinguish order from organization. Order and disorder express the terms of reference of the observer (interpreter, executant) rather than the nature of the thing observed, whereas organization refers to inherent properties of the object of attention: in the case of music, what we can determine from the evidence of the printed score. 'it might be said that order refers to the *quantity* of information (i.e. negative entropy) in a system, whereas organization refers to the *quality* of information. . . . Organization is often taken to imply an element of purpose or design.'[3]

Piece X is organized in orders of seven rather than six or five, with respect to a number of opposing musical criteria signifying relative order or absence of order: for example, sound and silence, movement and stasis, dynamic contrast or similarity, or tone and noise. Although the structural criteria are more extreme than ever before, they are nevertheless organized with typical purpose. For example, tone is defined as melodic and harmonic figures derived from a chromatic hexachord (which links this piece and VII and IX with the Webern Symphony, Op. 21); noise by contrast is expressed in terms of a range of note clusters extending in width from a major-second (three-note) cluster to a semitone short of three octaves (36 notes), and including diagonals (cluster glissandi played with the side of the hand). During the course of the piece tone material gradually comes to take precedence over noise material: the music expresses an organized determination in favour of a particular quality of material.

On the printed page, sound and noise represent instantaneous qualities measured on the vertical co-ordinate of pitch, and they also refer to instrumental timbre. The choice of instrument is part of the definition: 'The material itself must be part of the creative act. Which means that when I start a new piece, the selection of either a preformed sound source, an instrument, or sound material must be already

---

[3] Paul Davies, *The Cosmic Blueprint* (London, 1987), pp. 75–6.

organized or structured the way the whole piece will be structured.'[4] Order and disorder corresponding to sound and noise is a polarity we recognize in *Zyklus* as well; but a tempered keyboard instrument is structured for tonal and intervallic consistency, in complete contrast to a solo percussion ensemble, which to Western ears is inherently disorganized, noisy, and dependent on performer action for what qualities of order it may be heard to convey. Electronic sound likewise mediates between corresponding extremes of sine-tone single frequencies and white noise, which includes all frequencies.

In common with all the other pieces of the set V–X, however, X is essentially a pianistic discourse on time, the horizontal co-ordinate of the musical graph. X seems to issue from the condition of aperiodicity finally attained by IX, but it might be more accurate to say that it reoccupies the same territory rather than continuing in the same direction. Both IX and *Zyklus* are represented as structures in fixed albeit convoluted evolution from a primary to a secondary state. Both piano pieces operate within very large structural time values, but whereas IX is classically measured, outwardly objective, even meditative, X by contrast is highly subjective, technically virtuosic, and seemingly designed, like the grace-note figures of Piece VIII, to exploit a conflict between what the score demands and what the performer can realistically deliver. The more esoteric significance of 'disorder' is thus the extent to which the notated time-values are actually realized (Ex. 48).

Stockhausen had been impressed as early as 1957 by the way Cage's *Music of Changes IV* set the performer an impossible task of assimilation and execution: 'Frequently in this score the pianist is asked to follow *simultaneously* so many different instructions in a given measure of time that he is obliged to leave out particular actions, and to play less than the music indicates.'[5]

The piece's terms of reference are discovered at the critical point in *Zyklus* where statistical groups 'imperceptibly merge' with measured proportions (see Ex. 44 above). In X the distinction is not simply a visual shift in graphics from statistical to proportional notation to which the performer responds with a change from intuitive to precise timing. What tendency to instability there is lies with the performer: the music reckons with an inherent unpredictability of interpretation. There are two factors influencing a performer's accuracy of timing, which are brought together in Stockhausen's brilliantly ambiguous notation. The first is a mental ability to estimate the length of a structural unit of time (equivalent to a classical musical phrase); the second is a physical ability to execute the given notation in the estimated time. What the piece does is set these two criteria uncharacteristically in opposition, so that a condition of virtually continuous uncertainty of timing prevails.

Already in *Kontakte* Stockhausen had come to organize the range of musical time into frequency octaves (that is, scaled in powers of 2). The orders of seven in Piece X may correspond to the seven octaves in the pitch domain represented by the piano

---

[4] Jonathan Cott, *Stockhausen: Conversations with the Composer* (London, 1974), p. 37.
[5] Karlheinz Stockhausen, *Texte zur Musik*, ii (Cologne, 1964), p. 232.

Ex. 48

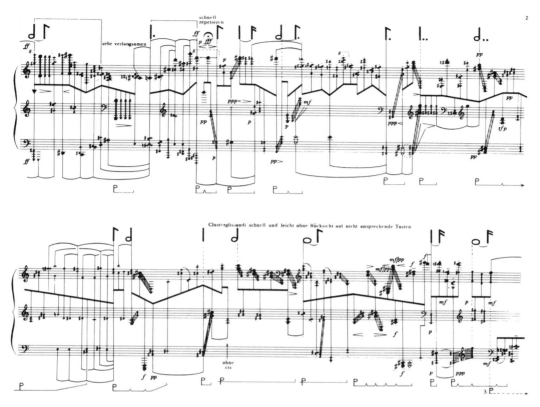

Piano Piece X, page 2. The time structure is indicated by the note-values above the stave; within these durations the performer fits the notated pitches, chords, and glissandi in relative proportion. The executed time values are a compromise between those indicated and the practically realizable.

© Universal Edition AG Wien.

keyboard, from c 28–4,000 Hz. As the time-scale descends below the limit of pitch perception, it enters a region of frequency quantified as metre and rhythm: approximately seven octaves of larger time-values defines the range of conventional note duration values from c $\frac{1}{16}$ to 8 seconds. Beyond 8 seconds, the scale articulates musical form for a further seven octaves from the length of a phrase to the duration of a movement or major compositional segment. At the boundaries between timbre and pitch, pitch and rhythm, and rhythm and form are regions of perceptual uncertainty, and it is these subjective ambiguities which determine the choice and organization of material in the present work.

Above the stave are note-values acting as time signatures. Because these precise structural durations are occupied by aperiodic grace-note figurations, and not by regular time units, they have to be timed as a whole, and not divided into convenient aggregations of beats. It follows that the shorter the structural time unit, the more likely the grace-note content will conform to the indicated duration, but the larger the structural time unit, the less accurately it is likely to be executed. On the other hand, as Piano Pieces VIII and XI have shown, difficulties of preparation and execution of the grace-note content also influence the accuracy of execution of notated time and speed values. The greater the quantity of information the performer has to assimilate, the more complex the musical material, the more difficult it will be to keep to the assigned structural durations, even if they can be mentally quantified. Stockhausen succeeds beautifully in subverting the very hierarchy of time-values singled out by Webern (in *The Path to the New Music*) as one of the glories of Western music, having first called it into question in a 1955 essay on the composer.[6]

Piece X unites the filigree intricacy of a Debussy (e.g. 'Voiles' or 'Feu d'artifice') with the energy and intensity of impulse-generated electronic sound. All the same, it is a work of considerable delicacy, which is why the description 'ecstatic' seems more appropriate than merely 'exuberant'. Although glissando intervals appear in the Bartók *Sonata for Two Pianos and Percussion* which he had analysed at considerable length as a student, the appearance of clusters and cluster glissandi in the new piece refer more particularly to discoveries at a late stage of realization of *Kontakte*, at XIIIE and XVIE. Interestingly, the electronic vertical clusters (impulses of densely compacted filtered noise) are drawn to look like nails and sound like hammer-blows, extremely forceful and concrete; the glissando clusters on the other hand have completely different connotations, appearing lightweight and transient, associated with feelings of floating and withdrawal. As with the recomposition of *Punkte*, the use of clusters creates an effect of shifting surfaces of sound, and may arouse in the hearer a renewed sense of the instrument as a totality of sound progressively mapped in patches and lines. Such a way of hearing leads directly to *Mikrophonie I*, where an entire range of timbres is derived from a single instrument.

Punkte 1952/62

1962–6: *Points* for orchestra.

3. 3. 3. 3. 3; 3. 2. 1; tubular bells, glockenspiel, vibraphone, marimbaphone, 2 pedal timpani (3 players); 2 harps, 2 pianos (+celesta); strings 8. 8. 8. 6. 4 ('all solistic'). Duration 22′.

In the new version the 'points' of the title are rarely simple note-points: they become the nuclei of groups, clusters, swarms, vibrating masses, *micro*-musical *organisms*.

---

[6] 'Structure and Experiential Time', *Die Reihe* (English Edition), 2 (1958), 64–74.

To distinguish the original points I use four formal types: a point expands upwards, or it expands downwards [into a band of pitches]; or a tone-mixture contracts upward or downward to a point. Both expanding and contracting types have characteristic textures (sostenuto, tremolo, trill; staccato, portato, legato, glissandi, chromatic melodies etc.), also characteristic timbres, intensities and relative speeds. The intervallic limits and tempi within which these transformations occur remain constant for longer or shorter periods and so link up to form larger structures.

During composition so many layers of sound sometimes accumulate the the volume of sound became too great for the available space. (Why must we always imagine music as note-structures in empty space, black notes on white paper? Could we not equally well begin from a homogeneously filled acoustical space and *carve out music*, revealing musical figures and forms with an eraser?)

So I composed *negative forms* as well, comparable with the positive forms mentioned above; holes, pauses, cavities of various sizes, their edges sharply or vaguely defined. At a further stage of composition I changed these back and forth: shaping leftover areas in one case, or making an empty space resound in another.[7]

The new version confirms, if that were needed, the view that instantaneous form is a derivation of pointillism. As the static moments of *Carré* can be interpreted as points translated into a larger time domain, so *Punkte 1952/62* retains its original title while expanding the original point structure into less stable, more dynamic textures and tone mixtures. Its basic sound-vocabulary is transferred from Piano Piece X into the orchestral domain: the original 1952 version having sought to establish a rational basis for serial differentiation of timbre, the new version underlines the concept of the orchestra as an extended keyboard by both increasing the complement of tempered percussion and adopting the piano piece's new strategy of integration through qualities of articulation. The original point structure is fleshed out into masses of sound (Ex. 49), producing occasional effects of a sensuality far removed from the asceticism of the earlier version.

After recomposition the score underwent a number of revisions; a new edition appeared in 1964, and a final edition in 1966. The 1964 version is chiefly notable for the removal of a page-'0' Ligeti-like introductory shimmy for full orchestra. Tempi are increased uniformly by one degree up the tempo scale, and the continuity is frequently interrupted by pauses, some of which incorporate a form of feedback repetition of the previous segment of music, for example at 66 and 114. Elsewhere one finds minor adjustments for ease of performance, such as the transposition of high trumpet trills at 27, and trumpet and horn parts at 35, the reshuffling of woodwinds at 139, and balancing of string dynamics between 79 and 115.

In the final 1966 version most of the pauses with feedback lose the element of repetition. Some pauses are lost altogether, while others are highlighted by harmonic or melodic elements, e.g. the string accents at 51 and 71, the trumpet signal at 58 and woodwind interruptions at 129. Harp and piano parts are

---

[7] Stockhausen, op. cit. iii (Cologne, 1971), p. 12.

Ex. 49

Punkte 1952/62. Contrasting mass textures are clearly visible.

© Universal Edition AG Wien.

strengthened, also longer structural durations reinforced by brass and woodwind harmonies. Also noteworthy are the filling-out of fragmentary points into continuous melodic lines in the first six pages of woodwind and again at 20, 92, and 123, in the string parts at 8, 26, 30, 35, and 48, and in piano and harps at 4, 15, 48, 54, and 58. The 1966 version reverts in fact to the 1962 concept of a dynamic continuum.

Momente

1961–72: *Moments* for soprano solo, 4 choir groups and 13 instrumentalists.

Four choir groups, each 3 or 4 × SATB; 4 trumpets, 4 trombones, 2 electronic organs (e.g. 1 Hammond or Lesley organ, 1 Lowrey organ); vibraphone, large and small tam-tams, 5 suspended cymbals, 5 antique cymbals (tuned F5–C6), 3 tom-toms, kidney drum (or 1 snare drum, 3 kidney drums), 3 tambourines (3 players).

Members of each choir group play percussion instruments: I, tuned cardboard tube drums; II, tuned claves; III, shot-rattles; IV, tuned metal claves.

Duration 90′.

This is Stockhausen's first full-scale composition for voices and instruments since the *Drei Lieder* of 1950, and only the second major work (after *Gesang der Jünglinge*) in which the voice and text convey an extra-musical message. Cantata-like in scale, it is operatic in scope, treating the subject of love in a vast and demanding stream-of-consciousness soliliquy of considerable emotional and stylistic range, from coolly spiritual aria to comedy and highly charged recitative. When Stockhausen writes for solo voice we may be sure he has something very personal to divulge, and is feeling especially confident. Like the early songs, *Momente* has elements of autobiography, which makes it something more interesting than just another of the many large-scale works for female voice and orchestra (call it the *genre* Cathy Berberian) which appeared at the turn of the sixties, signalling the coming-of-age of the post-war avant-garde and a change from the austere radicalism of the fifties to a more outgoing sensibility. Compared, not with Boulez' *Pli selon Pli*, nor with Berio's *Circles*, but with the electronic *Gesang der Jünglinge* of 1956, the earlier image of boyish innocence gives way to one of feminine, even feline experience, and the message of faith and self-mortification to a celebration, albeit partially biblical in spirit, of sensual delight. The new outlook compares with his change of musical orientation, already identified, from the ideal to the real.

Momente's literary antecedents are the stream-of-consciousness novel and its dramatic analogue, the radio play. The text is meditative in character and episodic in structure. It depends neither upon action nor upon chronological sequence for its effect. Events recollected order themselves by association, not by cause and effect, and the pattern of association can vary according to what attribute the memory may choose to recall. It is the essentially timelsss state of memory to which T. S. Eliot alludes when he speaks in *The Dry Salvages* of:

> the unattended
> Moment, the moment in and out of time . . .   (206–7)

Technically, *Momente* represents a comprehensive synthesis of the achivements of a decade: a mobile form, building on Piano Piece XI, and a moment-form, like *Carré*; integrating instrumental sound and noise with language, going a stage beyond *Gesang der Jünglinge* and *Kontakte*; and ranging from determinate to indeterminate in content, like *Zyklus*. In addition Stockhausen incorporates a new system of cross-referencing, to determine liasons between moments for whatever sequence is chosen. Everything about the form, including the rationale for the liaison scheme, ultimately derives from his acoustics and phonetics studies with Professor Meyer-Eppler. So much, so, in fact, as to make *Momente* a fitting memorial to his 'greatest teacher', whose untimely death in 1960 brought an extraordinarily fertile partnership of science and music prematurely to an end.

The work is dedicated to the painter Mary Bauermeister, who became Stockhausen's second wife in 1967. The first sketches were begun in January 1961 and the essential formal definitions were completed very rapidly. The structure is arboriform (Ex. 50), three principal branches representing the distinctive features K (*Klang*), M (*Melodie*), and D (*Dauer*) progressively ramifying in ever subtler combinations. K-moments are homophonic, characterized by vertical relationships, including timbre and harmony. They are associated with male voices, individually and in a group, with metal and skin percussion instruments, and with spoken consonants and noises.

M-moments are melodic, emphasizing the horizontal dimension in an active sense; they include continuous glissandi as well as heterophonic elements, where a number of different sources are moving in a similar shape, but are not precisely co-ordinated or in parallel (heterophony is a feature of folk-music). The solo soprano, the speaking voice and spoken texts, and the four trumpets and four trombones all identify M-moments, and a certain type of randomness associated with heterophony is also characteristic.

The D-moments emphasize duration, which is passive time articulation; out of the act of measuring time, expressed in mensural notation, comes the possibility of polyphony, and also silence. Female singing voices, high and pure in pitch, are identified with them, also the electronic organs, which are able to sustain pitches for precise durations without decay.

Linking the main K, M, and D branches are I-moments (amorphous or

Ex. 50

Momente. The moment-structure. Moments I and I(d) link the three M, K, and d moment-structures. K is the central pivot around which M and D structures may turn; likewise M(k) and M(d) structures may rotate about M, and higher branches around their respective centres.

indeterminate) which tend to neutralize distinctions between them and between the performance and the public. Interjections, hissing, clapping, and foot-stamping all form part of the musical fabric, and audience participation is an unstated but significant ingredient of the music-theatre experience:

The reaction to my music in Germany is as violently hostile as ever. Last year, for example, when I conducted my *Momente* in Cologne, the audience made so much noise I just gave up— stopped the performance. After about five minutes, I started again, and went through to the end, although they were yelling so that even *I* couldn't hear anything. At home, it is always that way.[8]

The I-moments are roughly eight minutes in length, M, K, and D four minutes, and higher levels two, one, and half a minute respectively, ensuring an equivalent exposure of each level throughout the entire work. The structure permutates like a Calder mobile, branches M and D revolving round moment K, which remains at the centre, and their smaller branches also pivoting round their respective higher centres. Needless to say, this complex mobility cannot be captured in a single performance, which is fixed like a photograph in a chosen order, reading from left to right. This means that whatever order of moments is selected, the hierarchical form remains relatively the same, in fact somewhat resembling the symmetry of a Sierpínski carpet,[9] with moments of each duration at each structural level evenly spaced throughout the work. Though the structure appears open and hierarchical,

[8] Id., Interview, 'Notes and Commentaries', *The New Yorker*, 18 Jan. 1964.
[9] Benoît Mandelbrot, *Fractals: Form, Chance and Dimension* (San Francisco, 1977), pp. 166–7.

in practice the system closes back on itself, the subtle distinctions of the highest-level D-moments merging imperceptibly with the I-moment flux.

A similar tree-structure governs the hierarchy of tone (Ex. 51), noise, and instrument categories. The 'Distinctive Features Theory' of Halle and Jakobson is its evident prototype. The latter system of speech-sound classification (Ex. 52) also defines five levels of binary definition, clearly analogous to the range of distinctions employed to classify texts, voices, and instrumental timbres. Note the plus–minus notation expressing successive levels of binary distinction, which becomes a hallmark of Stockhausen's transformational compositions in the coming decade.

By analogy with earlier examples of mobile form in music and system design elsewhere (architecture, furniture), one might imagine the essence of Stockhausen's connection scheme of 'inserts', which interlace the order of moments into a fixed sequence, to be that components fit naturally together in different combinations; they do not have to be forced (Boulez' criticism of the segments of Piano Piece XI not remaining fixed in their essential dimensions and internal characteristics reveals a similar misconception of the earlier piece as an essay in modular design). Why should it be necessary, the argument goes, having controlled the inner chemistry of moment types so meticulously, to stress a particular sequence by the relatively unsubtle means of editing in material from one moment to the next?

There are a number of ways of regarding the question. From a practical point of view, the technique of inserting is natural to Stockhausen; it springs from a habit of incorporating new ideas into his music at the time they happen, and since new ideas often appear during work in quite a different context, these inserts are resumed and developed more fully at a later point, while the earlier flash of insight remains as a momentary interruption anticipating the new event to come. In a similar way, earlier events can be recalled at a later point in a work. Piano Piece X is an example of a sectional form incorporating references and anticipations of adjacent changes of material.

Then there is the analogy from phonetics. A composer as *au fait* with phonetics as Stockhausen would certainly be aware of the principle of 'coarticulation', which says that far from being isolated components simply juxtaposed like letters on the page to produce words, spoken vowels and consonants actually influence one another, those that precede as well as those that follow them: in short, the sound of every phoneme is uniquely determined by its context as well as by its inherent composition. On that basis a system of liaisons between moments which takes the nature of particular juxtapositions into account is certainly arguable if the formal continuum is intended to represent an expansion of speech processes into macrotime.

But the inserts also have a dramatic purpose, which is to characterize the triangular relationship of *Karlheinz*, *Mary*, and *Doris*. The extent to which a character interpenetrates with another is an expression of its individuality and influence; hence 'The K-moments are all active. They influence others but are not influenced themselves. The strongest moment is the moment which takes the least and gives the least, and the weakest moment is the one you can hardly recognize for itself because it has so much in common with what has happened before and what is to follow.'[10] And yet, when all these factors are taken into account, the inserts still create enormous difficulties in practice, both in terms of printing and publishing, and also in obscuring the material distinctions and proportions on which the form-scheme is based (Ex. 53*a*, *b*). It is perhaps significant that neither *Mixtur* nor *Mikrophonie I*, subsequent pieces in which the order of moments can be varied, do such problems of page assembly arise. (This is not to say that *Momente's* pagination difficulties could not be solved in future, however: already the compact disc offers the technology for freely permutating moments (if all possible versions are prerecorded), and videodisc may well allow for the reproduction on screen of a suitably edited score compiled to correspond with the chosen sequence of moments.) On the question of general intelligibility, a case might be advanced for enlarging the structural time-values, so that a listener has a better chance to register distinctive qualities which identify individual moments and inserts, particularly where the mix of attributes is especially subtle. This was the case for slowing down the time constant of *Mixtur* from crotchet = MM 60 to MM 40.[11] Inserts would possibly appear less confusing were they prerecorded and played back over loudspeakers instead of being part of the live 'real-time' theatre experience. Stockhausen has since adopted such an idea (though he could hardly do otherwise) for incorporating the glimpses of *Carré* and *Momente* itself into the vocal fabric of *Mikrophonie II*. A parallel usage of recording technology to create layers of past and future occurs in *Originale*, Stockhausen's other essay in music-theatre.

Like *LICHT* and the *Tierkries* lyrics, Stockhausen's texts are decided according to a pre-existing compositional plan: they are chosen to fit the music, not the other way round. Nevertheless, the elided and volatile nature of the dramatic conception is entirely in character with his earlier music, as is evident when the essential features of the word-settings are compared with the early choral and vocal compositions of 1950–1. Solid four-part homophony, floating melodies for high voice, compression and dilation of time, a fondness for natural speech-rhythms, dialogue of male and female, low and high voices—even the essential symbolisms of masculine debauchery and feminine spirituality can be found in the works of Stockhausen's apprentice years.

Though universal in theme, *Momente* is distinctively local in character. For the first performance in May 1962, the 'Cologne' version, only about a third of the structure was realized, about 25 minutes of music comprising the central K-structure, moments M(m), MK(d), and three I-moments: I, I(m), and I(d). The remaining M- and D-moments were realized during the summer of 1963 and early

---

[10] Stockhausen and Maconie, op. cit. 70.

[11] Karlheinz Stockhausen, 'Stockhausen Miscellany', Translated by Sheila Bennett and Richard Toop, *Music and Musicians*, 21. 2 (1972), 32.

Ex. 51

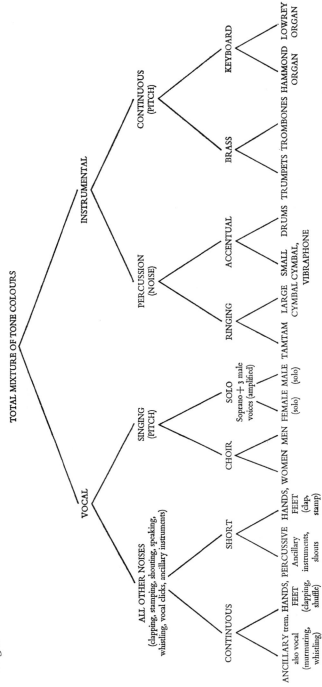

Momente: diagram of the tonal hierarchy (after the composer's sketch reproduced in his *Ein Schlussel für 'Momente'*, Kassel, 1971). The classification system tends from gross to increasingly refined distinctions in a similar pattern to the formal structure.

Ex. 52

Halle–Jakobson: 'Distinctive Features Theory'
Classification of speech sounds

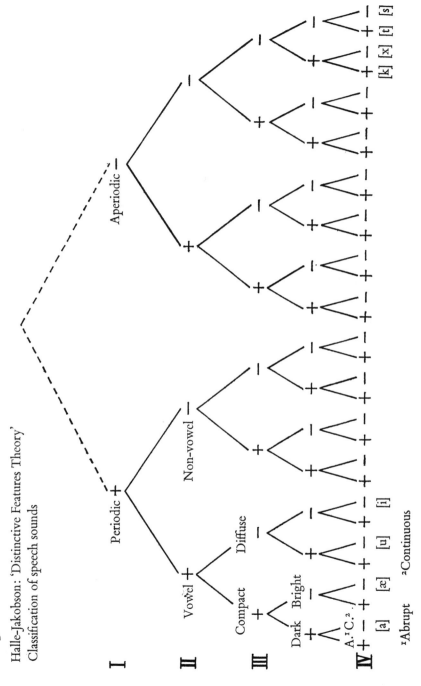

Structured classification of speech sounds, derived from the 'Distinctive Features Theory' of Halle and Jakobson (Roman Jakobson and Morris Halle, *Fundamentals of Language*, 2nd ed., New York, 1971).

Ex. 53

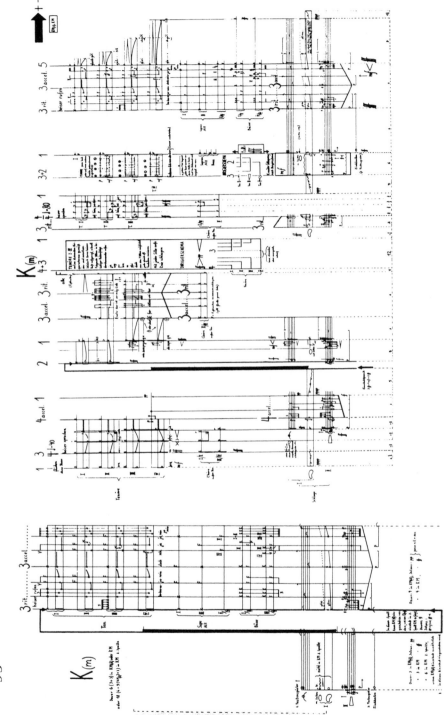

Momente. Einschub (Insert) K(m) at the left, is a 'memory' or 'anticipation' of the two penultimate measures of moment K(m) on its right; the solid arrow indicating that the *Einschub* segment is to be inserted into the chosen following moment, for example moment KM. The + and − signs after the arrow determine that KM is to be played first with the *Einschub* in place at either of the places indicated, and then a second time without it. *Einschub* K(m) itself has scope for interpolating material from yet other sources.

© Universal Edition AG Wien.

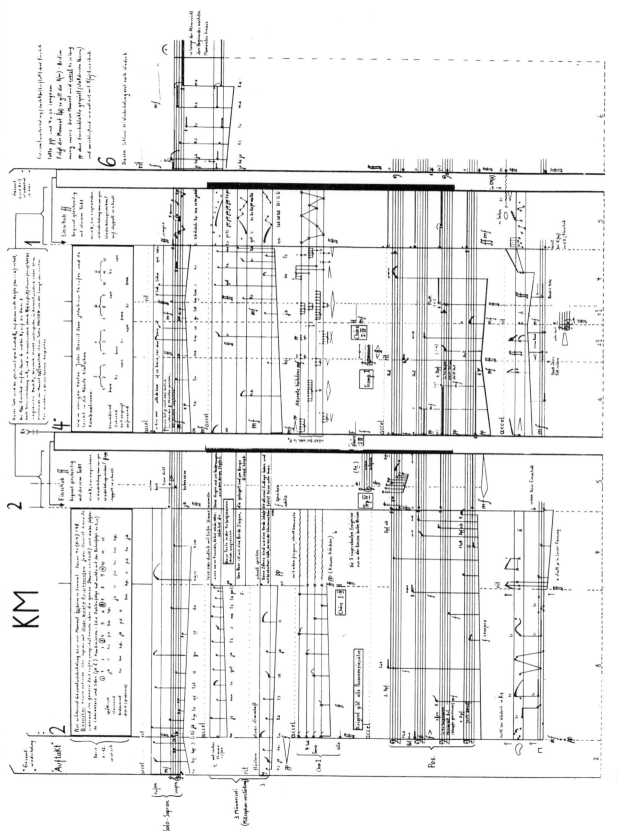

Momente: moment KM. The shaded vertical lines mark entry points for inserted material from earlier or following moments.

© Universal Edition AG Wien.

Ex. 54

Momente, 'Europa version': the continuous staves of I(k) suggest a departure from the earlier concept of moments as instantaneous.

© Universal Edition AG Wien.

1964; in October 1965 an enlarged 61-minute 'Donaueschingen' version, omitting the D-moments, was premièred at the Donaueschingen Festival and subsequently released on disc. In the original staging the solo soprano stands centre stage, closely surrounded by a defensive wall of electronic keyboards and percussion, with considerable empty space separating them from the four choirs and brass forming a semicircle at the stage periphery. The arrangement resembles a scaled-down, stage-mounted *Carré*, with the difference that this meditative music now has a voice and can speak for itself.

By 1969, however, when he resumed work on moment I(k) with a new series of performances in prospect, Stockhausen's attitude to the work had changed. An originally intimate theatre has now turned into something public and universal. The soprano character of the beloved, beset on all sides by a threatening public, has become transformed into a matronly 'Mother Earth surrounded by her chickens'. A revised stage setting has removed the tam-tam from a position of heliocentric pre-eminence to a mere silhouette presence at the stage rear. I(k), a new Fellini-like introduction, in which the choirs and brass, summoned by the soprano with a cheerful 'Komm' doch herein!' process down the auditorium aisles to take their places on stage, seems to contradict the very basis of moment-form (to have neither formal beginning nor ending), as well as representing a change of mood from contemplative to congenial (Ex. 54). It seems a pity if in adapting it to accommodate a more conciliatory world-view he has turned this exceptional dramatic form against itself.

9 *Live Electronic Music*

STOCKHAUSEN'S music during the latter half of the sixties is characterized by two objectives, one being to establish a workable discipline for the creation of electronic music live in concert, the other to develop performance notations and transformation skills appropriate to this new art. Having been forced to curtail both *Kontakte*, and before that *Gesang der Jünglinge*, for want of time, it was clear that ways would have to be found to speed up the synthesis process if electronic music was to remain practically viable. The equipment he was used to working with in the studio of Cologne Radio was not designed for creative use, and lacked the refinements necessary for compositional efficiency. Since the synthesizer industry was only just in its infancy, and studio effects devices in the transistor age were few and unrefined, any significant improvements would have to be sought in the method of working rather than in new equipment. An enormous amount of time and effort could be taken up in basic experimentation, and even when that yielded a positive result, it did not inevitably follow that the same procedure would work over a range of pitches or durations. If miscalculations occurred, it was virtually impossible to foresee or undo them. One section of *Kontakte* took three arduous months to synthesize, edit, and mix; when after all the work had been done and it could be heard in context, it turned out to be too fast and everything had to be resynthesized, edited, and mixed again from scratch.[1]

However, *Kontakte* had introduced Stockhausen to process planning as a compositional strategy. After years of being obliged to create electronic timbres by inspired guesswork, using serial determinations as a guide, he now had the option of defining a range of sound types in terms of a particular combination of studio equipment; a situation easy to describe, repeatable, and easily modified. It was a more structured approach: more importantly it led to a newly integrated perception of sounds and noises as localized-field events on a universal pitch–time continuum. Later, with *Momente* the same inclusive perception could be applied, thanks to the discoveries of phonetics, to natural sounds and noises. Since he now had a transformational procedure to relate any sound to any other, the philosophical basis of Stockhausen's musical processes, to start from opposite extremes and gradually bring them together, began to lose its fascination. The way was now open to explore,

---

[1] Karlheinz Stockhausen and Robin Maconie, *Stockhausen on Music* (London, 1989), p. 132.

in real time and with acoustic instruments and performers, transformational processes which *Kontakte* had articulated in the electronic domain.

Stockhausen refers to this changed perception of sounds in a cryptic programme note to the 1965 première of *Momente*. Brought up to conceive the world in dualistic terms, he says, he had come to doubt the reasoning behind many of the conventional polarities; the philosophy now was 'Homo and poly and homo and hetero and homo and mono and homo and. And and either and or and and. AND.'[2] To distinguish, to contrast, and to discover similarity in equal measure: this was the way ahead.

Mikrophonie I

1964–5: *Microphony I* for tam-tam, 2 microphones, 2 filters and potentiometers (6 players).
Duration at least 20'.

The composition of *Mikrophonie I* came about as a result of intuitive experimentation with a large (1.55 m. diameter) tam-tam originally purchased for *Momente* and installed in the back garden of Stockhausen's Kürten home. During 1964 he began a series of broadcasts for Cologne Radio under the title 'Do you know the music that can only be heard over a loudspeaker?' Among the earliest examples of tape music broadcast in the series was a 1950 concrete *étude* by Pierre Henry, called *Tam Tam IV*. In his radio introduction Stockhausen observed 'I understand from the title that Henry recorded the sound of a tam-tam for this composition on to tape and then worked further on it . . . Completely new sounds can be obtained by transformation of natural (or shall we say, familiar) sounds.'[3]

Perhaps stimulated by this example of music from the time of his student days in Paris, Stockhausen made a trial recording holding a microphone in his left hand and wielding items from a heteogeneous collection of kitchen and domestic implements as beaters in his right hand; his studio technician operated a variable-bandwidth filter and potentiometer more or less at random and the result was recorded on tape. 'I must say that what we both heard was so astonishing that we started embracing each other, and saying this is unbelievable, a great discovery. We heard all sorts of animals that I had never heard before, and at the same time many sounds of a kind I couldn't have possibly imagined or discovered, not in the twelve years I had worked in the electronic music studio up to the time of that experiment.'[4] It was a

---

[2] Karlheinz Stockhausen, *Texte zur Musik*, iii (Cologne, 1971), p. 32.
[3] Ibid. 244.
[4] Stockhausen and Maconie, op. cit. 78.

breakthrough, showing that using a single complex source it was possible to extract a range of sounds of entirely different types, some realistic, others unearthly, and all charged with an extraordinary animus.

On the basis of this experiment *Mikrophonie I* was composed. It is a stereophonic work. There are two teams of three performers, one team for each channel. They stand on either side of the tam-tam, which is placed edgewise to the audience. The first player excites the surface of the instrument with a weird variety of materials chosen with particular care to produce a specified sound character or quality. The resulting vibrations are monitored stethoscopically by a second player moving a microphone back and forth in relation to the tam-tam surface and to and fro across the point of excitation. The third team member operates a Cologne Radio in-house variable-bandwidth filter, letting more or less of the sound through, and also controlling the sound level with a potentiometer. The resulting dynamically varying sound then passes to loudspeakers either on the left or right of the auditorium. As the same resonator is employed for both layers of musical gesture, there is naturally some leakage of signal from left to right and vice versa, also modulated in turn by the movements of the two microphones and by the respective filters. What results is a dialogue of two channels with a composite third voice created by the interaction of both: a mystical union reminiscent of the concept of *Schlagtrio*. This third voice is intended to weave a mysterious dance between the speakers as a consequence of the constant change of balance and filtering between them.

The work is composed in 33 'moments', the action generally passing alternately between each team of three performers, with the exception of a *tutti* moment where both teams play continuously at once. The order of moments is variable according to a fixed 'connection scheme' of structural relationships, symbolized as in Example 55.

Ex. 55

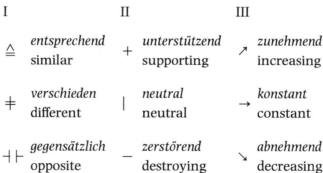

Note: Each liaison is defined by a combination of one of each of the three categories.

Mikrophonie I. Notations of structural relationships. Each liaison between moments is determined by a combination of one of each of the three categories.

Ex. 56

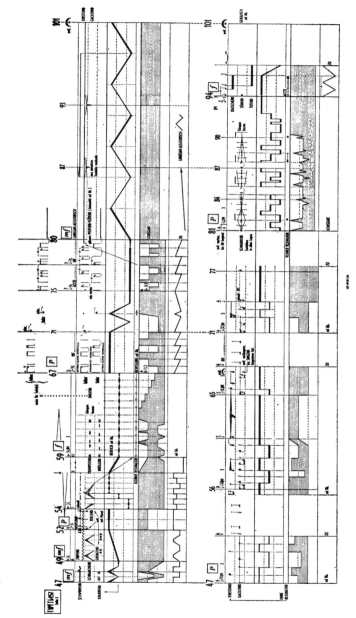

Mikrophonie I, 'Brussels version': page 2 of the 'Tutti 157' moment.
© Universal Edition AG Wien.

We are back with Pierre Schaeffer and 'l'objet musical', in particular the idea propounded in Schaeffer's 1952 essay of 'a sort of anti-melody' created by a succession of transformations of a so-called 'complex note' or musical ideogram.

Originally Stockhausen proposed to have each of the three performers in a team working completely independently in a production line resembling the team productions of *Gesang der Jünglinge's* aleatoric showers of impulses.[5] In due course he settled for a greater measure of co-ordination within each team, and the published 'Brussels version' score based on the CBS/DG recording is very precisely timed. In Example 56 there are two systems which play simultaneously, one system for each team of performers. Each system is made up of three layers, a top layer of notations for the musician exciting the tam-tam, a middle layer of symbols for the microphonist, and a bottom layer of cross-hatched shapes representing the variable bandwidth, over a white stave of symbols for the potentiometer. At certain times the two pairs of exciter and microphonist have to begin together, which requires some form of signalling as they normally cannot see their counterparts on the other side of the instrument.

Stockhausen worked hard on the question of notation. His first intention was to describe in meticulous detail every move involved in the generation of a given sound. This proved enormously complicated and ultimately counter-productive; the clinching argument being that having got all the details of the action right, there was still no guarantee that the intended effect would be produced. Thinking laterally, he decided instead to describe the result as clearly as possible, and leave the choice of materials and actions to achieve the result largely to the performers themselves. That involved compiling a list of words to correspond with the actions producing a wide range of sounds, or suggesting them onomatopoeically. It proved unexpectedly difficult to find a complete range of suitable words, a lesson in how much the language of timbres and sound types is identified with the objects making the sound, and not the quality of sound *per se*.

Mikrophonie I reveals a rich and varied sound-world within the compass of a single complex timbre. The gestural world strangely recalls Varèse's *Poème électronique*, but the force and eloquence of gesture is one of the work's exceptional strengths. In an odd kind of way the process of articulation actually resembles the mechanics of speech, the tam-tam representing the vocal cavity, the various modes of excitation consonants and vowels, and the filters and potentiometers shaping diphthongs and envelope curves. Adjusting to the sound-world so that one can hear the differences and not just the underlying similarities requires some practice on the part of the listener, but the rewards are great, just as they are with *Mikrophonie I*'s more feminine counterpart *Stimmung*. Integrated serialism may not be anything new, but a matching acoustic integration is quite an achievement.

---

[5] Jonathan Cott, *Stockhausen: Conversations with the Composer* (London, 1974), pp. 71–2.

Mixtur

1964–7: *Mixture* for five orchestra groups and 4 ring modulators and sine-wave generators.

Large ensemble, e.g. 3. 3. 3. 3. 5; 3. 3. 1; 3 suspended cymbals, 3 tam-tams (3 players), harp; strings 12. 12. 10. 8. 6; microphones, 4 sine-wave generators, 7 loudspeakers.

1967 version for small ensemble 1. 1. 1. 1. 2; 1. 1; percussion as above; strings 4. 4. 4. 2. 2.

Duration 28′.

It takes strong ears to ring-modulate an orchestra. The ring modulator is a very simple electronic device with drastic consequences for the signal modulated. If a reverberation circuit multiplies and shifts an acoustic image in the time domain, ring modulation does the same in the frequency domain; whereas the former phenomenon is recognized in the natural sound-world as a manifestation of acoustic space, the latter produces an effect which is the antithesis of spatial awareness. Under ring modulation the timbre distinctions of an orchestra are effectively neutralized by an iridescent overlay of additional harmonics, but distinctions of timing such as attack, rhythm, and texture are preserved, indeed enhanced. Ring modulation exists in nature on a microcosmic scale and is recreated at a macrocosmic dimension through the use of microphones and amplification.

So why ring-modulate an orchestra? Perhaps to transform it into a sort of electronic tam-tam by analogy with *Mikrophonie I*, a collective instrument having the whole complement of textural and gestural resources of an orchestra but within the confines of a single global sonority. Certainly, in the absence of orthodox timbre distinctions, and with even the normal pitch distinctions severely reduced, Stockhausen was obliged to reform his orchestral palette into a few broadly contrasted surface textures: woodwind, brass, pizzicato strings (including harp where appropriate), bowed strings, and percussion. The four groups of pitched instruments are separately amplified and ring modulated with sine tones of varying frequency. The percussion, which is not ring modulated, consists of three players each with a suspended cymbal and tam-tam amplified via contact microphones. The combination suggests a music in which the characteristics of one instrumental group may be imposed on, or transformed into, those of another, with the percussion acting as an intermediate stage.

Stockhausen sketched out the instrument and pitch content of the twenty shortish 'moments' rapidly and with graphic simplicity during July and August 1964 (Ex.57). Each moment has a name and is largely identified with a single gesture or musical image. The order of moments may be reversed. The notation of moments

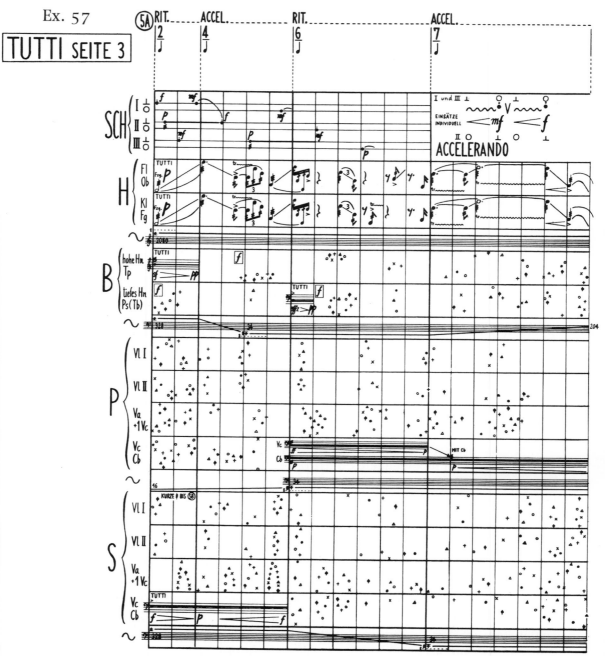

Mixtur : page 3 of the 'Tutti' moment. The five systems are SCH—percussion (cymbals and tam-tams), H—woodwinds, B—brass, P—pizzicato strings, and S—bowed strings. H, B, P, and S group outputs are ring-modulated via sine-wave generators, indicated by wave-form symbols. In this section woodwinds make strongly textured speech-like utterances in which the collective shape is more important than precise pitches: in effect, imitating the sound of ring modulation in unmodulated performance. Instruments from the B, P, and S groups examine similar interactions of pitches E and C with sine tones which converge on a low C♯. Simultaneously other players produce a spangled texture of modulated points; each player chooses one or two symbols and plays only where they occur (the height of the two-line stave representing the entire range of the instrument).

© Universal Edition AG Wien.

ranges from orthodox through a catalogue of relatively indeterminate pitch and time specifications to extremely indeterminate. In addition, each moment incorporates a speculation about the influence of sine-tone ring modulation upon chosen instruments or musical shapes. When the modulating sine tone is high in frequency the timbre is influenced; when its frequency enters the rhythm domain of 16 Hz or under, the instrumental texture is rhythmically modulated. In some moments, such as 'Ruhe' (Quiet) or 'Blech' (Brass), the use of ring modulation seems primarily for expressive coloration; in most others, however, the technique has obvious influence on the musical structure. 'Translation' is one moment where the contribution of ring modulation is evidently of structural significance: the two groups of instruments mimic the beat interference effect simultaneously being produced (or at least implied) by their associated sine-wave generators. Were ring modulation to be omitted, the moment would lose much of its point.

At times one feels that the composer is using ring modulation to 'tune' the instrumental body of sound to particular harmonic spectra, anticipating *Mantra*. Real tonal images—a hint of 'La Marseillaise', a fragment of folk-tune—are buried deep in the musical texture, elements of another phase of the natural world shortly to be assimilated in the composer's next stage of integration in *Hymnen* and *Telemusik*. *Mixtur* is a brash, physical, inquiring piece whose simple representational imagery is a sign of the times.

Mikrophonie II

1965: *Microphony II* for choir (6 sopranos, 6 basses), Hammond organ, 4 ring modulators, and tape.

Duration 15'.

Einfache Grammatische Meditationen by the poet Helmut Heissenbüttel[6] provides the vocal material for this next work, which applies a special kind of ring modulation to voices. The twelve voices are divided into four groups of three, two of sopranos, two basses; each is independently ring-modulated with the output of a Hammond organ. Though smaller in scale than *Mixtur*, the new work is nevertheless richer in sound potential: on both sides of the ring-modulation equation are found instruments of greater flexibility. Where the orchestral work employed more or less fixed pitches, the choirs here are asked to produce every kind of expressive nuance, and in contrast to the monophonic oscillators of *Mixtur* the Hammond organ is both polyphonic and

---

[6] Helmut Heissenbüttel, *Einfache Grammatische Meditationen* (Breisgau, 1955); trans. Michael Hamburger as 'Simple Grammatical Meditations', in Helmut Heissenbüttel, *Texts* (London, 1977), pp. 30–1.

polytimbral. The relative intimacy of the ensemble brings further benefits of immediacy and sympathy of response. In his comments on the work Stockhausen stresses the importance of continuous processes of transformation occurring within the musical material, rather than being imposed from outside, as with the earlier electronic pieces. Continuity is a feature of sounds in nature, and the search for more naturally continuous processes of integration and transformation of artificial timbres is an important new goal of live electronic music. Building on the example of *Mikrophonie I*, Stockhausen introduces higher levels of continuity to the musical process, of which the sense of a text is one, the characterization of a tone of voice another: these undoubtedly influenced his choice of texts and the unusually theatrical characterizations associated with them.

Clearly this is not music-theatre to be visualized on the stage like *Originale* or *LICHT*. For the première the singers were seated in a semicircle, their backs to the audience, the four channels of modulated sound being projected into the auditorium by groups of loudspeakers. At the centre, facing singers and audience, sat the organist on a raised dais; two timekeepers were seated in front of the organ, and the composer in the auditorium regulated the balance of modulated and unmodulated sound among the four speaker groups. But while it may not appear theatrical, the work is certainly dramatic in purely aural, quasi-radiophonic terms. The sound imagery of the piece draws on the choric textures of *Carré* and the crowd scenes of *Momente*, and taped extracts from these two earlier works and from *Gesang der Jünglinge* are heard at different times during the piece (Ex. 58). A slightly more sophisticated system of ring modulation is employed, allowing the sounds of the four groups of singers and Hammond organ to be separately combined and balanced. Only when a signal from both singers and organ is detected is the output of a channel ring-modulated: consequently either part is able to influence the quality and timing of the modulated output. In addition, unmodulated signal can be sent to each speaker to allow for continuous transitions between natural and modulated sound.

Radiophonic drama, unlike its stage counterpart, is essentially private and interior, and the associations of *Mikrophonie II* combine with the alien sound-world of ring modulation and the circular incantations of Heissenbüttel to create a relatively bleak and desolate world resembling the 'deserts of the spirit' evoked by Varèse in *Déserts*. These are caricature crowds from Grosz or Brueghel, whatever the acoustic interest may be in the timbre of voices 'like a confused, toothless old crone, enraged', 'like a typewriter', 'an affected snob', 'a Sicilian hawker, choked', or (for basses repeating the phrase 'oder und oder oder') '*à la* jazz, cool, fast—like plucked string basses'. Certainly the sound types and their descriptive notations serve a higher serial purpose whose rationale may well be indifferent to psychology, but so strong a cumulative impression surely cannot result entirely by accident.

Stockhausen had difficulties with the notation of *Mikrophonie II* just as with its earlier namesake, abandoning an early detailed and precise score for one more open to performer intuition and relying to a greater extent on verbal descriptions.

Ex. 58

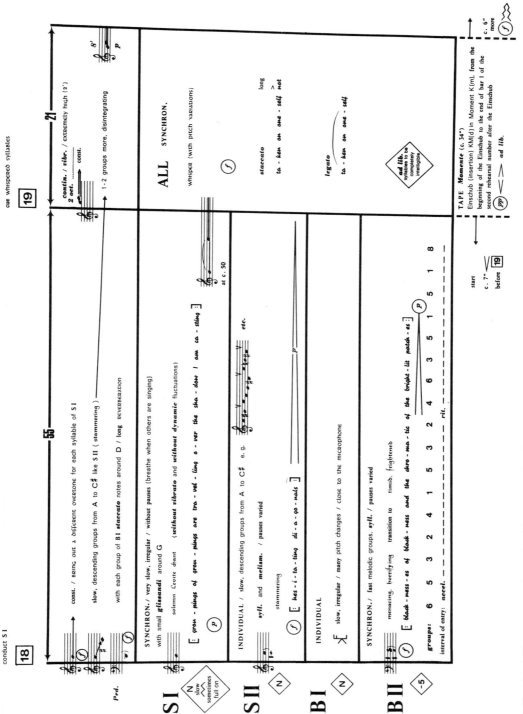

Mikrophonie II: moments 18–19. Stockhausen applies the same kind of verbal characterization to vocal delivery as previously to tam-tam sounds in *Mikrophonie I*. Note the 'sound-window' at 19 through which a taped excerpt of *Momente* is heard.

Technically, the piece represents an advance on the earlier *Mixtur*, and a necessary stage in the development of the transformational idiom of *Hymnen*, *Telemusik*, and *Mantra*.

Solo

1965–6: for melody instrument with feedback (4 assistants).
Duration 6–10′.

Microphones, filters, sine-wave generators, and ring modulation having been pressed into service as real-time instruments of live electronic music, Stockhausen turns his attention to the tape recorder, and especially the tape loop. *Solo* for melody instrument and feedback is designed to enable a single player to make polyphonic music. The compositional procedure can be referred back to the *Kontakte* experiments involving a reversal of the usual order of erase, record, and playback heads on a tape recorder to allow polyphonic complexes to be built up on a loop of tape by continuous overcopying. Unlike the electronic work, however, *Solo*'s cyclic recurrences of music are not intended to become the microstructures of accelerated strange new timbres; rather the work plays with the idea of simultaneity of different time strata, with images of decay and renewal, of erosion and regrowth (as in *Punkte* 1952/62)—temporal distances appearing as displacements in aural perspective.

In the original version the feedback is produced electronically, though subsequent devices developed by Koenig and Anderson do incorporate extended tape loops. A line of music is recorded continuously or intermittently on to one or both tracks of a two-channel tape by an assistant stationed at the record potentiometers (Ex. 59). As the tape travels toward the wind-up reel it passes six tape playback heads spaced at precise distances corresponding to time delays. Each is switched on in turn by a second tape assistant in an order determined by the chosen form-scheme. The prerecorded tape then passes under the control of a third assistant at the output potentiometers, who according to guidelines in the score either allows it to be heard continuously, intermittently, or not at all after the appropriate delay, feeding back a layer to the live solo which is then automatically rerecorded.

Using two channels instead of one for recording has certain advantages. A layer which is suppressed during one cycle can be preserved and reappear on the other channel. In this way a range of different cumulative structures can be executed. For example, by alternating channels a simple two-part canon can be produced, or an ostinato accompaniment created for an evolving theme; at the other extreme layers can be allowed to accumulate into dense noisy bands of sound. The assistants

Ex. 59

SCHEMATIC DIAGRAM:

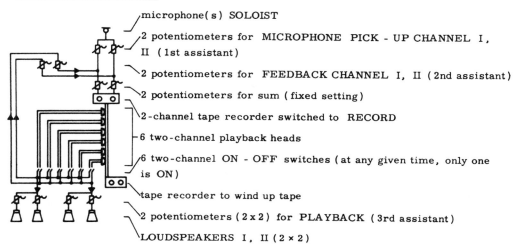

microphone(s) SOLOIST

2 potentiometers for MICROPHONE PICK - UP CHANNEL I ,
II (1st assistant)

2 potentiometers for FEEDBACK CHANNEL I, II (2nd assistant)

2 potentiometers for sum (fixed setting)

2 -channel tape recorder switched to RECORD

6 two-channel playback heads

6 two-channel ON - OFF switches (at any given time, only one
is ON)

tape recorder to wind up tape

2 potentiometers (2 x 2) for PLAYBACK (3rd assistant)

LOUDSPEAKERS I , II (2 × 2)

(Amplifiers must be added.)

The diagram shows how the sound picked up by the microphone(s) is fed back after a time delay, at the same time synchronised with new sounds, and played back over loudspeakers.

Solo : feedback circuit diagram.

© Universal Edition AG Wien.

controlling record and replay potentiometers play a major part, therefore, in cutting and shaping individual layers or groups of layers, creating gaps and voids, or slicing continuous aggregations of tone vertically into blocks or chords. Depending on the speed of their actions and the density of the accumulated texture the resulting cross-sections will sound more or less noisy or harmonious.

The score consists of six form-schemes and six melody pages. The performer chooses a form-scheme (Ex. 60) and allocates a melody page to each of its six subsections A–F, called 'cycles'. Each cycle repeats with a different periodicity corresponding to one of the six playback heads; that length of time is equivalent to the duration of each line of the melody page, so for the form-scheme illustrated where cycles A, B, and C repeat at intervals of 12, 24, and 6 seconds respectively, the same page of note material would be played on different occasions at tempi twice as slow as A (for B) or twice as fast as A (for C). The aggregate layer structure is shown in the system for Assistant 3. The symbols at the foot of the page are for the soloist and assistants, and indicate the development tendencies within a cycle: for example, for

149

Ex. 60

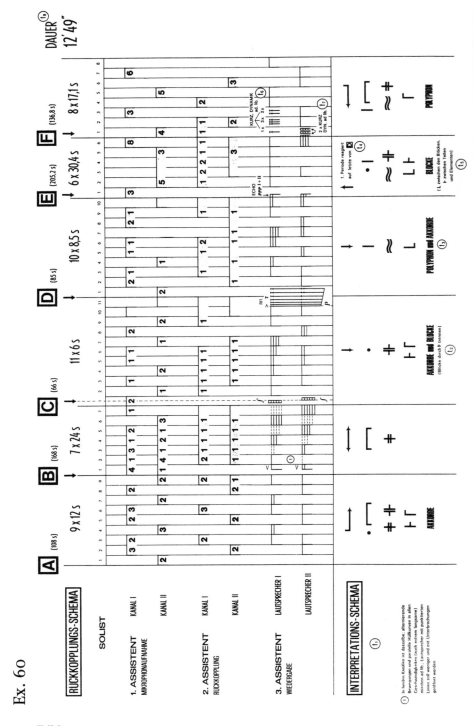

Solo: Formschema, Version II. In the upper system or 'Feedback schema' the shaded blocks indicate which channels are open, and the Third Assistant's part gives an indication of the increasing density and shape of the playback material, which at C, D, and F in this version is 'sliced' into vertical quasi-chords. At the top of the page indications '9 × 12s', '7 × 24s', etc. determine the number and duration in seconds of cycles in a given segment, and the associated time delay.

© Universal Edition AG Wien.

cycle A they signify in order: anticipation (cf. *Momente*), staccato and legato alternated (cf. Piano Piece XI), different and opposite conjunctions (cf. *Mikrophonie I*), middle and upper registers, and the production of chordal harmonies. Certain cycles develop toward dense, inchoate blocks of sound, others to open polyphony of melodies, still others to chord structures. These formal distinctions are reproduced in microcosm as degrees of noisiness, dynamism, and clarity of instrumental timbre.

Each melody page (Ex. 61) consists of a number of layers (the visual picture is exact since each line corresponds to one length of a cycle). The total is structured like a group from *Gruppen*: each layer has an underlying inner pulse corresponding to a different harmonic of the fundamental frequency of the cycle, and is also based on a different interval and central pitch. The same freedom to cut and shape group rhythms is evident here as in *Gruppen*, though the shaping in this case arises from feedback manipulations, and not from the outline of distant mountain ranges.

As with all of these live electronic compositions, the stakes are high and there are many imponderables, both technical and interpretative. *Solo* has had a rather chequered career, partly because the technical set-up requires some ingenuity, and partly because this is not a work in the virtuoso convention, but tends to attract those who would like to make it so.

Stimmung

1968: *Tuning* for six vocalists (SSATTB) and amplification.
Duration 70–80′ (recorded version 73′)

In German the word *stimmung*, literally *tuning* [transfers] from music to mental states. [It denotes] those peculiarities of mental condition which are capable of musical representation. I think we might appropriately define *gemüthstimmung*, or *mental tune*, as representing that general character temporarily shewn by the motion of our conceptions, and correspondingly impressed on the motions of our body and voice. Our thoughts may move fast or slowly, may wander about restlessly and aimlessly in anxious excitement, or may keep a determinate aim distinctly and energetically in view; . . . all this may be imitated and expressed by the melodic motion of the tones, and the listener may thus receive a more perfect and impressive image of the 'tune' of another person's mind, than by any other means.[7]

Stimmung's timeless meditation on a six-voice consonance belongs in this sequence of live electronic compositions even though the electronic intervention is reduced to microphone amplification alone. In a musical acoustic sense it is the harmonious counterpart of the 'noisy' *Mikrophonie I*: the harmonic basis of the work, built up of

[7] Hermann Helmholtz, *On the Sensations of Tone*, trans. Alexander J. Ellis (New York, 1954), pp. 250–1.

Ex. 61

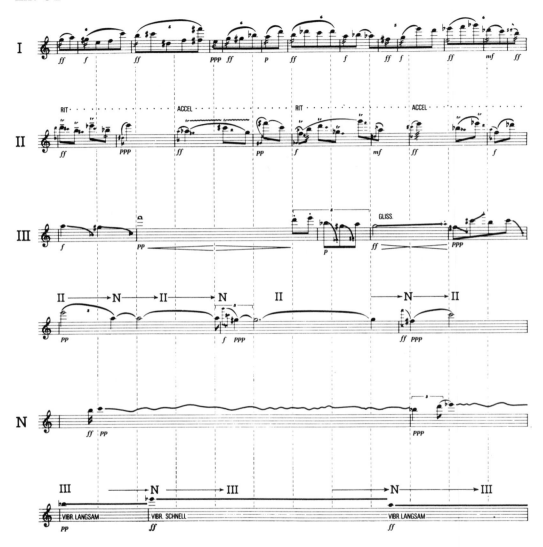

Solo: sample score part for the soloist. The tempo of a line corresponds to the time constant of the tape delay, so each new line should coincide with a potential repetition of the previous line(s) heard over the playback system.

partials 2–9 (omitting 6 and 8) of Bɪ flat (lowest note of the bassoon), playing a complementary role to the more complex spectrum of the tam-tam, and the 'magic names' and poems intoned by the six vocalists on the same pitches corresponding to the 'exciting' of the tam-tam by different materials, and also to the filtering stage. In a dramatic sense, however, its refined and shining composure stands at the opposite extreme from the dark and menacing world of *Mikrophonie II*, though it is equally private and untheatrical in its stage presentation (the six vocalists sit in a circle, again with their backs to the audience).

Amplification magnifies the voice: in addition to creating an atmosphere of shared intimacy, this also makes audible analogies between natural vocal effects and electronic modulation and filtering processes. The fact that the underlying harmony does not modulate in a conventional tone sense does not mean that the music is changeless, or that it does not modulate in other, quasi-electronic ways: indeed, because the harmony remains the same attention eventually wanders away from the chord itself, just as it would do when exposed to any constant background sound. When that happens the perceptions can spontaneously open to the liveliness, the movement, the constant activity going on in the music in consequence of the modulation of the 'carrier frequencies' by the chanted and spoken texts. There is always something in transition, and usually at quicksilver speed: syllables chasing one another in canon, condensing into words, fusing into vowel-based harmonic mixtures, or disintegrating in a tissue of consonantal percussion.

The work has a separate form-scheme which, like *Solo*, determines a fixed sequence of changes for the underlying harmony (number of voices audible in aggregate at any one time) through the work's 51 moments. Again, the inner balance of the stationary chord turns out to be surprisingly changeable. This predetermined curve of varying harmonic density is relatively freely disturbed by the introduction of the 'magic names' of exotic and ancient divinities. Six 'model pages' (Ex. 62) of magic names precisely notated in rhythm and tempo are distributed among the vocalists. At moments marked *N* in the form-scheme the vocalist whose pitch is emphasized takes the lead and introduces a new magic name in the indicated tempo and rhythm; the others follow the lead and one after another gradually metamorphose the previous pattern of intonation into the new pattern. At certain times the transformation of one into another is total, at other times certain aspects of the earlier model are retained, creating different degrees of transitional complexity.

The model incantations are themselves cyclical, repeating at different serial periodicities and also pulsing at serially varied internal tempi. At times the carrier pitches themselves are slightly distuned to produce quasi-electronic intermodulation effects. The four poetic texts incorporated in the model pages, one for a female voice, and one each for the three male vocalists, are musically spoken rather than sung, and introduce an erotic charge to the otherwise contemplative atmosphere of the piece.

A special 'microphone voice' is required of the vocalists, a head tone capable of

Ex. 62

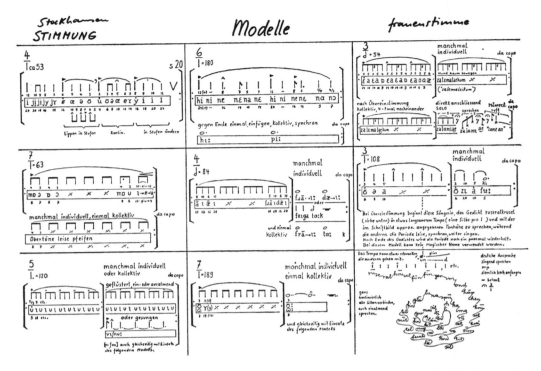

Stimmung : 'model page' for female voice. Each box represents a cyclic incantation of a 'magic name' or a syllabic pattern derived from one. Tempi and durations of cycles are 'harmonically' varied (compare *Solo*). From time to time a poem appears: heare the poem 'Ruseralkrusel . . .' may be seen spiralling inward at the bottom of the page.

© Universal Edition AG Wien.

producing strong high-frequency resonances, and being able to focus upon selected formant overtones at will. The magic names are transcribed very specifically in international phonetic script to ensure that the desired frequencies within the voice spectrum are in fact emphasized. Incidentally, both the vocal style and the associated character of intimacy recreate the musical ambience of Renaissance part-song, and act as a reminder of the rich aural interplay of pitch and verbal tone and texture to be discovered in the pre-Classical vocal repertoire. (At one time it was rumoured that Stockhausen was composing *Stimmung* with the Deller Consort in mind.)

One cannot help but be moved by the purity of the musical conception and by its inner composure. When agitators broke up a performance in Amsterdam in 1969, Stockhausen wrote: '*Stimmung* will yet reduce even the howling wolves to silence'.[8]

[8] Stockhausen, op. cit. 110.

10 *Metamusic: Process Planning and Intuitive Music*

CLASSICAL stave notation is a musical map, with pitch as latitude and time as longitiude. As the earth rotates in time, lines of latitude remain constant while those of longitude move past an external observer from east to west. It is the same for a musical stave: the passage of the music describes a continuous movement relative to the reader from right to left, while pitch relationships remain constant in the vertical plane. The grid of the musical map arises from the development of universal measures of pitch and time, embodied in tempered tuning and mensural notation, intellectual abstractions transcending individual instrument and performer limitations of intonation and memory. Standard notation evolve to its modern form at the same time as the science of cartography itself was coming to maturity, so it is not surprising that sixteenth-century European composers should take the same delight as their seagoing explorer contemporaries in charting the course of a melodic shape at will across the musical map into remote regions of chromatic tonality, inhabited by wild and strange dissonances.

Learned composers of the baroque period experimented with transformation processes in alternative dimensions, for example dynamic perspective (crescendo–decrescendo, echo-canon, stratified dynamics) and relative time-scale (accelerando–ritardando, augmentation–diminution). But modulation, expressing the restless and exploring spirit of classical Europe, has survived as the principal musical legacy of the concept of a uniform pitch space implemented in standard notation; even today modulation is virtually synonymous with musical progression as movement in the frame of reference of pitch. Dynamic and tempo transitions, while certainly capable of conveying a sense of purposeful direction in the short term, have tended to play a subordinate and more subjective role in musical expression, perhaps because the scope for continuous movement in one direction is so much more limited in dynamics and tempo than in pitch. Timbre modulation as a means of conveying momentum appears more recently in the history of music, but can be equally as powerful as conventional tonal modulation, as the *Bolero* by Ravel amply proves.

Navigation in a multidimensional musical space is the underlying theme of a series of metamusical process compositions which form an important second stream of Stockhausen's compositional activity in the sixties. But if traditional modulation is like moving musical shapes about on a map, Stockhausen's is more like navigating in conditions of weightlessness. Though without the gravitational attraction of tonality, his musical space is well provided with scalar co-ordinates not only for location in pitch and time, but also for relative magnitude (expansion and contraction of interval and duration values), dynamics, timbre (tone and noise), probability (determinancy or indeterminancy of pitch or time position), and even orientation and movement of music in physical space. Deriving from his studies in the fifties culminating in *Kontakte*, Piano Piece X, and *Momente*, these new co-ordinates equipped Stockhausen to pilot a musical image from any point in musical space (defined in pitch, timbre, intensity, duration, position, etc.) to any other point, through a series of intermediate steps representing precise transitional values. The question was whether suitable navigational skills could be developed for real-time applications in live electronic music. The first priority would be to develop suitable notations to put across the concepts of continuous transition in these unaccustomed dimensions, so that they could be interpreted as freely and inventively as figured bass in the Classical era.

Plus–Minus

1963: '2 × 7 pages for working out'.

For solo or small ensemble.

Duration unspecified.

For many years I had worked on the idea of writing a piece having such powers of metamorphosis that I might come across it one day and hardly recognize it as my own.[1]

Plus–Minus, the first process composition, is a piece in which certain essential transformational relationships are determined symbolically, allowing an interpreter to decide, within limits, what material expression may be assigned to them. Originally devised as an exercise for the composition class of the first of the series of 'Cologne New Music Courses' directed by Stockhausen from 1963 to 1968, the work consists of seven pages representing form-schemes and another seven pages of musical material. For every page of form-scheme used, a different page of note material is employed. It is not yet a question of playing directly from the symbolic notations: instead a conventionally notated score is composed on the basis of the symbol pages according to precise rules of interpretation.

Today we are able to understand the concept of such a music by direct analogy with a computer program which determines the way in which information is

---

[1] Karlheinz Stockhausen, *Texte zur Musik*, iii (Cologne, 1971), p. 40.

processed while leaving the choice of information to be processed to the individual user. Then it was not so obvious. The score is complex, and the complexity is a consequence of wanting to retain control, however remote, of the pitch-information content of the piece as well as the transformational process. Each form-scheme page (Ex. 63) consists of a cycle of 53 time frames or moments, reading in the conventional way from left to right, top to bottom (unlike some mobile pieces of the period which have a similar appearance, but are intended to be read in any direction from frame to frame). Each moment consists of a standard formula comprising symbols for a 'central sound' and 'ancillary notes' which stand in somewhat ornamental relation to it. The central sounds define the formal process, while the ancillary notes define the central sounds. The seven 'central sound' symbols are each assigned one of seven roman-numbered note groups from the note page (Ex. 64), and ancillary note groups are assigned note collections of the same arabic number. Thus whenever the same symbol recurs, the same note group recurs for central sound and ancillary notes, though the combination of central sound and ancillary notes may vary.

Symbolic controls extend to the duration and envelope curve of the note formula, its rhythmic regularity, accentuation, degree of reverberation, sound clarity, muting, whether it leads into the following event or is separated from it, and by how much. Where two or more form-scheme pages follow in succession, events from one page may be inserted into previous or following pages in empty frames left to receive them. Further instructions apply where two or more pages are realized polyphonically.

The name *Plus–Minus* refers to the systematic accretion or erosion of material from the combinations of central and ancillary notes, which give the piece something of the character of a board game. Central notes are able to expand to a point where they become elevated to a new status, or to be reduced to zero and have their place taken by a negative quantity. Ancillary notes proliferate and permutate, or simply disappear, During the course of a given interpretation the musical events associated with the symbol content will wax and wane, occasionally leading to the annihilation or promotion of material. A second order of transformations applies to the pitch content itself, and regulates transpositions in pitch, dynamic, and absolute duration of particular events.

If *Plus–Minus* were written today, logically it would be written as an intelligent-computer program which, having been set up with the appropriate form-scheme and note-page combinations, would then be able to configure the music according to the rules in general terms for an operator to reject or modify at will. As a compositional game it probably operates at a level too elevated and abstract for most composers; it is certainly a game for initiates, and ultimately for the 'Magister ludi' himself. It clearly indicates the enormous difficulties of defining continuous musical processes in a more open fashion, and points the way to the radical simplifications of later process compositions for direct interpretation by performers.

Ex. 63

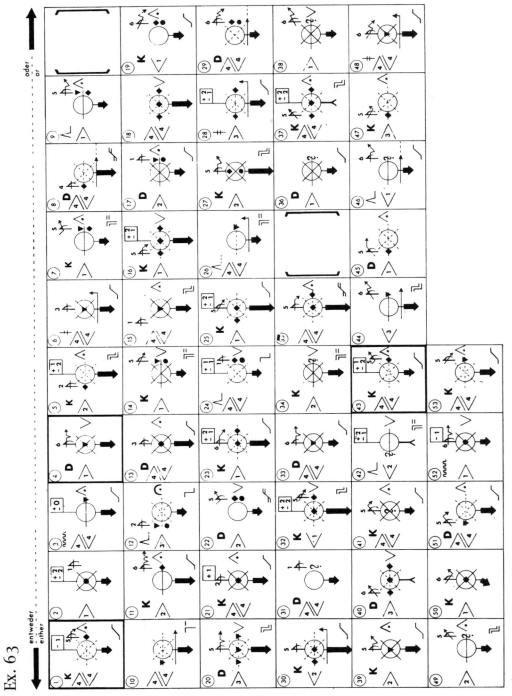

Plus–Minus: one of seven symbol pages. Each box corresponds to a musical unit: an empty box is a space for inserting material from another page. Every symbol page is characterized by the combination of its box 1, which constitutes a sort of refrain. Here for example there are close resemblances between boxes 1, 5, 21, 35, 37, 41, 43, and 53.

© Universal Edition AG Wien.

Ex. 64

Plus–Minus: sample note page. Roman numerals identify 'central sounds', arabic numerals groups of ancillary notes. Both reservoirs are derived from a starting note (D in the example) by interval displacements corresponding to a Fibonacci series, expressed in semitones (2 = tone, 3 = minor third, 5 = perfect fourth, 8 = perfect fifth, etc.).

© Universal Edition AG Wien.

Prozession

1967: *Procession.*

For tam-tam, viola, electronium, piano, 2 microphones, 2 filters and potentiometers (6 performers). Alternative instruments may be chosen, corresponding to the above.

Duration 30′ minimum.

Stockhausen returned to process planning in 1967, having assembled a regular team of players, the 'Group Stockhausen', with whom to work out the practicalities of notation, interpretation, and co-ordination of compositions expressed only as degrees of change from one moment to the next. In the meantime, after *Plus–Minus* he drastically simplified the notation of degrees of change in *Mikrophonie I* and *Solo*, also returning to the original Piano Piece XI format whereby the note content is fully determined and only the connection scheme is symbolically notated to allow variation of sequence. The new process pieces all work on the basis of starting with previously familiar, memorized material and systematically transforming it by stages into unknown new material. In *Prozession* the players draw on their knowledge of existing Stockhausen works; in later compositions 'sound-objects' are taken from short-wave radio.

Suppose we record a sound obtained by lightly stroking a few strings of the piano with the finger. . . . What can be done with such a sound? First of all, we can make a melody in the classical sense. Our equipment enables us to play with the pitch of this *complex note*, to give it rhythm, and so on. . . . But as an alternative to evolving a more or less commonplace melody, we can also attempt to create a family of objects similar to the prototype, but playing on an aspect of its form: a progression in intensity or brevity of attacks, progressive enlargement of the internal rhythm, or alteration of the dynamic envelope. . . . In such a way new musical

Ex. 65

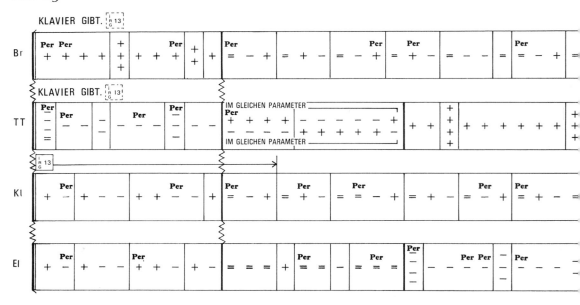

processes may be discovered . . . in the alignment of a series of musical objects bearing an intrinsic relationship one with another, like the materials of architecture. For this to happen, alternatives to pitch-evolution have to be recognized; at least, pitch must relinquish its supremacy. A *series* of identical sound-objects, but varied in intensity, might be considered not as a series, but as a *dynamic melody*. . . . A complex note, [representing] not only a point in the scale, a letter in the alphabet of sounds, [but] often a whole word, or even a phrase of a new musical language, . . . heard once, twice, three times in succession, describing any desired gradient of intensity, could amount in itself to a miniature work, or at least the self-contained fragment of a work.[2]

Prozession is a work for four strongly-contrasted timbres whose music may or may not interact. The notation of developmental trends between successive moments is reduced to the three signs +, −, and =, which may be interpreted in different ways and assigned freely to different aspects of a musical object:

+   higher or louder or longer or more sections (*Glieder* = 'limbs');
−   lower or softer or shorter or fewer sections;
=   the same pitch (register) and volume and length and timbre and number of sections.[3]

Higher and lower refer to pitch transposition, other aspects remaining the same.

[2] Pierre Schaeffer, 'L'Objet musical', *La Revue musicale*, Numéro Spécial No. 212 (1952), 69–71.
[3] Stockhausen, op. cit. 103.

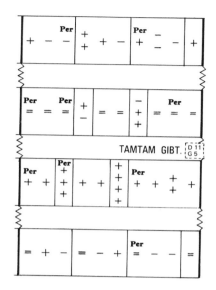

Prozession: reconstructed section of 'full score'.
'Br' = viola, 'TT' = tam-tam, 'KI' = piano,
'EI' = electronium. Symmetrical and reciprocal
formations between parts can be clearly observed.
© Universal Edition AG Wien.

Longer and shorter refer to duration, and do not imply slowing down or speeding up, but instead to repetition or removal of note content at the original tempo (as if the material were taken from a continuous length of tape). More or fewer sections *does* refer to tempo, because the duration remains constant, the note content being divided up into more sections, or aggregated into fewer.

No full score is published because the four parts do not regularly coincide, but if one is reconstructed (as in Example 65) obvious symmetries or reciprocal relationships appear between parts. Each part comprises a sequence of 250 symbols or symbol combinations, grouped in multiples of ten event-changes, and adding up in total to a balance of plus, minus, and equal tendencies. The superscript 'Per' indicates that the internal rhythm of the event should become periodic (that is, conform to a regular beat). These larger ten-event groupings are variously characterized as all-plus, all-minus, or an equally weighted combination of symbols. One special group recurs once in each part and appears to have a special 'refrain' significance, a five-degree rise in one parameter coupled with a complementary fall in another parameter; the trend then reverses for a further five changes (Ex. 66). Other symmetrical formations abound, for instance a group of ten plus-changes followed by ten minus-changes; sections 6–10 of the viola part form a super-symmetry of all-minus, all-plus, balanced, all-minus, and all-plus groups of ten changes.

Players are not restricted to imitating the material they begin with, but may

Metamusic

Ex. 66

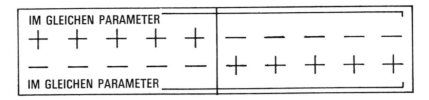

Prozession: a symbolic 'refrain'. 'Im gleichen Parameter' = parameters remain the same for each line, e.g. a five-unit expansion of dynamics is followed by a five-unit reduction of dynamics, simultaneously with a reciprocal reduction and expansion process in another dimension (for example, the number of sections).

© Universal Edition AG Wien.

connect with other players in imitative dialogues, trios, etc. Since the timing of individual events is free it is possible for the four instruments to advance at different rates; to maintain a measure of overall synchronization between parts each is assigned two of eight quasi-cadence points where the ensemble converges on the register (R), dynamic envelope (I), duration (D), or internal rhythm (G) of all call-sign given by the leading instrument.

Kurzwellen

1968: *Short Waves.*

For piano, electronium, tam-tam with microphone, viola with contact microphone, 2 filters, 4 potentiometers and loudspeakers, 4 short-wave receivers (6 players). Alternative instruments may be chosen, corresponding to the above.

Duration 50–60'.

In 1964 Frederic Rzewski and Cornelius Cardew prepared a version of *Plus–Minus*— one page each—for two pianos. Both decided to use an accessory instrument to perform the 'negative-band' music which appears when a 'central sound' is eliminated from play. Rzewski decided on a cluster played on harmonium, while Cardew opted to play static noise found between stations on a transistor radio. Stockhausen, who was not consulted on the matter and who was not particularly enamoured of either sound source, nevertheless expressed approval of the result:

Ex. 67

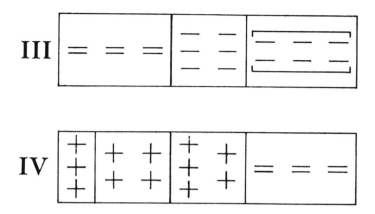

Kurzwellen: a complex symmetry between III and IV, section A.
© Universal Edition AG Wien.

When I heard the tape of the Cardew–Rzewski version of *Plus–Minus* for the first time, I was, in a truly unselfish sense, fascinated by it. . . . Sounds and sound combinations that, while recognizing their use by other composers, I had personally avoided (prepared piano and radio music), were now being brought by performers into my music, and in exact accordance with the functional sound requirements laid down in the score. The result is of a highly poetic quality, in consequence of the way *Plus–Minus* is constructed: when such a result is obtained, detailed considerations of sound and material become unimportant.[4]

With *Kurzwellen* Stockhausen comes round to using short-wave radios as sources of material for process transformation. Effectively, short-wave sound becomes a link between the various instruments, rather as ring-modulated sound is the link between the instrumental groups of *Mixtur*. So to the motivic assimilation and development processes of *Prozession* is added timbre imitation and transformation. And since each player has a short-wave receiver the incidence of untreated short-wave sound is inevitably bound to compete with that of any one instrument. Short-wave receivers can also be used as sound sources imitating instruments (for example, by tuning back and forth across a signal in the rhythm of another player). It follows that a player is able to imitate another either instrument to instrument, instrument to the other's short-wave event, short-wave receiver to the other's instrument, or short-wave to short-wave, giving equal ot greater prominence to radio events. Because the same repertoire of broadcasts will be found on each receiver, however, the possibility of random encounters of the same material by different players is so much the greater.

[4] Ibid. 43.

Ex. 68

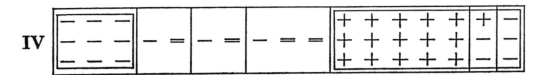

Kurzwellen: a symmetrical formation 'rotated' and interrupted.
© Universal Edition AG Wien.

The piece has a more open form than *Prozession*, but is stricter in time controls. Each part consists of 136 events, divided into sequences of 5, 20, 25, 35, and 51 events. There is a 'full score'; the ensemble comes together at the end of a sequence (indicated by a heavy barline) by each player repeating the last event until all have 'arrived', after which the designated leader gives a signal for all to proceed in step for a given number of events. As the piece proceeds and the distance between successive co-ordination points increases, so the paths of all four instruments will tend to diverge; nevertheless, the latent co-ordination of short-wave material will still be able to connect instruments whose transformational processes are otherwise out of synchronization.

The score reveals a number of new complexities. If we designate the five major sections as Introduction, A, B, C, and D, then the Introduction features a canonic sequence of miniature symmetries in parts II, III, and IV: staggered blocks of three plus followed by three minus-signs. Imitation continues in section A with successive entries of group events consisting of five plus-events, a sequence of minus-events, concluding with three equals, though II is disguised and III slightly varied. Brackets play a more prominent role in creating new and intricate internal symmetries. For instance, the basic 4×5 structure of the 20-event section is rendered in I as a symmetrical sequence 1-4-3-2-2-3-4-1, whereas in II brackets create an expansion structure of 2-3-4-5-6. Symmetries of signs before and after in the same part and between parts are less exposed than in the earlier piece. The final eight events of III and IV provide a simple example (Ex. 67).

Section B divides into five subsections each of 5 events. The symmetries and imitations here are more regular. Section C is more polyphonic in emphasis: each part is assigned two solo groups, one larger, the other smaller, which suggest independent but overlapping structures involving major continuous transformations. In IV, for example, the larger solo group involves an interrupted three-tier transformation sequence of minus-plus-minus (Ex. 68), and the smaller solo, enclosed by a long bracket, is restricted to a single parameter (Ex. 69).

In D, the final section, symmetries between parts are less obviously exposed, but a

Ex. 69

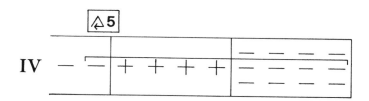

Kurzwellen: another rotation of symmetry, bracketed to limit the curve of growth and decay to a single parameter.

© Universal Edition AG Wien.

degree of complementarity may initially be seen between I and IV, and between II and III, in terms of complexity. At 17 before the end all four parts come together in a simple two-pair symmetry incorporating positive, negative, before, and after like the four identities of a classical twelve-tone series O, I, R, and IR. The piece ends with recapitulations of processes (or their negative inversions) from earlier in the piece (compare *Plus-Minus* in this respect). Part I's final 14 events reflect its first 14 of A; II's final four bars are a variant mirror-image of its section-A 2–4; III's last two bars recapitulate the last two bars of A, while IV's final minus grouping recalls the end of A in Part I and bars 2–5 of A in III.

In 1970 Stockhausen was invited to lecture on Beethoven as part of Dusseldorf's celebration of the bicentenary. Instead he imagined a performance of *Kurzwellen* in which miraculously every short-wave channel would be transmitting Beethoven material. For this performance he substituted tape recorders with specially prepared tapes for short-wave receivers. The tapes, which are simply faded up and down as required, are composed of recorded excerpts of selected Beethoven compositions, interspersed with readings from the Heiligenstadt Testament. To give the effect of short-wave, Stockhausen subjected this material to a variety of electronic transformations based on processes employed in *Hymnen* and also including a new Modul A ring modulator, immediate predecessor of the special Modul B circuit employed in *Mantra*.

Kurzwellen mit Beethoven, also known as *Opus 1970* and *Stockhoven–Beethausen*, marks a relaxation of Stockhausen's original ban on the use of 'totally unmodulated short-wave events' (i.e. recognizable music). In fact, it comes closer, as we shall see, to the original concept of *Hymnen*, being a work for four instrumentalists, each manipulating, imitating, and transforming events pre-recorded on a tape which is only heard intermittently by the audience.

Spiral

1968: for a soloist with short-wave receiver.

Duration indeterminate.

Spiral was composed at the request of a young American guitarist. The new score provides for the possibilities of a harmonic instrument, and also appeals, since it is a solo work, to the interpretative spirit of the performer. To the plain arithmetical notation of *Prozession* and *Kurzwellen* it brings a further vocabulary of symbols, most of which are global in implication, in contrast to the selective transformations of the $+$, $-$, and $=$ signs. For example, there are 'expand' and 'contract' symbols applying to every parameter in a form of spatial perspective; at least five new types of repetition are allowed for, from simple echo to exponential repetition and distortive feedback; there are also new signs for recollecting a past event and anticipating a future event. The global symbols, interestingly, presuppose a quality of detachment from the player's sound image, which the earlier plus–minus signs appeared calculated to dispel. If one returns to the navigational analogy, it is as though the

Ex. 70

Spiral: a complex structure of interlocked symmetries, indicated below by brackets. The score incorporates new 'global' transformation symbols.

© Universal Edition AG Wien.

earlier signs are performer-centred, and represent clear alternatives of direction, while the newer signs are from the point of view of an external observer, such as a sound projectionist, for example, who sees all tendencies within a single frame of reference. Of all the new symbols, however, the most provocative is certainly the 'spiral-sign' which gives the piece its name, and which instructs the performer to transcend all previous limitations of material and technique. Lest this be thought a peculiarly sixties feature, one need only point to the extraordinary restrictions placed on the performer. Stockhausen's experience of working within the extremely tight constraints of serial predetermination has been that it produces its own reaction in the form of sudden flashes of inspiration, 'musical visions', completely tangential to the music in hand, yet which demand to be incorporated. The spiral sign is perhaps intended as a safety-valve for the imagination in this case.

In Example 70, the spiral-sign is the box of plus-signs enclosed by repeat-signs; the subsequent symbols in repeat-brackets are global 'contract', 'expand', and 'repeat with interpolations'. The sequence is typically flamboyant, and exploits the ambiguities of the additional symbols to maximum effect, as may be seen from the quasi-symmetrical pair formations bracketed below. Heinz Holliger has made a virtuosic recording of *Spiral* which is also one of the funniest, with magical imitations of short-wave static and some wonderful slapstick humour at the expense of an unfortunate piece of light music. But there are indications too that the composer himself is taking some wicked enjoyment in setting his performer an impossible task.

Pole für 2

1969–70: *Poles for 2.*

For two soloists with short-wave receivers and optional amplification (the score includes a part for sound distribution).

Instruments unspecified.

Duration indeterminate.

Composed at short notice to supplement Stockhausen's programmes for the German Pavilion at Expo '70 in Osaka, *Pole für 2* and *Expo für 3* complete the sequence of process scores with a return to simplicity. As its title suggests, *Pole für 2* revives the game plan of the reconciliation of opposites. As one might expect, mirror-image processes and dialogues form the basis of a symmetrical composition that one might almost describe in terms of a classical formal dance where male and female partners execute complementary patterns of movement, sometimes alternately, sometimes together. Compared to *Spiral* the score appears neither tentative nor burdened with symbolic overkill. The piece falls into seven sections, ending with a 'da capo' allowing for a continuation of the cycle at a higher level of transformation. The sections alternate dialogue sequences where the lead passes from player to player on signal, with duos where symmetrical processes occur simultaneously: both dialogue and duo forms are reflected in the parts for sound distribution, designed with the Expo '70 dome auditorium in mind, but adaptable to smaller speaker systems (a minimum of eight (4 × 2) separately addressable outputs) (Ex. 71). Where the two parts form a symmetrical duo, the underlying implication is that their opposite natures are emphasized, and these sections all terminate with 'spiral-sign' cadenzas which are oppositely charged. The dialogue sections, on the other hand, suggest convergence and exchange of material, and the point of maximum reconciliation, as such, appears to be at 17 toward the end of section 3, where I and II play in parallel, II leading, followed at 18 by a codetta in which echoes of the previous event predominate. A rather more brusque encounter occurs in the first section at 8, where I leads and II plays in parallel, but this is followed by a reassertion of I and a codetta of equal-signs which could just as well suggest agreement to differ as reconciliation, making the gesture less conclusive than that of 17–18.

Expo Für 3

1969–70: *Expo for 3*.

For three soloists with short-wave receivers and sound projection, instruments (or voices) unspecified.

Duration indeterminate.

Closely synchronized gestures and canonic imitation feature prominently in *Expo für 3*, an altogether more relaxed piece in which solo leads and synchronized accompaniments suggest a high level of mutual understanding among the players. A combination of factors gives the work its cheerful aspect: one is the hybrid sign language, which incorporates conventional verbal instructions and notated rhythms, accents, and dynamics along with plus and minus signs (Ex. 72). Another is the relative simplicity of the individual parts, in which imitation features prominently. Once again the co-ordination and sequence of events is fairly tightly controlled, and the individual parts are not only relatively uncomplicated, but also individually characterized. There are touches of evident humour: III is given a lengthy solo passage consisting of single plus-signs followed by quadruple minuses, which looks suspiciously like self-parody; and two 'inserts', one slow, one fast, in which all players synchronize to a common beat and periodically repeat (with

Ex. 71

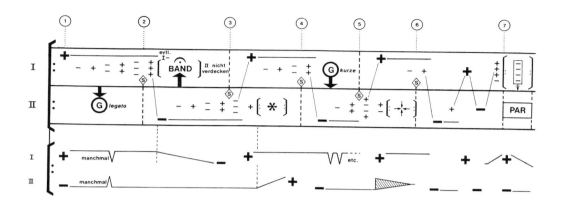

Pole für 2. Mirror-symmetries abound, alternating with passages where the initiative passes back and forth from player to player. The score contains staves for two channels of sound projection.

© Universal Edition AG Wien.

Ex. 72

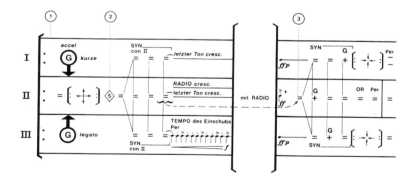

Expo für 3 : moments 1–3. II is in charge: a preponderance of equal-signs means a high proportion of imitation and interaction. Note the symmetry between I and III.

© Universal Edition AG Wien.

syncopations) a fragment from a previous event, suggest choruses of laughter. The seven-times-repeated cadence at the 'da capo' repeat, in strict time, suddenly imposed on all three players who have been independently playing at top speed (BAND means to assimilate previous events into a continuous blur of sound), has the mock finality of Satie (Ex. 73). 'One almost wishes', said Stravinsky of *Zyklus*, 'it

Ex. 73

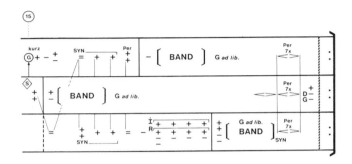

Expo für 3 : moment 15. The cycle ends with what appears to be a Satiesque seven-times-repeated final chord.

© Universal Edition AG Wien.

didn't have to be *translated* into sound but were a kind of hand-drawn photo-electric sound (after a spectrum).'[5] Reading the process scores and sensing the thought, elegance, wit, and humour in them, one almost wishes that they, too, could find a means of expression uncompromised by performers. That possibility comes closer as computers and sound-sampling devices come into wider use. At present, using live performers, the position resembles that of early electronic tone synthesis, where one has to accept the results of a serially determined configuration in default of being able to sample more widely. One advantage the computer offers is that of allowing the composer of process pieces to establish, by repeated trials, the values a performer may consistently assign to a plus or a minus (or any other symbol) in a given context in order not to run out of room in which to manœuvre. While one would be reluctant to hand over all the decision-making to a machine, the fact remains that Stockhausen's transformations are substantially expressions of quasi-mechanical processes, such as are available on synthesizers, or they relate to such processes. The arrival of formula composition in the seventies, in which an entire composition is proportioned and constituted from a single melodic kernel, effectively restored an audible frame of reference to transformations which were in danger of becoming lost in their own exuberance.

If the process pieces represent a distillation of development and differentiation

[5] Igor Stravinsky and Robert Craft, *Memories and Commentaries* (London, 1959), p. 118 n.

tendencies, Stockhausen's text compositions *Aus den sieben Tagen* and *Für kommende Zeiten* focus on integration and harmony: 'In 1968 all of a sudden I reached the moment in my composing where I gave practically nothing to the performer, even to myself as one of the players of my group. Then and there I wrote fifteen texts.'[6] The fifteen *Aus den sieben Tagen* texts, written during a week of total withdrawal in May 1968, are inspirational restatements of certain fundamental expressive goals, intended to polarize the thoughts of his group of players in a common direction. It is perhaps a measure of the degree of concentration demanded of the players of the process compositions, and the dangers of losing the thread or lapsing into banality that arise even among players of goodwill, that Stockhausen may have felt it necessary to compose exercises in pure meditation of this kind. The late sixties witnessed a growth in 'group improvisation' and so-called 'free jazz' ensembles. He was very critical of what he saw as merely mindless and purgative aspects of improvisation, and that it encouraged strident competition and demagoguery particularly among classically trained musicians whose natural self-expression had been repressed and who had never learned to meditate, listen, articulate ideas, and generally make musical conversation in a civilized way.

As ever, the texts all contain a transcendental exhortation to spur the imagination and technique. The first requirement is to draw the performer out of the familiar physical frame of reference of improvisational music, that is, away from the complacent enjoyment of vocal or technical prowess for its own sake. The alternative frames of reference are those of the astronomer or the particle physicist: observers who contemplate physical processes at the extremes of the humanly conceivable and measurable universe. What kind of music can express that world of the infinitely great or infinitely small, or the thoughts of those who inhabit it? A supernova erupts in a distant galaxy: what music conveys the magnitude of such an event as it appears to those who have been preparing for it for the whole of their working lifetimes? A direct consequence of that distant event is the detection of neutrons deep in a zinc mine in Japan: the infinitely large gives rise to events of infinite power at the other end of the scale of magnitude. Musical events as dedicated as these are, and to objectives as grand and as absolute, are capable of attaining a purity of expression virtuous in itself and necessary, one feels, for the proper execution of Stockhausen's process pieces and his other music.

Aus den sieben Tagen

1963: *From the Seven Days.*

Fifteen text pieces: *Richtige Dauern* (Right Durations), *Unbegrenzt* (Unlimited), *Verbindung* (Connection), *Treffpunkt* (Meeting-Point), *Nachtmusik* (Night Music),

[6] Karlheinz Stockhausen and Robin Maconie, *Stockhausen on Music* p. 114.

Abwärts (Downwards), *Aufwärts* (Upwards), *Oben and Unten* (Above and Below—theatre piece), *Intensität* (Intensity), *Setz die Segel zur Sonne* (Set Sail for the Sun), *Kommunion* (Communion), *Litanei* (Litany), *Es* (It), *Goldstaub* (Gold dust), *Ankunft* (Arrival).

For ensemble (numbers variable).

Durations 4–60'.

Two texts address the player directly: 'Give all that up, we were going about it the wrong way,' he says in *Ankunft*. The musician must learn stillness, to open the mind and spirit to external influence (a Fritz Lang image of a life-giving electrical discharge here). And in *Litanei* he says in effect 'I do not make *my* music, I am simply the radio receiver by which vibrations are intercepted. I am not asking you, the performer, to become a composer in the old sense . . . I'm doing this for you, . . . I'm switching you on as a receiver. Whether you sound good or not is up to you.'

The other texts define particular fields of awareness which are recognizably descriptive of processes in his previous music. Polarities abound: think large, think small; reconcile the two, reconcile both with the dimensions of human experience. Think duration, think communication, think reconciliation, think nasty, think virtuous. Most provocative of all is the text *Es*, which counsels the musicians to:

Think NOTHING

Wait until it is absolutely still within you

When you have attained this

begin to play

As soon as you start to think, stop

and try to reattain

the state of NON–THINKING

Then continue playing

'Not only the music critics, but intellectuals in general were thinking that I had become a dangerous influence.'[7] Nevertheless, this particular text has inspired a remarkable consistency of intuition in performance:

I have compared numbers of different performances of the same texts, and have found that they often share very similar characteristics. All the different versions of *It* have started with very brief, short, sound actions; then gradually you get here and there a longer sound, which stops as soon as another sound starts, which shows that sounds are cutting off each other. Later in all the versions there is a gradual superimposition of sustained sounds: you have one musician playing, then another starts playing a sound or certain pattern, and the first is able to keep going. Then it builds very quickly, in every version I have heard: all of a sudden there is a situation reached where they are obviously taken all together by something that is in the air, . . . and then very dense structures come about. These last for some time, until at some point one of the musicians plays a sound that goes out of context: then abruptly there are

[7] Ibid. 120.

long silences. After that, they try to recapture what they were doing before, but it doesn't work any more.[8]

These pieces are studies: their value is as great as any technical set of studies, or any other meditative regime employed by performance artists. Stockhausen speaks in this context of training the mind in order to prolong the moment of intuition indefinitely. It has been his experience that intuitions, sudden flashes of inspiration, can produce the most extraordinary and transcendental musical images. Film actors have long practised meditation as a means of getting into the mind of a character so completely that it will be revealed in action and in close-up without words, and even without conscious effort of expression. It goes more or less without saying that Stockhausen's intuitive pieces ought to be practised in conjunction with recording and listening.

Für kommende Zeiten

1968–70: *For times to come.*

Seventeen texts for intuitive music: *Übereinstimmung* (Unanimity), *Verlängerung* (Elongation), *Verkürzung* (Shortening), *Über die Grenze* (Across the boundary), *Kommunikation* (Communication), *Ausserhalb* (Outside), *Innerhalb* (Inside), *Anhalt* (Halt), *Schwingung* (Vibration), *Spektren* (Spectra), *Wellen* (Waves), *Zugvogel* (Bird of Passage), *Vorahnung* (Presentiment), *Japan*, *Wach* (Awake), *Ceylon*, *Intervall* (Interval).

For ensemble, instruments unspecified.

Durations unspecified.

Stockhausen wrote several more texts during 1968—his composition seminar at Darmstadt that year studied the *Aus den sieben Tagen* texts—and these, together with others written at various times on his travels between then and July 1970, make up a second collection entitled *For times to come.* By and large these texts display little of the emotional tension of the earlier sequence. As his self-confidence returns, so the pathetic tone diminishes and his thoughts take on a more practical character:

Waves

Overtake the others
Hold the lead
Allow yourself to be overtaken
Less often

[8] Ibid. 120–1.

Across the Boundary calls for a performer to impersonate 'a Humorous Master-Interpreter', offering intriguing scope for magical virtuosity (and, on a time-scale of at least 'one earth-hour', prodigious comic talent). While some texts, such as *Harmony*, *Waves*, *Prolongation*, and *Shortening* relate directly to the earlier text pieces, being concerned with specific perceptions, others (*Ceylon*, *Japan*) are tone images, and one, *Interval*, hovers on the borderline between high ritual and comedy.

II *Radiophony*

RADIOPHONIC imagery features strongly in the electronic and instrumental compositions of the late sixties. From being an incidental by-product of electronic transformation of live instrumental sound in *Mixtur* and *Mikrophonie II*, the poetry of radio gradually asserts itself in works directly imitating a radio environment. The formal and aesthetic implications of short-wave are interesting. The totality of information broadcast at any one time is structured in layers of frequency bands; some channels of sound are occupied by noise, some by speech, others by music of various kinds. Some broadcasts are weak and distant, others strong and near. Many are interrupted or occluded by rhythmic or harmonic distortion. When a listener tunes across the frequency range, the different programmes are revealed individually, with occasionally more than one superimposed. The time perceptions a listener brings to radio are altered: when tuning from one channel to another, one's sense of before and after is greatly attenuated, events being perceived as virtually simultaneous, although heard non-simultaneously. The analogy with moment-form is useful.

Radio imagery has its own tonal laws, based on noise and signal tensions rather than dissonance and harmony. In between the extremes of unmodulated signal and noise can be found a range of mixtures, distortions, filter effects, and modulations. Even silence has a new meaning: not simply the absence of music, because sound can still be heard in such cases (hence the concept of the 'negative band' of *Plus–Minus*), and not loss of channel (since the music does not necessarily cease but simply passes out of hearing). Silence in a radiophonic sense, a real absence of *sound*, means a total loss of transmission, which is a perceptual metaphor for loss of hearing—a perceptual loss. 'The longest silences I have used in my pieces are up to a minute in length. A radio broadcast would be switched off if that happened, because the engineers are instructed that when a silence is longer than fifteen seconds they have to switch off because something is wrong with the equipment.'[1] In a radio context, such as a radio play about radio communication, these same tonal laws have also established conventional sentimental associations, related to the emotions of separation and communication across long distances and in adverse conditions.

---

[1] Karlheinz Stockhausen and Robin Maconie, *Stockhausen on Music* (London, 1989), p. 24.

Stop

1965: For orchestra divided into 6 tonally characterized mixed groups of similar size.
Duration 15'.

Devised as a further exercise for his 1965 composition class of the Cologne New Music Courses, this is a simple composition designed to test a number of basic expressive and notational requirements for the new aesthetic. The division of an orchestra into groups of clearly distinguishable timbre is fundamental to the idea of programme layers occupying different frequency bands. Stockhausen is still very wary of using intelligible material, i.e. music in any conventional idiom, at this stage, so the efforts of the different groups are largely directed toward the production of coloured and modulated noises, out of which harmonic and very occasional melodic signals may briefly emerge (Ex. 74).

In addition to monitoring the production, distribution in time, and dynamic and rhythmic modulation of serially permutated noise types, the conductor has a special responsibility for cross-fading between successive moments (= channels). Changes vary from instantaneous to hazy, and there are occasional encroachments of new materials while others continue to be heard. Such a role for the conductor is more like sound-mixing at a control desk than beating time; we have already seen it operating in *Mixtur*, and *Stop* takes the development a stage further.

Telemusik

1966: *Telemusic*.
Electronic music.
Duration 17' 30".

Telemusik is a purely electronic piece: small, polished, beautifully precise, standing in jewel-like contrast to the generally sombre background of Stockhausen's music in the mid-sixties. Realized remarkably quickly in the electronic music studio of NHK Tokyo during the first quarter of 1966, it unites the sounds of classical Japanese music and pre-recorded ceremonial music from other ancient cultures with structurally similar idioms from his personal repertoire. The unambiguous message is of a hidden unity of world musical traditions which may be demonstrably integrated through the medium of the composer and electronic sound processes.

176

Ex. 74

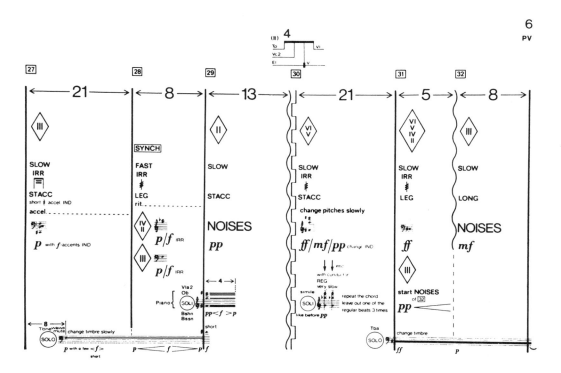

Stop, 'Paris version'. The transitions between successive instrumental textures are as significant as the textures themselves, against which isolated tones and chords are heard. Roman numerals in lozenges refer to contrasting instrumental combinations; wavy lines to degrees of blending of adjacent textures.

© Universal Edition AG Wien.

Formally, the composition is episodic, a sequence of 32 musical moments, their durations proportioned according to Fibonacci between 13 and 144 seconds. Each moment was designed to be realized in a single day's work, and the final order of moments, with one minor exception (track I of 24 and 25), follows the order of composition. The speed of working and consequent simplicity of musical gesture lend a freshness and immediacy to the music, aided in turn by the brighter sheen of the Japanese sound. Technically, the work uses an advanced 6-channel tape recorder, with the possibility of track-to-track recopying to a maximum of five separate channels mixed down to the sixth. On this machine material copied from one track to another is delayed by c 0.3 second, representing the time during which the tape travels between replay and record heads. This characteristic leads to some interesting discoveries, later to be exploited in *Hymnen*. In addition, he had the use of a special linear amplitude modulator, one which imposes the *amplitude* envelope of input signal A upon the *sound* of second input B: the output is a mix of A unmodulated and the amplitude-modulated B signal which resembles its acoustic shadow. Standard ring modulation and a tape recorder of continuously variable speed add to the repertoire of transformational possibilities.

Stockhausen's formal vocabulary begins with attack and resonance characteristics, resuming the percussion-orientated researches of *Studie II*, and also further developing his investigations of the possibilities of ring modulation. *Telemusik* continues and refines the procedures employed in *Mixtur* and *Mikrophonie II* for generating and mediating between timbres which include pre formed elements of speech and music. Stockhausen uses the opportunity to exploit, in effect to make punning allusions to, resemblances between his ready-made folk material and strictly technical acoustic processes. Wailing temple chanting at 22, for instance, is compared to the oscillatory timbre distortion of a vibrating gong, and at 9 (Ex. 75) the entry of a fragment of Hungarian folk-music is geared to enmesh with an accelerating beat-interference pattern produced by two slowly diverging ring-modulated sine waves (itself an electronic shadow of the *gagaku* drum *mokugyo*).

Each moment is announced by the sound of a Japanese ceremonial drum or gong: dry-sounding *bokusho* or *taku* beats for shorter sections, ringing *rin* or *keisu* strokes for longer moments, with the characteristic accelerating beat pattern of the *mokugyo* drum injecting dynamic relief from time to time. Each initial stroke marks a time change, sounding the divisions, and signalling the onset of a new process of intermodulation or style of resonance. Allusions to radio can be heard from the beginning: at 2 ordered frequency strata are progressively cross-modulated into a tangle sounding like random tuning, a scene-setting gesture comparable with *Hymnen* 'Region I'; later at 5 African folk-music is heard fading in and out like a distant radio broadcast. Certain formal aspects of *Telemusik* recall processes in *Mixtur*, for instance passages of compression and attenuation of statistical point complexes, or the fact that percussion in both works perform a similar role. The impulse-like character of much of the work's percussive material also refers back on occasion to *Kontakte*: for instance, the famous transformation of pitch into rhythm at 17′ 0.5″, the long study of reverberation thereafter, and the 'splitting of the sound' episode, recalled here at 19. Other parts seem temperamentally very close to *Adieu*: long stretches of the latter work appear to draw on *Telemusik*'s ritual ululations.

Low and high frequency extremes are more noticeable in *Telemusik* than in Stockhausen's Cologne electronic works. The Cologne sound is dense and solid, whereas the Japan sound is more transparent, interiorized, and enveloping. An example is the hypnotically evocative study in irregular heartbeats at 11, followed in 12 by a sequence where the copied sound is actually pulled by hand past the record head (a sound with extremely potent physical associations). Then, too, there is the extraordinary ascent heavenward at 15, where twelve layers of material taken from earlier sections soar upward one by one to merge into a hissing chroma of sound at

Ex. 75

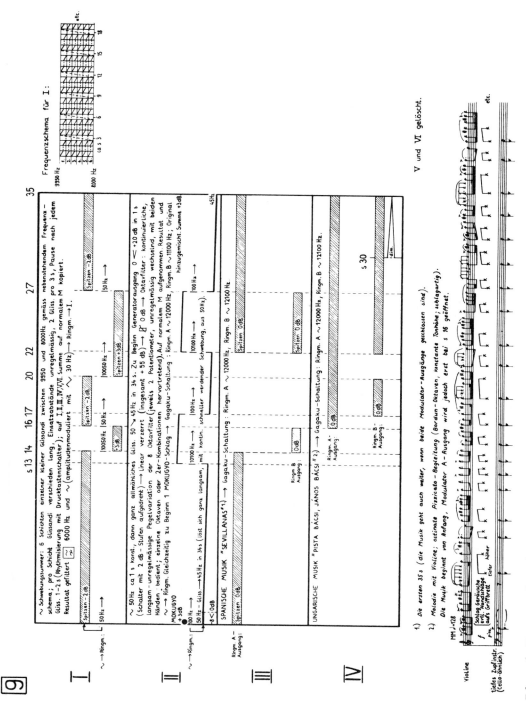

Telemusik. At 9 a recording of a Hungarian folk-dance (notated below the electronic stave) combines with an electronic beat pattern produced by the interaction of modulating sine frequencies in I and II.

Ex. 76

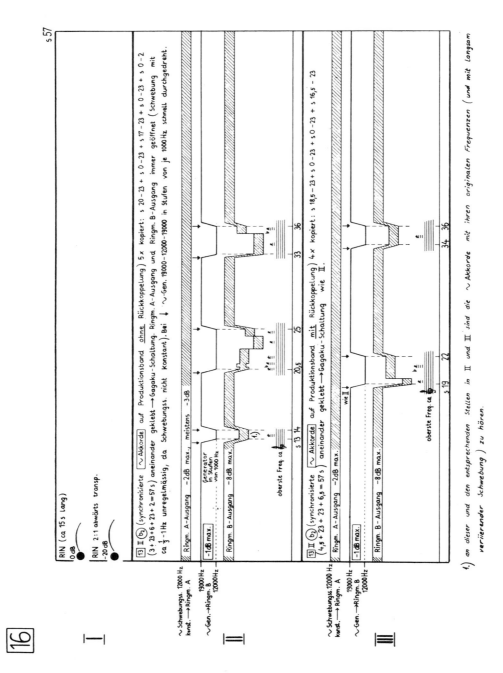

Telemusik.

the upper limit of audibility, followed in 16 by a twilight sequence in which tiny arpeggiate figures descend like fingers of St Elmo's fire, and then retreat again over the top of awareness (Ex. 76). At 29 a classic recapitulation of the four interlocutory percussion is heard as a series of formal exchanges; then a long (144-second) meditation on the sound of temple bells concludes with a rush of upward glissandi like a flock of birds taking flight (reminiscent of *Kontakte*) and the triumphant 'Yoho!' cry of a Noh percussionist.

Stockhausen has described his stay in Tokyo between January and March 1966 as a time of excitement and elation. He identified very readily with the formality of Japanese life and culture, their greatly expanded awareness of time (compared to European cultures today), encompassing very slow and very fast actions often in the same context (as in sumo wrestling), and their rightness of timing as well (as in the tea ceremony). *Telemusik* reflects that elation, and retains even today the sense of heightened perceptions of that initial encounter.

Adieu

1966: for wind quintet (flute, oboe, clarinet, horn, bassoon).
Duration 11–15′.

For this memorial piece, to the memory of a young musician killed in a motor accident, Stockhausen returns to the imagery of transition and obliteration of *Stop*. The work is given added sharpness by his incorporation of glimpses of tonal music, which happen to be final cadences, but played with a delicacy and lightness which belies their symbolic meaning (Ex. 77). Indeed, all but the last cadence are themselves interrupted by music which appears to represent a timeless harmonic limbo, static textured chords of considerable astringency, distorted harmonic counterparts perhaps of the noises of the earlier orchestral study. Music flowing along horizontally is suddenly invaded or arrested by vertical sound complexes which convey a sense of perpetual present, representing death as the negation of movement.

Painstakingly arranged right-angle intersections belong to the expressive poetry of Mondrian's paintings, a retrospective of which Stockhausen visited while pondering the commission for a wind quintet. The example of Mondrian also helped to persuade him that such a composition should not inevitably have to involve him in a long period of concentrated work. In fact *Adieu* was composed in a weekend burst of activity. The structural outline is based on four principal sections of 144 time units. Each is introduced by an interrupted tonal cadence. The first section is divided

Ex. 77

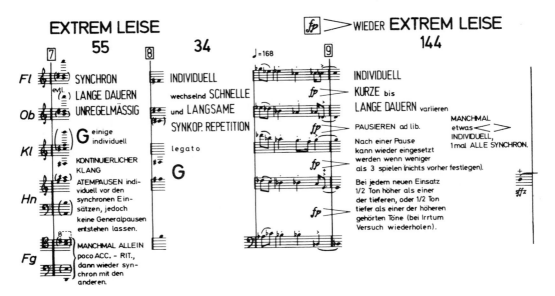

Adieu, showing the tonal cadence leading to the third major subsection at 9. There is some procedural similarity to *Stop*, in that the element of drama resides in the transitions between 'timeless' block textures, which after 9 begin to succeed one another very rapidly.

© Universal Edition AG Wien.

into 2 proportioned subsections, the second into 6, the third remains undivided, and the fourth breaks down into a remarkable 22 subdivisions. Indeed, so rapidly do synchronized changes succeed one another in the fourth section that it becomes a problem for players to do so without reintroducing a sense of momentum when the image is rather based on the 'chaotic' metaphor of random tuning between stations, as if to erase even the image of timelessness of those interminable tone mixtures:

The music looks simple enough on paper, but I found out in 1969, rehearsing it myself for the first time in Paris, how difficult the work actually is. The dynamic balance between the instruments, free glissandi around a pitch, synchronized groups and fairly frequent fast changes of playing technique, require an ensemble in complete understanding and agreement.[2]

A third ingredient is silence. Silent fermatas of unspecified duration regroup the smaller divisions of the piece into larger structural units (Fig. 4). Each 'General Pause' occupies the place of the last element of a symmetrical formation, and this gives it a nominal duration (which is not to say that it should be counted for that

---

[2] Karlheinz Stockhausen, *Texte zur Musik*, iii (Cologne, 1971), p. 93.

Fig. 4.

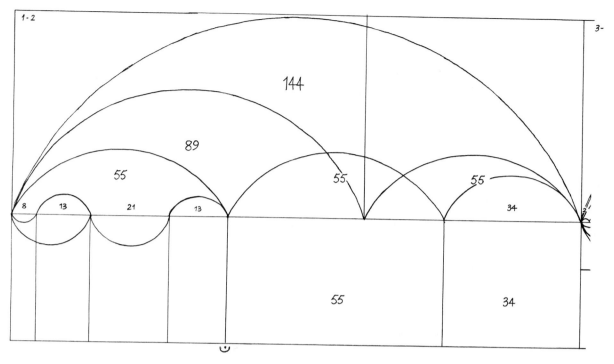

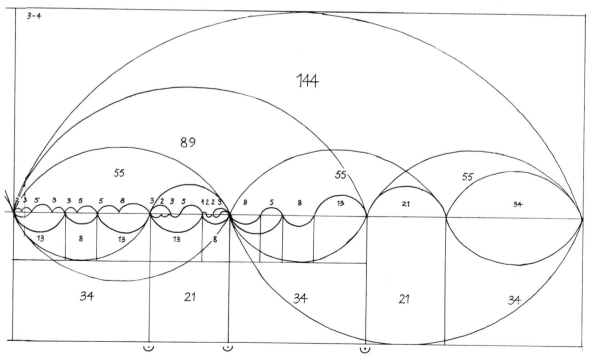

length, but that the symmetry of the larger formation will be influenced by the performers' intuitive estimate of its length). At 6 the missing proportion is as in brackets 8-13-21-13-[9]; at 17 the pattern is 2-3-5-(3+3)-(5+5)-(8+[8]); the 'sehr lang' after 25 connects with the succeeding group as [13]-8-5-8-13; while the fermata at 29, together with the four pauses of varying length which break into the closing cadence, may be interpreted as a descending series of silence durations (8-5-3-2-1) edited into the last section of a rising series of music durations (5-8-13-21-34).

Adieu belongs to the collection of inward-focusing chamber works which also include *Mikrophonie II* and *Stimmung*. The music asks to be amplified, being written effectively for a 'dead' acoustic and with the kind of subtle inner tonal interactions that amplification ideally reveals.

Hymnen

1966–7: *Anthems*, electronic and concrete music in four 'Regions'.
Duration 113'.

Hymnen mit Solisten

1966–7: *Hymnen with soloists*.
Duration 125'.

IIIe Region der Hymnen

1969: *Third Region of Hymnen with Orchestra*.
4. 4. 4. 4. 8; 4. 4. 2; strings 10. 10. 10. 5. 5. Alternatively, triple or duple winds with correspondingly fewer strings.
Duration 38'.

A vast, contradictory work, an enormous tapestry of national anthems, *Hymnen* is Stockhausen's grandest electronic composition in scale, if not in scope. Realized in the Cologne Radio electronic studio in 1966 and 1967, it marks the composer's long-delayed acknowledgement of familiar musical idioms as valid material, not simply as radiophonic illustration, but for full-blown metamusical anamorphosis. The electronic music at present consists of four regions having a combined duration of about 113 minutes. This, however, represents only a fraction of the potential of the material, only about forty of the 137 national anthems originally collected being used. While the version for tape alone is a fully autonomous work (the composer invites artistic collaboration in its visual realization, and is rash enough to permit it to be edited to any such requirement), the true destiny of the tape is almost certainly as a continuous tape memory for structured instrumental imitation, in the manner of his original intention for *Kontakte*. The tape has the same monumentality as *Carré*, evoking visions of limitless spaces, both empty and populated. The anthems are supplemented by other recorded material of people and animals: crowds in the market-place, cheering scenes of pageantry, the noise of excited football crowds, together with bird sounds (real and synthesized) and farmyard noises. It could be music expressly designed for Stockhausen's 'new halls for meditative listening', first proposed at the time of *Gruppen*.[3]

Each region of *Hymnen* has several centres, usually selected anthems, which act as points of reference and convergence for demonstrating the transformational processes employed. The first region, dedicated to Boulez, has two centres, the *Internationale* and *La Marseillaise*. It begins with a babel of short-wave (Ex. 78) and gradually resolves into a rigid and orderly form (perhaps an interpretation of Boulez'

Ex. 78

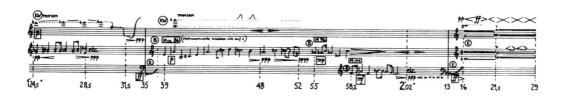

Hymnen: Region I. No attempt is made to indicate the full texture of the tape music, which here is a babel of short-wave; instead essential cues and timings are given. Anthems are indicated by their melodies or top voices: violent 'tearing' sounds suggesting tape being pulled past the playback head by hand, are indicated at 1' 08", 1' 35", and 2' 13".

© Universal Edition AG Wien.

[3] Id., 'Music in Space', *Die Reihe* (English Edition), 5 (1961), 67–82.

citation of Artaud: 'considérer le délire, et, oui, l'organiser').[4] The radiophonic introduction actually sounds like the mixture of signals heard in a Cologne taxi-cab.

The second region, dedicated to Henri Pousseur, has four centres: the West German anthem, a composite of African national hymns, alternating with (and no doubt influenced by) the beginning of the Russian anthem, and fourthly an 'individual centre' which cuts through the electronic music to reveal a discussion between Stockhausen and his assistant David Johnson about whether or not the Horst Wessel Song ought to be incorporated. Stockhausen is practising a moment of interpolated commentary responding to the misgivings of the director of Cologne Radio, Otto Tomek: 'Otto Tomek said . . . But . . . it is only a memory . . .'. The right inflection is hard to find; Johnson reveals that the tape is still running: 'Ach, so!' says Stockhausen, and one can hear the smile breaking. In this peeling away of time layers the process of synthesis is laid bare, and in Stockhausen's words 'present, past, and ulterior past all become simultaneous'.[5]

The third region is dedicated to Cage. Its centres are the Russian anthem, this time standing alone, the American anthem, and the Spanish anthem. The Russian anthem is unique in being composed of electronic tones, and is heard on a vastly distended time-scale, 'the greatest harmonic and rhythmic expansion of anything I have composed to date'.[6] In contrast to the bare grandeur of the Russian anthem, the American anthem attracts round itself a colourful, cosmopolitan medley of national and festive pieces, affectionate and descriptive. The third centre, the Spanish anthem, is a highly edited composite subjected to progressively greater acceleration, out of which the anthem emerges through a shift of focus, as a figure suddenly coalesces out of elements of a Dali landscape. Region IV, dedicated to Berio, is in many ways the most remote in character; Stockhausen recounts how it was influenced by events in his personal life.[7]

As early as 1964 he was working on an idea of a work for three pianos and tape based on anthem material. The pianos would be situated along three sides of an auditorium, with the tape operator on the fourth side. Following the precedent of *Kontakte*, it is reasonable to suppose that the role of the three pianists was intended to be to comment on and musically connect different anthems, as the earlier work makes transitions between different timbres, in a symbolic gesture of political reconciliation. However, there is a practical relevance in using national anthems, and that is to illustrate the new transformation procedures he has developed in an idiom more immediately intelligible to both players and audiences. A piece to be performed all over the world would logically need local signposting for as many countries as possible.

In addition to the anthems themselves, there are allusions to processes of musical forming which can be identified with *Hymnen*'s four dedicatees. The Boulez image of

---

[4] Pierre Boulez, 'Son et verbe', in *Relevés d'apprenti* (Paris, 1966), p. 62.
[5] Stockhausen, op. cit. 96.   [6] Stockhausen, op. cit. 97.
[7] Jonathan Cott, *Stockhausen: Conversations with the Composer* (London, 1974), pp. 142–4.

sublime delirium is one: the music also comments indirectly on Boulez' preoccupation with Mallarmé's multidimensional poetry and on Berio's with James Joyce, whose recreation of a universal oral culture resonant with cross-cultural references and multilingual wordplay is in many ways a literary equivalent of *Hymnen*. Cage is naturally identifiable with the Third Region's 'fleeting collages and pluralistic mixtures'.

The character of the Croupier, played by the composer himself, belongs in the same tradition of cabaret as the Ringmaster of Berg's *Lulu*, the Joker of Stravinsky's *Jeu de Cartes*—itself a masterpiece of musical montage with chance as a dramatic ingredient—but refers especially to the Mephistophelian figure of the stage manager in Henri Pousseur's opera *Votre Faust*, who invites the audience to vote at critical moments on the fate of the composer-hero Faust, whose name is also Henri (Heinrich). The very first interpolation by Stockhausen as croupier, in Region I at 4′ 33.5″, is transcribed in the score with the words 'Faîtes votre jeux, messieurs-dames, s'il vois plaît', an unaccountable solecism unless a cross-reference between 'votre jeu'—the game of chance—and *Votre Faust* were the reason behind it. (Even if it is a miscopying of the grammatically correct 'votre jeu', the call still departs from the normal plural form 'Faîtes vos jeux'.) The spoken 'Rouge, rouge' meditation on the reds of the Communist world is similar to Pousseur's litany on the word 'Hélas!' in his electronic composition *Électre*, and there is a certain procedural resemblance between Stockhausen's manner of building anthems into a continuous melodic stream and the Belgian composer's *Le Tarot d'Henri*, a one-movement history of European music, played as a piano soliliquy by the composer-hero Faust at a major turning-point of the opera.

There is a further underlying affinity between *Hymnen*'s stream-of-consciousness imagery and literary allusions, and Stockhausen's functional intentions for the electronic tape in relation to live performers. Beneath the surface of simulated radio, complete with morse, static, intermodulations, and sideband distortions, is an information flow as elusive and immaterial as thought itself. Spontaneous creation plays as much a part in the electronic music as in the intuitive responses of the performers in the version with soloists: like *Telemusik*, *Hymnen* was an exercise in composing electronic music at speed. For a work of such monumental proportions, it made an extraordinarily rapid gestation compared with the electronic compositions of the previous decade. Naturally the use of pre-recorded material is calculated to save preparation time, but it also places correspondingly greater reliance on the quality of mixing and editing. The music has to transcend the superficial banalities of the national anthems themselves, limited resources for signal transformation, and old-fashioned turntable speed and pitch transposition. Out of the spontaneity of invention that comes with composing at speed comes the sort of emotional charge that may inspire soloists to heights of intuition:

[The soloists] comment freely on what they hear on tape, using a score which contains a transcription of the tape. Actually this freedom is relative, because I've rehearsed the work quite a lot with musicians I've worked with over a number of years. So it is a matter of very precise mutual agreement . . . What you have to do today is develop a technique of getting in touch with the intuitive, whenever you want and for as long as you want.[8]

In the *Third Region of Hymnen with Orchestra* quite a different procedure is adopted. Stockhausen has designed a score and some simple transformational notations which are capable of being understood and acted upon by orchestral musicians unused to intuitive performance and even sceptical of what they are being asked to do. These simple processes, by virtue of superior numbers, are calculated to generate large-scale impressionistic effects emitted at a tangent to the electronic flow of events. Sometimes the texture consists of showers of lines or points thrown off the surface of the tape, like sparks from a grindstone; at other times the texture is denser and unrolls more continuously. The instruments act individually or in groups, and may simply prolong selected notes or figures from the anthems on tape or develop them—again singly or collectively—in shape, pitch, or complexity (Ex. 79). The orchestral music as a whole is a succession of contrasting episodes cut to the proportions of the electronic matrix and completely dependent on it as a source of starting material. The orchestra, in short, acts as a resonating device, or group of devices, to the tape.

Stockhausen's orchestra is interesting in that he includes no fixed-pitch keyboard instruments, nor any percussion instruments of indefinite pitch. Winds, brass, and strings are all expected to be able to adjust their tuning to follow the microtonal shifts of the taped music. The orchestral music starts at the third centre of Region II, following the spoken words 'Wir können noch eine Dimension tiefer gehen' ('We can go still one dimension deeper'). It begins with a composite of African anthems, imitated first discreetly, then more assertively by the orchestra. As the Russian anthem comes into the foreground, its metallic harmonies are reflected by the orchestra in constantly changing instrumental timbres, and quasi-short-wave effects break surface at sporadic intervals.

At 17 there is a moment of surface pointillism against a background of sustained harmonies that is strikingly reminiscent of *Spiel* or *Punkte 1952*, with the difference that the 'points' are now melodic fragments which repeat over and over, gradually disintegrating in the general flux. At 7′ 39″ an upward surge in the tape is accompanied by a three-part glissando of string harmonics in the first of several appearances of an image of radio static and change of tuning. In the version for tape alone, this point marks the end of Region II and a short intermission for the tape to be changed. When the tape resumes, the music surges downward to 'tune in' again to the Russian anthem. In the version with orchestra this gap between the two Regions is spanned by the orchestra alone in a five-minute process entitled the 'Russian bridge'.

[8] Karlheinz Stockhausen, 'Spiritual Dimensions', Interview with Peter Heyworth, *Music and Musicians*, 19. (1971), 32.

Ex. 79

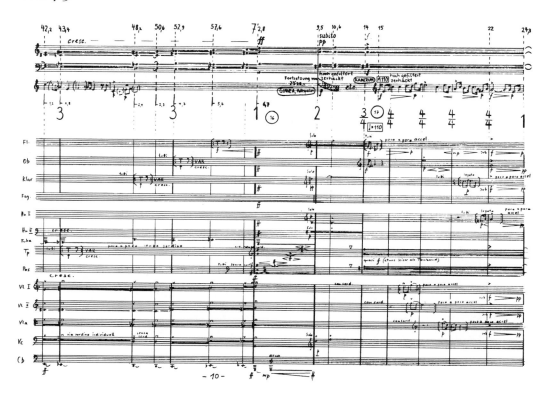

Third Region of Hymnen with Orchestra. The players listen to the tape, and imitate what they hear. The symbol T means 'pick out a tone and repeat it' (woodwinds, trumpets). Strings, then brass take turns to reinforce the tape harmonies. At 17 muted strings repeat notated fragments of the Cameroon anthem.

© Universal Edition AG Wien.

This section (Ex. 80) consists of three overlapping processes: (1) a sustained, slowly expanding chord played by muted strings, leading from the pitches of the Russian anthem; (2) repetitions of these same pitches at irregular intervals by woodwind and brass, gradually diverging individually in pitch and repetition frequency to give the effect of a halo of sound; and (3) fragments of melody, played by woodwinds and brass in mixed pairs, uniting the Russian anthem and the Internationale. The string glissando 'bridge' eventually reconverges on the electronic pitches of the beginning of Region III. As the anthems return the orchestra reverts to an imitative role. As the music on tape becomes increasingly complex, so the orchestra's becomes more and more diverse and perhaps intentionally Ivesian.

At the second transition (13′ 24″) the orchestra resumes its *Adieu*-like commentary. Gunfire clusters punctuating the electronic continuum at 14′ 53″ are answered

Ex. 80

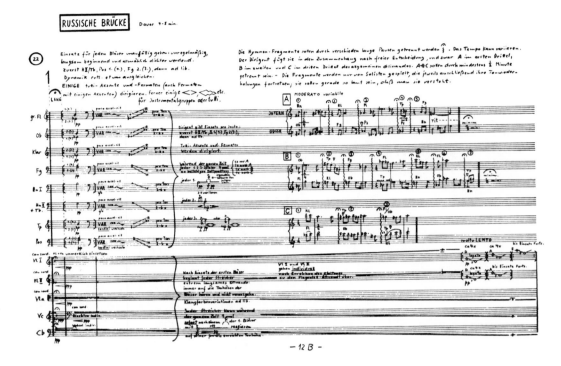

Third Region of Hymnen with Orchestra: the 'Russian Bridge'.
© Universal Edition AG Wien.

by instruments in what is perhaps the score's most rhythmically concerted and aggressive passage. A new type of mimicry appears at 101, where the strings imitate the recorded guitar strumming of the Spanish introduction with clattering *col legno battuto* playing, and the winds pick out melody elements and transpose them freely to different octave registers. The Daliesque composite anthem appearing at 19' 15" gives rise to another *Adieu*-like complex of overlapping responses by winds in groups, then later by ostinato figures against a sustained harmonic background of a immense chord which rises in the bass, expands into the treble at 20' 58", and relapses into the bass again as a 3-part *organum*. Following a fortissimo climax, the orchestra begins to weaken from 137, and gradually the tape moves into the foreground, while low strings sustain an open fifth and high strings continue to add harmonic coloration up to and beyond the tape fade at 23' 40".

The fourth Region has two centres, the Swiss anthem and a Stockhausen 'hymn associated with the realm of *Hymunion in Harmondie unter Pluramon*, which is the longest and most penetrating of them all: the final chord of the Swiss anthem is shaped into a calmly pulsating bass ostinato, over which are heaped gigantic blocks, surfaces and highways, in whose clefts the calling of names, with their many echoes, is heard'.[9] This unearthly sound vision is bathed in a continuous downward glissando cluster of extraordinary richness and radiance, like a jet aircraft perpetually passing overhead. (Psychologists may recognize it as an example of the Shepard illusion, albeit in descending rather than ascending form).[10] This sound eventually yields to that of slow, steady breathing, with which the region and the work ends. Here, as too in the deliberately informal treatment of his electronic material, Stockhausen detaches himself from the programmatic implications of universal harmony. *Hymnen* is neither a manifesto nor a latter-day 'Choral' Symphony; the music does not moralize. Rather it meditates, and it meditates ultimately alone. The composer draws the music round him like a shroud until all that is left is that sound of amplified breathing, perhaps an image of man the explorer, Cortez as astronaut, silent and alone at the moment of encounter with a new world.

During 1968 Stockhausen was invited to propose an auditorium as part of West Germany's contribution to the Osaka World Fair Expo '70. The project came to act as a point of convergence for his researches in live electronic, intuitive, and radiophonic music during the sixties. With *Kurzwellen* in particular, he attempted along with his Group Stockhausen players to develop the transformational processes of *Hymnen mit Solisten* in a consistently structured way. At the same time, he was also engaged with technical advisers in the development of the projected auditorium, and of two new pieces of technical equipment: a 'sound mill' panoramic potentiometer for rotating an output through a speaker array, on the same basic principles as a joystick, but more massive and more complicated; and an improved form of ring modulation to give a cleaner output: the Modul 69A and 69B. The earlier 69A is heard in the version of *Kurzwellen* with prepared tapes of Beethoven material. The 69B circuit incorporates a signal compresser, filter, and amplitude follower (after the Tokyo model used in *Telemusik*) with the result that second and third harmonic distortion is suppressed and the high-frequency halo attenuated.[11]

As the names indicate, the development work for this new apparatus took place in 1969, and Stockhausen's preparation of the tapes for *Kurzwellen mit Beethoven* involved some experimentation in the modulation of piano timbre. A new composition for two pianos was already taking shape in his mind; a year later, after the Osaka experience of daily performances of intuitive music, he was seized with an urge to compose a fully determinate work once more. Abandoning a project for two pianists, *Vision*, in which the players signal the note configurations they are to play in dumb show, so an audience may hear them better having seen them visually

[9] Id., *Texte zur Musik*, iii, p. 97.
[10] John R. Pierce, *The Science of Musical Sound* (New York, 1983), p. 194.
[11] Karlheinz Stockhausen, 'Die Zunkunft der elektroakustischen Apparaturen in der Musik', *Musik und Bildung*, (1974), 412.

expressed (an idea which returns in amplified guise in *Inori*), he came back to the earlier plan for a music germinated from a single formula. The piano timbre, however, is modulated with sine tones using the Modul 69B device, which adds a radiophonic dimension to the composition, both in terms of the range of 'distancing' distortions which colour the piano timbre, and also in the music-theatre sense that the players each have to 'tune' a sine-wave generator to different frequencies as though to receive the music on different wavelengths.

Mantra

1970.

For two pianists, short-wave radio receivers (or tape-recorded short-wave sounds), Modul B modulation circuits. Chinese woodblocks, and antique cymbals. An assistant is required for sound projection.

Duration 65'.

This is a masterpiece. It defines Stockhausen's musical aims for the seventies as surely as *Mikrophonie I* for the previous decade. In his great work for solo tam-tam Stockhausen addressed himself to the audio-tactile qualities of sound, and to the achievement of exactly defined musical ends by flexible and collaborative means. With *Mantra* the polarity is abruptly reversed. The music is synthetic rather than analytic, active not passive, and detached rather than involved. There is coolness and reserve implied in the composer's return to the neutral sonority of the piano, to the world of equal temperament, and to a rigorously conventional notation which uses verbal indications for tempi and few excursions into modern 'irrational' values. The pay-off, however, is music of action and high spirits which by some marvellous alchemy succeeds in 'tuning in' to a succession of different classical and modern idioms.

The mantra, or basic formula, is a melody based on the series A, B, G♯, E, F, D, G, E♭, D♭, C, B♭, G♭, returning to A again. The melody is ornamented, so that each pitch becomes the seed of an expansion process; it is divided in four phrases by rests of different lengths, and is accompanied in the left hand by a form of mirror inversion. At the outset (Ex. 81), one hears the mantra compressed into a fanfare of four chords; following a tremolando on the A, which is the musical compass point on which the whole work turns, it is stated again in open form, but still confined within the space of little more than an octave. The entire work grows from this kernel of rhythm and interval, image and reflection. Woodblock signals, antique-cymbal flourishes, sine-wave tunings, and tremolando ostinati (a rhythmic feature of the

Ex. 81

Mantra. Piano I announces the mantra in full in bars 3–9. At 12 a tremolo statement of the mantra is superimposed on a dotted-rhythm version, derived from the dotted value which forms the rhythmic kernel of the second note of the original mantra. Note the exchange of the tremolo voice between the pianos, which presents the series A–B–A♭ (G♯)–E etc. in expanded form. Antique cymbals announce sections with the same mantra-derived gestures: tremolo A at 2, dotted-rhythm B at 11.

first note of the mantra) all articulate, in their different ways, the original proportions and pitches of the mantra in various expansions. Time expansions range from the entire length of the work to the inner proportions of the smallest mantra statements; pitch expansions range up to half of the piano keyboard (leaving the other half for the mirror image). A Stravinskian passage in dotted rhythms (recalling the neoclassical *Concerto for Two Pianos*) represents a modest expansion; it is followed soon after by a maximum expansion, which not unexpectedly sounds rather like Boulez' *Structures Ia* for two pianos.

Indeed there are many allusions to the Paris of 1952, from Stockhausen's revival of *personnages rythmiques* and permutation squares to the crystalline ideal whereby every aspect of form ought to be derivable from an initial serial configuration, and to the melody-based structures of *Formel*. Stockhausen even reclaims the idea of transforming the piano sound from the limbo to which it was consigned by Cage: 'It is significant', Stockhausen remarked in 1957 apropos the prepared piano, 'that a composer should undertake himself preparation of the sounds for a composition, to some extent composing the timbres along with the music, as far as that may be achieved with instruments already in existence'.[12]

The effect of modulating the piano tone with a sine tone of a particular pitch is to create an electronic tonal polarity centred on the sine tone. Piano notes which are consonant or in simple harmonic relationship with the modulating sine tone are reinforced in pitch; as they diverge from near-consonance to remoter intervals (their dissonance exaggerated by equal temperament) the combination gives rise to increasingly complex sum and difference tones, increasingly metallic and percussive to the ear. Where the modulating sine tone is of medium or high pitch, additional pitch resonances are created; if, however, the modulating tone is set at a very low frequency, the intermodulation takes the form of a regular pulsation agitating the piano sound. Such a passage occurs at 132, where II lowers the sine frequency to 5–7 Hz, and the effect is magical.

Using two pianists, Stockhausen is able to exploit the familiar polarities: differentiation-harmonization, analysis-synthesis, static-dynamic. There is an additional reciprocity in the relationship of each piano part with its electronic modulation: this latter symmetry is beautifully expressed at 110, where a slowly descending scale in II is followed by an equally slow rising scale in I, each accompanied by its modulated mirror image. Stockhausen described working on *Mantra* as 'the happiest composition time I have ever spent in my life'. Time and again the high spirits bubble to the surface, as for example at the Zen-like target practice at 212, an 'insert' arising from the composer's own difficulty in striking notes simultaneously at both extremes of the keyboard. And there is high exultation too at 421, where gigantic chords played by both pianos simultaneously are swept back and forth by sine tones, and intersected consonances leap forth from the sustained resonances.

[12] Id., *Texte zur Musik*, ii (Cologne 1964), p. 147.

Ex. 82

Mantra: part of the presto 'fast résumé'.
© K. Stockhausen.

At the end of the formal exposition of the serially ordained transmutations of the mantra, Stockhausen has added a concentrated reprise (Ex. 82) in which 'all expansions and transformations are gathered, extremely fast, into four layers, gradually condensing into vertical harmonies'.

As a study in temperament and harmonic relationships *Mantra* may be identified, along with *Stimmung* and *Sternklang*, as a work of the composer's 'Helmholtz' phase. Something equivalent to a return to a tonal hierarchy is implied by his use of modulation, and yet if we look at the 'Spiegel' moment in *Mixtur,* or the opening of *Mikrophonie II,* we see the intention to use ring modulation as a means of enhancing tones consonant with the modulating frequency. More significant perhaps is the inauguration of a new period of melody-based composition, and of a new art of melody, more approachable to the public and more confident in itself.

12 *Projections*

Two spatial images dominate Stockhausen's music. One, derived from electronic studio practice, is a continuous, panoramic space within which sound-events are distributed to interact antiphonally, as in *Gesang der Jünglinge*, or move, as in the orchestral compositions *Gruppen* and *Carré*, and in *Kontakte*. Dynamic movement of sounds in space begins in reality with the development of the four-channel 'rotation table' which gives a more realistic impression of movement than electronic pan-potting. Then there is a gap until 1970, when Stockhausen's interest in circular movement of sounds around the listener revives with the development of the dome-shaped Expo '70 pavilion and associated new equipment, in particular the hand-operated rotary potentiometer, the 'sound mill', allowing an operator to spin sounds rapidly in any direction and at any desired angle. Here the shifts in location are accomplished purely electronically and the signal is not subject to the same Doppler and phase shifts perceived when real sound sources actually move in space. In 1977, for the composition of *Sirius* for voices, instruments, and electronic tape, an improved, motorized rotation table was developed, enabling sounds to be rotated and re-recorded on to eight channels at speeds of up to 50 rotations per second.[1] At rotation speeds approaching the reaction time of the auditory nerves, the illusion of rotational motion ceases and the music itself begins to dissociate into harmonic regions concentrated in different locations of the auditorium:

With fourteen or fifteen revolutions per second you still hear the movement circling around you. But suddenly you get an effect like that which you sometimes see in movies—where a chariot wheel, which isn't exactly aligned with the number of frames per second, appears to go backward . . . [The sound] starts dancing completely irregularly in the room—at the left, in front, it's everywhere. It's no longer periodic though the sound produced is revolving around your head. And if you go still faster something extraordinary happens: the sound stands still; it's no longer heard outside of you, you hear completely within your body. You *are* the sound physically.[2]

Since *Sirius*, Stockhausen has composed the *Unsichtbare Chöre* (Invisible Choirs) from

---

[1] Karlheinz Stockhausen, 'Die Zunkunft der elektroakustischen Apparaturen in der Musik', *Musik im Bildung* (1974), 416.
[2] Jonathan Cott, *Stockhausen: Conversations with the Composer* (London, 1974), p. 98.

Donnerstag aus LICHT as a 16-channel tape composition of voices in surround-sound polyphony.

All of these explorations of musical space presuppose a spatial unity with the listener at the centre: musical events and movements are charted and navigated in the same way as celestial bodies in the heavens.

The second spatial image derives from radio, consequently from his radio-inspired compositions of the sixties. According to this concept, space is discontinuous; it arises from the coexistence of musical events which are already distributed and do not a priori interact, though they may signal their isolation musically and make individual efforts at communication. Ideally, to recreate the isolation of musical sources of short-wave radio involves a distribution of players to locations remote from one another in the same building, or out of doors. Such a distribution of sources is no longer experiencable as a unified space, either by players or audience. Even if an intercommunication network is set up, by land-line or satellite link, the perceptual consequence of impoved co-ordination is not continuity of space so much as coincidence of timing.

Among the musical consequences of composing for widely separated players, in addition to the need to incorporate signalling conventions, are a loss of fine co-ordination and the creation of multiple aural perspectives. Because sound does not propagate instantaneously, it follows that where different sources are heard sounding together, those further away are actually chronologically earlier than those from more nearby sources. It also follows that listeners on opposite sides of the performance area will hear polyphonies which are different both in relative dynamic emphasis and in their timing. The conventional criteria of simultaneity no longer apply. For such a composition to work effectively, it must be calculated to work from a multiplicity of possible audience locations, and not just one. If that requirement appears esoteric, we have only to examine the liaisons among different groups of players and singers in, for example, the polychoral compositions of the Gabrielis and Schütz. These works are themselves designed to be performed in spaces so vast that the same variables of perspective and relative time of arrival of music from different sources have to be taken into account.

An early indication of Stockhausen's interest in this new area of spatialized music is found in sketches for an unfinished work for orchestra, *Projektion für Orchester*, dating from 1967. A symphony orchestra is 'layered' into nine mixed groups of 8–10 players. The whole 25-minute work is sketched in short score and a few pages have been fully orchestrated. The music is relatively densely written, and incorporates parallel harmonies in the style of *Trans*. It was Stockhausen's intention to perform the work simultaneously with a filmed performance of the same work, which itself would incorporate a further filmed performance, giving it a simultaneous 'present' and two levels of anterior 'past' tense. To this end the music is designed to allow for differences in relative timing and tempo among the three time layers, and also for the 'perforation' of foreground music to allow the background layers to filter through.

Ensemble

1967.

Collective composition by members of the composition class, Darmstadt International Vacation Courses for New Music.

Duration 4 Hours.

At Darmstadt the same year Stockhausen's composition class collaborated in the production of a multiple environment enitled *Ensemble*. In Stockhausen's words, it was:

an attempt to transform the traditional concert format into something new. We are accustomed to comparing compositions played one after another. In *Ensemble*, 'pieces' by twelve different composers are performed at the same time. . . . These 'pieces' are not perfectly worked out musical objects ('works') but images in sound (produced on tape or by short-wave receiver), with individual rules, forms of action and reaction, and notated 'events', which their composers bring into play in the process of the collective performance. . . . The resulting four-hour process is more than the sum of its 'pieces'; it is a composition of compositions, fluctuating between the total isolation of individual events and the total interdependence of all levels, mediating also between extreme determinacy and unpredictability.[3]

Stockhausen's sketch-plan (Ex. 83)[4] reveals a superordinate time structure within which the component 'pieces' are assigned relative priorities ('Ps' = trombone, 'Fl' = flute, 'Sch' = percussion, etc.). *Mikrophonie I* symbols are intended to 'colour' the interactions of the non-solo performers. During the performance there are eight *Einschübe* (E-moments or 'inserts') which break the continuum and focus all the players on very simple unified procedures (for example, in E3 pianissimo slow chords, in E4 fortissimo periodic rhythms).

The performance took place in a large assembly hall, an open-plan rather than ideally compartmentalized environment. Each player was microphone-linked to one of four mixing desks, and its output sent to a speaker located at a distant or opposite point in the auditorium, superimposing an additional radiophonic dimension on the live sound.

[3] Karlheinz Stockhausen, *Texte zur Musik*, ii (Cologne, 1971), p. 212.
[4] Stockhausen, op. cit. (above, n. 3), p. 215.

Ex. 83

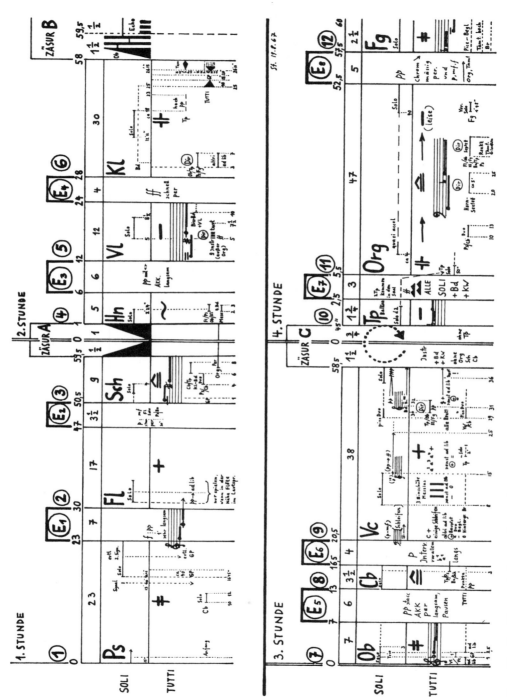

Ensemble: Stockhausen's 'score of scores'.

Musik für ein Haus

1968: *Music for a house*.

Collective composition by members of the composition class, Darmstadt International Vacation Courses for New Music.

Duration 4 hours.

The following year Stockhausen's composition class at Darmstadt sudied the *Aus den sieben Tagen* text pieces, and collaborated on a further multiple-space composition.[5] On this occasion a two-storey hunting lodge with basement was made available as a performance area in which individual players or groups of a collective composition could be relatively isolated one from another. A miniature communications network was set up, allowing players to interact as though via radio, using call-signs. Fourteen players took part, in groups of up to seven at once:

Ideal conditions for the 'House Music' are provided by a cluster of rooms of various sizes on two floors, connected and acoustically isolated by a network of passages. Each listener comes and goes in his own time and is able to change his listening perspective within the house at will. . . . What the instrumentalists play is picked up by microphones in each room and relayed at varying amplification over loudspeakers. The players not only react to one another, but also to the music emanating from the other rooms. In a fifth room ('Klangbox' [in the basement]) may be heard a continuous relay of the music from all four rooms over four separate speakers.[6]

Hinab–Hinauf

1968: *Downward–Upward*.

Audio-visual project for the German Pavilion, Expo '70, Osaka, Japan.

For small ensemble, electronic and concrete music, film and light projection.

Duration 13′ 31″.

This project for the Expo '70 spherical pavilion was intended to provide a model example of the kind of audio-visual presentation Stockhausen envisaged for performance environments of the future. It is clear from his initial specification that visual images were intended to provide a fixed line of evolution to which the

---

[5] Fred Ritzel, '*Musik für ein Haus*', *Darmstädter Beiträge für Neue Musik*, 12 (1970).
[6] Stockhausen, op. cit. (above, n. 3), p. 226.

musicians would respond with intuitive music in calculated parallel or opposing relationship. The music would be able to evolve from performance to performance, gaining in subtlety and refinement throughout the period of the exposition. The concept is very much in the familiar 'Glass Bead Game' mould of mediating between opposites: visual/aural, exalted/debased, sublime/degenerate, spiritual/material:

Beginning with bright, exalted, nameless happenings, a first phase of concerted light, sound and spatial movement leads through a panorama of abstract forms, then technical-objective images, then living-organic forms, then surreal and dreamlike, then fauna and flora, then mineral and organic images through to the unimaginable level of the atoms. In subsequent phases, sound, light and spatial movements diverge more or less from one another, passing independently through the various levels, meeting again from time to time and ultimately coming together in a long, contrapuntal upward movement out of the deepest sphere of decaying and lifeless things, finally reaching the highest attainable level, a region of calm, pure, lasting brightness of sound and light (Ex. 84).[7]

Ex. 84

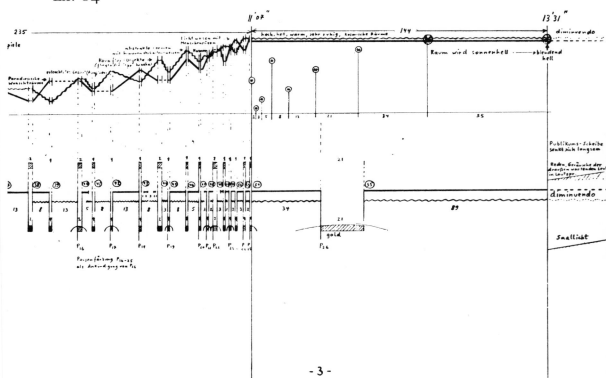

Sketch score for *Hinab–Hinauf*. The ascent to the highest level of enlightenment at 11' 07" incorporates a barely visible reference to 'flying carpets–ha ha!'

[7] Ibid. 155–8.

Dr. K-Sextett

1969.

For sextet (flute, bass clarinet, piano, vibraphone/tubular bells, viola, cello). Duration 3′ 28″.

In January 1969 the London office of Universal Edition requested a number of the firm's house composers to contribute a short chamber piece for performance by the Fires of London ensemble at a birthday concert for the firm's director Dr Alfred Kalmus. Stockhausen's contribution, the Dr. K-Sextett, sketched on the back of the publisher's letter, is a tiny masterpiece: a slow-motion study of a wave in 26 eight-second 'frames' (Ex. 85). The piece's image of a shock wave emitting and reflecting back through itself is caught in the test piece 'Waves' in the collection *Für kommende Zeiten* (q.v.), though the piece antedetates the text by some eighteen months.

Dr. K is a structure of eights: eight voices, eight dynamics, eight divisions of the fundamental time frame, which corresponds to a periodically renewed sample of a continuous process, scanned at a constant speed, like a wave-form on an oscilloscope. (This is essentially the same procedure as he used in the earliest pointillist compositions.) A time frame is articulated as a fixed ritardando beat pattern into which the note content gradually disperses; it eventually reflects back on itself as an accelerando which telescopes inward on itself. However, the pitch collection continues to ripple outward from an original cluster to a chord spanning six octaves, only clicking back to an aggregation of thirds in a final cadential gesture.

By way of adding interest to a fairly austere musical process, and also to give necessary cues to performers in the absence of a conductor, Stockhausen has introduced a number of deviations, certain pitches being prolonged unexpectedly, others agitated by trill or tremolando. The grace-notes in 7, 11, and 18 are identified in the original sketch as 'deliberate mistakes'. The piece belongs in the context of spatial compositions because its time-point displacement process is so clearly a metaphor of spatial movement, and indeed anticipates *Ylem*, another cyclic exposition of expansion and contraction of musical points in which the performers themselves also physically disperse and reconverge.

Fresco

1969: *Wall Sounds* for meditation, for four orchestra groups.

One orchestra is divided by the conductor into four distinctively characterized mixed

Ex. 85

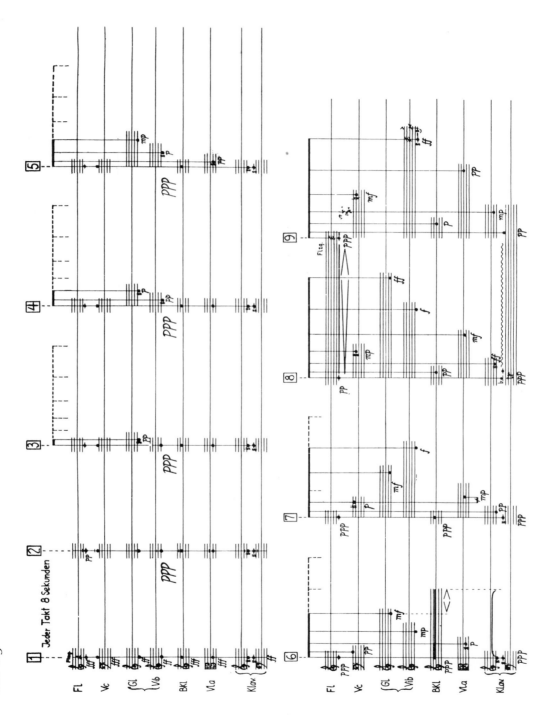

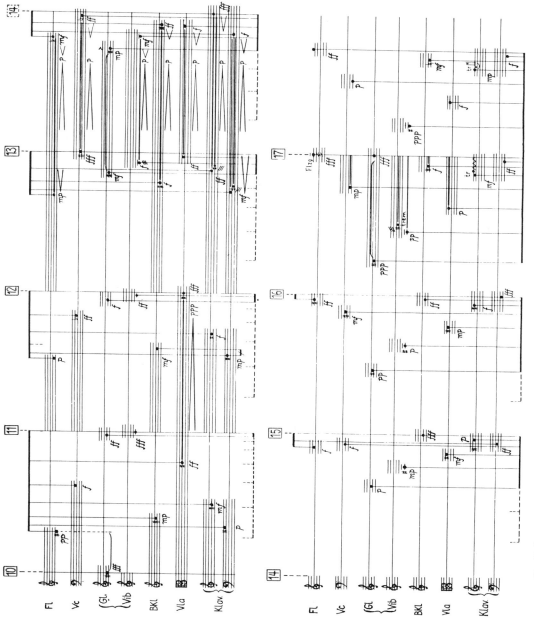

Dr. K-Sextett: score. An initial chord ripples outward from the down beat and from the middle octave. As each note drifts to the edge of its 8-second time frame, it is bounced back.

© Universal Edition (London) Ltd.

Projections

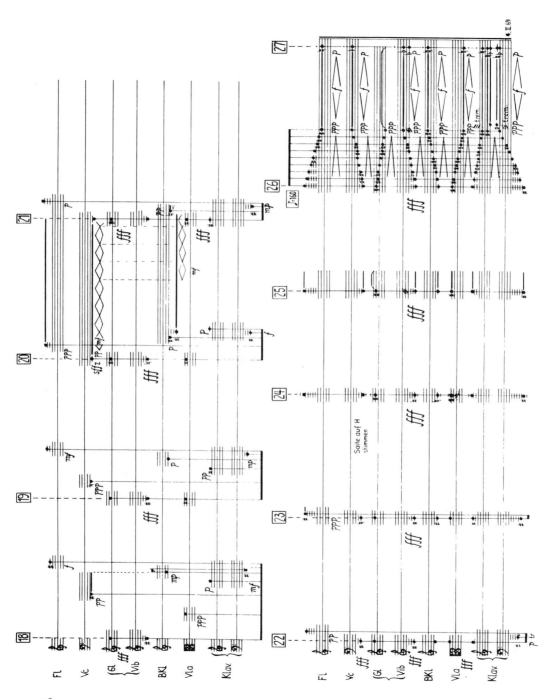

206

groups. Three additional co-conductors are required. The work should preferably be performed in four foyers or four different rooms of the same building.
Duration: 5 h 40 min.

Invited by Volker Wangenheim, general music director of the newly opened Beethovenhalle in Bonn, to take over the complex for an evening of music on 15 November 1969, a Saturday, Stockhausen jumped at the chance of mounting a four-hour non-stop simultaneous concert in the three principal concert-halls. The three programmes would be co-ordinated and timetabled to allow the public to change halls between items should they so wish. It was a concept about which he had often spoken, to have halls of music where the public would be able to come and go at will, as to the cinema or church, and take time off from everyday business to listen to music.

The resulting evening's music represented a virtually complete résumé of Stockhausen's output over the previous fifteen years from *Gesang der Jünglinge* of 1955–6 to 1969, comprising rarely heard multichannel play-backs of *Gruppen* and *Carré, Momente, Mikrophonie I, Mikrophonie II,* and *Mixtur,* live performances of *Kontakte, Hymnen mit Solisten,* the *Klavierstücke I-XI, Zyklus, Refrain, Spiral, Kurzwellen, Prozession,* and *Stimmung,* readings from *Aus den sieben Tagen,* and filmed performances of *Mikrophonie I* and *Momente.*

By removing areas of seating in the concert-halls and laying mats and rubberized carpets, the complex was adapted to allow relatively noiseless movement of the public from place to place between items, though not during them.

In addition to the concerts, Stockhausen envisaged filling the exterior corridors and public spaces with musical sounds to create an appropriate atmosphere throughout the complex from the moment the public entered, and sustain it during moments of transition between concert-halls, until they finally left. The composition of *Fresco* is designed to meet a specification for a music functionally similar to, but aesthetically completely the opposite, of, piped music. The prescription is for intentional musical sounds which colour an environment acoustically but are themselves relatively featureless. Stockhausen borrows the example of *Hymnen* Region IV's descending cluster of electronic sounds, and orchestrates it. There are four basic triangular formations and two directions of movement: a cluster expands from a point or contracts to a point, the point being at either the upper or lower extreme of range, and the full expansion covering the entire pitch range of the group. The movement of pitch articulating the triangular shape is either ascending or descending. The timing of entries is according to the clock (Ex. 86).

The four orchestral groups were located along walls near the main entrances and by the two cloakrooms. For the première groups of contrasting texture and timbre were chosen, I consisting of woodwind, brass, and tuned percussion (two pedal timpani, marimba, and vibraphone), II and IV, directed by harmonium and accordion (alternating with mouth-organ), consisting of strings. Group III, led by

Ex. 86

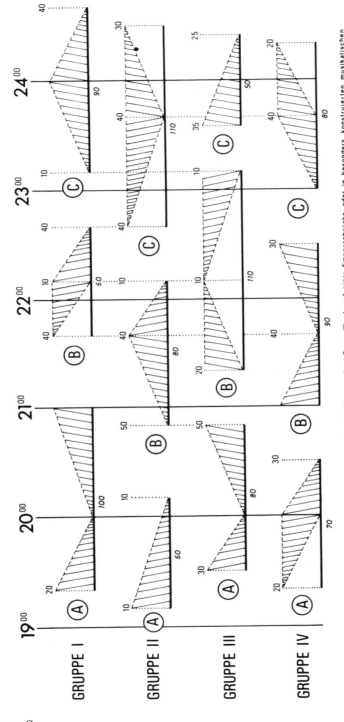

Fresco. Overall form-scheme co-ordinating the four separated instrumental groups.

© Universal Edition AG Wien.

Aloys Kontarsky on piano, was made up of winds and strings but no other percussion. The distribution of instruments in line followed their pitch range from low to high, so that as the cluster tended toward either extreme, a corresponding lateral shift in the ensemble's centre of gravity would also be audible.

To perform such outwardly featureless music is far from easy. Production effects of walls or curtains of sound which are commonplace in studio recordings of light orchestral music are nowhere near as simple a task for live instrumentalists working in a non-engineered acoustic environment. Stockhausen was to confront similar problems of fatigue and concentration with the strings who create the curtain of sound for *Trans*. Nevertheless, some psychological relief is offered by fairly regular changes of articulation of the cluster, from smooth legato to shimmering trills, to gritty fluttertongues and fast tremolos. These are calculated to emphasize a sensation of greater compression and density as the cluster diminishes to a point, or of increasing lightness as it expands to fill the entire pitch range.

Tunnel-Spiral

1969.

Solo for reader, Japanese temple bells, and short-wave receiver for performance in a multiple-delay 'sound tunnel'.

Duration unspecified.

Late 1969 provided Stockhausen with an extraordinary range of opportunities for spatial projection of his music. Close on the heels of the Beethovenhalle experience came an invitation to devise a circuit plan and music for a 200-speaker 'sound tunnel' in Los Angeles; shortly afterward he and his group of players made the trip to Lebanon to perform process and intuitive compositions, and also *Stimmung*, in the vast underground caves of Jeita. The 'sound tunnel', 40 feet long and over 6 feet high, but only $3\frac{1}{2}$ feet wide, appears to have resembled an acoustic shooting-gallery, with fairly massive Altec speakers at either end, and 200 smaller speakers ringing the intervening space at regular intervals. It was claimed to be a virtually anechoic enclosure, though that is a little difficult to believe. Stockhausen responded with a plan for a speaker circuit designed to produce a spiralling output, rapidly at first, but progressively slowing in speed of rotation during the total of 16 seconds it took for a signal to pass from end to end. With the slowing-down of rotation an impression of a trumpet-shaped expansion of the acoustic space might also be created.[8]

[8] Ibid. 190–3.

Since he could not be on hand to test the arrangement in person, Stockhausen kept his sound specification simple: a reading (by a deep male voice) from *The Synthesis of Yoga* by Sri Aurobindo, punctuated from time to time by strokes on the *rin*, bowl-shaped Japanese temple instruments first heard in *Telemusik*, sporadic short-wave signals of 'scarcely comprehensible speech' briefly faded up and down, and very occasionally by single handclaps to test the acoustic.

As always, there is a kernel of technical interest. It arises from the continuous change of delay in the feedback circuit from an initial $\frac{1}{12}$-second to a final $\frac{1}{3}$-second interval between successive speakers. Somewhere in between these two extremes a transition occurs between a continuous spiralling sweep of sound and a 'flutter echo' of discrete repetitions, and this point of transition will conceivably vary with the degree of continuity, pitch, and noisiness (such as consonants) of the source signal. Unfortunately the results of this exercise are not recorded.

Sternklang

1971: *Star Sound.*

Park music for five groups of four players, percussionist, and optional amplification. Instrumentation unspecified.

Duration at least 3 hours.

The translation of meditative works such as *Stimmung* or the *Aus den sieben Tagen* text pieces into an open-air environment has an immediate effect of altering their focal length and direction from a common centre to an unspecified outer limit. A particularly dramatic example, which the composer still recalls with pride, was a performance of the text 'Unlimited' in the grounds surrounding the chateau of St-Paul-de-Vence which lasted a whole evening. The performance tends away from the production of inwardly focused individual and collective images, to the generation of a larger collective response, attuned not only to the text or musical object of contemplation but also the environment and its acoustic character.

Sternklang is Stockhausen's first composition specifically designed for out of doors. It is intended to be performed in a park 'during the warm summer weather, under a clear starry sky, preferably at a time of full moon'. The five groups of players are distributed around the park; each is 'tuned', as in *Stimmung*, to a specific overtone series on to which 'magic names' are modulated, though this time the magic names are those of zodiacal constellations (Ex. 87).

Instruments imitate voices by variations in timbre, relatively simple with synthesizers and already an established technique for brass instruments such as the

Ex. 87

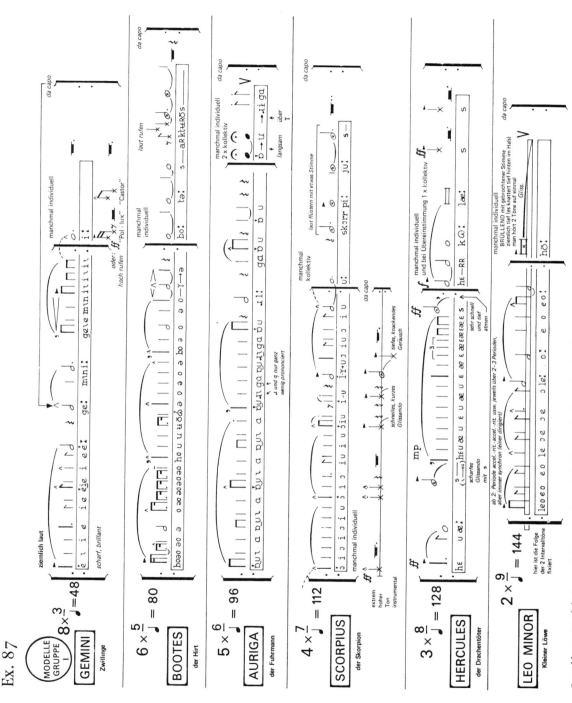

Sternklang: Model Group I. Names of constellations substitute for the divinities of *Stimmung*. Note the Noh percussionist's 'Yo-ho!' cry which is incorporated into Leo minor (the composer's sign).

© K. Stockhausen.

trombone. The percussionist at the centre provides tempo and pitch references from time to time. The pitch E4 (330 Hz) is common to all five harmonic spectra, and the tempo crotchet = MM 144 is also common to the five analogous structures of harmonically related tempi to which the groups also conform (Ex. 88). The time structure is extraordinarily calculated, like intricate clockwork (Fig. 5). Each notated 'model group' of names of constellations comprises six intonation phrases which are continuously repeated for a specified number of times, together with cadence phrases. The *periodicities* of each set of six phrases, determined by their respective durations, are harmonically related (Ex. 89). The *tempi* of intonation within the phrases are also harmonically related. And of course, the pitches in which the names are intoned are harmonically related. So Stockhausen has reproduced analogous frequency relationships in all three time domains of pitch, pulse, and structure.

An unusual feature is the use of individual performers as runners to carry musical messages from group to group, the pitch and rhythm of which are then incorporated in the receiving group's music. At predetermined times all five groups cease their ritual intonations and focus their attention on the visible constellations in the evening sky, playing their shapes as intervallic figures. ('Think Cassiopeia or the other constellations of the stars,' (Stockhausen to Aloys Kontarsky, having difficulty

Ex. 88

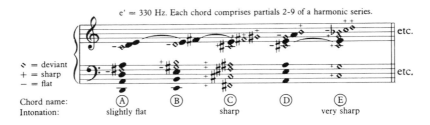

Sternklang. The five harmonic series tuned to E4.

Fig. 5

Group tempi:

I.	MM = 16	: 48	: 80	: 90	: 112	: 128	: 144	
II.	MM =	18	: 54	: 90	: 108	: 126	: 144	: 162
III.	MM =		20.6	: 62	: 103	: 124	: 144	: 165 : 186
IV.	MM =			24	: 72	: 120	: 144	: 168 : 192 : 216
V.	MM =				29	: 87	: 144	: 174 : 204 : 232 : 261

Ex. 89

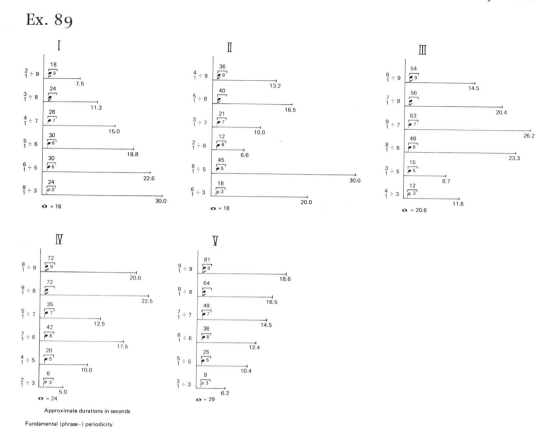

Sternklang : harmonic phrase structures.

with the text 'play a vibration in the rhythm of the universe' from the text piece 'Connections'). 'Oh', he said, 'you mean Webern? Well, okay, let's start.')[9]

On one occasion in 1980, a performance scheduled to take place in the Rheinauen Park in Bonn was threatened with cancellation because of unseasonal rain. It had been planned for two years, and would otherwise have occurred under a full moon as ideally stipulated. The whole performance was moved into a large hall some 50 m long and 25 m wide. Two hundred and fifty trees of all shapes and sizes were brought into the hall, and rugs and cushions laid on the floor, to simulate the atmosphere and, as far as possible, the acoustic of a park. So successful was this that Stockhausen published an account with photographs as an addendum to the score, and now permits indoor performances which follow his guide-lines.

[9] Karlheinz Stockhausen and Robin Maconie, *Stockhausen on Music* (London, 1989), p. 119.

Alphabet für Liège

1972: *Alphabet for Liège*.
'Visible music', 13 musical images for soloists and duos.
For performance in separate rooms of the same building, e.g. an art gallery.
Duration 4 hours.

As *Originale* eleven years earlier had turned the composer's spotlight on the self-revealing spontaneous actions of a number of his artist friends and colleagues, so in *Alphabet für Liège* Stockhausen composes a musical event out of observing natural phenomena (again including musician friends). This time, however, it is not what they do but how they respond to music. People and things are altered by the musical vibrations they receive and transmit. The quality of being a medium which the texts for intuitive music express acoustically, is now demonstrated visually.

The work brings together science, meditation, and music in a simultaneous exhibition of thirteen 'situations'. The première took place in the ideal environment of a large basement complex of rooms in the newly constructed RTB radio and television headquarters in the Palais de Congrès, a resonant labyrinth of concrete and breeze-block walls and ceilings freshly painted in white but still awaiting the refinements of windows, doors, and carpets. As this is a composition of 'visible music', and arrangements had been made to film the presentation for television, it is interesting to see how Stockhausen approaches the composition in visual terms. It is the first occasion in which he has had to rely primarily on a visual choreography to give meaning and shape to acoustic processes, and thus a significant precursor of those subsequent compositions which are precisely visualized for film and television reproduction.

Of the thirteen situations only the first, '*Am Himmel wandre ich . . .* ' ('In the sky I am walking') for two singers, is through-composed. The others, paraphrased below from Stockhausen's notes, are documentary images of the physical world responding to the influence of sound vibrations.

2. Tone vibrations made visible in fluid, light rays, and flames. Generate visible models in fluid by the influence of specific sound vibrations and project them on a screen.

3. Make sound spectra visible in solid material (flour, iron filings, etc.)

4. Bring glass to breaking-point with the aid of tones.

5. Magnetise foodstuffs with tones, making the magnetisation visible with the aid of a pendulum.

6. Massage a human body with sounds (a female dancer translates the vibrations of a musical instrument into her body, which becomes a living loudspeaker).

7. Self-extinguishing tones (for example, by bringing the bell of a trumpet ever closer against the wall, which is bare or hung with a variety of materials).

8. 'Make love' with tones (e.g. generate beat frequencies of varying speed and intensity by bending the unison vibration of two opposing recorders and/or voices, possibly showing the beat frequencies on an oscilloscope).

9. Bring the seven centres of the body into harmony with the aid of tones (Mantra-technique).

10. Use tones to repel thoughts and keep thinking at bay [compare the text piece 'It'].

11. Use [pulsed] tones to vary continuously the respiration and heartbeat rhythms of living creatures (fish).

12. Invoke and supplicate the spirits of the dead in tones (until in a trance).

13. Pray in tones (sometimes intelligibly); listen to and study sung prayers of all religions from tape recordings.[10]

The title 'Alphabet' arises from a list of actions which associate with the letters of the alphabet (Anrufen, Begleiten, Chaos, Dudeln, etc.). These actions, allocated at random, are the basis of hourly excursions by the human performers to visit other designated players or situations, communicate in tones something of what they are doing, and bring back tonal or rhythmic information from the visit which is incorporated in the resumption of normal play.

Unlike *Musik für ein Haus*, where an elaborate electronic intercommunication network linked the various rooms, here events are co-ordinated to a master time plan by acoustic signals which are the responsibility of the musical leader. Japanese chimes mark the minutes, sustained tones the moment sequence. There are two general pauses in each hour, when movement ceases and the musicians freeze in mid-action; these are signalled by camel-bells (strings of nesting cup-shaped bells). Bundles of tiny Indian bells are shaken to 'erase' sustained pitches at the end of their time.

'*Am Himmel wandre ich . . .*' (*Indianerlieder*)

1972: '*In the sky I am walking . . .*' (*Songs of the Indians*).
Twelve songs from American Indian poems, for two voices, male and/or female.
Duration 50'.

I chose twelve poems or sayings or prayers, however you like to call them, from an anthology, *American Indian Prose and Poetry*, edited by Margot Astrov. . . .[11] These sayings I have completely transformed in a manner conforming to music, expanding and composing them

---

[10] Karlheinz Stockhausen, *Texte zur Musik*, iv (Cologne, 1976), pp. 194–5.
[11] Margot Astrov (ed.), *The Winged Serpent: American Indian Prose and Poetry* (New York, 1946).

215

into a more complex new text. [The work] consists of *twelve scenes* which succeed one another without interruption and form a musical whole. For each scene there is one Indian song. The first is composed with only one tone, the second song with two, and so on to the twelfth, with twelve different tones [Ex. 90].[12]

For all their austerity, these twelve songs are rich in implication. They begin with rhythmic counterpoint on a unison, already a music of ritual meditation; then the next song, on two notes, refers to the two-note signals of *Sternklang*. Melodies of three and four notes evoke the words of plainchant and folk-song, which with the addition of notes five and six becomes distinctly oriental in character (Ex. 91). As more and more pitches come into play the melody range expands upward, and the melodic character changes from modal to diatonic, and finally chromatic. The concept refers to a kind of new oral tradition by which a listener is able to tell which point in the

Ex. 90

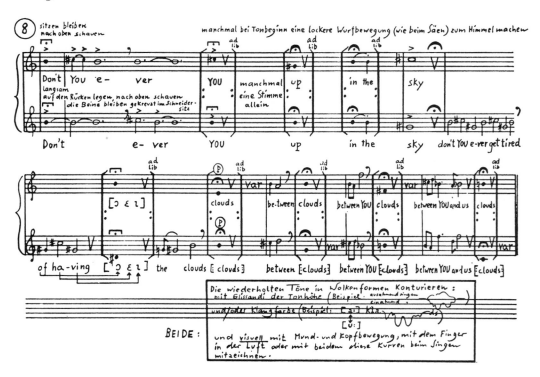

'Am Himmel wandre ich . . .' (*Indianerlieder*), 8: 'Plaint against the Fog'. Stockhausen compares the progression to that of Western music from monotone to chromatic melody. Here at 8 the music is appropriately diatonic.

© K. Stockhausen.

[12] Stockhausen, op. cit. (above, n. 10), pp. 202, 205.

Ex. 91

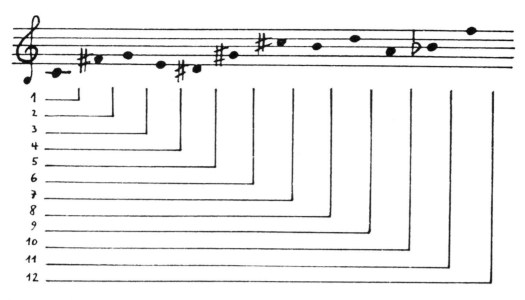

'Am Himmel wandre ich . . .': the series. Each of the twelve lieder employs the number of pitches corresponding to its place in the sequence.
© K. Stockhausen.

cycle has been reached by counting the number of different tones. That point represents not only an elapsed duration of performance time—useful if you need a reminder of what time it is—but also symbolizes a point in the historical evolution of music, on a rising dynamic curve, and a level of spiritual enlightenment.

Both the visual images of materials in contact with sound vibrations, and the acoustic imagery of the *Indianerlieder*, invite comparison with Stockhausen's *Hinab–Hunauf* project. The choreography of gesture in the songs and of movement through the acoustic labyrinth are, however, a foretaste of an entirely new development in the lyric and dramatic visualization of Stockhausen's music.

Ylem

1972: for ensemble of 19 or more players and/or singers.
Four electric or amplified instruments at the rear of the stage; non-portable

instruments including a large tam-tam at the front edge of the stage, piano stage centre; ten or more players of portable instruments. Instrumentation variable. Duration 22′.

The cyclic attenuation and compression of a constellation of musical 'points' over a lengthy period of time is a recurrent image in Stockhausen's music, from *Spiel* of 1952, though *Gruppen*, *Mixtur*, 'Translation', *Adieu* at 9, the 'Russian Bridge' from *Third Region of Hymnen with Orchestra*, right up to the *Dr. K-Sextett*. Here the image is stated with medieval directness. 'Ylem' means the primordial flux of elementary particles out of which the universe has expanded into existence and into which it is doomed to return; it also refers to the period of oscillation between chaos and destruction of the universe, and thus to the ultimate fundamental vibration of which all other cycles are mere harmonics.

The music begins literally with a 'Big bang' on the tam-tam, round which (Ex. 92) the players of portable instruments are grouped (flute, oboe, cor anglais, clarinet, bass clarinet, bassoon, horn, trumpet, trombone, and violin in the London Sinfonietta version). Immediately the players jerk into life and begin to pour out streams of repeated notes at maximum intensity, choosing either E3♭ or A3, or the same an octave higher. The players of portable instruments gradually disperse out into the auditorium to take up positions along the walls, where they continue to play with eyes closed.

There follows a general but non-uniform ritardando lasting eleven minutes, during which time the repetition rate of individual players gradually falls to around one note every 90 seconds. Commensurate with the time-expansion is an expansion of the pitch space from the original tritone octave in mid-range upward and downward as appropriate, to the extremes of range. As the rate of repetition slows, players are asked to bring the pitches to life through small variations of pitch, intensity, attacks flourishes, or timbre. They come to symbolize, as Stockhausen remarks, 'the diversity of quite differently animated planets in the universe'.

The four players of electric instruments (in the Sinfonietta version they are an electronium, a keyboard synthesizer, amplified cello, and saxophone doubling bassoon, each modulated by a VCS-3 synthesizer) contemplate the action like Greek gods from their celestial vantage-points, from time to time executing melodic 'interstellar voyages' between chosen pitches and timbres. Each of them also has a short-wave receiver, which is switched on once during the expansion cycle, and once during the period of contraction. Melodic links are also forged between pitches encountered in the radio signal and those in the air.

After eleven minutes, by which time the density of 'points' has attenuated to about one every six seconds, one of the four players of electric instruments calls the syllable 'Hu!' and is answered by the other players (the cry 'Hu, Hu' is also found in *Telemusik*, taken from a Suyai Indian chant). From this point the music begins to contract: players very gradually begin the equally long process of descent and

Ex. 92

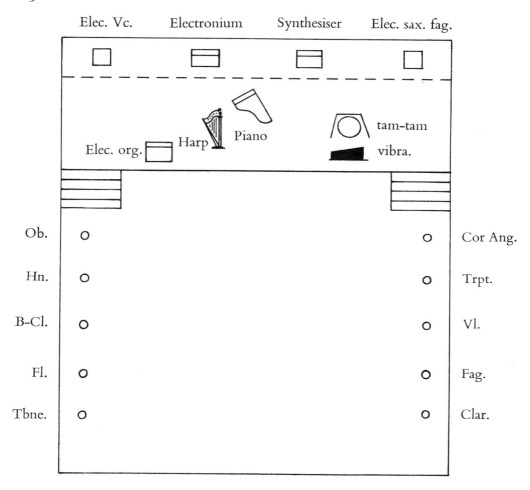

Ylem: stage plan for the 1973 London Sinfonietta première.
© K. Stockhausen.

acceleration of pitches back to fast repetition of the original tritone, at the same time reconverging on the tam-tam. At the climax point there is a second 'Big Bang', but this time the tritone leaps a tone higher, into another dimension of pitch space, and the players once more begin the expansion cycle, but instead of moving into the auditorium, all withdraw from the platform, players of fixed instruments taking up portable instruments such as melodicas, and continue playing while moving out of the building until no more is heard.

13 *Theatre of Melody*

ACOUSTIC space is the first dimension of music, but the last to submit to musical control. At the most basic level every sound we hear confirms something of the nature of the environment, and since music is organized for hearing, it tends to communicate that basic information the more coherently and immediately. The question we have to decide is whether musical space expresses the actual acoustic environment of a musical performance, or imitates acoustic reality, or merely exploits the spatial dimension as a convenient visual or aural metaphor for other co-ordinates of musical expression, for instance distributing pitch levels or polyphonic layers to different locations. We may call 'real' those spatial relationships in music which draw attention to actual acoustic conditions, and 'virtual' expressions of spatial relationships which are either simulated or metaphorical.

The musical space most familiar to Western audiences is also the most sophisticated: the suggestion of aural perspectives through instrumental colour and dynamics. Like painting, musical perspective has developed in response to a two-dimensional 'picture-frame' style of musical presentation which has dominated Western music since Classical times. Of course there are other, more real expressions of spatial relationship in music: for instance antiphony, which exploits contrasts of distance and direction of sound to dramatic effect, and processional music, in which the passage of performers signals direction and movement relative to the listener. Both survive in ceremonial contexts, antiphony in the fanfare, and processional music in church and in the march past.

An impression of acoustic extent arises from a combination of distance and directional cues, and of a connected space by common resonance characteristics among sounds originating from different locations, or describing a continuous movement between separated points of reference. Each indicator of the perceived space may be a feature of the actual performance acoustic or a simulation: in music it is usually a combination of both. Thus Berlioz' kettledrums in the *Symphonie Fantastique* express actual distance, being situated at the back of the orchestra, and virtual distance inasmuch as they imitate distant thunder. When we locate a solo flute in the centre of the orchestra its position is real but normally of no representational significance; on the other hand, an off-stage trumpet is a dramatic event precisely because it introduces an element of potential acoustic realism into conventional orchestral perspective. Movement in space expressed as a continuous change of direction of a source of sound can either be real, when the source actually moves in relation to the listener (or when the listener is moving), or virtual, when the signal is merely cross-faded from one instrument or speaker to another elsewhere.

The arrival of stereophonic recording in the late fifties was widely promoted as introducing a new degree of spatial objectivity to recorded music. In fact, as Stravinsky was quick to remark, the benefits of stereophony had very little to do with acoustic realism.[1] The stereo image provided by widely spaced microphones bears little or no relation to what two human ears six inches apart hear in reality. For the purposes of harmony and ensemble, moreover, and in terms of what Wagner sought to achieve at Bayreuth, stereo separation of parts can actually be counter-productive. Polyphonic and polychoral music, on the other hand, may benefit from the greater dynamic range and clarity of detail available with two-channel reproduction. The superficial attractions of greater part definition do not always coincide with a composer's musical intentions, nor is the illusion of space necessarily any less imaginary in stereo than in mono.

Dance is another means of expressing musical relationships in visual and spatial terms. Here again the spatial dimension is metaphorical rather than real; however, by virtue of the connectedness of the visible action, dance has the added advantage of suggesting continuities of relationship which may not be immediately apparent in a music alone. Compared to the instrumental performer whose actions are mainly determined by the written score, a dancer or group of dancers enjoys considerably greater liberty to impose a human frame of reference and an embracing continuity of movement on a music which might otherwise appear intellectually abstract or fragmentary. An ability to resolve aural complexities of music in terms of a simpler visual imagery is perhaps why contemporary dance has become so successful as a promotional vehicle for more difficult new music.

Stockhausen's compositions during the seventies are distinguished by a number of innovations aiming to project musical relationships more clearly in spatial and, more importantly, visual terms. During the fifties his energies are concentrated on purely aural antiphonal relationships: exchanges back and forth among spatially separated groups of similar instrumentation, or cross-faded continuously from group to group or speaker to speaker in the case of electronic music. In the sixties his attention moves from real space to the metaphorical spaces of frequency and timbre, a series of transformational scores exploring the transitional areas between pitch and rhythm, and between natural and electronically modified sound. With the arrival of the Modul B circuit in *Mantra* we observe the emergence of a clearly audible hierarchy of consonance and dissonance operating for electronically modulated sound; a hierarchy furthermore in general agreement with the laws of classical harmony.[2]

---

[1] Igor Stravinsky and Robert Craft, *Memories and Commentaries* (London, 1960), pp. 123–6.

[2] Not to mention Hindemith's theory of interval consonance based on difference tones (*The Craft of Musical Composition* (New York, 1942)), itself derived from Hermann Helmholtz, 'Degree of Harmoniousness of Consonances', in *On the Sensations of Tone*, trans. Alexander J. Ellis (New York, 1954), p. 193.

The seventies are marked by further developments into melody based formula compositions, and into new visual domains of lighting, stage design, and choreography.

Stockhausen's adoption of the formula may be seen in one way as a necessary, or at least predictable consummation of earlier techniques. Formula composition encapsulates all of the essential structural features of an entire work in an easily remembered melodic sequence. The formula is more than a seed: it is an aural navigational aid superseding the cantus firmus, fugue or sonata subject, Wagnerian leitmotif, or Schoenbergian series, allowing the listener to follow the expansions and contractions of musical expression from the smallest detail to the largest structural component. The idea of melody on a human scale materializing in the region where pointillistic layers are perceived to overlap in pitch and time, is intuitively established as early as *Kreuzspiel*, and by the time of *Kontakte* we find melodic fragments made into tape loops and accelerated into the timbre domain, mediating continuously between different timbres representing alternative perceptual time-scales.

As a compositional device formula composition may be seen as similar in kind, if stricter in application, by comparison with Stockhausen's earlier serial procedures. To regard it merely as a personal invention, however, is to ignore a profounder, more universal relationship between formula composition and the structural and mnemonic function of melody in folk- and art music generally. There is clearly a sense in which Stockhausen is adopting formula composition as a means of tuning in to oral musical cultures, as he had already unconsciously tapped in to Spanish flamenco idioms in *Momente*[3] and had pursued others with greater deliberation in *Telemusik* and *Hymnen*.

The function of melody as an aural—and cultural—*aide-mémoire* is not yet fully understood, though its efficacy is not in any doubt. What is acknowledged is that a melody is recognized by its general shape, not in terms of its component pitches, intensities, and so forth; as long as certain essential relationships are preserved, a melody can be identified even though distorted in a great many ways.[4] So the same melody can be recognized in a different key, or mode, or intervallic scale, in a different tempo or rhythm, or even in different forms, when notes are added or taken away. Unlike a Beethoven variation theme, or Schoenberg series, the Stockhausen melody formula both prefigures all the structural and expressive transformations which go to make a composition, and determines the order in which they will be heard. And because melody retains its perceived identity through all of these transformations, it is both a natural vehicle for musical structures based on dimensional variation and its own justification for such compositional procedures.

Early in the seventies Cologne Radio's electronic music studio obtained an EMS Synthi 100 synthesizer. A feature of this synthesizer is the sequencer, a digital memory programmable as a sequence of instructions expressible in different musical

[3] Karlheinz Stockhausen, *Texte zur Musik*, ii (Cologne, 1964), p. 133.
[4] See, for example, John Booth Davies, *The Psychology of Music* (London, 1978), pp. 141–55.

parameters including pitch and duration. A melody stored on a sequencer can be recycled indefinitely, like a superior tape loop, and may also be influenced in various ways. It can be stretched or compressed in time, and its succession of intervals can also be expanded or reduced to correspond to virtually any scale or temperament, including microtonal inflections. Without doubt the Synthi 100 was a catalyst for Stockhausen's conversion to formula composition and his adoption of a new style of notational determinism. Note information is stored in the sequencer as exact numerical values, and the operations performed on this information are also numerically determined. In addition to stretching and compressing an original melody, the sequencer offers the crucial advantage of allowing the composer to explore, with previously undreamt-of precision, contrapuntal relationships among melodies subject to variable degrees of expansion and contraction; in other words making possible the composition and notation for conventional instrumental forces of a music of multiple time layers.[5]

Just as the melodic template makes it easier for the listener to gauge different scales and degrees of transformation, so Stockhausen's introduction of scenic and gestural specifications during the seventies is aimed at allowing the viewer to follow musical relationships visually in progressively greater detail. Because the theatre is based on the music, and not the other way round, it appears mythic and symbolic rather than realistic: indeed the provision and working-out of a continuous narrative framework (comic interludes apart) is altogether less important to Stockhausen's music theatre than the awakening of appropriate modes of listening among his audiences, apprehensions of mystery, magic, and revelation, out of a sense that these actions, whatever they seem to suggest, are divinely ordained. His earlier spatialized compositions and projects such as *Sternklang* and *Alphabet* appear to be based on an initial principle of separation upon which the composer subsequently imposes a choreographic web of spatial interconnections by way of compensation. The new works, by contrast, are concerned with realizing a visual scenario already inherent in outline in the musical structure, which has only to be fleshed out in word and gesture to make contact with and exploit potential affinities with existing theatrical conventions (for instance, the Balinese shadow play in *Donnerstag aus LICHT*, which is a theatrical metaphor of a musical component expressing the idea of 'negative action').

To the visible choreography of live sound sources Stockhausen adds further unseen dimensions of pre-recorded and electronically modified sounds. So in his music-theatre the acoustic space is both actual (the visible auditorium) and imaginary (the reproduced soundscape), and the contrast between the two worlds is an important ingredient of Stockhausen's dramatic art.

From 1968, when the record industry abandoned the rule that stereophonic recordings should be mono-compatible, Stockhausen began to mix his stereo

---

[5] Karlheinz Stockhausen and Robin Maconie, *Stockhausen on Music* (London, 1989), pp. 158–62.

recordings in a way calculated to simulate four-channel surround-sound from only two channels. Shortly thereafter, commercial quadraphonic recording began to appear on the market in various formats, creating new problems, and possibilities for record producers, many of whom did not know how to manage space as a dimension of musical expression. The early seventies was a time of erratic experimentation with the layout and distribution of orchestral forces, choirs, and soloists, both in the studio and in the final mix, in order to justify a spread of audience attention around four channels. Given the psychoacoustically suspect rationale of much quadraphonic reproduction, not to mention the doubtful production practices to which it gave rise, it was clearly in Stockhausen's creative interests at this time to establish firmer artistic control over the spatial dimension of his compositions, if only to prevent his musical conception being corrupted or undermined by a record producer with the wrong ideas (or indeed by a video producer, since videotape was also becoming a force to be reckoned with). By embracing the theatrical dimension, and integrating scenario and choreography with his musical schemes, Stockhausen can be seen as preparing for the eventuality of full audio-visual recording, and guarding his work against the possibility of interpretative distortion in the visual domain.

Trans

1971: for orchestra, orchestral soloists, and tape.
  I. 4 flutes, bass clarinet, amplified celesta, percussion (5 cinelli, Indian bell garland).
  II. 4 oboes, trombone, percussion (vibraphone, bass cowbell, sizzle cymbal, cymbal on stands).
  III. 4 clarinets, bassoon, contrabassoon, percussion (tubular bells, 2 gongs with domes).
  IV. 4 B♭ trumpets with cup mute, tuba, percussion (3 tom-toms, bass drum, tam-tam, 'infantry drum').
Strings 22. 0. 8. 6. 4: electronic organ with low C ($C_1 = 32$ Hz).
Duration 26′ 15″.

Trans is the first of a series of works examining particular aspects of musical space. Here it is the longitudinal dimension, the aural equivalent of the sight-line of traditional perspective, with its suggestion of overlapping planes at increasing distances. Later, in *Inori*, he redefines the lateral dimension, left to right; in *Musik im Bauch* he articulates a space of lines and circles around a centre, and in *Sirius* the emphasis is reversed, to focus outward instead of inward, and the musical action takes place at an imaginary periphery. The stage and lighting plan of *Trans* (the title suggests 'trance' and 'transition') represents musical space as a multilayer aural perspective which seeks to draw the listener out of the 'inner space' of an auditorium and through a perceptual gateway into a mysterious auditory hinterland. 'Music-theatre' may be too strong a term for a composition the dramatic interest of which is still overwhelmingly aural. Listeners, among them hospice patients, have written to the composer of out-of-body and afterlife experiences from hearing this music. Its aural effect is unexpectedly and intensely physical. Not here the dreamlike shades of Ravel, Debussy, or even Boulezian impressionism. Rather, a combination of tunnel vision and interiorized, amplified polyphony. The audience sees and hears a wall of string players, scarcely moving, bathed in red–violet light, playing a succession of static note clusters, behind which unseen musical forces can be discerned surging and writhing in response to a measured flagellation of amplified time strokes of a recorded weaving-shuttle. Though much more powerful in impact, the sound-action of the shuttle resembles an amplified slide projector, or stills camera with automatic shutter, and it sections the musical action into 'frames' in a comparable way.

Trans creates an initially dramatic situation out of confounded expectations and ambiguities introduced into the conventional concert-hall relationship of orchestra and audience. Normal visual cues are removed or reduced; the light is more than usually dimmed, there is no conductor visible, and, interpolations apart, very little performer action to be seen. The concealed orchestral groups are self-evidently 'behind' the string orchestra; a logical inference of the scenario also being that they are to be heard as layers of musical backdrop at successively greater distances. The image is consistent with the layered instrumental perspectives of American big-band jazz to which Stockhausen used to tune in secretly at night as a cadet during the war, an image of alternating and opposing parallel harmonies perceived through a haze of shortwave interference, where the saxophones appear to be on a plane behind the clarinets, and cup-muted trombones and trumpets stepped back at still greater distances.

On the other hand, the aural imagery of *Trans* is contradictorily enhanced, the hidden layers of parallel harmonies being relayed through speakers placed above the proscenium arch. What the wall-of-sound scenario suggests a listener is going to hear, namely a play of musical perspective based on real distance effects, is not what actually happens. Everything in the orchestra is amplified and brought forward to the plane of the proscenium; instead of being heard as layers into the distance behind the strings, the four wind groups emerge from equidistant points above the strings, arrayed left to right. In his notes on the work the composer makes a theatrical point of the ambiguous nature of these musical layers: are they live or tape recorded, he asks, as if an audience's primary concern would be whether it was getting value for money at a live orchestral concert. But that is simply to divert attention from the larger contradiction between what the music appears to profess and what it actually delivers. The polyphony of layers at different physical distances is interiorized, the image of external perspective transformed into a mind-invading cocktail of musical actions distinguishable not by an instinctive apprehension of the acoustics of space, but only by an intellectual apprehension of harmonic and rhythmic relationships.

Coincidentally, at this time Stockhausen was lecturing widely on the malign dominance of the visual sense in Western culture, and asking audiences to put more trust in their ears, and in what the sounds of new music actually revealed. So, apropos *Kontakte*:

> When they hear the layers revealed, one behind the other, in this new music, most listeners cannot even perceive it because they say well, the walls have not moved, so it is an illusion. I say to them, the fact that you say the walls have not moved is an illusion, because you have clearly heard that the sounds went away very far, and that is the truth. Whether the walls have moved at all has nothing to do with this perception, but with believing in what we hear as absolutely as we formerly believed in what we see.[6]

Perhaps the reason for *Trans*'s change of perspective, if change there were, is that a live acoustic perspective along the lines suggested by the visual scenario (and prefigured in his electronic compositions) cannot be guaranteed in a normal concert-hall environment. Given the nature of the scenario, an opera-house stage, with its greater depth, would seem to be necessary for the four hidden groups of instruments to be placed behind one another at acoustically meaningful distances. But there would then be the danger that the sound of the wind groups would be lost, unable to penetrate the physical barrier of string players and dissipated upward into the flies. A system of amplification could be made to simulate, by filtering and other means, the perspective effect desired, but Stockhausen has not done this, preferring to give an equivalent close-microphone sound to every layer. This does not make the concept invalid, but, for the sake of ensuring that the work is widely performable, it does change the rules. (It is instructive to see how he subsequently deals with the longitudinal dimension in *Jubiläum*, by the use of off-stage wind bands, and in *Samstag aus LICHT*, which is given in an opera-house or large church.)

At the outset organ and strings slowly build a shrill screen of pitches from bottom to top of the normal six-octave range. Because the cluster is musically featureless, modulating neither in density nor in intensity from one shuttle-stroke to the next, it is eventually assimilated as an incidental noise to be mentally 'filtered out' from the auditory field of reference. To return to a radio analogy, it becomes the short-wave interference through which a target transmission (or overlapping signals occupying the same band) is discerned. Incidentally, the device of a static organ cluster has long been associated, in radio and film, with characterizations of dreamlike or delirious states, and is indeed employed by Stockhausen in *Momente* during the 'amorphous or indeterminate' moment I(d), in which all formal distinctions are temporarily dissolved: a literal *idée fixe*, perhaps.

[6] Ibid. 109.

But the imagery of a static trance only persists as long as the listener continues to perceive the cluster as a featureless tinnitus, which the music reveals is not the case. As the piece progresses, the cluster varies in density, now becoming more attenuated, now notched and pierced to reduce the level of distraction and allow more of the masked layers to be heard. These changes of cluster density are themselves partly masked by the whizz and crunch of time's guillotine slicing above (or even, for the listener equipped with headphones, seemingly through) one's head. But they are discernible all the same, and they change the dramatic balance of the music significantly, from what the composer calls 'tragic'—the working-through of a preordained situation of conflict—to a subtler, measured, and potentially 'comic' (humanly influenceable) dialogue between concealment and revelation, 'hearing' and the 'heard'. (We may also perceive it as a dialogue between the cluster as a form of 'negative music' (remembering the erasures of surfaces of sound during the composition of *Punkte 1962*, for instance) and the 'positive' and dynamically articulated chord mixtures of the four wind and percussion layers.)

As music-theatre, *Trans* does pay homage to Japanese culture, and to *gagaku* music in particular. The extended time-scale of Japanese culture, able to embrace greater extremes of contrast of slow and fast action than cruder and more impatient Western sensibilities, made a lasting impression on Stockhausen during his visits in 1966 and 1970. With *Telemusik* he had come to identify his use of percussive markers to signal formal divisions with Japanese musical convention. He was not the only one to be impressed; in 1963 Messiaen attempted to render the 'féroce mais immobile' sonorities and intensities of *gagaku* in European instrumental combinations, in the evocative if misconstrued *Sept Haï-kaï*.[7] The piece entitled 'Gagaku' in fact incorporates a Western version for ensemble of violins of a particular feature of the Japanese classical orchestra, the mouth-organ called *sho*, which along with the Chinese *sheng* is the ancestor of Western free-reed instruments such as the accordion and harmonium. The *sho* is employed in the *gagaku* ensemble as a source of sustained harmonies which, to Western ears, appear to have no ordinary harmonic function. Unlike Western drones, they lie in the upper register, beyond the range of tonal or modal attraction. Though modally determined, they are not (to Western ears) modally perceived, instead providing a sustained harmonic infill giving continuity and dramatic tension to the musical and mimed action. The harmonies change periodically as the piece progresses, but always simultaneously with percussion strokes, and since every chord in the instrument's repertoire sounds like a cluster at this high register, a comparison of *gagaku* with the changing clusters and time strokes of *Trans* is quite suggestive. 'There is in Gagaku no concept of harmonic progression. Instead there is one harmonic structure for each of the tones of the Togaku [modal] system. The *shō* part simply outlines the main melody with these harmonic clusters.'[8]

[7] Messiaen's *haiku* are much longer pieces which have been cut short.
[8] Robert Garfias, *Music of a Thousand Autumns: the Tōgaku Style of Japanese Court Music* (Berkeley, 1975), p. 65.

In many ways the compositional drama of *Trans* reciprocates the visual and aural tensions of its scenario. As the listener strives to penetrate the visual and acoustic screen to make sense of what is going on behind it, so too the hidden instrumental groups alternately divide and combine among themselves to suggest musical ideas and gestures in ferment, trying to assert themselves, to break through into the consciousness of the listener. The atmosphere is similar to *Sternklang* but more heated. In the earlier piece, too, there are separated groups of players, each group articulating around a given harmonic structure and all structures related to a common focal pitch, independently striving to make contact with an unseen audience, but in a very laid-back manner. On this occasion, however, the struggle is more violent, there is more argumentation among the groups, and, although the idea of a common focal pitch uniting the various group harmonic spectra is retained, the harmonies themselves are tensed to a far greater degree. Each group comprises a bass instrument representing a fundamental, second, or fourth harmonic (Stockhausen's registrations are octave transposable, like an organ), above which is superimposed a cluster of four higher harmonics or their tempered equivalents. The first musical 'frame', for example, has the central tone E (the same as *Sternklang*). The four flutes of Group I form a cluster of harmonics corresponding to 14, 15, 16, and 18 of a fundamental E1; the Group II oboes to harmonics 13, 15, 16, and 19, and the clarinets of Group III to harmonics 16, 17, 21, and 22 of a second harmonic at the same pitch; finally the cup-muted trumpets of Group IV approximate to harmonics 20, 21, 23, and 28 of a fundamental of which E1 is the fourth harmonic. The bass notes of each group are prominent and the role of the higher instruments is self-evidently coloristic. Stockhausen's transposition of the melody register into the sub-bass range is a remarkable feat: against expectations the bass melodies remain articulate and volatile, and despite the interval gap separating bass and upper harmonics, the latter occupying a more prominent range of the tonal spectrum, group identity and internal balance are consistently preserved.

Under repeated assaults from the hidden groups the string and organ tonal fabric suffers a variety of stresses, changes in the texture of pitches as well as temporary ruptures. On the other side the groups also show signs of stress, if that is the way we interpret degrees of loss of co-ordination among the four groups and of disintegration among individual groups. Tension and anger spill over into laughter, however, as one by one the groups dissolve into fragments floating gently down or up through the pitch space in a textural imagery similar to *Fresco*. And in the work's only overt manifestations of theatre, the visible action is similarly interrupted from time to time by solo cadenzas seemingly in spontaneous reaction to the tensions of the situation.

These episodes mark larger divisions in the six-part musical form. To signal the beginning of part II a military drummer marches on to the stage to inspect the strings. He fixes his attention on a hapless viola player who stands to attention and promptly goes berserk, playing a wild parody of a cadenza until saved by the next time stroke. Part III, at cue 12, is prepared by an orchestral tutti during which a

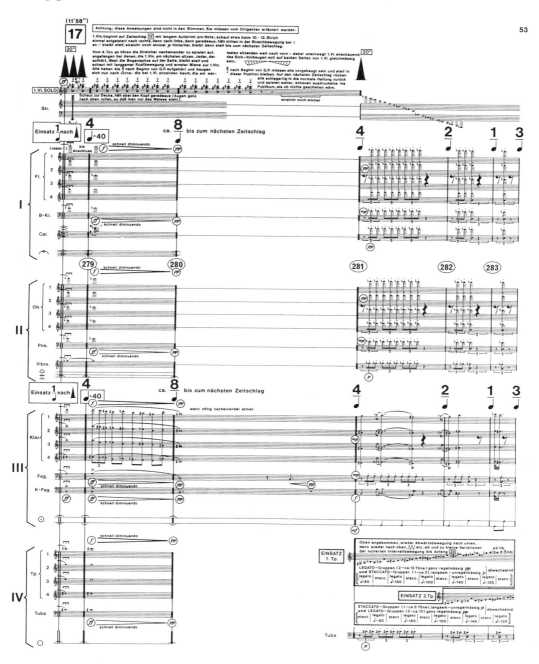

53

Trans: the concert-master's interruption at 17 (see text). The witches' hats denote passes of the recorded weaving shuttle; below the solo violin stave may be seen the string cluster which forms the acoustic screen at the front of the stage. Groups I–IV are concealed behind the violins. Note the disintegration of layer IV after the interruption: trumpets begin one after another to create a rising texture of note points.

© K. Stockhausen.

concert assistant enters with music and stand for the principal cello, whose smooth performance is switched on and off along with the light on the stand. At cue 17, part III begins with the leader of the orchestra himself seemingly succumbing to a nervous tic, his bowing arm breaking into a mechanical twitching on a high-pitched harmonic (Ex. 93). All other musical action grinds to a halt; one by one his companions turn slowly on him with reproving eyes while he in turn averts his gaze as if disclaiming responsibility for his arm's unseemly behaviour.

At cue 23, the beginning of part V, a solo trumpet appears from behind the wall of strings and mounts a ladder to play a joyful reveille. Wake up, they are real players behind there after all, he crows, ending his piece with an unmistakeable raspberry directed at the doubters in the audience.

A marvellous, typically Stockhausen gesture marks the climax of the work. Two strokes before the end of V all music stops. In the public concert performance which occupies one side of the first recording, this vacuum is predictably filled by audience protests which have been building in intensity from the opening bars. It is almost as though the music were deliberately winding up the audience to a point where it would catalyze the very process of self-expression inherent in the work itself; to today's listener to the recording, the shutters open on the past, and in that moment the past is vividly revealed. The piece concludes with a coda bringing the whole ensemble, including the recorded time strokes, into a dignified unity and repose as telling as the coda of Stravinsky's *Symphonies of Wind Instruments*, which it passingly resembles.

Inori

1973–4: *Adorations* for one or two soloists and orchestra.

The orchestra is divided into two groups: treble instruments to the right of the conductor, bass instruments to the left, with piano and *rin* between.

4. 4. 4. 4. 8; 4. 2. 1. tuba; 14 sound plates, 16 *rin* (Japanese temple bells), vibraphone, antique cymbals, piano; strings 14. 12. 10. 8. 8.

Duration 70'.

The word *inori* is from the Japanese, and means 'prayer, invocation, adoration', hence the subtitle 'Adorations for one or two soloists and orchestra'. The element of prayer is manifested on two levels: visually in the leading role played by the soloists, and aurally in the music itself. The solo part may be played by an instrument, and indeed is notated in the score as melodic line elaborated from the underlying formula. For preference, however, it is interpreted by two dancer-mimes, who translate the

Ex. 94

Inori: form-schema.

© K. Stockhausen.

notes and inflections of the solo line into an 'action melody' of silent gestures drawn from world religions.

These prayer gestures are exactly reflected in the music for orchestra, which rises and falls in pitch, expands and contracts in amplitude, and is excited and depressed in tempo like a living entity. The orchestration is enormously sensitive, and introduces a seductive emotional and gestural continuity and an expressive suppleness and opulence to the music, which are unexpected from a composer of normally austere and uncompromising character.

The entire composition is derived from a basic formula, lasting about one minute, which encapsulates the underlying proportions of pitch, dynamics, tempi, and duration (Ex. 94). The formula divides into five segments and occupies a range of about an octave above middle C4. The formula's central tone, and tonal pivot of the whole work, is G4, associated with prayer gestures indicating the heart, and with the magic syllable 'HU', invoked at the high point of the composition. The thirteen notes of the formula (which includes a lower and higher C) are associated as well with thirteen tempi, thirteen dynamic levels, thirteen timbres, and thirteen prayer gestures.

The formula is 'projected' on to the much larger scale, about 70 minutes, of the whole work. Its five segments are matched by five formal divisions in about the same proportions, of about 12, 15, 6, 9, and 18 minutes' duration respectively, with extra time for ritardandi, fermatas, and events of indeterminate duration, together with a transcendental moment in the 'Spiral' section and the final exit. These larger divisions are ordered in a stepwise progression from lower to higher complexity reflecting the birth and growth of consciousness and action, in the composer's words 'like a history of music, from its primeval beginnings until the present.'[9]

The first section, 'Rhythm' ('In the beginning was Rhythm'—Hans von Bülow), is an orchestral study on one note which may be perceived by some as an extended meditation on the implications of Berg's famous 'Interlude on the Note B' from *Wozzeck*, much discussed in the golden Darmstadt years of the fifties.[10] Others may hear it as an orchestral meditation in the spirit of monotone plainchant: either way, the effect of reducing the pitch dimension to a single note is to focus the mind and open the hearing to modulations of timbre and dynamic emphasis that would normally pass unnoticed. The section includes a 'tempo melody' or sequence of tempo changes which expresses the pitch frequencies of the formula in the rhythmic domain.

It is succeeded by an unfolding of dynamics, conventionally signifying intensities of emotion and action, and also aural perspective. Here the composer has prepared a surprise. His scale of dynamics is expressed as a *lateral* expansion, from the orchestral extremes cumulatively into the centre: as the level rises, more instruments gradually

[9] Sleeve notes to the recording (DG 2707 111), p. 2 (translated by Suzanne Stephens).
[10] See Pierre Boulez, *Boulez on Music Today*, trans. Susan Bradshaw and Richard Rodney Bennett, (London, 1971), pp. 61–2.

join in a controlled implosion of sound energy, and as the music fades, it also correspondingly recedes from the middle to the edges of the orchestra. Stockhausen has gone to immense pains to orchestrate scales of 60 levels of dynamic from the fringes of audibility to the loudest *fortissimo*, an effort which has further involved redisposing the orchestra to put section leaders at the back instead of the front. The end result is a dynamic dimension of remarkable ductility, but how well the curve is perceived by a concert audience as a directional fluctuation is hard to say. What the conductor is ideally placed to hear as an approaching or receding of amplitude in direct response to his own gestures, a concert-goer in mid-auditorium is invited to hear as lateral movement; but unfortunately concert-halls are not designed to assist lateral discrimination. That is not to say that it could not be made to work (although it is rather reminiscent of the Boulez/CBS panoramic productions of Bartók studio-engineered during the brief heyday of quadraphonic recording). It simply poses a challenge to promoters (and recording engineers) to explore alternative arrange-ments, for instance different acoustic environments and use of electronically assisted reverberation. Certainly in the last resort, a suitable recording, expressing the viewpoint of the conductor and engineered with appropriate acoustic enhancement, should be able to offer the listener using headphones or good surround-sound playback equipment the kind of perspective experience the music promises.

In 'Melody', the third section, which begins after about half an hour, elaborations of the basic formula in its melodic form start to appear; here Stockhausen's lateral orientation of orchestal forces—bass instruments to the left, treble instruments to the right—begins to come into its own, as part-writing assumes a more obviously antiphonal character. Once again nature appears to imitate art as the orchestral arrangement conforms to the two-handed division of the keyboard reproduced in the composer's piano recordings. Sections four and five, devoted respectively to 'Harmony' and 'Polyphony', develop the formula by transposition and expansion in its several dimensions with progressively greater complexity to a symbolic cadenza or 'Spiral' moment in 'Polyphony' where the orchestral texture and hierarchical structure is dissolved in a teeming flux of individual self-expression.

Though commissioned by a Japanese patron, *Inori* reveals fewer overt affiliations with Japanese music than the title might lead one to expect. Stockhausen's concern to develop a more dynamic harmonic idiom based on the relative composition of different timbres at different intensities was bound to excite comparisons with familiar Western idioms, whether Mussorgsky or Gershwin (Ex. 95). It was briefly rumoured that the solo part would be taken by the conductor in a symbolic affirmation of the priestly character and responsibility of a role lately declined into self-serving and spiritually empty ostentation. There is much to compare in the gestural language of *Inori* with the expressive conventions of the podium. In assigning the solo part to a mime, the composer is able to preserve the prayerful nature of the part more intact, one suspects, that it would otherwise be; and the performer is also free to face the audience. The soloist is raised on a precariously high

Ex. 95

-78-

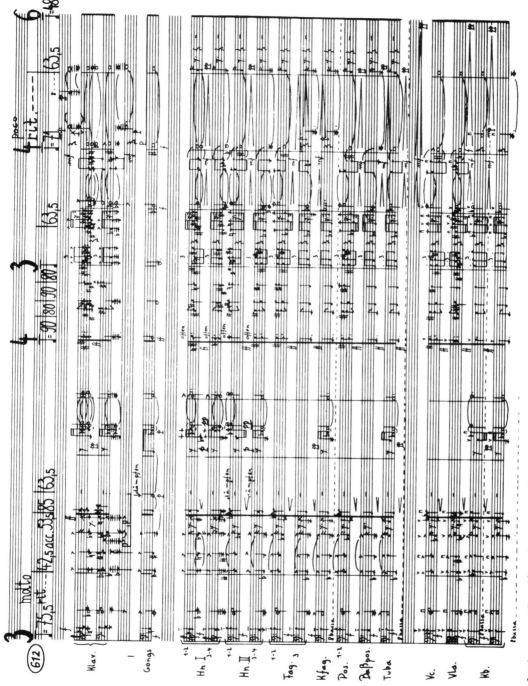

Inori: score at 612. The solo part is marked 'Be' (*Beter*: 'one who prays'): numbers in circles refer to a repertoire of prayer gestures. The unusual graphic notation in the treble strings and woodwinds indicates the rhythm and dynamic nuances of the constant pitch shown at the top of the page.

© K. Stockhausen.

and small platform, reached by ladders of twelve steps; beneath the platform, at ground level, stands the real conductor in a position of suitably reduced status.

By and large, the prayer gestures present, in their seamless continuity, effective stylizations of Stockhausen's own clearly articulated conducting movements. The notations of the prayer gestures are an invention of great importance for the future choreography of the composer's opera cycle *LICHT*. Although one might suppose the relationship between the soloist and the orchestra to be self-evident, it transpired after a number of early premiéres that audiences were perceiving the soloist as improvising to the music, and his subsequent use of two soloists in parallel has aimed to counter this mistaken impression by making it obvious that the gestures are fully composed.

Spiritually, *Inori* relates to *Momente*. The tone is meditative rather than extrovert, the expressive dimension instrumental rather than vocal—the mute mime an exact antipode to the cheerful garrulity of the solo soprano in the earlier work. If *Momente* in part represents the tensions of the relationship of the artist and society, personified by the choirs, *Inori* in part expresses the analogous tensions between the composer and orchestra—tensions manifested dramatically in the orchestra strike of *Samstag aus LICHT*. Here the 'disturbances' are relatively minor: in a scene recalling the orchestrated cat calls of *Momente* a bass tuba interrupts with the musical equivalent of derisive exasperation, puncturing the atmosphere of ritual at a critical point and distracting the soloist during a particularly intricate sequence of moves. She glowers at him, and stamps her foot.

In a 'Lecture on HU', listed as a separate work for a singer (preferably female), the composer provides an appropriately dignified introduction to the *Inori* formula and its implications.

14 *Fables and Incarnations*

STOCKHAUSEN'S compositions after *Inori* are united in the pursuit of a theatrical imagery expressing musical concepts in spatial and visual terms. This common pursuit links pieces that superficially appear totally unrelated in style or content; indeed their differences are a consequence in part of a systematic evaluation of specific technical problems.

'Atmen gibt das Leben . . .'

1974–7: *'Breathing Gives Life . . .'*
Choral opera with orchestra (or tape).
Duration 49′ 30″.

The choral opera *'Atmen gibt das Leben . . .'* is the first of a group of compositions which examine the problems of composing for an ensemble with cheoreographed stage movements. It began life as a short piece for unaccompanied mixed choir, sketched during one of the composer's regular composition seminars at the Cologne Musikhochschule in response to a request for a piece suitable for amateur choir. Stockhausen made a class assignment of it, specifying the music should be adaptable for more than one text, and that the text should be neither Christian nor political. For his own exercise he chose a text by the Sufi philosopher Hazrat Inayat Khan:

> Breathing gives life,
> But only singing gives the form . . .

—with an alternative text also by Inayat Khan entitled *Schlafend ist erquickened* (Sleeping is reviving).[1] The sounds of breathing and sleeping become a starting-point for a glossary of interesting new vocal sounds based on huffing and puffing, and unusual ideas such as singing while inhaling (Ex. 96).

[1] Stockhausen found these texts in Hazrat Inayat Khan, *Die Schale des Schenken* (Berlin, 1948).

Ex. 96

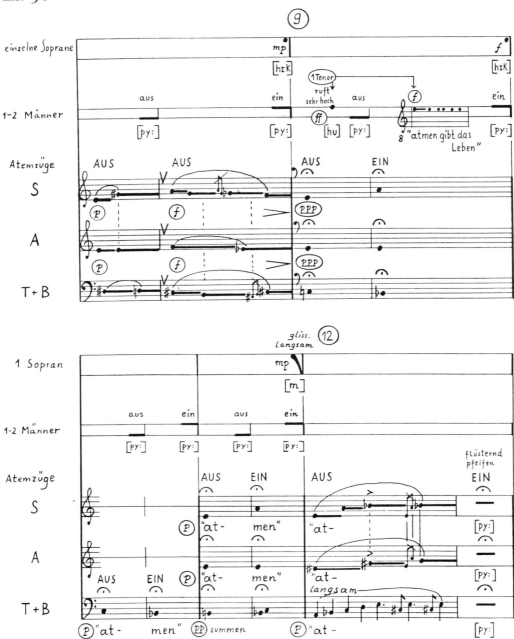

'Atmen gibt das Leben. . .'. Page from the 1974 version for unaccompanied choir.
© K. Stockhausen.

The normal repertoire of natural vocal noises is considerable, and their meanings (many of them rude) universally recognized, from the hiccup to the sharp intake of breath through pursed lips. These sounds are clearly fruitful material for an international vocal music: it is just that they have never been properly acknowledged, notated, or otherwise incorporated into Western written music. Other aspects of the music (the harmonic idiom, polarization of male and female voices, solo voices 'floating' over the ensemble, and a certain literalness in interpreting the text), take the listener back sharply to the a-cappella pieces of the composer's youth, the *Choral* and the *Chöre für Doris*.

In December 1976 he revised and expanded the work, discarding his original alternative text and adding a sequence of new texts, including citations from Socrates, the Gospel according to St Thomas, and Meister Eckhart. Much of the text material suggests ideas, situations, and characters to be later assimilated into *LICHT*. An orchestral part, which may be performed from tape, was composed to accompany the new material. The complete work comprises a sequence of scenic attitudes, the texts alluding, rather like the intuitive text pieces of 1968–70, to states of contemplation rather than to a specific theme. Dramatically, one could say the piece is literally about 'inspiration' and the images of dreams that remain in the mind upon awakening. Stockhausen's choreography is reserved, even cautious, incorporating the fixed expressions and frozen double-takes which are features of the composer's productions since *Mantra* and refer as much to German expressionist films of the thirties as to the style of Noh drama.

Herbstmusik

1974: '*Autumn Music*'

Actions for four players, two of whom play viola and clarinet.

1. 'Ein Dach vernageln' (Nailing a Roof) (duo with accompaniment)
2. 'Holz brechen' (Breaking Wood) (quartet)
3. 'Dreschen' (Threshing) (trio)
4. 'Laub und Regen' (Leaves and Rain) (duo)

Duration 70'.

Performances of this composition have been widely misunderstood. Stockhausen has taken a television or radiophonic conception into the concert-hall (Ex. 97), outraging critics conditioned to expect a narrower range of sounds, and possibly a greater decorum of behaviour, in 'their' cultural preserves. The idea of a tone-poem

Fables and Incarnations

Ex. 97

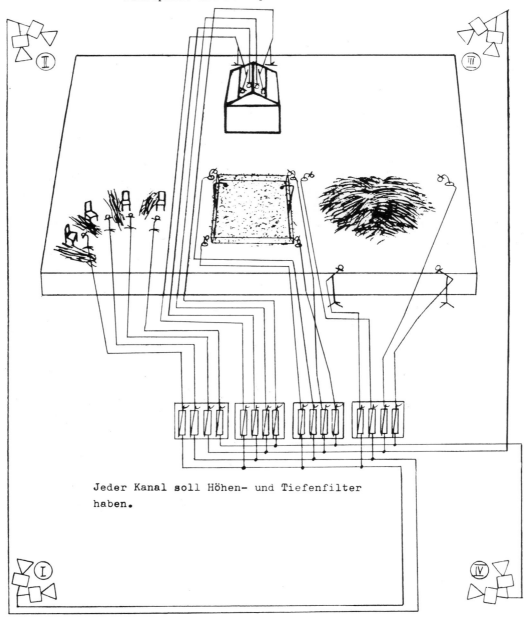

Abbildung 2: Aufstellung des Instrumentariums und Verteilung der Mikrophone und Lautsprecher mit technischer Schaltung.

Jeder Kanal soll Höhen- und Tiefenfilter haben.

Herbstmusik: stage plan showing amplification circuitry.
© K. Stockhausen.

in sound, or wordless play of incidental noises, is as old as radio itself. As early as 1924 C. A. Lewis, Programme Organizer of the fledgling BBC, foresaw 'a new form of drama evolving, . . . given in a series of sound pictures. [It] would depend largely for its effect on the realism of the atmospheres produced by the noises transmitted'.[2] German radio drama has an equally long and imaginative tradition of scene-painting in sound which Stockhausen, as an employee of Cologne Radio, was bound to absorb. There is nothing intrinsically peculiar in a composition of sound-actions. All one asks is that the sounds be sufficient in themselves to convey what the author intends. On this occasion the message of the sounds is a musical statement often far removed from the dramatic implications of the visible actions, which seem to range from polemical reportage of a kind associated with Jean-Luc Godard, to silent comedy, by way of Samuel Beckett. There is a hint of mischief in Stockhausen's translation of an intrinsically non-visual radiophonic idiom on to the stage, a move virtually guaranteeing that the work will be immediately misconstrued as a piece of visual theatre. The comedy does not end there. Soundscapes in radio and television tend to be purely expository, any developing 'narrative' normally arising from the succession of images and not from their content. On this occasion, however, Stockhausen has taken great care to choose sound-actions with their own dynamic of evolution; so whereas the visual actions may appear static and repetitive, the sounds produced (if the listener would only pay attention to them instead of ignoring them as a mere by-product) actually evolve and change in a musical way.

Ostensibly a celebration of rural life, the work grapples head-on with the challenge of reconciling the live equivalent of 'concrete sounds' with the world of live music-making. Natural sounds, like the consonants of '*Atmen gibt das Leben . . .*', constitute a vast repertoire of creative material, made accessible through recording technology, and only denied to the serious composer by outdated and unnecessary taboos. The work is in four scenes which are performed as a continuous sequence. The first, 'Nailing a Roof', consists largely of a two-part polyphony of hammering nails. The pattern of rhythmic relationship between the two hammerers is richly varied from totally synchronized to complete independence, and is defined with great precision in the score, which of necessity is verbal rather than notated. Hammers and nails alike are exactly described: the hammers have claws of unequal length, the nails comprising a series of five different lengths and thicknesses for musical variety.

Hammering is the natural 'concrete' equivalent of Stockhausen's beloved impulses. The sound of two diverging trains of hammering is vividly evoked in *Telemusik* (the *taku* beats at 19), and hammering is also implicit in the composer's writing for conventional percussion. Pure hammering as musical material was first introduced by Stockhausen into the recording of the intuitive composition *Intensität*, in the sleeve note to which he remarks:

[2] Cecil A. Lewis, *Broadcasting from Within* (London, 1924), pp. 121–2.

First I cleaned the timber with periodic [i.e. rhythmically regular] sandpapering and rasping. I then knocked in long nails one after another: at first individual ones completely, then groups of nails to different depths, and finally deeper till they were right in (big differences in pitch) . . . The 'intensity' of my playing . . . which I first interpreted as the purely physical one of hammering and sweating, turned suddenly into an extremely spiritual one, into a wealth of rhythmic polyphony.[3]

The second action consists of four players breaking brushwood in front of microphones; the sound is amplified and reproduced from the four corners of the auditorium space. The players draw their sticks from separate piles, organized so that the thickest are at the top, and the thinnest twigs at the bottom of each pile. The resulting sound composition is a 'concrete' version of the kind of instrumental texture composed for *Fresco*, namely a field of indeterminate points of sound gradually reducing in range toward the treble. Since each stick naturally tapers, the breaking of it defines a pitch range from a low snap at the thicker end to a high splintering at the thin end, and since the sticks are graded in thickness from the top of the pile to the bottom, it follows that the degree of pitch variation will change as the piles are exhausted, till at the end the sound texture will be concentrated in the upper register. The texture also relates to electronic transformations of pointillistic textures, with the difference that no acceleration accompanies the upward transposition, and the sound quality is also relatively unaffected by the change of pitch.

'Threshing', the third scene, involves a stylized swishing of thin switches through the air on to a pile of straw. Their sound relates to continuous sibilants, as the stick-breaking sounds relate to stopped glottals and palatals, and nail-banging to plosives; in addition, however, these 'elegant, wonderfully far-out' movements incorporate dynamic curves which have distinct associations with the rotational movement and extreme acceleration of electronic music. The fourth and last episode, 'Leaves and Rain', is played by a couple in amorous rough-and-tumble on freshly raked leaves. The thump of bodies hitting the ground is predictably low and muffled, but of high amplitude. We are now in the real world of low-frequency sounds and their physical associations, a world encountered before in *Kontakte* and *Telemusik*. These greatly amplified bumps are offset by the officious tread and heel-click of a third member of the ensemble, introducing a note of danger and a suggestion that the couple's behaviour might have an illicit dimension. It begins to 'rain': sprinkers start to play on the bodies and leaves. Gradually the pile of leaves becomes more compacted; equally gradually the players' actions acquire clearer acoustic contours and richer overtone spectra as the soft thumps give way to sharper slaps of wet bodies on one another and on firmer ground. Towards the end they assume a stylized rhythm which transforms magically into a closing duet for viola and clarinet.

---

[3] Sleeve note to LP set DG 2720 073 (trans. Richard Toop).

Tierkreis

1974–5: *Zodiac*, twelve melodies for musical boxes.

1. 'Aquarius'
2. 'Pisces'
3. 'Aries'
4. 'Taurus'
5. 'Gemini'
6. 'Cancer'
7. 'Leo'
8. 'Virgo'
9. 'Libra'
10. 'Scorpio'
11. 'Sagittarius'
12. 'Capricorn'

Durations between 24.4 and 30.4 sec.

These twelve melodies introduce a new flexibility of scale and expression to the concept of a melody formula. They are longer and conform more nearly to existing classical and folk-melody idioms; with their simple accompaniments they also appear more natural in cadence and rhythm than the severe, concentrated formulas of *Mantra* or *Inori*. They are also simpler, omitting serial dynamic and attack specifications, and abandoning the stop—go structures, with interpolated fermatas, of the earlier melodies.

Considering their celestial names one thinks of *Sternklang* and the idea of substituting composed melodies at the point where the players look heavenwards and improvise melodies to the shaps of the visible constellations. Such an idea would imply a collection of melodies designed to make musical sense in any combination or sequence, which is an attractive challenge. The wider implications of having a range of interrelating melodies instead of only one formula are considerable. In an operatic context, for example, characters could be associated with their own distinctive melodies, and their dramatic interactions be exactly reflected in appropriate contrapuntal combinations.

Stockhausen has to some extent designed the twelve melodies after the *Sternklang* 'models'. Each is composed as an indefinitely repeating cycle, each is based on a different tonal centre ('Aquarius' = E♭, ascending in a chromatic scale via 'Leo' = A to 'Capricorn = D), and each pulsates at a different degree of a tempo scale between crotchet = MM 71 and 134 (which is a minor-third transposition of the scale MM 60–120). There is more. Composed for musical boxes, their high tessituras, cyclic structures, and relatively limited range of durations are also associated with the parameters of musical box construction. There is therefore an additional mechanical dimension influencing their composition and notation, and the concept of mechanically recurring melodies has significant further implications.

If we analyse the new melodies (Ex. 98) we see that the distribution of pitches in time, meaning the number and pattern of repeats of individual pitches as well as the pattern of intervals they form in combination, is quite unlike the decorated but

Ex. 98

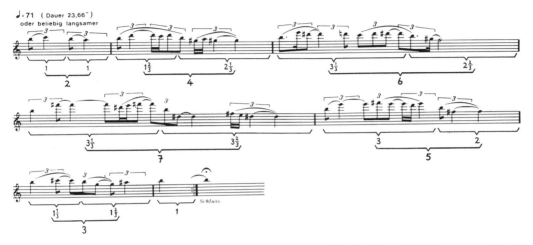

'Libra' melody from *Tierkreis*, analysed. The starting note B divides the melody into proportional sections, and the melody interval content also pivots around the same note.

© K. Stockhausen.

essentially literal serialism of his orthodox formulas (though there are striking resemblances to certain melodies of *Formel*):

In the LIBRA melody, B is the central pitch, and all of the other pitches swing out from it: up, down, up, etc. The durations of the measures are as follows: 2, 6, 6, 7, 5, 3, 1. Think of LIBRA, the balance, and how this large rhythm swings out and back over the entire melody . . . Now let's see what makes this melody so rhythmically special. Always short, long, short, long . . . The 'new' pitches . . . have the following progression of intervals in respect to the central note B: +1, −2, +3, −3, +4, −6, +7, −8, +5, −5, +2, −4, −1, 0. . . . The principle is that in each *limb* there are two new pitches. This aspect is also like a balance.[4]

The inner composition of these *Tierkreis* melodies is much closer to the pitched

---

[4] Karlheinz Stockhausen, *Stockhausen in Den Haag*, Documentation of the Karlheinz Stockhausen Project (English edn.), Michael Manion, Barry Sullivan, and Frits Weiland. Koninklijk Conservatorium te Den Haag (The Hague, 1982), pp. 19–20.

impulse sequences of *Kontakte*, which were of course designed to be accelerated enormously until their inner rhythms were transformed into timbres. So in an important respect these new melodies also correspond to wave forms, designed to be capable of making the transition from the human scale of pitch and rhythm to the time-scale of tone colour. Evidently, the immediate pretext for this aspect of melody composition is the composer's work with the Synthi 100.

A number of editions of the melodies have been published, both for instruments and for accompanied voices (to texts by the composer). A version for chamber orchestra, in which the complete cycle of twelve melodies is performed, dates from 1977, and a shorter form incorporating only six melodies is also authorized and has been recorded. An especially beautiful version dates from 1984, created for his co-workers Markus Stockhausen (trumpet and piano), Suzanne Stephens (clarinet), and Kathinka Pasveer (flute and piccolo), which is also recorded.

These versions keep to the human time-scale of the original melodies. In *Musik im Bauch* and *Sirius*, on the other hand, the possibilities of combining melodies in polyphonic structures of varying time proportions are examined in greater detail.

Musik im Bauch

1975: *Music in the Belly*.
Musical fable for six percussionists and musical boxes.
3 crotala keyboards (C6–B7)(or 2 plus glockenspiel), glockenspiel, 3 switches, marimbaphone (2 players), bell plates, tubular bell (or musical spinning top producing a loud overtone chord on the note E4), 12 musical boxes (of which 3 are chosen for any one performance). In the centre stage is suspended MIRON, a larger-than-lifesize mannequin, male, with the head of an eagle, garlanded in small Indian bells, and containing the three musical boxes in a cavity in the belly.
Duration 45′

Dedicated to his daughter Julika and inspired by an attack of collywobbles which caused her great excitement one day when she was just 2 years old, this entrancing musical fable employs imagery of the nursery as dramatic illustration of a new modular polyphony allowing for different structural combinations of the *Tierkreis* melodies. perhaps the subject-matter reflects a spirit of innocent experiment: certainly there is much in the actions to delight and charm the listener. A performance is based on three chosen melodies from the *Tierkreis* cycle. *Musik im*

Bauch unfolds simultaneously on different time-scales. The marimba, with two performers acting in concert like automatons, plays a stretched version of one of the chosen melodies which lasts the entire length of the performance; on the opposite side of the stage the bell-plate player performs stretched versions of all three chosen melodies in sequence, each in turn determining the duration of one scene.

On to this formal skeleton is superimposed the flesh-and-blood ritual actions of the other three players. Their behaviour has elements of the fairy-tale convention of three brothers on a mysterious quest, each undergoing the same experiences, encountering a mysterious figure, and gaining a prize, though it is left to the child in the audience to guess, or rather invent, the true meaning.

In scene 1 the three 'brothers' are discovered practising their different melodies at the rear of the stage. In the second scene, they approach and circle the mannequin, flexing switches and grimacing like practising samurai; each player using the rhythm of his own birth-sign melody. Very tentatively at first, then with increasing vigour, they begin to pat, then swat the MIRON figure, adding a crescendo of thuds and coruscation of tiny bell sounds to the increasingly vigorous swish of the switches through the air.

On a loud signal from the tubular bell (or spinning top) everyone freezes. Followed by the fixed stares of his companions one of the 'brothers' runs in a straight line off the stage with a clatter of footsteps (recalling a famous scene from *The Goon Show*), to return after a short pause (the bell or top still audible) with an enormous pair of shears as big as those of the scissor-man in *Struwwelpeter*. Deftly inserting them between the buttons of MIRON's shirt, he makes a couple of giant snips and reaches into the cavity to remove a small musical box. Moving to a low table at the left front of the stage, he opens the musical box: it begins to play his melody, and he moves to kneel at a glockenspiel and play along with the musical box melody. He is interrupted by a loud bang from a bell-plate and runs off the stage.

The second 'brother' repeats the action of extracting musical box, places it on a centre-front table, and again plays along with it. As he leaves he sets both boxes playing. The third 'brother' also finds a musical box in the belly of the mannequin, advances, stops the other boxes, sets his own box playing on the table at stage right, and plays along with it on the glockenspiel. Finally, having rewound the first musical box, he sets all three boxes playing simultaneously, salutes MIRON with an elegant bow, and exits. Gradually the boxes run down, and their music slows into hesitant isolated tones. As their music also comes to an end, the two marimba players turn and take their leave, walking with the exaggerated stiffness of mechanical dolls. The piece ends with the three musical boxes slowly running down against a background of tolling bell-plates. The moral seems to be that what we take to be humanly inspired is in fact entirely preordained in the divine melodies of which the composer, in his guise as bird-man, is the mysterious messenger. Music is the ultimate meaning of the visible drama.

Sirius

1975–7.

Electronic music and trumpet, soprano, bass clarinet, bass.

Duration 96'.

Commissioned by the government of the Federal Republic of Germany in honour of the United States' bicentennial in 1976, *Sirius* is Stockhausen's most substantial tape electronic composition, and in many ways the most radically new. The new work has symbolic importance as a statement of faith in synthesized electronic music (just as Boulez's *Répons* was to make a similar public affirmation of IRCAM's computer technology in 1981) and as a defence of the idealistic values of the post-war generation of composers to a younger generation increasingly disaffected with technology. *Sirius* is also, inevitably, a statement about the state of the art, especially one particular piece of technology, the Zinovieff-designed EMS Synthi 100. Almost all of the technical interest is focused, however, on the sequencer which inspired the composition of the *Tierkreis* cycle of melody constellations, and which now demonstrates its transformational prowess.

The relationship of the four live players to the electronic music is the same as for *Kontakte* or *Hymnen mit Solisten*. Like the melodies they play, the live players are represented as human incarnations of a transcendental reality expressed by the electronic music. The latter ranges across and beyond the time and pitch scales of the original melodies and their sung versions, to encompass time scales as fast as the wind or as slow (metaphorically) as the seasons, and pitch inflections as slight as the buzzing of an insect or susurration of the breeze. Like *Hymnen*, the electronic treatment of recognizable themes is impelled by a dynamic of speed and associated transformations of scale and perspective of objects in the environment. In the earlier work, the listener is transported across the Atlantic in an instant; for the new work Stockhausen has lifted his sights to the stars as their changing patterns reflect the orbital motion of the earth on its journey through the cosmos.

Cyclic formations dominate the work at every level. The cycle of the seasons, the zodiac, the elements air, earth, fire, and water, even the cycle of human life itself, express a terrestrial fabric of experience and belief which connects with a universal order of cycles within cycles mediated by the electronic polyphony.

The work begins with a 'Presentation' of the four soloists, who appear at the four compass points (bass north, soprano south, trumpet east, and bass clarinet west). Their principal melodies, which form the basis of the electronic music, are 'Capricorn' (winter), 'Cancer' (summer), 'Aries' (spring) (Ex. 99), and 'Libra' (autumn) respectively. They appear out of four bursts of sound whizzing round the

247

Ex. 99

'Aries' melody as it is sung in *Sirius*. Compare with the *Formel* melody for vibraphone, Ex. 7.
© K. Stockhausen.

audience like an acoustic cyclotron, creating weird aural illusions (see above p. 197). Each rotational descent is marked by a final burst on the throttle recalling the sound of Cocteau's motorbike-riding messengers of the gods in *Orphée*. As they mount their platforms at north, south, east and west, the four arrivals are accompanied by recorded natural sounds of footsteps in the snow and breaking ice, crackling and burning of a wood fire, the gurgling of a brook, and the whistling and howling of the wind—aural talismans of a richer seasonal tapestry of which *Herbstmusik* could conceivably have been a preliminary sketch.

There follows the centre-piece of the work: 'The Wheel', a musical cycle of the seasons. A performance can begin at the point in the cycle appropriate to the time of year, reviewing the zodiacal melodies in sequence and ending on completion of one revolution. 'Each of the four main melodies reigns for approximately $\frac{1}{4}$ hour, and all 12 melodies divide the hour like the 12 numbers of a clock.'[5] The work ends with the section 'The Annunciation', to a visionary text by Jakob Lorber, greeting humankind on behalf of an extraterrestrial intelligence, a notional close encounter with which the musical conception is clearly in sympathy.

The music of *Sirius*, in particular 'The Wheel', shows Stockhausen in a new contrapuntal guise. For all its textual allusions to directional separation, the four-part solo and accompanying electronic music forms a dense sound web demanding the greatest concentration of a listener. One is made aware how important a component of the music the spatial dimension has become, both to allow the different parts to be clearly distinguished, and to give the music (and the listener) room to breathe. The necessary reduction of an original circle of eight play-back channels to stereo undoubledly makes listening to the published recording more

[5] Sleeve notes, DG album 2707 122, p. 3 (trans. Suzanne Stephens).

248

Ex. 100

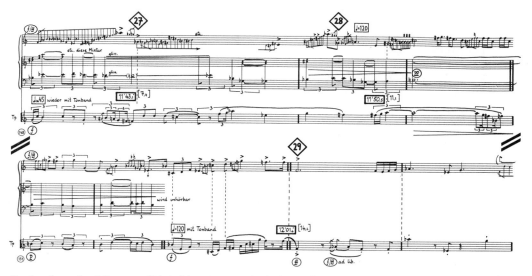

Section from the full score of '*Aries*' (concert version). At 29 the trumpet re-establishes contact with the 'Aries' melody.

© K. Stockhausen.

difficult than to a live performance; but another equally powerful factor is the penetrating intensity of the electronic sounds themselves, which glister in the acoustic darkness of multitrack tape with the disorientating brightness of polished chrome. The Synthi 100 is not famous for its range of timbres.

In 1980 Stockhausen prepared a concert version of *Aries* for trumpet and tape (Ex. 100), and in an introductory lecture he leads the listener through the melodic transformations which mark the movement of the seasons from spring to autumn:

This version of ARIES begins with the ARIES melody heard with the rhythm of CAPRICORN. It is increasingly sped up, and the CAPRICORN melody is added to, or mixed with, the melody of ARIES. During this accelerando process, the rhythm of CAPRICORN is transformed to become the ARIES rhythm, and the rhythm and melody of CANCER is slowly introduced. After about two minutes the melodies disappear and a hissing sound appears, because it is no longer possible to analyze either the melody or the rhythm: they are too fast.[6]

The sound divides into two layers; one is further accelerated, throwing off bright fragments of the 'Aries' melody like sparks, while the other dense band, compounded from the three melodies 'Cancer', 'Capricorn', and 'Aries', is gradually compressed until only a monotone A4 pitch is heard pulsating in the melody rhythm. Then, in a process reminiscent of Messiaen, the shorter rhythmic values are gradually

[6] Stockhausen 'Musical Metamorphosis', op. cit. 31–2.

249

lengthened and the longer values gradually shortened, to leave a regular pulsation. This too slows down, and the individual pulses are gradually lengthened until they merge into one continuous timbre:

Here at last is the great survivor, the timbre. And the timbre disappears like the wind which whistles behind the corner of a house. [Be] careful here not to lose the residue of melody which conceals itself between two vowels, within the timbre, precisely between the *i* and the *u* . . . Then from the depths of the progressive annihilation, the timbre rises once more, and this time with a completely different melody.[7]

Stockhausen's own seemingly improvised texts to the melodies and for the solo singers deserve notice in view both of the composer's youthful prowess as a poet, and in the light of his sensitivity to words, and to the texture of language, in previous works. He is evidently concerned in this work not to allow words to dominate; rather, they are ritual invocations, marker buoys on a musical tide, commenting on rather than leading the musical action. Indeed his way with words appears more idiomatic in French than in English; perhaps because the French language is structured in a more sympathetic way, perhaps because the fragmented, allusive style is one more readily associated with French poetry and surrealist word-painting. Of course, it is equally important to Stockhausen that the text should also be free of especial ties to any one language: these are universal sentiments which should be equally attuned to all languages. The matter is of some importance because the same considerations also underlie the texts of *LICHT*.

A more personal form of celestial messenger arrives in the figure of Harlequin as female clarinet player. Suzanne Stephens, a young American, became associated with Stockhausen in 1974, at the start of her professional career. The clarinet parts in *Herbstmusik* and *Sirius* were written for her, and since that time she has become a permanent member of the composer's musical household, as soloist and collaborator in developing the art of the clarinet and basset-horn, and as the musical incarnation of Eva in the opera cycle *LICHT*.

Harlekin

1975: *Harlequin* for clarinet.
Duration 44'.

---

[7] Mya Tannenbaum, *Conversations with Stockhausen* trans. David Butchart (Oxford, 1987), p. 62.

Ex. 101

Harlekin: melody formula 'Der verliebte Lyriker'.

© K. Stockhausen.

Der Kleine Harlekin

1975: *Little Harlequin* for clarinet.
Duration 8′ 42″.

Harlequin is the personification of mischief and magic: a human, sensual, comic counterpart to the austere divinities of *Sirius*. These pieces for Suzanne Stephens are both affectionate portraits of virtuoso high spirits, and further developments of a more fluid, secular art of music-theatre, fully and continuously choreographed and consolidating the relationship between visual and musical actions.

Harlekin is composed as a large-scale wave form in both music and action. It begins in the high register, expands downwards to cover the pitch range, descends to lurk briefly in the low register, only to ascend again to the extreme upper register by a reverse process of expansion and retreat upward in pitch. The transformational journey across the registers—which has much in common with the spirit of the composer's earliest pointillist works—is measured by a series of staging posts at which a principal formula, 'the enamoured lyrist' (Ex. 101), is heard at different registers and tempi. Connecting these are cyclic *moto perpetuo* figurations based on the pitch sequence of the formula, condensing out of an initial trill and gradually increasing in number of pitches and dynamic spread to fill the entire range of the instrument. These musical processes are also associated with rotational movements by the performer; it is as though the imagery of Stockhausen's 'rotation table' heard in *Sirius* were being translated into human terms. Their almost baroque figurations relate too to the continuous transformation processes of the Synthi 100 sequencer as encountered in the version of *Aries* described above, and subsequently in *Jubiläum* for orchestra.

In 1977 'Harlequin's Dance', part of the larger work, was developed as a separate piece. In it, the choreographic possibilities of a comic foot-stamping dialogue with the clarinet (marking the moment of ultimate contact with the low frequencies of the real world) are further extended and elaborated.

Amour

1976: Five pieces for clarinet.
  1. 'Sei wieder fröhlich' (Cheer up)
  2. 'Dein Engel wacht über Dir' (Your guardian angel watches over you)

3. 'Die Schmetterlinge spielen' (Butterflies are playing)
4. (Ein Vöglein singt an deinem Fenster) (A little bird sings at your window)
5. 'Vier Sterne wiesen Dir den Weg' (Four stars light your way)

Duration 23′ 30″.

These five character pieces continue Stockhausen's exploration of formula transformation as a vehicle for figurative representation of a kind we are more used to associating with the nineteenth century than with twentieth-century serialism. Unlike romantic character pieces, however, these are not inventions inspired by the object of affection as much as musical discoveries which awaken particular associations and thus assume a special identity. We are not quite yet back in the *Sturm und Drang* world of Viennese expressionism—the tempi are still numbers rather than words—but Stockhausen's softer-centred titles are clearly aimed at inspiring and directing the interpretative sympathies of the solo performer in a positive way.

'Sei weider fröhlich' unfolds from a musical bud into a fully opened formula, at the same time conveying a familiar middle-eastern melancholy. 'Dein Engel wacht über Dir' is a two-part invention in which initially separated versions of the same formula, one low and expansive, the oher high and compressed into homogeneous time values, gradually merge and interact. A musical image of courting butterflies is the visual referent of 'Die Schmetterlinge spielen', a virtuosic exercise in rapid interval transposition in pianissimo, a sound level allowing an agreeable 'fluttering' quality to be heard. In 'Ein Vöglein singt an Deinem Fenster' (Ex. 102) a four-limb formula floats on the surface of a fluctuating-tempo melody, its intervals gradually closing together with each recurrence into a gently bobbing middle range, and trills at the same time becoming 'teased out' into grace-note figures. 'I remember sitting for hours, for days, at a pond when I was very small. I used to throw stones into the pond and watch my reflection become completely distorted. Processes like this have never been possible in music.'[8] He gets close to it with this intriguing study. The last piece, 'Vier Sterne weisen Dir den Weg' follows a continuous process of transformation of a four-note figure in the low register. The player is asked to discover nuances in the transition between periodic and rhythmicized repetitions which are too subtle to notate. The distillation of rhythm from rapid periodicity derives from a feature of digital sequencing mentioned already, which gradually eliminates distinctions of rhythm as a consequence of time compression (gradually all duration values are reduced to 1). The piece is dedicated to Doris, the 'four stars' symbolizing their four children. However it also appears to be making a more sardonic reference to his first wife's early aspirations as a music student. While this bumblebee buzzes and struggles, unable to take flight, high above it a larger transformation of the same interval pattern effortlessly soars.

---

[8] Stockhausen, op. cit. (above, n. 5), p. 33.

Ex. 102

Amour, 'Ein Vöglein singt . . .': the melody stretched to its fullest extent.
© K. Stockhausen.

Jubiläum

1977: *Jubilee* for orchestra.

4. 4. 4. 3. contrabassoon. 4; 3. 4. 1; 2 glockenspiels, glass chimes, 5 triangles, chromatic bell-plates (or gongs and tam-tams) C2–C3♯, piano, celesta; strings 8 (10). 8 (10). 8. 6. 6.

Duration 15′.

This short (for Stockhausen), festive piece for orchestra was commissioned for the 125th Anniversary Jubilee of Hanover Opera. To arrive at an idea of its sound imagery, we may borrow the example of a football crowd (one of the structured noises Stockhausen employs in *Hymnen*). This type of noise-event can often be perceived as a structure of musical layers. First there is a layer of applause, a dense noise filling the frequency spectrum, and within which the sound of individuals clapping at different speeds may be heard, sometimes increasing in speed, sometimes slowing down. Against this background a second layer may occasionally appear, as groups among the crowd begin to synchronize their applause in regular periodic clapping. This change from unstructured to structured noise is often accompanied by singing, which, however, does not usually last for very long: when it ends after a short while the periodic clapping either spontaneously dissolves back into individual applause, or sometimes one hears it starting to increase in speed to a point where it breaks up once more into unstructured noise.

A third layer can be heard during the intermission, when a band plays an item of music. Depending on the item, the crowd may ignore the music or clap and sing along with it.

Imagine such a sound-event with its layers of speeds, degrees of noise and music, degrees of indeterminacy and integration, and superimposed transitions from more disordered to more orderly and back, expressed in orchestral terms and you have an idea of the sort of music Stockhausen has composed for *Jubiläum*. The main orchestra is divided into four mixed-instrumental frequency bands. At the top of the range are the two glockenspiels, piano (treble stave only, always with sustaining pedal), and celesta: this use of keyboards as marking the extreme treble harks back to the 'star-sound' convention of *Formel*. Flutes, clarinets, and violins with mutes constitute a second frequency band in the mezzo-soprano range; trumpets, horns, violas, and cellos occupy the tenor layer, and bassoons and contrabassi, aided by tuned bell-plates, sit firmly in the bass. All instruments are chromatically tuned with the exception of the glass chimes and five triangles, though they too are heard as pitch collections.

The banded divisions of the orchestra are reflected in a layout which once again organizes treble instruments to the right and bass instruments to the left. Technically, the musical structure is an orchestral realization of a four-layer polyphony of formulae in perpetual motion and perpetual transformation, of a kind encountered in the electronic music of *Sirius*. At the centre is a solemn, harmonized formula (Ex. 103), punctuated by pauses filled with 'coloured noises' of wind and string overtone glissandi, the whole 'in the character of a hymn'.

Not since *Zeitmasze* has Stockhausen addressed with such care—and obvious concern for ease of assimilation and rehearsal—the problem of notating and co-ordinating multiple tempi in continuous variation. The score is masterly: an object-lesson for composers. And like *Zeitmasze*, the music itself is full of humour. While the three upper instrumental layers independently slow down and converge on to the time frame of the hymn, or accelerate and dissipate away from it, the fourth extreme bass layer acts as a permanent time reference, underpinning the hymn whenever it appears, providing a base for a layer descending into its time-scale, and a launch pad for a layer ascending back into the stratosphere. It is, as it were, the cantus firmus for the conductor and the route map by which those playing independently are able to navigate.

At the outset the tenor instruments occupy the time frame of the two-minute hymn, played firmly and loudly at crotchet = MM 30. During this time the two higher instrumental layers are heard in the background playing octave bands of melody noise consisting of periodic 15-note figures derived from the formula and independently repeating at different tempi. The tenor instruments then begin to accelerate, still playing in harmony but gradually becoming quieter, until a tempo twice as fast is reached. At the same time the two other bands are expanding in time, their initial periodicity giving way to structured rhythms. At 33 the whole process is

Ex. 103

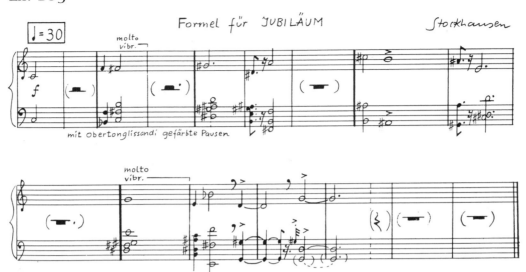

Jubiläum: formula 'in the character of a hymn'.
© Universal Edition AG Wien.

suddenly interrupted by the first of two 'sound-windows'. Through an open door at the rear left of the orchestra platform a brass quintet of trombones and tuba is heard playing the hymn at the new higher crotchet = MM 60 tempo.

The interruption is dramatically effective and a useful tactic for covering both the final co-ordination of the flutes and violins layers, and an otherwise tricky transition of the tenor layer from harmonized co-ordination to unison gradual uncoordination. Now the mezzo layer is 'in tempo', the tenor layer accelerating, and the keyboards still slowing down. After its moment of contact, the mezzo layer begins to accelerate again and a second moment of truth is reached at 94, where a second 'sound-window' opens, this time at the rear right, and a quartet of oboes is heard playing a higher octave transposition of the harmonized formula.

Now the treble keyboards are 'in tempo' with the bass cantus firmus, but at the higher speed; while they descend to the original tempo the two middle layers continue accelerating and compressing their rhythms into periodic values (Ex. 104). At the end of this process the orchestra comes together in a gesture of unity similar to *Trans* and salutes the audience with a final chorus of the formula at a briskish crotchet = MM 50.

After the first performance Stockhausen made some additions to the score. Some discreet changes of texture and colour are introduced to enhance formal divisions, for example the string tremolos at 17 at the start of the acceleration process. The bare architecture of the hymn is also given some decorative additions which, in addition

Ex. 104

Jubiläum: full score at 107. Flute, oboes, and violin soli add ornamental counterpoint based on the pitches of groups I and II. The high keyboards have slowed down to the tempo of the group-IV 'ground bass', and continue to decelerate; the group II woodwinds and violins simultaneously begin to accelerate from MM 30 back to an eventual maximum, while group-III brass and lower strings are already well advanced on their own acceleration process, in which rhythmic distinctions are gradually lost and co-ordination is likewise progressively obliterated in a turbulent band of sound.

© K. Stockhausen.

to enlivening the musical action, do useful duty in co-ordinating the rank and file, for instance the standing first-horn solo at 17 and concert-master at 62, whose roles and mannerist ornamentation are derived unashamedly from classical practice. Stockhausen has also aded considerably to the polyphonic texture from 107, including a birds' chorus of flute, oboe, and violin and scalic flourishes on piano to enhance the brilliance of triangles and glass chimes. It is a fresh, exuberant piece, but the real achievement without doubt is in its design and notation.

In Freundschaft

1977: *In Friendship* for clarinet.
Duration 15′.

Stockhausen's reworking of pointillist ideas to take account of the principles of formula composition finds particularly clear expression in another solo work for Suzanne Stephens, *In Freundschaft*. Its formal principle is very similar to the outwardly very dissimilar *Schlagtrio*: the music describes a coming together of two melodies from extremes of register into the mid-range, and a resolution (though not a levelling out) of the contrasts between them. This reconciliation is effected through a sevenfold repetition of a formula representing the two components as alternate voices in a solo two-part invention (Ex. 105). It will be seen that the lower layer is a retrograde of the upper, two octaves down, compressed in time, and at the other dynamic extreme (Even the old pointillist association of loud dynamics with short

Ex. 105

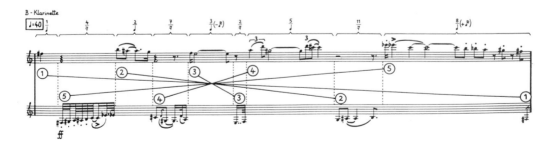

In Freundschaft formula analysed. Stockhausen dovetails a second, mirror-image in the measured silences punctuating the higher-pitched statement of the formula.
© K. Stockhausen.

Ex. 106

In Freundschaft: score, page 5. The two extremes begin to come together.

© K. Stockhausen.

durations, and soft with long, makes a come-back.) The idea of convergence is also inherent in the reciprocal tendencies of the two layers. We are back in the world of the Glass Bead Game, but this time in an idiom closer to the baroque music of proportions Hesse's novel evokes. And from Stockhausen's viewpoint, there is the important new consideration that the 'polar opposites' of earlier times have given way to polar transpositions of identical material. The work of reconciliation now concerns changing the frame of reference rather than the object. Since that reconciliation is achieved more or less automatically by closing the register gap between the two layers (Ex. 106), the dramatic interest of the composition shifts from the process of evolution itself to the expressive potential of exchanges arising along the way, and how these may be exploited. 'In most of the music that has been composed since 1951 the idea of development has been abandoned, which to my mind is a shame. In the future I think we need more layers within compositions which have a strong directional orientation, and clearer developments.'[9]

This dramatic potential is added to in a number of ways. In performance, events derived from the lower layer of the formula are directed to the player's right (and audience's left), while those in the upper layer (whatever their pitch transposition) are pointed in the other direction. Actual register is distinguished by performer movement in the vertical plane, lower pitches being aimed at the floor and higher pitches correspondingly higher up. The mid-point in pitch is signalled by a trill on A4, which also serves to divide alternate events from the two layers; it is associated with a point in mid-elevation directly in front of the player.

In addition, the constituent limbs of each layer of the formula are subject to order transposition from one cycle to the next, like changing partners in an old-fashioned dance. In these *Veränderungen*, as in his frequent figural and textural elaborations of the underlying structure, Stockhausen allows himself considerable leeway to shape his material in a manner consistent with expressive objectives (his lecture *The Art of Listening*[10] goes into delighted detail over the extent of these unscripted alterations). Two major interpolations are the 'explosion' between cycles 4 and 5 (Insert 9), and the trill cadenza after cycle 6. Out of the combination of structural and interpretative forming—what Boulez would call 'the bones and the flesh' of the composition—is derived a three-dimensional sound calligraphy capable of further expansion and development on the operatic stage.

[9] Karlheinz Stockhausen and Robin Maconie, *Stockhausen on Music* (London, 1988), p. 56.
[10] Karlheinz Stockhausen, op. cit. (above, n. 5), pp. 35–41.

15 *The Passage to LICHT*

It is strange that we are not able to inculcate into the minds of many men the necessity of the *distinction* of My Lord [Francis] *Bacons*, that there ought to be *Experiments of Light* as well as of *Fruit*. It is their usual word, *What solid good will come from thence?* . . . It were to be wished, that they would not only exercise this vigour, about *Experiments*, but on their own *lives*, and *actions* . . . But they are to know, that that in so large and various an *Art* as this of *Experiments*, there are many degrees of usefulness; some may serve for real, and plain *benefit*, without much *delight*; some for *teaching* without apparent *profit*; some for *light* now, and for use hereafter; some only for *ornament* and *curiosity*.[1]

STOCKHAUSEN has worked on the composition of the opera cycle *LICHT* (Light) since 1977. The seven-day project is planned to be completed by the year 2002, its 25-year development both complementing the period of assimilation and discovery of 1952–77 and, more importantly, integrating the manifold and seemingly incompatible aspects of his musical output during that period. The complete sequence of seven music-dramas will form a mythical 'life cycle', the individual music-dramas revealing themselves, in their proportional and musical relationships, their principal actions, characters, and even their colour preferences, as stations of a larger process. As a summation of the composer's art and philosophy *LICHT* invites comparison with such earlier masterpieces as the Bach *St Matthew Passion*, Mozart's *The Magic Flute*, Wagner's *Ring* cycle, and Schoenberg's *Moses und Aron*, as well as Stravinsky's more recent *The Flood* and Pousseur's *Votre Faust*. The autobiographical dimension expressed in Schoenberg's depiction of Moses and Pousseur's of Henri Faust is equally present in Stockhausen's triple characterization of Michael, Eva, and Luzifer.

The work's full title, *LICHT*: *die sieben Tage der Woche* suggests a wealth of meanings and associations. Like *Sirius*, the musical structure is cyclic, and in the image of a natural cycle in the earthly calendar. But whereas the earlier work is structured as a scale model of the seasons of the year, *LICHT* is designed as a real-time marriage of musical and natural time, based on a fundamental cycle of the week, and its seventh harmonic, the day.

---

[1] Thomas Sprat, *History of the Royal Society*, ed. Jackson I. Cope and Harold Whitmore Jones (London, 1959), p. 245. The Royal Society identified a ninth category of '*Experiments of Light, Sound, Colours, Taste, Smell*: . . . of *Ecchos* and reflected *Sounds*: of Musical *sounds*, and *Harmonies*' (op. cit. 225).

261

On to this natural *Eigenton* or reverberant frequency of one week Stockhausen has constructed a three-layer superformula, divisible into seven 'limbs'. The frequency interval expressed by the ratio 1 : 7 is the (dominant) seventh, which in conventional tonal practice has very special properties. As a natural consonance from the overtone series, the dominant seventh is inherently stable; within the tonal tradition, however, the seventh interval and chord has come to embody a dynamic impulse or progression, the combination of dominant seventh and tonic, V^7–I, thus bearing an additional connotation of imminent finality. These complementary perceptions of the seventh interval: simultaneously vertical and horizontal, movement and stasis, purpose and fulfilment, are in paradoxical accord with the triple characterization of Stockhausen's musical drama. The three layers of the tone formula (Ex. 107) correspond to the three identities, or (to paraphrase Messiaen) *personnages musicaux*, around whom the drama unfolds. They are spiritual absolutes in human guise: Michael, Eva, and Luzifer. The name Michael—meaning 'a face like gold'—has herioic connotations: 'In Altenberg, where I was brought up, is a

Ex. 107

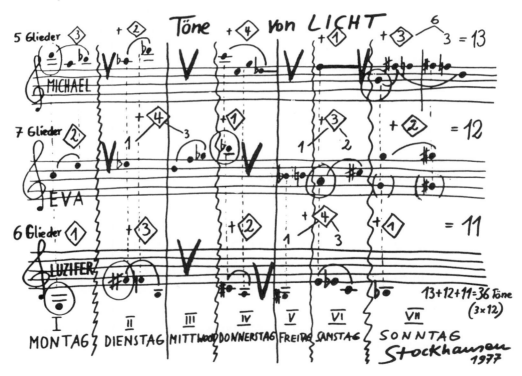

The three-layer tone formula of *LICHT*, showing the Michael, Eva, and Luzifer melodies of 13, 12, and 11 notes respectively.

© K. Stockhausen.

beautiful sculpture in the cathedral: Michael fighting the dragon'.[2] He embodies imagination, action, daring, vision, progress: the dynamic impulse. Luzifer is the total idealist: fastidious, exact, proud, dedicated to perfection, mistrustful of mortality, rejecting human weakness, unmoved by the fact of death and the promise of recincarnation. Eva is the mediator and teacher of mankind: through her, beauty and wisdom are conveyed to humanity in musical expression. In the 36-tone superormula, these characteristics are underlined by the fact that Luzifer is assigned 11 tones, 11 being prime and indivisible, but less than the chromatic total, indicating that there is something about him that remains unrevealed; Eva is given 12, which is a perfect total and a number fertile in combinatorial possibilities; and Michael has 13, also a prime, but greater than 12 and charged with additional magical associations.

The implications of the title are many and rich. Stockhausen's symbolism extends to the physical properties of light as much as to its metaphysical associations. As the light of Newtonian rationalism can be split into seven spectral colours, so the seven days of *LICHT* are interpreted as partial refractions of a total spectrum. (The dominant colour of Monday is silver-green, of Tuesday red, Wednesday yellow, Thursday blue, Friday orange, Saturday black, and Sunday golden.) *Montag* is Eva's day, the day of fruitfulness; *Dienstag* (in French *Mardi* or Mars' day) is the day of conflict between Michael and Luzifer. *Mittwoch* brings the three personae into co-operation; *Donnerstag* is Michael's day; *Freitag* the day of Eva's temptation by Luzifer. *Samstag* is Luzifer's day of reckoning, and *Sonntag* brings about a mystical union of Michael and Eva.

Stockhausen has employed the device of a human trinity as emanations of a mystical and musical unity once before. In *Momente* the K, M, and D archetypes allude not only to a triple division of a musical totality (*Klang*, *Melodie*, and *Dauer*) but also (as we have noted) to human embodiments of their associated characteristics and degrees of influence which they exercise on one another, or receive. To that extent *Momente*'s formal interrelationship of elements in varying proportions and combinations constructs a divine rationale for an essentially private and human interplay of relationships at a particular time is the composer's life. It is also, implicitly, a message of reconciliation.

A key to *LICHT*'s more volatile chemistry of good and evil is the emergence of Luzifer as a force to be reckoned with in the enchanting theatrical invention *Der Jahreslauf* of 1977. This commission for the Japanese Imperial *Gagaku* Ensemble appears to have provided the final impetus for Stockhausen's grand conception of the *LICHT* cycle. The aesthetic rules governing this music are very strict. Stockhausen has responded not as an imitator but as an observer, tempering the formality with distinctive humour.

---

[2] 'MICHAEL is the protector angel of the Germans (and I know this since I was a small child). MICHAEL is also the protector angel of the Hebrew people (Recha Freier, director of the Jerusalem TESTIMONIUM, commissioned MICHAELS JUGEND, which was premiered in Jerusalem' (Karlheinz Stockhausen, private communication to the author).

Der Jahreslauf

1977: *The Course of the Years* (Scene from *LICHT*).

For performance as an opera scene, as a ballet, or as a concert piece. Tenor, bass (opera version); 4 dancers, 14 musicians, actor, 5 impersonators (dancers or mimes or silent actors), 4 musical assistants, tape, sound projectionist (ballet version).

Japanese (Western) instrumentation:

  I. 3 *sho* (harmoniums);
 II. 3 *ryuteki* (piccolos); *shoko* (anvil);
III. 3 *hichiriki* (soprano saxophones); *Kakko* (bongo);
 IV. *gakuso* (electric harpsichord), *biwa* (electric guitar); *taiko* (bass drum).

Duration (opera scene or ballet) 1 hour, (concert version) 50′.

On his visits to Japan Stockhausen was greatly impressed at the country's successful assimilation of Western industrial culture, and by the traditions of Japanese indigenous culture, its striking tensions and attenuated perceptions. In Japanese arts he found a ready response to his own serially derived preoccupations with extremes of scale and awareness. A familiar example is the juxtaposition of superhuman bulk and quickness of reflexes of sumo wrestling. In many of the traditional arts, for instance calligraphy, one finds a methodical, slow, and overwhelmingly conscious ritual of preparation leading to a spontaneous, as it were uncontrolled, release. To Western observers it is as though the formal discipline is designed to contain and thereby accumulate an intensity of spiritual energy suddenly discharged in an instant of inspired creative action. At his first encounter with the Japanese tea ceremony, Stockhausen was fascinated to discover that what it was about was not manners, nor even tea, but rightness of timing, about knowing precisely when and how to drink, in order to experience the moment of perfection.

Extremes of scale are also characteristic of Japanese classical dance. To discover anything like it in European tradition one has to go back to the court dances of the late Renaissance and early Baroque, when action followed formal trajectories expressing a divine grace above mere athleticism, and celebrated the symmetry of organization in space and time of an orderly and harmonious universe. The same combination of predestined path and solemn gait with individual spontaneity of gesture are evident in the Japanese dance, their effect heightened by imposing costumes and make-up. Long, slow actions and subtle tremors are interrupted by breathtaking trance-like pauses, where the action is suspended in mid-gesture. The dance is offset by music of astringent power, acoustically weighted (to Western ears) towards the higher extremes of frequency.

Japanese timing is supremely a recognition of the time-scales of nature: of pulse, growth, and reaction among living things and natural processes. In directing attention in *Der Jahreslauf* to a Western decimal system of counting, albeit chronometric, Stockhausen appears to be making an ironic commentary both on the nature of Western orgnizations of time, and on the implications of Japanese assimilation of a Western culture organized by the clock. This mischievous aspect is what subsequently led him to place the work in the 'Tuesday' opera of the cycle, the day of contest between discipline and anarchy.

Anybody who has watched a sports event on television and observed the dance of the digits of the computer timer will have an image of the polyphony of time-scales which is the essence of Stockhausen's conception. It could not be simpler. The stage is laid out with four paths in the form of four numbers corresponding to the digits of the year in which the performance takes place. A dancer, or runner of the years, is assigned to each path. Accompanied by an appropriately responsive body of instruments, each runner traverses his path at a speed corresponding to its position in the temporal hierarchy, the units (accompanied by harpsichord and guitar) moving noticeably faster than the decades (soprano saxophones), the decades faster than the centuries (piccolos), and the runner of the millenia (harmoniums) scarcely moving at all. (In practice the time-scales do not correspond to powers of ten, but to the actual digital values of the year in question. Thus, for the 1977 performances the successive time-scales were $1 : \times 9 : \times 7$ (63) : $\times 7$ (441) rather than $1 : 10 : 100 : 1,000$, bringing the extremes into a more manageable relationship. For 1988, the paths of the two runners of the years and decades become eights, and the time-scales also change, to $1 : 9 : 72 : 576$. Fortunately, this does not mean that a performance in the year 2000 will consist of one very slow-moving dancer and three stock-still, nor that the extremes of time-scale are set to double in value. Given that the ratios return to powers of ten and not zero, the extreme values of $2 : 1,000$ come down to $1 : 500$, returning to within the time-ranges of 1977 and 1988.)

There the matter would rest, were it not for the fact that this ceremonial march (or skedaddle) of time is interrupted four times by devilish temptations, to be restarted again by four divine incitements. After a formal beginning in which the players process on to the stage in a respectful imitation of Japanese protocol, the digital clock of the years is started at null, and the course of time begins. Stockhausen's humour gradually rises to the surface in the struggle of the four runners of the years to maintain a ritual decorum while at the same time co-ordinating body movements regulated to their unnatural extremes of speed. To use a televisual analogy, they have to move respectively at the pace of a freeze frame, slow-motion replay, normal play, and fast forward.

The first temptation is signalled by the sound of a ship's bell, the appearance of a giant devil's visage at stage right, and the sound of running feet. A male voice announces the offering of flowers to the four runners. It is the traditional artiste's bouquet, implying that the performance is over and the course of time may be halted. One by one they refuse. An angels' visage appears stage left, and a girl enters running. Clap hands for the artistes, she cries, making a pantomime appeal to the audience to help break the spell and allow the performance to resume. In the DG recording the resulting applause is exquisitely matched to the sound of the stage footsteps, effecting a punning transition from an image of clockwork regularity (running feet) to one of aleatoric freedom (many hands clapping).

At the second temptation a food trolley rolls on to the stage, pushed by a chef. The action stops, and three of the four runners are lured from their posts to crowd around the steaming pans. The millenium-runner, turning at a snail's pace, is about to rouse himself and join them when a stage lion bounds in and with a mighty roar bites the other three behind, at which they hastily resume their positions. (It is all too much for the year-runner, who can't resist stealing a sausage.) The third temptation brings the arrival of an ape riding a motorcycle, who circles the stage with a great deal of noise, revving his engine and honking furiously on four klaxons (their pitches, in another Daliesque illusion, just happening to coincide with those of the harmoniums at this point). The sound of the motorcycle, we recall, resembles that of the rotating sound table at the start and end of *Sirius*, and it is tempting to interpret this scene as a parodistic allusion to the solemn arrival and annunciation of the earlier work's more celestial visitors. It is succeeded, in any case, by a reappearance of the girl, whose skipping entry imitates the irregular rhythms of the motorcycle. Her stimulus to the musicians this time is the financial incentive of a prize of 100,000 Yen (or equivalent sum) to the best performer.

Once more the course of the years resumes. By now it is becoming a test of faith, not to say endurance, a hint of the spiritual trial to which the Psalmist of Stravinsky's *Symphony of Psalms*—'Exspectans exspectavi Dominum' . . .—patiently refers. However, despite obliquely alluding to another celebrated composition, both in its four-part isorhythmy and divine aspitation (not to mention the longueurs of a greatly-extended time-scale), this is no *Quartet for the End of Time*—or at least, not yet. There is still a final temptation to come, a soothing distraction of soft lights, saccharine background music, and a leering suggestion of off-stage strip-tease. It summons forth the suitably Jovian rebuke of a mighty thunderbolt to electrify the players back to lively consciousness of their duty (Ex. 108). In stroboscopic disarray the music starts again, and as the course of the years approaches the present the stage gradually fills with light from above, and the performance ends in a blaze of glory.

Stockhausen has suggested a coda in which a judge and panel of arbitrators arrive on stage to congratulate the performers and reward the most deserving musicians with the prize money left behind after the third temptation, to be used to further their musical training. Would that other deserving performances of new music were rewarded on the spot in a similar way!

In *Der Jahreslauf* Stockhausen confronts and attempts an accommodation with the two sides of his nature as a composer, the one painstaking and methodical, relentlessly dedicated to working through a preordained serial plan, the other a subversive propensity to break the spell, and go off on impulse in an entirely different direction:

Ex. 108

54

Der Jahreslauf, immediately following the fourth temptation and incitement (thunder and lightning). 'Tänzer IV' is the runner of the years, timed by *taiko* and *biwa* strokes; the other three runners, representing (in ascending order) decades, centuries, and millenia, are accompanied by musical processes which evolve proportionately more slowly. © K. Stockhausen.

The whole *Einschub* 'insert' technique goes back to the *Kontra-Punkte* and even to the *Drei Lieder* . . . which I wrote very fast during the college vacation and which is based directly on the overwhelming experience of inner sound visions which are stronger than your own will . . . On the other hand, you are an engineer, you do mental work, and there is sometimes a conflict between the two: you have overall visions, images which make demands of a kind you cannot yet realise, and they lead to the invention of new technical processes, but then the technical processes go their own way and become the starting point for other techniques which in turn provoke new intentions and you find yourself bombarded with images again.[3]

Commenting on the character symbolism of *Der Jahreslauf*, he adds:

We should not forget that the devil is himself a fallen angel—Lucifer, 'Bearer of Light' as his name indicates. Then he turned rebellious, wishing to tempt the greatest possible number of other spirits to resist, to hold back, to deny—even to *stop* the very flow of time, the *Course of the Years* itself, and bring the music of the universe to silence. . . . And yet: were it not for the temptations of Lucifer and consequent incitements of the angels, *Der Jahreslauf* would be theatrically monotone, humourless, without any salt. So even the devil has a part to play in the creative process, and in the ascent of the spirit.[4]

In more ways than one, 1977 was a decisive year. It was the year in which, after experiencing considerable difficulties with the EMS Synthi 100, he brought *Sirius* to completion. He enlarged the choir operal '*Atmen gibt das Leben. . .*', developing the choreography of the group on the platform and incorporating new, pre-recorded orchestra material. He conceived and orchestrated the festive turbulence of *Jubiläum*. Then, with *Der Jahreslauf* he concluded a working truce with his own maverick creative spirit. Almost certainly it was the philosophical issue, rather than any practical breakthrough, that was the catalyst on which the chemistry of *LICHT* ultimately depended. Having finally decided on the place of wickedness in the spectrum of human nature, it became clear how he would now be able to develop the character of Luzifer and the role of adversity and temptation in his planned epic treatment of the progress of virtue. In a month of great activity following the first sketches he made while still in Japan (Ex. 109), Stockhausen researched and decided on the basic lineaments, relationships, and levels of meaning of the entire seven-day opera cycle, and the place that *Der Jahreslauf* was destined to occupy in the overall plan.

The design and construction of *LICHT* follows the pattern established and elaborated in earlier compositions. *LICHT* extends the Corbusian analogy observed in the context of *Piano Piece XI*: the composer designs the structure of the mansion according to a harmonious scale of proportions, and then elaborates the individual rooms in diminishing values of the same scale, gradually working down to the fine detail of decoration. As the emphasis of the design changes scale from larger structural features to smaller, more decorative aspects, naturally the degree of

---

[3] Karlheinz Stockhausen and Robin Maconie, *Stockhausen on Music* (London, 1988), pp. 135–6.
[4] Karlheinz Stockhausen, *Texte zur Musik*, iv (Cologne, 1978), p. 357.

Ex. 109

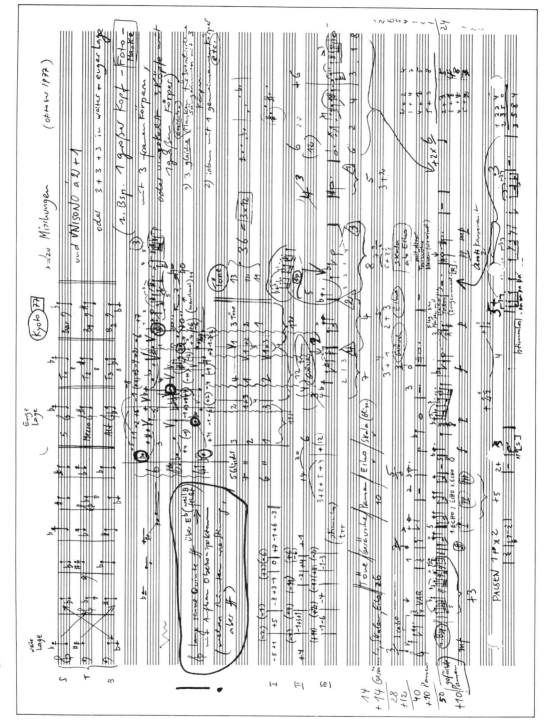

An early sketch page for *LICHT*, dated Kyoto, October 1977.

© K. Stockhausen.

flexibility increases in the interpretation of the plan: it takes on the character of the occupant and becomes more adaptable to individual choice of textures and style. A designer has to allow that the furniture be moved around, for example, or that the lighting arrangements may vary from one room to another. Nevertheless, by adhering to the principle of a regulatory system of scales and proportions, he is able to reconcile freedom of manœuvre with overall harmony of relationships within a room, and of individual rooms within the schema of the whole dwelling.

The superformula for *Donnerstag* (Ex. 110) fleshes out the bare interval structures of the tone formula for the entire week. Because it is Michael's day, his layer of the superformula is in the dominant position, on the highest stave. The transpositions of the three layers throughout *Donnerstag* are determined by the pitches of the Thursday segment of the Michael layer of the tone formula, the first of which, C, represents a descent of a whole tone in relation to the initial D of the Michael tone formula for the entire week. The three layers are characterized according to the traditional iconography of Western melody, 'assertive' fourths and fifths identifying the Michael leadership qualities, 'emotion' glissandi and 'soft' third-intervals the feminine attributes of Eva, and 'dissonant' chromatic intervals the persona of Luzifer. The stylization is deliberately exposed, in order for the obvious symbolism to be recognized, constantly recalled, and by accumulation of contextual association, ultimately transcended.

In addition to their real-time identity, the three layers of the superformula, by a familiar process of expansion, also determine the pitch transpositions and dynamic, instrumental, and rhythmic character of each major act and scene. The resulting austere and luminous music, characterized by bright and dark winds (trumpet and basset-horn) and brittle and timeless keyboard sonorities (piano and synthesizer, or harmonium or pre-recorded tape) yield an acoustic imagery which compares with the idealized and timeless aesthetic of a Mies van der Rohe if one thinks of the Barcelona pavilion, for instance, which expresses a similarly exalted purity of conception in slabs, surfaces, and high columns of polished lapis lazuli, glass, and steel.

Donnerstag aus LICHT

1978–80: *Thursday from LICHT.*

Opera in three acts, a greeting, and a farewell, for 14 musical performers (3 solo voices, 8 solo instrumentalists, 3 solo dancers), choir, orchestra, and tapes.

Donnerstags-Gruss (Thursday Greeting)

Act 1: Michaels Jugend (Michael's Youth)
  'Kindheit' (Childhood)
  'Mondeva' (Moon-Eve)
  'Examen' (Examination)

Act 2: Michaels Reise um die Erde (Michael's Journey around the Earth)

Act 3: Michaels Heimkehr (Michael's Return Home)
  'Festival' (Festival)
  'Vision' (Vision)

Donnerstags-Abschied (Thursday Farewell)

Duration 3 h. 10′, with 2 intervals *c.* 4 h.

Donnerstag is the day in which goodwill, in the character of Michael and in terms of the worldly ideals and experience of the composer himself, is most clearly in the ascendant. It is the day in which the human upbringing of Michael provides the composer with an opportunity to initiate the audience into the mysteries of the musical language and imagery of the entire opera cycle. It is an appropriate point in the week, therefore, for the composer to begin.

The story of Michael is carved on to the musical ground like a bas-relief on to marble. Stockhausen's telegraphic text often seems detached from the action, like an inscription, or the titles of a silent film; indeed it is arguably intended to impress the listener as a message from a remoter time. An instrumental prelude encountered in the foyer forms an intervallic arch through which the audience enters the place of celebration. The opera unfolds in a series of vignettes. Act 1, Michael's Youth introduces Michael, Eva, and Luzifer as a human family. In her identity as a mother-figure, Eva initiates the child into the mysteries of word-play through the syllables and resonances of names and their permutations. Later she appears in the figure of a dancer, and the boy learns that the world of the flesh as well as that of the spirit is capable of inventing games of intermingled identities. The father, Luzimon (Luzifer + Mond (Moon)), a school-teacher, is a punctilious character, full of facts, doing everything by number, fascinated by numerological coincidences. From him Michael learns of life and death (the hunt), of the reality of the supernatural (prayer) and of its opposite, illusion (theatre). In a series of rapid exchanges the parent-figures are shown gradually deteriorating in their relationship and in their individual personalities, from domestic happiness to isolated and obsessive extremes. Throughout the scene the 'Invisible Choirs', singing to texts from the Apocalypse of Baruch and from Leviticus, are heard as a distant 'sound horizon' from sixteen loudspeakers surrounding the auditorium.

In the next scene a female spirit, Mondeva, appears to the youth Michael and communicates with him in a seductive alliance of melody and dance. Guided by her, he is instructed in love and in the meaning of the melody formula which represents his identity and character. During this scene the parent-figures die, leaving their

Ex. 110

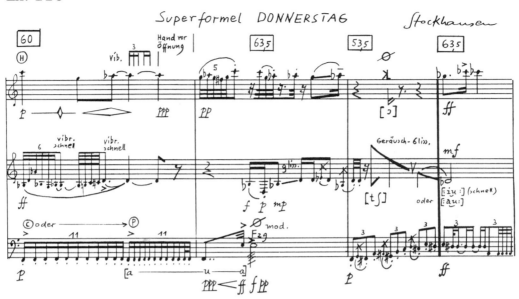

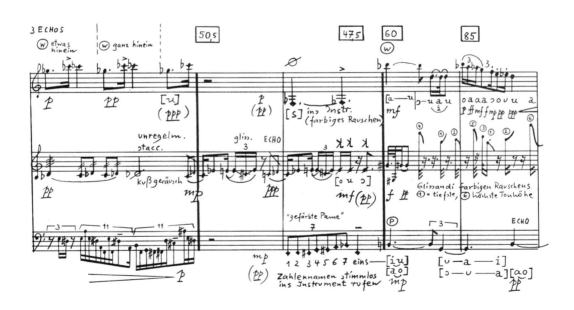

Superformula for *Donnerstag aus LICHT*. Note the intervallic and textural characterization of individual layers.

© K. Stockhausen.

Ex. III

Michaels Reise: beginning of the Fifth Station. The giant globe, centrepiece of the Act, ceases to rotate and a window opens in India. The orchestration is clearly layered in three registers corresponding to Michael, Eva, and Luzifer. © K. Stockhausen.

mortal existence to return to the spiritual domain. The scene changes to Michael's examination for admission to music school. In three guises as singer, trumpeter, and dancer he displays high virtuosity, and is admitted by unquestioning acclamation.

Act 2, Michael's Journey around the Earth, is a strikingly visualized instrumental movement for trumpet, additional soloists, and orchestra. Michael as trumpeter enters a huge rotating terrestrial globe, appearing at seven different openings to play his music in a manner identifying with the idiom of each of the seven regions at which he emerges (Ex. 111). His terrestrial pilgrimage (equivalent to a one-movement concerto of 48 minutes' duration) leads into an extended duo with Eva as basset-hornist in which they once again exchange intimacies in the other-worldly language of melody. The lyric tenderness of this music is interrupted several times by cheerfully rowdy elements who poke fun at the orchestra (the latter dressed, incidentally, as penguins), and the lovers.

The third and final Act, Michael's Return Home, reveals Michael in his threefold persona in his celestial home. In 'Festival', the first scene, Eva presents him with symbolic gifts to reimind him of his time on earth. The music of the Invisible Choirs also returns, gradually swelling to an amplitude that makes the stage action appear to diminish in scale to Lilliputian size. An ever-sceptical Luzifer tries once more to disrupt the ceremony, and is rebuked, then shamed into silence by the virtuoso playing of two youthful angels on soprano saxophones. An old woman emerges from the audience to berate the entire assembly in yet another heart-stopping action from life.

'Vision', which follows, is dominated by Michael as singer addressing the audience directly in a measured commentary on the events which have been presented. They reappear visually as seven shadow plays, images inverted, accompanied by taped flashbacks of music, in a form of coda (Ex. 112). As the audience leaves the opera-house, five trumpeters on high rooftops and balconies perform the five 'limbs' of the Michael formula in its unadorned intervallic form, as signals of farewell (Ex. 113).

Samstag aus LICHT

1981–4: *Saturday from LICHT.*

Opera in a greeting and four scenes for 13 musical performers (1 solo voice, 10 solo instrumentalists, 2 solo dancers), wind orchestra, ballet or mimes, male voice choir, organ.

Samstags-Gruss (Saturday Greeting)
Scene 1: Luzifers Traum (Lucifer's Dream)

Ex. 112

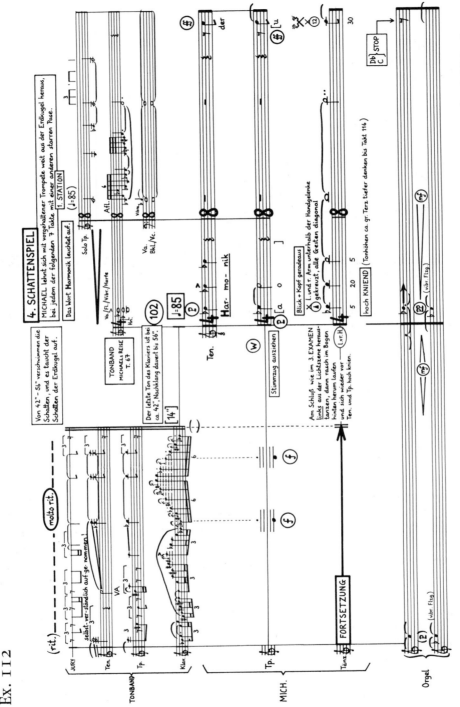

'Vision' from Michaels Heimkehr. Shadow plays from Michael's life on earth are seen: here taped excerpts from 'Examen' and 'Michaels Reise' are heard in the background. Note the writing for dancer.

© K. Stockhausen.

276

Ex. 113

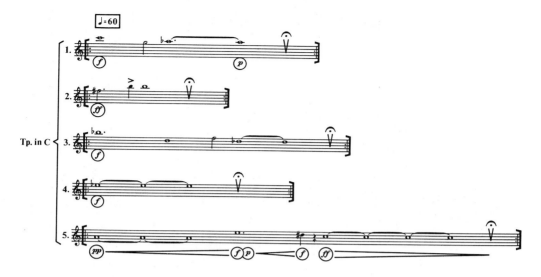

Donnerstags Abschied: five trumpets signal to one another from high vantage-points outside the auditorium, their melodies segments of the Michael formula.

© K. Stockhausen.

Scene 2: Kathinkas Gesang als Luzifers Requiem (Kathinka's Chant as Lucifer's Requiem)

Scene 3: Luzifers Tanz (Lucifer's Dance)

Scene 4: Luzifers Abschied (Lucifer's Farewell)

Duration *c.* 3 h. 15′, with 2 intervals *c.* 4 h.

Samstag aus LICHT is dedicated to Luzifer, spirit of exactitude. Michael's colour was heavenly blue; Luzifer, the antithesis of light, is associated with blackness (though not of complexion: Stockhausen's favoured female singers have always been black). The theme of *Saturday*, 'Saturn-day', is the sleep of reason, or unmasking of rational modes of thought to set free innocent perceptions. It is also physical death and spiritual resurrection viewed as an analogously natural process of release and renewal of consciousness.

This mind-expanding process is expressed in the opera as a progressive enlargement of the musical space and frame of reference (Ex. 114). 'The dimensions of art', said Klee, 'are dot, line, plane and space', and dot, line, plane, and space define the dimensional reference of each of the four scenes: the first is a static piano solo, the second a mobile flute solo with accompanying 'musical robots', the third expresses a musical plane in the vertical, and the fourth moving and being in both

277

Ex. 114

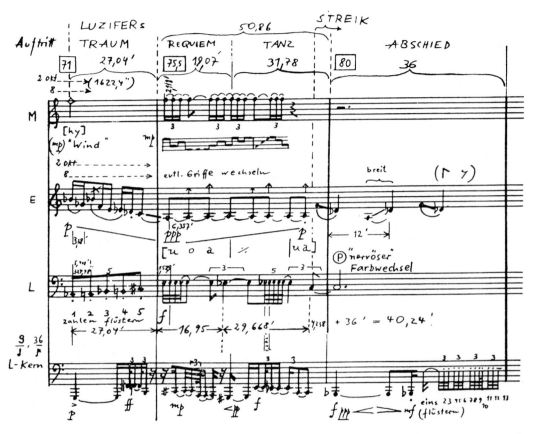

Formula-excerpt for *Samstag aus LICHT*, corresponding to segment VI of the Ex. 110 superformula above. Stockhausen has divided this segment into subsections on whose note content and time proportions the scenes of the *Samstag* opera are based.

© K. Stockhausen.

the horizontal and the vertical.[5] Not only outward, but inward as well, as Stockhausen expands the domain of melody from the rational scales and vowels of classical convention to embrace microtonal inflections, consonants, cries, and noises of nature. Following an introductory 'Greeting' by widely-spaced brass choirs, by turns exhilarating and terrifying (trombone glissandi roaring like lions), the first

[5] Boulez had considered a similar 'form of evolution' for *Pli selon Pli*: 'Early on I had thought about an evolutionary structure: starting with a piece for piano, then *Improvisation I* for a small number of instruments, *Improvisations II* and *III* for instrumental ensemble of increasing importance, ending in a grand *tutti* with *Tombeau*. I wanted it to express a sort of crescendo of instrumentation, and I'm confident that, had it been better realized, it would have worked' (in Claude Samuel (ed.), *Eclats/Boulez* (Paris, 1986), p. 22).

278

Ex. 115

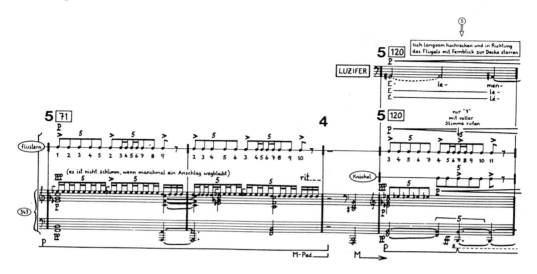

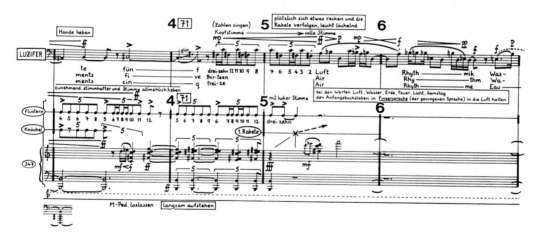

From Luzifer's Dream, Scene 1 of *Samstag aus LICHT*. The pianist nervously counts *sotto voce*, knocks on the piano woodwork, and, beginning at 349, fires off small rockets to signal the beginning of an expansion of the acoustic space.

© K. Stockhausen.

Ex. 116

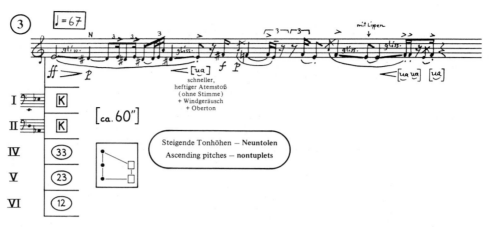

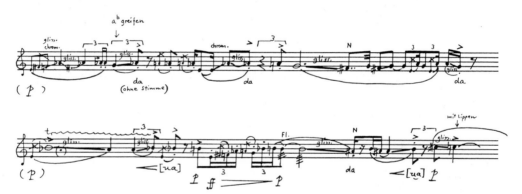

Kathinkas Gesang als Luzifers Requiem: Scene 2 of *Samstag aus LICHT*. The hyperactive flute part is offset by menacing percussionists (I–VI), whirring and buzzing like clockwork toys.
© K. Stockhausen.

scene has Luzifer caught in a trance, centre stage, perhaps like a spider in the middle of his own web, the latter a restless but curiously static piano solo (the piano an appropriate symbol of science applied to musical nature). As a visual set piece it concentrates the action to a Beckett-like monologue at a single point in space and time; the piano sound is also amplified, confusingly perhaps, to put the listener inside the player's mind, where we can hear the manic undertones of counting and whistling that lurk beneath the façade of virtuoso self-control. Tiny rockets are set off to begin a process of expansion of consciousness and physical space (Ex. 115). The conception begs for a filmic interpretation in the style of Meliès.

A piano-shaped coffin is the appropriate centre-piece of Scene 2, (Kathinka's Chant) for solo flautist dressed as a cat, spiritual accomplice of witchcraft. Its skittish

Ex. 117

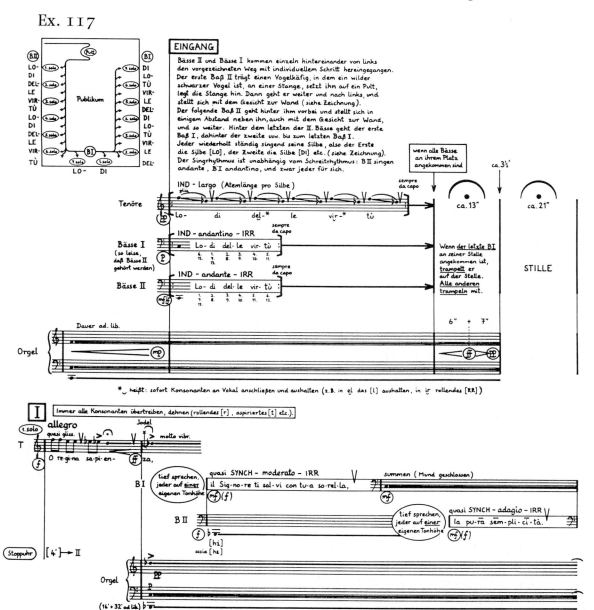

Samstag aus LICHT: Luzifers Abschied. The singers take up their places around the audience, facing the walls in a directional inversion of the inward-focused piano solo of Scene 1. Stockhausen's employment of classical tempo indications ('largo', 'andantino', 'andante') is unusual for him but part of a continuing amelioration of his notational style for non-virtuoso performers.

© K. Stockhausen.

perpetuum mobile accompanies a scampering exploration of the dramatic space, opening out the horizontal dimension, and summons the assistance of six automaton-like percussionists, dressed all in black and whirring and chirping like clockwork toys. (Ex. 116). The composer has since made an electronic version of the percussionists' parts at IRCAM in Paris.

Lucifer's Dance, the third scene, introduces a fabulous visual invention—a symphonic wind band, arrayed in ten groups on six stages rising almost vertically, and depicting a giant Lucifer face. Urged on by Luzifer, walking high on giant stilts, the various features—eyebrows, eyes, nose, cheeks, and chin—one by one come to life. As the counterpoint of features becomes progressively more uninhibited, Michael, playing piccolo trumpet, makes a brief appearance to appeal brilliantly but in vain for decorum, and is laughed out of court by Kathinka in a teasing piccolo cadenza. (In staged performances, this scene ends abruptly with a walk-out by the musicians, a further illustration from life of the destructive consequences for the spirit of living by the clock.)

The final scene extends the musical performance around and above the audience (Ex. 117), ultimately leading the way out of the auditorium (or church) into the open air, and into the light. A setting of St Francis of Assisi's *Lodi delle Virtù* (Hymn to the Virtues) is intoned in Italian by bass and tenor choirs wielding jingles and ratchets, and punctuated by the terrifying clatter of wooden sandals running clockwise and anticlockwise round the periphery. It is music drawing on the literally inspirational (breath-taking) and mind-cleansing functions of ancient musical ritual, ending with the release of a black bird, representing the spirit, and the splitting of coconuts on a resonant tablet of stone in a Zen-like rite of head-cracking awakening.

Montag aus LICHT

1984–8: *Monday from LICHT.*

Opera in three acts, a greeting, and a farewell, for 21 musical performers (14 solo voices, 6 solo instrumentalists, 1 actor) and modern orchestra (electronic keyboard instruments, percussion, various instrumental ensembles, choir groups, pre-recorded solo voices, concrete and electronic sounds).

Montags-Gruss (Monday Greeting)
Act 1: Evas Erstgeburt (Eva's First Birthgiving)
Act 2: Evas Zweitgeburt (Eva's Second Birthgiving)

Ex. 118

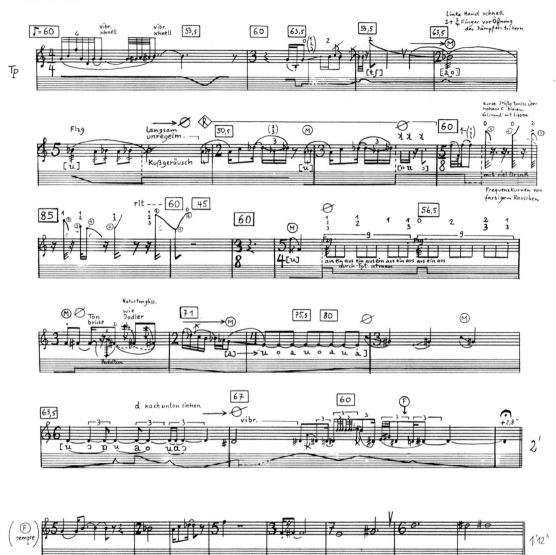

Montag aus LICHT: Evas' formula, as played by trumpet. The high-pitched glissandi of coloured noises express a spectrum of emotions from grief to anger (the lion's roar of the massed trombones of Saturday Greeting), and from pain to ecstasy.

© K. Stockhausen.

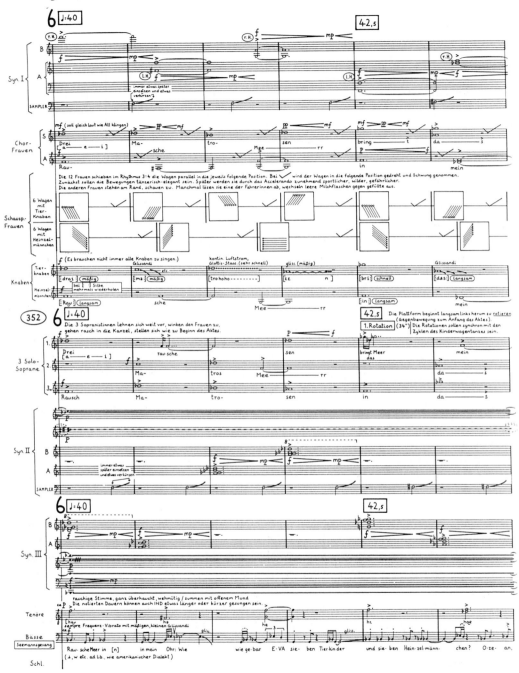

Montag aus LICHT. The boxes indicate the dance of the prams ('Baby-buggy-boogie') around the stage in two sets of six, each moving line abreast. A novel spatial counterpoint is observable in the 3 sopranos; the D♭ moving in one direction, the F in the other direction, more slowly. Such spatial interactions introduce new subtleties into a music which, on the surface at least, appears considerably simplified.

Act 3: Evas Zauber (Eva's Magic)
Montags-Abschied (Monday Farewell)
Duration *c.* 3 h. 30′.

After *Samstag* and death, *Montag* and birth. Monday, Eva's day, 'is characterized principally by female voices. They have to be clear as well as high in range. . . Also electric organs'. The prescription refers actually to the D-moments of *Momente*,[6] but tallies remarkably with this day dedicated to the feminine mystique, and even suggests a pretext for Stockhausen's adoption of the keyboard synthesizer in place of the string orchestra, as the Hammond and Lowrey organs had previously served in 1962. Here, too, we see 'Mother Earth surrounded by her flock'. The dominant colour is green and mother-of-pearl, the dominant imagery of abundance, living creation and fruitfulness infused by a certain eroticism. The musical imagery is elevated in pitch, richly harmonious and inconstantly undulating, like the sea in the scenic background, in articulated microtonal sweeps and broader glissandi (Ex. 118). The libretto is also exceptionally rich, drawing upon all the composer's experience of phonetics and verbal texture with Meyer-Eppler, and beyond it to the verbal sensualities of Tristan Tzara's dadaist 'mots vaporisées' and the mystical verbal counter-culture of Raoul Haussmann and Kurt Schwitters.

Entering the opera-house foyer, the audience has the illusion of being underwater. The stage setting depicts a giant translucent female form, by Epstein out of Niki de Sainte-Phalle, supine by a rolling sea. It is attended by a band of 21 women, who prepare it for birth. The growth of a human embryo is seen projected in the sky above. A triple-voiced Eva sings from the larynx of the statue. As the embryo develops, its musical analogue, a melody formula, also grows in size and shows increasing signs of independent life.

The statue brings forth fourteen strange creatures: seven small boys with the heads of animals and birds, and seven aged dwarves. Three sailors disembark from boats and bring gifts of flowers, juices, and fresh fruit.

The children and manikins are wheeled around the stage in a dance of the prams (Ex. 119). Suddenly Luzifer appears, a repellent double-image, singer and awkward mime, joined amoeba-like by a greyish web (Ex. 120). He heaps scorn on the company and is eventually buried in the sand by the women, only to re-emerge at the end of the Act as devilish *régisseur*: 'Now then! Back to your places! Once more, rrrright from the top!!!'.

Act 2 begins: the sun is shining, the sea frozen over. The women crack the ice with axes. Suddenly the lights go out, exactly like a power cut. Voices cry: 'Light!' and singing voices are heard approaching from the rear of the audience. Three lines of young women costumed as lilies move toward the stage, bearing lighted candles.

---

[6] Stockhausen and Maconie, op. cit. 69.

Ex. 120

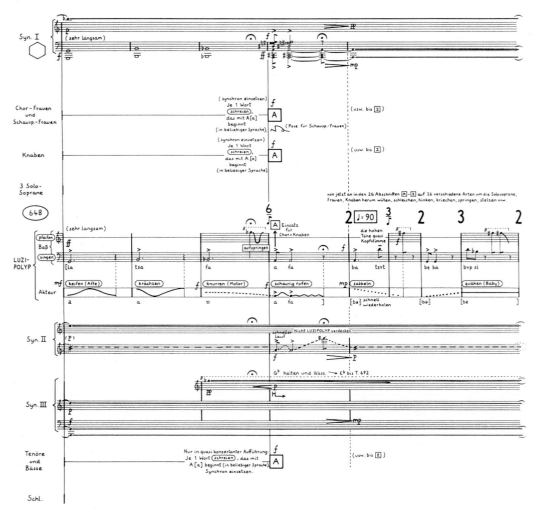

Montag aus LICHT. The amorphous Luzipolyp clowns in front of the women and children.
© K. Stockhausen.

They perform the ceremony for the statue Eva's second birthgiving. To the accompaniment of a piano solo (played by the boy-budgerigar) the statue-Eva ripens and, 'glowing like a Christmas crib', gives birth to seven more little boys. These reveal themselves as musical geniuses, perfect at mimicry. A door opens over the statue's heart, and the Eva basset-hornist appears dressed in a heart-shaped costume. She teaches the newcomers the musical meaning of the seven days of the week, then metamorphoses into a trio of basset-hornists who entice them away.

In the final act, the ice has melted and green grass is sprouting around the Eva-statue. The boys, now grown to manhood, and their female companions sing a hymn of praise to the coming of a wonderful musical being, one with magical powers. A new persona, Ave, mirror image of Eva, appears, dressed as a male. Mutually attracted, Eva and Ave perform a graceful duet in which their two melodies gradually entwine (Ex. 121). The children approach and stare curiously. Ave beckons them, Eva draws back. Ave, transformed into the Pied Piper, draws the children under the spell of her piccolo playing until they trip after her like marionettes. As taped scenes of music and children's fun and games are heard, Ave leads the children off the stage and for a long time their singing can be heard getting fainter, as they ascend to 'a higher world where the clouds are green'. Finally the piccolo and children's voices are transformed into bird-song, and the Eva-statue into a work of Nature: a mountain bursting with trees, shrubs, flowers, and streams.

The distinctive and dramatic novelties of the music of *LICHT* can be said to arise from what for Stockhausen is a new awareness of temporal continuity (of which the melody-formula device is the principal intimation), and pleasure in counterpoint. We begin to see the development of a number of processes of continuous transformation through the seventies: in *Sirius*, for example, the impression of continuous momentum is exceptionally strong, together with the counterpointing of different *Tierkreis* melodies, a merging of melodies by interpolation one into another (a process reminiscent of early American experiments in computer-modified melody), and also extremely subtle and gradual transitions, markedly in *Aries*, of time-scale and intervallic expansion of cyclic melodies. Earlier, in *Inori*, an actual continuity of choreographed gesture reinforces an intentional continuity of musical flow. The perception of sound textures in continuous evolution over time is of course dramatically significant in both *Jubiläum* and *Der Jahreslauf*, expressed in a counterpoint of time-scales and complementary oscillations between aleatoric and co-ordinated rhythms, effected on a time-scale and with a degree of finesse which makes even a Boulez' essays in degrees of aleatory (for example, in *Rituel*) seem by comparison merely playful, if not scrappy.

It is this underlying sense of continuity—melodic, structural, and procedural—which distinguishes *LICHT* above all from the earlier *Momente*. Paradoxically, it is corresponding apparent absences of continuity, or of material consistency, among other aspects of the opera cycle which have drawn a certain amount of fire from the public domain. How, for instance, it is said, can an opera be composed in segments for different groups under different commissions, and yet pretend to form a coherent unity? Or, alternatively, how can the composer claim that individual scenes or parts of scenes are realistically presentable as self-contained concert works?

LICHT, on the evidence of *Donnerstag* at least, is a Wagnerian enterprise only in scale. It has nothing otherwise to give it any manner of Wagnerian shape or coherence; no narrative to speak of; no development, no consistency of approach, or of instrumental or vocal forces, no

Ex. 121

Montag aus LICHT : 'Ave' duo from Evas Zauber. The characteristic glissandi of the Eva formula are the basis of a microtonal idiom of varying degrees of intervallic refinement.

© K. Stockhausen.

Leitmotive, no sense (nor even any attempt to lend a sense) of the gradual unfolding of a grand design.[7]

To live in Cologne is to experience how the physical shape of the city and the lives of its inhabitants are influenced and directed by the great cathedral at its centre. It is possible to detect a kind of town-planning mentality among those arguing the virtues of consistency, a convention probably owing more to the demands of early radio broadcasting in this century than to any historical aesthetic imperative. It was of the cathedral-building culture of the Middle Ages and Renaissance that Herbert Read remarked that it belonged to a period of history without aesthetic preconceptions. Harmony of spirit is more important than consistency of roof-line, as town planners themselves now concede.

Stockhausen's use of pre-recorded choirs and instrumental groups, and the high profiles accorded to trumpet, basset-horn, flute, and synthesizer have also been interpreted as wilful impoverishments of opera traditions of numerical and auditory luxury. There is admittedly an element of self- and family portraiture in Stockhausen's choice of soloists which is part of the narrative conception as much as a reflection of their merits as artistic collaborators. By and large, however, the prejudice in favour of numbers seems based on nineteenth-century market expectations which have survived in opera but have long been superseded elsewhere. We have only to look to the present, or to the more distant past, to realize that large-scale orchestral forces are no longer necessary for the sake of audibility in today's large auditoria, nor were they ever a prerequisite for large-scale rituals, mass or masque, in pre-industrial times.

Stockhausen employs audio technology not only to amplify small sounds into large, but also to project the stage perspective into the main auditorium, and to create surround-sound effects as part of the dramatic design.[8] Inevitably complications arise in managing the spatial and aural perspectives of the same music in simultaneously live and amplified form. Given that his concern is for the best acoustic projection of his music, Stockhausen could hardly fail to take note of the superior quality of a conventionally recorded opera by comparison with the sound of a staged performance, a superiority due to audio technology and to the freedom producers have to distribute the singers and orchestra in a panoramic arc around the studio.

In giving priority to the microphone Stockhausen once again acknowledges the aural culture of radio drama as a parallel reality to the visible performance (and even a preferable reality in the medium of recording). To interpret Stockhausen's theatre as radio made visible rather than as conventional theatre set to music is one way of appreciating the counterpoints of perspective and scale, of close-up and background, of interior imagination and exterior representation, which derive their meaning

---

[7] Dominic Gill, *Financial Times*, 6 Apr. 1981.
[8] See Mya Tannenbaum, *Conversations with Stockhausen* (Oxford, 1987), pp. 37–41.

from radio and contribute to the richness of Stockhausen's operatic language: 'the visible world of the theatre and the invisible world of the angels and spirits, the invisible singers and choirs, are all developed in the opera to the same degree.'[9]

The stylized but relatively easy intimacy of visualized movement and music in *LICHT* shows Stockhausen becoming increasingly confident of his choreographic skills, of which his development of a precise notational vocabulary for stage movement and gesture in three dimensions (Ex. 122) should be recognized as especially significant. Refined visual gesture goes hand in hand with refinement of musical gesture, hence solos in preference to the orchestral mass. 'Tonal colour is

Ex. 122

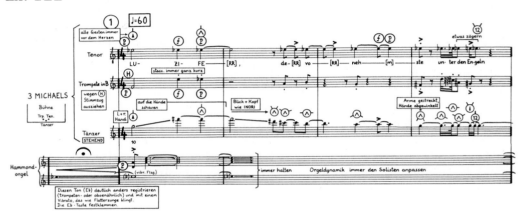

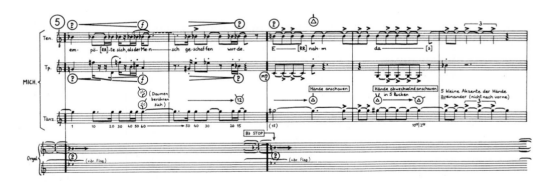

'Vision' from *Donnerstag aus LICHT*, showing a further refinement of the gestural notation of *Inori*. © K. Stockhausen.

[9] Stockhausen and Maconie, op. cit. 146.

never used for its own sake [in *nagauta*]. It is always related to the text or dancing in a rigid manner little known in the Western concept of orchestration.'[10]

Stockhausen's solo instrumental writing is highly volatile, especially in the dynamic and timbre domains. It makes up in variety of inflection what it may appear to lack in motivic variation. This flexibility is especially apparent in the writing for trumpet. Stockhausen had hoped to develop a portable electronic device to modify the trumpet sound in a controllable way, and for a time a number of research and development personnel at IRCAM were involved in the project. It was not a whole-hearted success, however, and a battery of different mutes is employed for the time being to enlarge the instrument's range of tone colour. Stockhausen's initial apprehensions concerning the orchestral use of commercial synthesizers, on the other hand, were sufficiently allayed by the time of *Montag aus LICHT* to enable these instruments to play a very prominent part. (Perhaps a certain amount of *force majeur* as well, since synthesizers are among the best-equipped instruments to manage the chordal glissandi which are significant to the character of Eva (Ex. 123).)

In the same way that his choreography mediates between informal naturalness and ritual without getting locked either into the Pavlovian subjection to music of conventional ballet or into the Thespian insensibility to movement of conventional grand-opera production, so too Stockhausen's melody writing with its interruptions, hiccups, gasps, and related noises is intended to occupy an intermediate level of existence between speech and song, and between song and vocalize. The solo instruments may be imagined as voices speaking a supernatural language which only sometimes distils into comprehensible speech (as it was in *Gesang der Jünglinge*). This metalanguage is intended to embrace all the communicative noises of all living things: the mew of the cat, the roar of the lion, the chirping of birds and insects. All communicable sound employs the same basic gestures: repetition, rising and falling inflections, pauses, irregular rhythms. All of the composer's knowledge of phonetics and information theory is brought to bear on the libretto, which assigns equal value to levels of organization of text from burbling and scat-singing to factual utterance to sung poetry.

These works belong to an unbroken tradition of religious theatre, which is to say they represent the human condition as the expression of a higher, divine purpose. Central to any drama is the relationship of individual perceptions; what gives religious theatre its special significance is the way in which human differences of perception are represented and ultimately reconciled.

Composers are apt to conceal a message within the medium of music as well as any moral that may be floated upon its surface. Bach's affirmation of equal temperament in the 'Well-Tempered Clavier' has an intriguing philosophical dimension—whether a composer is morally justified in accepting corrupted tuning in exchange for freedom of modulation—which bears significantly on the symbolism of key

---

[10] William P. Malm, *Nagauta: The Heart of Kabuki Music* (Tokyo, 1963), pp. 112–13.

Ex. 123

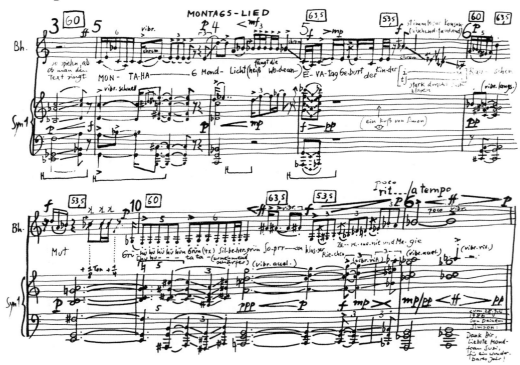

'Montags-Lied' from *Montag aus LICHT*. Elements from Eva, Michael, and Luzifer melodies are incorporated in the basset-horn part. In *Montag aus LICHT* Stockhausen discovers new areas of expression in vocal consonants, whistled and aspirated, in glissandi and microtonal scales, and in the use of block chords, of which the glissando chords for synthesizer are a good example.

© K. Stockhausen.

changing in his religious works. Schoenberg's Moses, driven to despair ('O Word, that I lack!') at the frailty of faith among God's chosen people, is also Schoenberg's Schoenberg venting his frustration at popular resistance to the Word of serialism. '*The Flood*', said Stravinsky, 'is also The Bomb', but the equally relevant message of the music is its defence of serial method in the face of a burgeoning aesthetic of musical chaos. For Pousseur, the Faust story is explicitly the tragedy of a contemporary music which appears to have lost its social role and aesthetic direction.

We do Stockhausen's conception and our own chances of reaching an accommodation with it an injustice to expect *LICHT* to conform to a classical narrative convention at odds with his musical practice, or indeed, to the entertainment convention that music is secondary to a good story-line. At the same time, there remains more than a hint of old-fashioned existentialism in the composer's vision of a world in which things appear to happen illogically or at random but implicitly conform to a mysterious master plan.

Of the work's pedigree there need be no doubt. If it differs from earlier masterpieces, it is in perspective rather than essence. This is not a traditional hero's life, a linear narrative dedicated to the principle of action and the single-minded pursuit of individual fame. Equally it is not a Passion: the issue here is not so much physical suffering and death as the spiritual tussle between the visionary and the rational spirit. Stockhausen's biblical model is closer to Jacob than Moses or Christ.

Nor is Stockhausen's drama primarily about courage, though the examination of Michael in *Donnerstag* may be understood as a token gesture in the direction of the initiation rites of *The Magic Flute*. Indeed, in many ways *LICHT* is the precise antithesis of Mozart's contemplative vision of an already doomed Age of Enlightenment. Where Wagner's cycle evokes the past, summoning the shades of cultural memory, Stockhausen's reconstructs the essential perceptions of myth in an imagery and idiom intended to be both timeless and transcultural. Where the normal perception of drama is of human situations through which divine truths are intermittently revealed, for Stockhausen the divine vision is paramount and its expression in human actions necessarily fragmented, even gratuitous. He seems to delight in confronting operatic convention, only to turn it inside out.

Certainly Stockhausen's Michael has none of the doubts of Schoenberg's Moses, though elements of the drama between Moses, Aron, and the chosen people are as evident in *LICHT* as in the crowd scenes from *Momente*. Stockhausen's Luzifer also shares certain engaging personality features with Stravinsky's Lucifer in *The Flood*, a piece with which he was certainly familiar.[11] And whereas Pousseur's Faust succumbs to temptation by Mephistopheles in order to secure temporal power, influence, and public acclaim, in *LICHT* it is Luzifer who is challenged by the imaginative brilliance of Michael, and who finally has to concede defeat. Stockhausen's view of the conflict is itself untraditionally good-humoured, thanks to which *LICHT* is anything but solemn. For all its monumentality of scale, there is as much of the comic life and rhetoric of the European cabaret tradition, of Dada and surrealism, the magical and the bizarre, in Stockhausen's conception as there is of the pomp and circumstance of church and operatic ritual.

The image of light is also linked with Stockhausen's serial ideals of the early fifties. At a time when public attention was turning back to neo-classicism, in his essay '1952/3: Orientation' Stockhausen contrasted the moral implications of a system based on the old principles of variation and differentiation (divide and rule) with those of a serial principle of equality and complementarity. 'No Neo . . .! Not the

---

[11] *The Flood* was among a very small collection of tape-recorded works on file in the electronic studio of Cologne Radio in 1964, when I was a student there. In addition to similarities of subject and dramatic treatment, *The Flood* is also close to Stockhausen in matters of technique, being not only cyclical—the music ending as it begins—but also a remarkable instance of Stravinskian moment-form.

same *Gestalten* in a changing light. Rather, different *Gestalten* in the same light, that penetrates everything.'[12]

By extension of the same analogy, the ultimate message of *LICHT* may thus be identified with the fall and redemption of mankind from a condition of original sin owing less to the temptations of the flesh than to those of the intellect. Not the apple, but the naming of creation is identified as the first step along the path to an orderly human world based on categories and distinctions, entailing science and power, but also division and war. The moral imperative of *LICHT*, therefore, is of redeeming humanity from a condition of fragmented consciousness and restoring a primal intuition of the divine relatedness of all creation.

[12] Karlheinz Stockhausen, *Texte zur Musik*, i (Cologne, 1971), p. 37.

Bibliography

ASTROV, MARGOT (ed.), *The Winged Serpent: American Indian Prose and Poetry*, New York, 1946.

BOULEZ, PIERRE, *Boulez on Music Today*, translated by Susan Bradshaw and Richard Rodney Bennett, London, 1971.

—— 'Eventuellement . . .', *La Revue musicale*, Numéro Spécial No. 212 (1952).

—— 'Music and Invention', *Listener*, 22 January 1970.

—— *Relevés d'apprenti*, Paris, 1966.

—— 'Schoenberg is Dead', *Score*, 6 (1952).

CAGE, JOHN, 'Indeterminacy', reprinted in *Silence*, Cambridge, Mass. 1966.

CARDEW, CORNELIUS, 'Report on Stockhausen's *Carré*', *Musical Times*, October and November 1961.

COTT, JONATHAN, *Stockhausen: Conversations with the Composer*, London, 1974.

DAVIES, JOHN BOOTH, *The Psychology of Music*, London, 1978.

DAVIES, PAUL, *The Cosmic Blueprint*, London, 1987.

EIMERT, HERBERT, 'How Electronic Music Began', *Musical Times*, April 1973.

EISENSTEIN, SERGEI, *The Film Sense*, translated and edited by Jay Leyda, London, 1948.

ERNST, DAVID, *The Evolution of Electronic Music*, New York, 1977.

GARFIAS, ROBERT, *Music of a Thousand Autumns: The Tōgaku Style of Japanese Court Music*, Berkeley, 1975.

GEHLHAAR, ROLF, 'Zur Komposition *Ensemble*', *Darmstädter Beiträge für Neue Musik*. (1968).

GILL, DOMINIC, 'Stockhausen's *Donnerstag aus Licht*', *Financial Times*, 6 April 1981.

GOLÉA, ANTOINE, *Rencontres avec Olivier Messiaen*, Paris, 1960.

—— *Rencontres avec Pierre Boulez*, Paris, 1958.

GRIFFITHS, PAUL, *A Concise History of Modern Music*, London, 1978.

—— *A Guide to Electronic Music*, London, 1979.

HARVEY, JONATHAN, *The Music of Stockhausen*, London, 1975.

HEIKENHEIMO, SEPPO, *The Electronic Music of Karlheinz Stockhausen*, translated by Brad Absetz, Helsinki, 1972.

HEISSENBÜTTEL, HELMUT, *Einfache Grammatische Meditationen*, Breisgau, 1955.

HELMHOLTZ, HERMANN, *On the Sensations of Tone*, second English edition translated by Alexander J. Ellis, new printing, New York, 1954.

HENCK, HERBERT, *Karlheinz Stockhausens* Klavierstück IX: *Eine analytische Betrachtung*, Bad Godesberg, 1978.

HESSE, HERMANN, *The Glass Bead Game*, translated by Richard and Clara Winston, London, 1972.

HINDEMITH, PAUL, *The Craft of Musical Composition*, New York, 1942.

Bibliography

KARKOSCHKA, ERHARD, *Notation in New Music*, London, 1969.

KHAN, HAZRAT INAYAT, *Die Schale des Schenken*, Berlin, 1948.

KULTERMANN, UDO, *Art-Events and Happenings*, London, 1971.

KURTZ, MICHAEL, *Stockhausen: Eine Biographie*, Kassel, 1988.

LE CORBUSIER (Charles-Edouard Jeanneret), *The Modulor*, London, 1954.

LEWIS, CECIL A., *Broadcasting from Within*, London, 1924.

MALM, WILLIAM P., *Nagauta: The Heart of Kabuki Music*, Tokyo, 1963.

MANDELBROT, BENOÎT, *Fractals: Form, Chance and Dimension*, San Francisco, 1977.

MANNING, PETER, *Electronic and Computer Music*, London, 1984.

MYERS, ROLLO (ed.), *Music Today: Journal of the International Society for Contemporary Music*, 1 (1949).

OESCH, HANS, 'Interview mit Karlheinz Stockhausen', *Melos/Neue Zeitschrift für Musik*, 1. 6 (1975).

'L'Oeuvre du XXe siècle', *La Revue Musicale*, Numéro Spécial No. 212, (1952).

PIERCE, JOHN R., *The Science of Musical Sound*, New York, 1983.

RICHTER, HANS, *Dada: Art and Anti-Art*, New York, 1965.

RITZEL, FRED, 'Musik für ein Haus', *Darmstädter Beiträge für Neue Musik*, 12 (1970).

SABBE, HERMANN, *Karlheinz Stockhausen: '. . .Wie die Zeit verging. . .'*, Munich, 1981.

SAMUEL, CLAUDE (ed.), *Eclat/Boulez*, Paris, 1986.

SCHAEFFER, PIERRE, 'L'Objet musical', *La Revue musicale*, Numéro Spécial No. 212 (1952).

SCHARF, AARON, *Art and Photography*, London, 1968.

SCHILLINGER, JOSEPH, *The Schillinger System of Musical Composition* (2 vols.), New York, 1946.

SCHNEBEL, DIETER, 'Karlheinz Stockhausen', *Die Reihe* (German Edition), 4 (1958).

SPRAT, THOMAS, *History of the Royal Society*, ed. Jackson I. Cove and Harold Whitmore Jones, London, 1959.

STOCKHAUSEN, KARLHEINZ, 'Actualia', *Die Reihe* 1, Pennsylvania, 1958.

—— 'The Concept of Unity in Electronic Music', *Perspectives of New Music*, 1. 1 (1962).

—— 'Electronic and Instrumental Music', *Die Reihe* (English Edition), 5 (1961).

—— '. . .how time passes. . .', *Die Reihe* (English Edition), 3 (1959).

—— Interview, *Frankfurter Allgemeine Zeitung*, 18 July 1980.

—— Interview, in 'Notes and Commentaries', *New Yorker*, 18 January 1964.

—— 'Music in Space', *Die Reihe* (English Edition), 5 (1961).

—— 'Speech and Music', *Die Reihe* (English Edition), 6 (1964).

—— 'Spiritual Dimensions', Interview with Peter Heyworth, *Music and Musicians*, 19. 9 (1971).

—— *Stockhausen in Den Haag*, Documentation of the Karlheinz Stockhausen Project (English edn.), ed. Michael Manion, Barry Sullivan, and Frits Weiland, Koninklijk Conservatorium te Den Haag, The Hague, 1982.

—— 'Stockhausen Miscellany', translated by Sheila Bennett and Richard Toop, *Music and Musicians*, 21. 2 (1972).

—— 'Structure and Experiential Time', *Die Reihe* 2, Pennysylvania, 1958.

—— *Texte zur Musik* (4 vols). i–ii (ed. Dieter Schnebel): Aufsätze 1952–1962 zur musikalischen Praxis. *Zur elektronischen und instrumentalen Musik*, Cologne, 1963; ii: *Zu eigenen Werken, zur Kunst Anderer, Aktuelles*, Cologne, 1964; iii (ed. Dieter Schnebel): *Texte zur Musik 1963–1970*, Cologne, 1971; iv (ed. Christopher von Blumroder): *Texte zur Musik 1963–1977*, Cologne, 1978.

—— 'Die Zukunft der elektroakustischen Apparaturen in der Musik', *Musik und Bildung*, 7–8 (1974).

—— and MACONIE, ROBIN, *Stockhausen on Music*, London, 1988.

—— *et al.*, *Stockhausen in Calcutta*, a commemorative collection of writings selected by Hans-Jürgen Nagel, translated by Sharmila Bose, Calcutta, 1984.

STRAVINSKY, IGOR and CRAFT, ROBERT, *Conversations with Igor Stravinsky*, London, 1959.

—— —— *Memories and Commentaries*, London, 1960.

—— —— *Themes and Episodes*, New York, 1966.

STROBEL, HEINRICH, '*Verehrter Meister, lieber Freund. . .*': *Begegnungen mit Komponisten unserer Zeit*, Stuttgart, 1977.

TANNENBAUM, MYA, *Conversations with Stockhausen*, translated by David Butchart, Oxford, 1987.

TOOP, RICHARD, 'Karlheinz Stockhausen, Music and Machines', Introduction and programme notes, BBC Concert Series, Barbican Centre, London, 8–16 January 1985.

—— 'On Writing about Stockhausen', *Contact*, 20 (1979).

—— 'Stockhausen's *Konkrete Etüde*', *Music Review*, 37. 4 (1976).

—— 'Stockhausen's Other Piano Pieces', *Musical Times*, April 1983.

TUDOR, DAVID, 'From Piano to Electronics', *Music and Musicians*, 20. 12 (1972).

VINTON, JOHN (ed.), *Dictionary of Twentieth-Century Music*, London, 1974.

WEIZSÄCKER, VIKTOR VON, *Gestalt und Zeit*, Göttingen, 1960.

WOLFF, CHRISTIAN, 'New and Electronic Music', *Audience*, 5. 3 (1958).

WÖRNER, KARL H., *Stockhausen: Life and Work*, rev. edn., trans. and ed. Bill Hopkins, London, 1973.

Discography

Adieu   London Sinfonietta/Stockhausen   DG 2530 443

'*Am Himmel wandre ich. . .*' (*Indianerlieder*)   Hamm-Albrecht, Barkey/Stockhausen
DG 2530 876

Amour   Stephens/Stockhausen   CD DG 423 378-2

"*Atmen gibt das Leben*" (1974)   NDR chorus/Stockhausen   DG 2530 641

"*Atmen gibt das Leben*" (1974-7)   NDR chorus, NDR SO/Stockhausen   DG 410 857-1

Aus den sieben Tagen Es—Aufwärts—Kommunion—Intensität—Richtige Dauern—Verbindung—Unbegrenzt—Treffpunkt—Nachtmusik—Abwärts—Setz die Segel zur Sonne—
Goldstaub   Ensembles/Stockhausen   DG 2720 073 (7-LP set)

—— Es—Aufwärts   as above   DG 2530 255

—— Kommunion—Intensität   as above   DG 2530 256

—— Goldstaub   as above   DG 410935-1

—— Unbgrenzt   as above   Shandar SR 10 002

—— Setz die Segel zur Sonne—Verbindung (different versions)   Ensembles/Stockhausen
Harmonia Mundi 30 899 M

—— Setz die Segel zur Sonne   Negative Band   Finnadar SR 9009

—— —— Zeitgeist Sound Environment Recording Corporation 37662

Carré   NDR chorus, NDR SO/Kagel, Stockhausen, Markowski, Gielen   DG 137 002

Choral   NDR chorus/Stockhausen   DG 2530 641

Chöre für Doris   NDR chorus/Stockhausen   DG 2530 641

Dr. K-Sextett   Ensemble/Halffter   Universal Edition 15043

Donnerstag aus LICHT   Various/Eötvös, Stockhausen   CD DG 473 379-2; DG 2740 242
(4-LP set)

Drei Lieder   Anderson, SWF SO/Stockhausen   DG 2530 827

Ensemble   (Stockhausen composition studio)   Wergo 600 65

Formel   SWF SO/Stockhausen   DG 2707 111

Für kommende Zeiten Japan—Wach   Bojé, Caskel, Eötvös   EMI Electrola C 165-
02 313/14 (2-LP set)

—— Spektren—Kommunikation—Übereinstimmung   Pro Musica Da Camera   Thorofon
Capella MTH 224

—— Ceylon—Zugvogel   Ensemble/Stockhausen   Chrysalis 6307 573 (CHR 1110)/CHY
1110

Gesang der Jünglinge   (mono)   DG LP 16 133

—— new stereo version, 1968   Harmonia Mundi DMR 1007-09/DG 138 811

Gruppen   WDR SO/Stockhausen, Maderna, Geilen   Opus Musicum 116-118/DG 137 002

—— WDR SO/Stockhausen, Maderna, Boulez   Harmonia Mundi DMR 1010-12

298

Harlekin   Stephens   DG 2531 006
Hymnen   electronic music   DG 2707039
In Freundschaft   Stephens/Stockhausen   CD DG 423 378-2
Inori   SWF SO/Stockhausen   DG 2707 111 (2-LP set)
Der Jahreslauf   Ensemble/Stockhausen   DG 2531 358
Klavierstücke I–XI   Kontarsky   CBS S77 209/32 21 0008 (2-LP set)
—— Henck   Wergo 60135/36 (2-LP set), Wergo 60135/36-50 (2-CD set)
—— Wambach Schwann   Musica Mundi VMS 1067/68 (2-LP set)
—— Klavierstücke I–IV, VII–IX, XI   Klein   Point 5028
—— Klavierstück VI (earlier version)   Tudor   Vega C30 A278
—— Klavierstücke VI, VII, VIII   Schroeder   hat ART 2030
—— Klavierstuck VII   Bärtschi   Rec Rec Music 04
—— —— Damerini   Frequenz 3 DAN
—— Klavierstück VIII   Burge   Vox Candide STGBY 637/31 015
—— Klavierstück IX   Heim   Duchesne DD 6064
—— —— Körmendi   Hungaroton SLPX 12569
—— —— Letschert   Musik am Alten Gymnasium Flensberg FL. 286-48535
—— Klavierstück X   Rzewski   Wergo 600 10/Hör Zu SHZW 903BL/Heliodor 2 549016
—— Klavierstücke IX–X   Bucquet   Philips TC 6500 101
—— Klavierstück XI   Takahashi   EMI EAA 850 13-15
Der Kleine Harlekin   Stephens   DG 2531 006
Kontakte   electronic music   DG 138 811
Kontakte   electronic sounds, piano, and percussion   Tudor, Caskel/Stockhausen   Wergo 600 09
—— Kontarsky, Caskel/Stockhausen   Vox Candide CE 31 022/STGBY 638/Harmonia Mundi DMR 1013-15
Kontra-Punkte   Domaine Musical/Boulez   Vega C30 A66
—— Ensemble/Maderna   RCA SLD-61 005/VICS 1239
—— London Sinfonietta/Stockhausen DG 2530 443
Kreuzspiel   London Sinfonietta/Stockhausen   DG 2530 443
Mantra   Alfons and Aloys Kontarsky   DG 2530 208
Mikrophonie I (1965)   Ensemble/Stockhausen   CBS 32 11 0044/S77 230/72 647
—— new edition   DG 2530 583
Mikrophonie II   WDR   chorus/Schernus;   Kontarsky,   Fritsch,   Stockhausen   CBS 32 11 0044/S77 230/72 647
—— new edition   DG 2530 583
Mixtur (1964–7)   Ensemble Hudba Dneska/Kupkovič   DG 137 012
Momente (1965)   Arroyo,   WDR   chorus   and   Orchestra/Stockhausen   Wergo 600 24/Nonesuch 71 157
—— (1972)   Davy, WDR   chorus, Ensemble   Musique   Vivante/Stockhausen   DG 2709 055
Musik im Bauch   Percussions de Strasbourg   DG 2530 913
Oberlippentanz   M. Stockhausen Acanta 40.23 543
Opus 1970 (Kurzwellen mit Beethoven)   Ensemble/Stockhausen   DG 139 461
Pole   Bojé, Eötvos   EMI Electrola C 165-02 313 (2-LP set)

Discography

Prozession Ensemble/Stockhausen Vox Candide 31 001/STGBY 615/CBS S77 230
—— different version (Vox) Fratelli Fabbri Editori mm-1098
—— Version 1971 Ensemble/Stockhausen DG 2530 582
Punkte (1962) SWF SO/Boulez DG 0629 030
—— (1966) NDR SO/Stockhausen DG 2530 641
Refrain Kontarsky, Caskel, Kontarsky Mainstream 5003
—— Kontarsky, Caskel, Stockhausen Vox Candide CE 31 022/STGBY 638/Fratelli Fabbri
    Editori mm-1098
Schlagtrio Kontarsky, Batigne, Gucht DG 2530 827
Sirius M. Stockhausen, Meriweather, Stephens, Carmeli DG 2707 122 (2-LP set)
—— Cancer—Libra from *Sirius* (same recording) Harmonia Mundi DMR 1028-30
Spiel SWF SO/Stockhausen DG 2530 827
Spiral Vetter Wergo 325/Hör Zu SHZW 903 Bl
—— Holliger DG 2561 109
—— Bojé, Eötvös (two versions) EMI Electrola C 165-02 313/14 (2-LP set)
Sternklang Intermodulation, Gentle Fire, various artists Polydor 2612 031
Stimmung Collegium Vokale Cologne DG 2543 003
—— new recording 1982, same ensemble Harmonia Mundi DMR 1019-21
—— Singcircle/Rose Hyperion A 66115
Studien I und II electronic music (mono) DG LP 16 133
Telemusik electronic music DG 137 012
Tierkreis (musical boxes) DG 2530 913
—— Stephens, Pasveer, M. Stockhausen Acanta 23 531
—— Calame (violin) Pavane Records ADW 7142
—— 6-melody version Kremer (violin) Ariola-Eurodisc 201 234-405
—— 6-melody version Rogoff (violin) CBS/Sony AC 1188–9
Trans (two versions) SWF SO/Bour; RSO Sarbrücken/Zender DG 3530 726
Traum-Formel Stephens/Stockhausen CD DG 423 378-2
Unsichtbare Chöre WDR chorus, Stephens DG 419 432-1/CD DG 419 432-2
Ylem London Sinfonietta/Stockhausen DG 2530 442
Zeitmasze Domaine Musical/Boulez Vega C30 A139
—— Ensemble/Craft Philips A 01 488/L/CBS Odyssey 32 160 154
—— Danzi Quintett, Holliger Philips 6 500 261
—— London Sinfonietta/Stockhausen DG 2530 443
Zyklus Caskel Mainstream 5003
—— Neuhaus Columbia MS 7139
—— Caskel, Neuhaus (two versions) Wergo 600 10/Heliodor 2 549 016/Mace S 9091
—— Neuhaus (version as Wergo) Hör Zu SHZW 902 BL
—— Gualda Erato STU 70 603
—— Yamaguchi CBS Sony Japan SONC 16012-I
—— Yoshihara, Fry (two versions) RCA RDC 1
—— Yoshihara (as above) Camerata (Tokyo) CMT 1040
—— Fry (as above) EMI CFP 40207/CFP 40205
Stockhausen Festival of Hits excerpts from *Gesang der Jünglinge, Kontakte, Carré, Telemusik,*
    Stimmung, Kurzwellen, Hymnen DG 139 461

Stockhausen: Greatest Hits   excerpts as in *Festival of Hits,* also from *Gruppen,* 'Es', *Spiral, Opus 1970, Mantra,* 'Aufwärts'   Polydor 2612 023 (2-LP set)

Stockhausen conducts:

Joseph Haydn: Concerto in E flat major for trumpet and orchestra   M. Stockhausen, RSO Berlin/Stockhausen   Acanta 40.23 543

W. A. Mozart: Concerto in A major for clarinet and orchestra, KV 622   Stephens, RSO Berlin/Stockhausen   Acanta 23 531

W. A. Mozart: Concerto in G major for flute and orchestra, KV 313   Pasveer, RSO Berlin/Stockhausen   Acanta 40.23 543

Chronological list of works

UE = Universal Edition; SV = Stockhausen Verlag, 5067 Kürten, West Germany

1950	*Chöre für Doris* for unaccompanied choir UE15135
1950	*Drei Lieder* for alto voice and chamber orchestra UE15154
1950	*Choral* for four-part unaccompanied choir UE15169
1951	*Sonatine* for violin and piano UE15174
1951	*Kreuzspiel* for ensemble UE13117
1951	*Formel* for orchestra UE15157
1952	*Konkrete Etüde* (concrete music)
1952	*Spiel* for orchestra UE15915
1952	*Schlagtrio* UE15943
1952–62	*Punkte* for orchestra UE13844c
1952–3	*Kontra-Punkte* for ten instruments UE12218
1952–3	*Klavierstücke I–IV* for piano UE12251
1953	*Elektronische Studie I* (electronic music)
1954	*Elektronische Studie II* (electronic music) UE12466
1954–5	*Klavierstücke V–X* for piano UE13675
1955–6	*Zeitmasze* for five woodwinds UE12697
1955–7	*Gruppen* for three orchestras UE13673
1956	*Klavierstücke XI* for piano UE12654
1955–6	*Gesang der Jünglinge* (electronic music)
1959	*Zyklus* for a percussionist UE13186
1959–60	*Carré* for four choirs and orchestras UE14815
1959	*Refrain* for three players UE13187
1959–60	*Kontakte* (electronic music) UE13678
	—— version with piano and percussion UE12426
1961	*Originale* (music theatre with *Kontakte*) UE13958
1962–4–9	*Momente* for soprano, four choirs, and thirteen instrumentalists UE15151
1963	*Plus–Minus* '2 × 7 pages for working out' UE13993
1964	*Mikrophonie I* for tam-tam and six players UE15138
	—— 'Brussels version' (realization score) UE15139
1964	*Mixtur* for orchestra, sine-wave generators, and ring modulators UE14261
1967	—— version for smaller ensemble UE13847
1965	*Mikrophonie II* for twelve singers, Hammond organ, 4 ring modulators, and tape UE15140

1965	*Stop* for orchestra UE14989
1969	—— 'Paris version' UE14989
1965–6	*Solo* for melody instrument with feedback UE14789
1966	*Telemusik* (electronic music) UE14807
1966	*Adieu* for wind quintet UE14877
1966–7	*Hymnen* (electronic and concrete music)
	—— version with soloists UE15143
1969	—— version with orchestra UE15145
1967	*Prozession* for four players UE14812
1968	*Stimmung* for six vocalists UE14805
	—— 'Paris version' UE14805
1968	*Kurzwellen* for six players UE14806
1968	*Aus den sieben Tagen* 'fifteen texts for intuitive music' UE14790 (Performable individually): 1. *Richtige Dauern* for *c.* 4 players; 2. *Unbegrenzt* for ensemble; 3. *Verbindung* for ensemble; 4. *Treffpunkt* for ensemble; 5. *Nachtmusik* for ensemble; 6. *Abwärts* for ensemble; 7. *Aufwärts* for ensemble; 8. *Oben und Unten* theatre piece for Man, Woman, Child, 4 instrumentalists; 9. *Intensität* for ensemble; 10. *Setz die Segel zur Sonne* for ensemble; 11. *Kommunion* for ensemble; 12. *Litanei* for speaker or choir; 13. *Es* for ensemble; 14. *Goldstaub* for ensemble; 15. *Ankunft* for speaker or speaking choir
1968	*Spiral* for a soloist with short-wave receiver UE14957
1969	*Dr. K-Sextett* UE(hire only)
1969	*Fresco* for four orchestra groups UE15147
1969–70	*Pole* for two players/singers with short-wave receivers SV
1969–70	*Expo* for three players/singers with short-wave receivers SV
1970	*Mantra* for two pianists, percussion, and electronic modulation SV
1968–70	*Für kommende Zeiten* 'seventeen texts for intuitive music' SV (performable individually): 1. *Übereinstimmung* for ensemble; 2. *Verlängerung*; 3. *Verkürzung*; 4. *Über die Grenze* for small ensemble; 5. *Kommunikation* for small ensemble; 6. *Intervall* for piano duo, 4 hands; 7. *Ausserhalb* for small ensemble; 8. *Innerhalb* for small ensemble; 9. *Anhalt* for small ensemble; 10. *Schwingung* for ensemble; 11. *Spektren* for small ensemble; 12. *Wellen* for ensemble; 13. *Zugvogel* for ensemble; 14. *Vorahnung* for 4–7 interpreters; 15. *Japan* for ensemble; 16. *Wach* for ensemble; 17. *Ceylon* for small ensemble
1971	*Sternklang* park music for five groups SV
1971	*Trans* for orchestra SV
1972	*Alphabet für Liège* 'thirteen musical pictures' for soloists and duos
1972	*'Am Himmel wandre ich . . .'* 'Indian songs' for two voices SV
1972	*Ylem* for nineteen players or singers SV
1973–4	*Inori* for one or two soloists and orchestra SV
1973–4	*'Vortrag über HU'* for a singer. (Musical analysis of *INORI*) SV
1974–7	*'Atmen gibt das Leben . . .'* choir opera with orchestra (or tape) SV
1974	*Herbstmusik* for four players SV
1974	*'Laub und Regen'* closing duet (*Herbstmusik*) for clarinet and viola SV
1975	*Musik im Bauch* for six percussionists and musical boxes SV

Chronological List of Works

1975–6   *Tierkreis* 'twelve melodies for the signs of the Zodiac' for a melody and/or chord instrument   SV: 1. 'Aquarius'; 2. 'Piscies'; 3. 'Aries'; 4. 'Taurus'; 5. 'Gemini'; 6. 'Cancer'; 7. 'Leo'; 8. 'Virgo'; 9. 'Libra'; 10. 'Scorpio'; 11. 'Sagittarius'; 12. 'Capricorn'

          —— alternative versions for voice and chord instruments SV

1977   —— version for chamber orchestra SV

1975   *Harlekin* for clarinet SV

1975   *Der kleine Harlekin* for clarinet SV

1975–7   *Sirius* (electronic music and trumpet, soprano, bass clarinet, bass) SV

1977–80   *Aries* for trumpet and electronic music

1976   *Amour* (five pieces for clarinet) SV

          —— version for flute

1977   *Jubiläum* for orchestra SV

1977   *In Freundschaft* for solo player SV

          —— versions for clarinet, flute, recorder, oboe, bassoon, basset-horn or bass clarinet, violin, cello, saxophone, horn, trombone

Cadenzas:

1978   For Mozart's Clarinet Concerto in A major, KV 622 SV

1984–5   For Mozart's Flute Concertos in G major, KV 313 and D major, KV 314 SV

1984   For Leopold Mozart's Trumpet Concerto SV

1983–5   For Haydn's Trumpet Concerto in E flat major SV

1977–   *LICHT: Die sieben Tage der Woche* for solo voices, solo instrumentalists, solo dancers, choir, orchestra, ballet and mime, electronic and concrete music

1977   *Der Jahreslauf:* scene from *Dienstag aus LICHT* for ballet, actor, orchestra and tape or for orchestra alone SV

1978–80   *Donnerstag aus LICHT:* opera in three acts, a greeting, and a farewell for 14 musical performers (3 solo voices, 8 solo instrumentalists, 3 solo dancers), choir, orchestra and tapes. Donnerstags-Gruss; Act I: Michaels Jugend ('Kindheit'—'Mondeva'—'Examen'); Act II: Michaels Reise um die Erde; Act III: Michaels Heimkehr ('Festival'—'Vision'); Donnerstags-Abschied

Individual pieces from *Donnerstag aus LICHT* for concert performance:

1978   *Michaels Reise um die Erde* (Act II) for trumpet and orchestra SV

          Eingang und Formel (from *Michaels Reise*) for solo trumpet SV

          Halt (from *Michaels Reise*) for trumpet and double bass SV

          Kreuzigung (from *Michaels Reise*), for trumpet, basset-horn (also clarinet), 2 basset-horn, 2 horns, 2 trombones, tuba, electronic organ SV

          Mission und Himmelfahrt (from *Michaels Reise*) for trumpet and basset-horn SV

          Donnerstags-Gruss for eight brass instruments, piano, three percussionists SV

          Michaels-Ruf for variable ensemble (8 orchestra players) SV

1978–9   *Michaels Jugend* (Act I) for tenor, soprano, bass; trumpet, basset-horn, trombone, piano; electronic organ; three dancer-mimes; tapes with choir and instruments   SV
            Unsichtbare Chöre for sixteen-track a-cappella tape and eight- or two-track play-back   SV
            Kindheit (Scene 1 of *Michaels Jugend*) for tenor, soprano, bass; trumpet, basset-horn, trombone; dancer, tapes   SV
            Tanze Luceva! (from *Michaels Jugend*) for basset-horn or bass clarinet   SV
            Bijou (from *Michaels Jugend*) for alto flute and bass clarinet   SV
            Mondeva (Scene 2 of *Michaels Jugend*) for tenor and basset-horn plus ad lib. soprano, bass, trombone, mime, electronic organ, two tapes   SV
            Examen (Scene 3 of *Michaels Jugend*) for tenor, trumpet, dancer; basset-horn, piano; plus ad lib. 'jury' (soprano, bass, two dancer-mimes), two tapes   SV
            Klavierstück XII ('Examen') solo piano (from *Michaels Jugend*)   SV
1978–84   Version for soloists of *Michaels Reise* for a trumpeter, 9 other players, and sound projectionist   SV
1980   *Michaels Heimkehr* (Act III) for tenor, soprano, bass; trumpet, basset-horn, trombone, two saxophones, electronic organ; three dancer-mimes, old woman; choir and orchestra, tapes   SV
            Festival (from *Michaels Heimkehr*) for tenor, soprano, bass; trumpet, basset-horn, trombone; two soprano saxophones; three dancer-mimes, old woman; choir and orchestra; tapes   SV
            Drachenkampf (from *Michaels Heimkehr*) for trumpet, trombone, electronic organ (or synthesizer), 2 dancers ad lib.   SV
            Knabenduett (from *Michaels Heimkehr*) for two soprano saxophones or other instruments   SV
            Argument (from *Michaels Heimkehr*) for tenor, bass, electric organ (or synthesizer); ad lib. trumpet, trombone, percussionist   SV
            Vision (from *Michaels Heimkehr*) for tenor, trumpet, dancer; Hammond organ; tape; plus ad lib. shadow plays   SV
            Donnerstags Abschied for five trumpets (or one trumpet in a five-track recording)   SV

1981–4   *Samstag aus LICHT*: opera in a greeting and four scenes for 13 musical performers (1 solo voice, 10 solo instrumentalists, 2 solo dancers), wind orchestra, ballet or mimes, male-voice choir, organ. Samstags Gruss (Luzifer-Gruss); Scene 1: Luzifers Traum; Scene 2: Kathinkas Gesang als Luzifers Requiem; Scene 3: Luzifers Tanz; Scene 4: Luzifers Abschied

Individual pieces from *Samstag aus LICHT* for concert performance:
1981   *Luzifers Traum* (Scene 1) or Piano Piece XIII for bass and piano   SV
            Traum-Formel (from *Luzifers Traum*) for basset-horn   SV
1982   *Luzifers Abschied* (Scene 4) for male choir, organ, seven trombones (live or on tape)   SV
1982–3   *Kathinkas Gesang als Luzifers Requiem* (Scene 2) for flute and six percussionists, or flute solo   SV

<table>
<tr><td></td><td>——— version for flute and electronic music   SV</td></tr>
<tr><td></td><td>——— version for flute and piano   SV</td></tr>
<tr><td>1983</td><td>*Luzifers Tanz* (Scene 3) for bass (or trombone or euphonium), piccolo trumpet, piccolo flute; wind orchestra or symphony orchestra; plus a stilt-dancer, dancer, ballet or mimes for scenic performance   SV</td></tr>
<tr><td></td><td>*Linker Augenbrauentanz* (from *Luzifers Tanz*) for a percussionist, flutes, and basset-horn(s)   SV</td></tr>
<tr><td></td><td>*Rechter Augenbrauentanz* (from *Luzifers Tanz*) for a percussionist, clarinets, bass clarinets   SV</td></tr>
<tr><td></td><td>*Linker Augentanz* (from *Luzifers Tanz*) for percussionist and saxophone   SV</td></tr>
<tr><td></td><td>*Rechter Augentanz* (from *Luzifers Tanz*) for a percussionist, oboes, cors anglais, bassoons   SV</td></tr>
<tr><td></td><td>*Linker Backentanz* (from *Luzifers Tanz*) for a percussionist, trumpets, and trombones   SV</td></tr>
<tr><td></td><td>*Rechter Backentanz* (from *Luzifers Tanz*) for a percussionist, trumpets, and trombones   SV</td></tr>
<tr><td></td><td>*Nasenflügeltanz* (from *Luzifers Tanz*) for a percussionist and ad lib. electronic keyboard instruments   SV</td></tr>
<tr><td></td><td>*Oberlippentanz* (from *Luzifers Tanz*) for solo piccolo trumpet, or for piccolo trumpet, trombone or euphonium, two percussionists, and four or eight horns   SV</td></tr>
<tr><td></td><td>*Zungenspitzentanz* (from *Luzifers Tanz*) for piccolo solo, or for piccolo, ad lib. dancers, a percussionists, and euphoniums (or electronic keyboard instruments)   SV</td></tr>
<tr><td></td><td>*Kinntanz* (from *Luzifers Tanz*) for trombone or euphonium, 2 percussionists, euphoniums, alto trombone(s), baritone (tenor) saxhorn(s), bass tuba(s)   SV</td></tr>
<tr><td>1984</td><td>*Samstags-Gruss* for 26 brass players and 2 percussionists   SV</td></tr>
<tr><td>1984–8</td><td>*Montag aus LICHT*: opera in three acts, a greeting, and a farewell for 21 musical performers (14 solo voices, 6 solo instrumentalists, 1 actor), modern orchestra:[1] Montags-Gruss; Act I: Evas Erstgeburt; Act II: Evas Zweitgeburt; Act III: Evas Zauber; Montags-Abschied</td></tr>
</table>

Individual pieces from *Montag aus LICHT* for concert performance:

<table>
<tr><td>1984</td><td>*Klavierstück XIV* ('Geburtstags-Formel' from *Evas Zweitgeburt*) for solo piano   SV</td></tr>
<tr><td>1984</td><td>*Evas Spiegel* (from *Evas Zauber*) for basset-horn   SV</td></tr>
<tr><td></td><td>*Susani* (from *Evas Zauber*) for basset-horn   SV</td></tr>
<tr><td>1984–5</td><td>*Botschaft* (from *Evas Zauber*) for basset-horn, alto flute, choir, modern orchestra   SV</td></tr>
<tr><td></td><td>——— version for basset-horn, alto flute, choir   SV</td></tr>
<tr><td></td><td>——— version for basset-horn, alto flute, modern orchestra   SV</td></tr>
<tr><td></td><td>*AVE* (from *Evas Zauber*) for basset-horn and alto flute   SV</td></tr>
</table>

---

[1] Electronic keyboard instruments, percussion; various instrumental ensembles, choir groups, solo voices (recorded on tape); 8-track tapes of concrete and electronic sounds; 40-channel sound system, 16-channel sound projection.

1984–6   *Evas Zauber* (Act III) for basset-horn, alto flute and piccolo, choir, children's choir, modern orchestra   SV

1984–7   *Befruchtung mit Klavierstück* (from *Evas Zweitgeburt*) for piano, girls' choir, modern orchestra   SV

1984–7   *Evas Zweitgeburt* (Act II) for 7 solo boys' voices, solo basset-horn, 3 'bassettinists' (2 basset-horns, 1 voice), piano, choir, girls' choir, modern orchestra

1984–8   *Montags-Gruss* ('Eva-Gruss') for multiple basset-horns, electronic keyboard instruments   SV

1985   *Susani's Echo* (from *Evas Zauber*) for alto flute   SV

1986   *Evas Lied* (from *Evas Zweitgeburt*) for 7 solo boy's voices, basset-horn, 3 'bassettinists' (2 basset-horns, 1 voice), modern orchestra, ad lib. female choir   SV

         Wochenkreis ('Die sieben Lieder der Tage' from *Evas Zweitgeburt*) duet for basset-horn and electronic keyboard instruments   SV

         Der Kinderfänger (from *Evas Zauber*) for alto flute and piccolo, ad lib. basset-horn, ad lib. children's choir, modern orchestra   SV

         Entführung (from *Evas Zauber*) for piccolo, ad lib. modern orchestra   SV

         Xi for basset-horn (from *Montags-Gruss*)   SV

         —— version for alto flute or flute   SV

1987   *Evas Erstgeburt* (Act I) for 3 sopranos, 3 tenors, bass, actor, choir, children's choir, modern orchestra   SV

         Mädchenprozession (from *Evas Zweitgeburt*) for girls' choir, ad lib. choir, modern orchestra   SV

1988   *Montags-Abschied* ('Eva-Abschied') for children's choir, multiple voices and piccolos, electronic keyboard instruments   SV

Unpublished, Lost, or Unfinished Compositions

?1950	*Scherzo* for piano solo, in Hindemith style
?1950	*Drei Chöre* 'Three Choruses' (two- and three-part): 1. *'Gottes Krippen'* (God's Cradle) (Stockhausen); 2. *'Maria'* (Stockhausen); 3. *'Bei dem Kinde'* (With the Child) (Stockhausen)
1950	*Burleska*, a musical pantomine (concept and libretto by Stockhausen): a collective composition with Detmar Seuthe and Klaus Weiler. For speaker, 4 solo singers, chamber choir, string quartet, piano, and percussion. First performance: ?24 July 1950, by students of the Music Education Course, Cologne Musikhochschule; Detmar Seuthe (percussion), Karlheinz Stockhausen (piano), cond. Klaus Weiler
?1950	*Sechs Studien* (Six Studies) for piano solo (destroyed)
1951	*Präludium* (Preludium) for piano solo (identical with the piano part of the *Sonatine* for violin and piano, first movement)
1951	*Sonate* for piano (destroyed)
1951	*Ravelle* for clarinet, violin, electric guitar, piano, and contrabass. First performed in Freiburg, 14 June 1974
1952	*Studie über einen Ton* (Study on one tone) (two-part *musique concrète*). The work does not survive, and some doubt remains over whether it was ever completed
1954	*Klavierstück 5 ½*, *Klavierstück 6 ½* (Piano Pieces 5½, 6½). First performed in Cologne, 18 January 1974, by Aloys Kontarsky
1960–	*Monophonie* for orchestra (uncompleted)
1967–	*Projektion* (Projection) for nine orchestra groups and film (uncompleted)
1968–9	*Hinab–Hinauf* (Downward–Upward). Electronic and concrete music with solo performers and light show
1969	*Tunnel-Spiral*. Project for reader, Japanese *rin*, and short-wave receiver, for a feedback speaker system ('sound tunnel') developed for the Los Angeles Department of Municipal Arts Junior Arts Center
1969–	*Vision* for piano duo (uncompleted)
1970–	*Singreadfeel* for a singer with 'touch instruments'

Selected Films

1. *Musical Forming* 165' English 16 mm. colour and b/w
2. *Mikrophonie I* 90' English 16 mm. colour and b/w
3. *Moment-Forming and Integration* 120' English 16 mm. colour and b/w
4. *Intuitive Music* 60' English 16 mm. colour and b/w
5. *Questions and Answers on Intuitive Music* 35' English 16 mm. colour and b/w
6. *Four Criteria of Electronic Music* 105' English 16 mm. colour and b/w
7. *Questions and Answers on Four Criteria of Electronic Music* 105' English 16 mm. colour and b/w
8. *Telemusic* 60' English 16 mm. colour and b/w
9. *Mantra* 120' English 16 mm. colour and b/w
10. *Questions and Answers on Mantra* 60' English 16 mm. colour and b/w
11. *Momente* 45' 51" English 16 mm. colour and b/w
    —— in French
    —— in German
12. *Mikrophonie I* 21' 06" French 35 mm. and 16 mm. colour
13. *Stockhausen und die Höhlen von Jeita* Stockhausen and the Caves of Jeita 30' English 35 mm. and 16 mm. colour
    —— in French
    —— in German
14. *Stockhoven–Beethausen Opus 1970* 49' 17" German 16 mm. b/w
15. *Ich werde die Töne—die Weltschau des Karlheinz Stockhausen* (I become the sounds—the world-view of Karlheinz Stockhausen) 30' 44" German 16 mm. b/w
16. *Internationale Ferienkurse für Neue Musik, Darmstadt 1970. Dokumentation einer Misslungenen Revolution* (International Vacation Courses for New Music, Darmstadt 1970. Documentation of a Failed Revolution) (Excerpts from Stockhausen's seminars 'Feedback' and 'Expansion of Dynamics') English 16 mm. colour
    —— in French
    —— in German
17. *Mantra* 56' 28" German MAZ colour
18. *Mantra* 56' 28" English 16 mm. colour
    —— in French
    —— in German
    —— in Spanish
    —— in Arabic
19. *Trans . . . und so Weiter* (Trans . . . and so forth) 58' 43" 16 mm. colour
20. *Alphabet für Liège* 60' French 16 mm. colour
21. *Inori* 70' German MAZ colour

Selected Films

22. *Inori* 28′ 35″ German MAZ colour
23. *Inori* c. 75′ Italian 16 mm. colour
24. *Michaels Reise um die Erde* c. 50′ Italian 16 mm. colour
25. *'Tuning In' with Stockhausen and Singcircle* c. 49′ English 16 mm. colour
26. *TG L'UNA* c. 20′ Italian MAZ colour
27. Donnerstag aus LICHT *im Teatro alla Scala* (*Donnerstag aus LICHT* at La Scala) Italian 16 mm. b/w
28. *Notenschlüssel: Stockhausen und seine Kinder* (Keynotes: Stockhausen and his Children) 43′ 58″ German MAZ colour
29. *Stockhausen and seine Werke* (Stockhausen and his Works) 44′ 27″ German MAZ colour
30. *Musique et Electronique avec Karlheinz Stockhausen et George Lewis* (Music and electronics with Karlheinz Stockhausen and George Lewis) 26′ French video BVU/PAL colour
31. Samstag aus LICHT *im Teatro alla Scala* (*Samstag aus LICHT* in La Scala) Italian 16 mm. colour
32. *Blitz* c. 30′ Italian Maz colour
33. *Samstag aus LICHT—Karlheinz Stockhausens Zweiter Schöpfungstag* (*Samstag aus LICHT—* Karlheinz Stockhausen's Second Day of Creation) 29′ 45″ German U-matic colour
34. *Das Welttheater des Karlheinz Stockhausen* (The World-Theatre of Karlheinz Stockhausen) 60′ 23″ German MAZ colour
35. *Hymnen mit Solisten und Orchester* (*Hymnen* with Soloists and Orchestra) c. 125′ Hungarian video SECAM colour
36. Kathinkas Gesang *de Karlheinz Stockhausen* 33′ 21″ French BVU/PAL colour
37. Donnterstag aus LICHT *in Covent Garden* c. 45′ English 16 mm. colour
38. *Evas Lied* c. 42′ German U-matic colour
39. *Evas Zauber* c. 60′ French video BVU/PAL colour

Addresses:

Films 1–10: Allied Artists, 42 Montpelier Square, London SW7.
Films 11, 12: Marie-Noelle Brian, INA GRM, Service Diffusion France, Tour mercuriales, 40 rue Jean Jaurès, F-93170 Bagnolet
Film 13: MIDEM, 42 Avenue Ste. Foy, F-92 Neuilly
Films 14–16, 33, 34: Westdeutscher Rundfunk, Fernseh-Musikabteilung, Appellhofplatz 1, D-5000 Köln 1
Films 17, 21, 28, 29: Werbung im SWF, Produktionsverwertung, Postfach 1115, D-7570 Baden-Baden
Films 11, 18: German representatives and Goethe Institutes outside West Germany
Film 19: Alfred Schenz, Neuhauser Strasse 3, D-8000 München 2
Film 20: RTB, Palais de Congrès, Esplanade d'Europe, B-400 Liège
Film 22: ZDF Redaktion Musik I, Essenheimer Landstrasse, D-6500 Mainz 1
Films 23, 24: Direttore Braun, RTI, Via del Babuino 9, I-00100 Roma
Films 25, 37: BBC, Music Department (Television), Yalding House, 156 Great Portland Street, London W1

Films 26, 32: RAI, Service segretaria, Viale Mazzini 14, I-00195 Roma
Films 27, 31: Teatro alla Scala, Archivio fotografico, I-20121 Milano
Films 30, 36: IRCAM/Diffusion, 31 rue Saint-Merri, F-75004 Paris
Film 35: Magyar Radió Zenei Föösztalya, Bròdy Sàndor uka 5–7, 1800 Budapest, Hungary
   0133-039X
Film 38: Stockhausen-Verlag, D-5067 Kürten
Film 39: Jean Pierre Lannes, France Régions 3, 14 route de Mirecourt, F-54042
   Vandoeuvre, Nancy Cedex

Index

Note: Stockhausen's works are listed in the main A–Z sequence, and not within the composer's own entry.

317

Index

Xenakis, Iannis 15

Ylem 203, 217–19

Zeitmasze 9, 44, 72, 82–6, 87, 93, 119, 255

Zen Buddhism 196, 282

Zinovieff, Peter 247

Zyklus 9, 57, 60, 100, 102, 108–12, 120–1, 128, 170